BY JALEIGH JOHNSON

DUNGEONS & DRAGONS

The Fallbacks: Bound for Ruin
Honor Among Thieves: The Road to Neverwinter
The Howling Delve
Mistshore
Unbroken Chain
Unbroken Chain: The Darker Road
Spider and Stone

MARVEL

Triptych: A Marvel: Xavier's Institute Novel
School of X: A Marvel: Xavier's Institute Anthology

WORLD OF SOLACE SERIES

The Mark of the Dragonfly
The Secrets of Solace
The Quest to the Uncharted Lands

ORIGINAL FICTION

The Door to the Lost

DUNGEONS & DRAGONS

THE FALLBACKS
BOUND FOR RUIN

DUNGEONS & DRAGONS

THE FALLBACKS

BOUND FOR RUIN

JALEIGH JOHNSON

RANDOM HOUSE WORLDS

NEW YORK

Published in the United States by Random House Worlds, an imprint of Random House, a division of Penguin Random House LLC, New York.

RANDOM HOUSE is a registered trademark, and RANDOM HOUSE WORLDS and colophon are trademarks of Penguin Random House LLC.

Hardback ISBN 978-0-593-59954-9
Ebook ISBN 978-0-593-59955-6

Printed in the United States of America on acid-free paper

randomhousebooks.com

2 4 6 8 9 7 5 3 1

First Edition

Book design by Alexis Flynn

To Tim, for all the adventures we've had and all the ones still to come. Love you always.

DUNGEONS & DRAGONS

THE FALLBACKS
BOUND FOR RUIN

CHAPTER 1

"It's probably harmless," Lark said.

The party surveyed the stretch of multicolored stone floor that lay between them and the pair of treasure chests situated on the opposite end of the ruined worship hall. There was no furniture remaining in the room. Shreds of rotting carpet still clung stubbornly to the floor in places, and the air smelled of mildew and smoke from the torches burning on the walls.

"That's what we thought about the last chamber," Tess said. She moved past Lark as he leaned against the doorframe, adjusting his busking hat and quill. His apple-red skin was covered in a thin layer of dirt and a film of salt water from the cave they'd been exploring in their search for the entrance to the lost temple of Oghma, the god of knowledge.

Standing to Tess's right, Cazrin pushed her long dark hair out of her face and held up her staff. The purple stone at its tip hovered above two silver points and glowed with soft light to illuminate the corridor and the worship hall beyond. At the back of the party, Baldric and Anson watched for threats approaching from behind.

Tess crouched on the floor in the doorway, examining the flag-stones carefully. She'd tied her shoulder-length blond hair back behind her pointed ears so it wouldn't get in her way, and she carefully ran her fingers over the seams between the stones, searching for concealed wires or pressure plates.

"Two silver says the chest on the left is a mimic," Baldric said. "You a betting man, Anson?"

Tess glanced back and saw the burly dwarf flash two silver coins at Anson, waggling his eyebrows as he ran his other hand through his thick black beard.

Anson studied the two chests like a man contemplating the mysteries of life. The young fighter was human like Cazrin, with short, straight dark hair and warm beige skin, but closer in build to Tess, with wide, muscled shoulders and hips. He rummaged in one of his pouches and came up with two silver coins of his own. "I'll take that bet," he said.

"They can't all be mimics, can they?" Cazrin asked as they shook on the wager. "I know the last three were, but statistically speaking, surely . . ."

"All that really matters right now is that *someone* is keeping watch while I concentrate on disabling the deadly spike trap I've just found right here," Tess said, shifting position on the floor so they could all see the outline of the pressure plate.

"There *is* a trap?" Lark's tail lashed back and forth in Tess's peripheral vision, distracting her from her work. "I'll be damned! I had a good feeling about this floor."

"Don't worry, Tess," Anson said easily. "Uggie's on guard duty. She's keeping a great watch back here. Aren't you, girl?"

He gestured to the squat figure at the back of the group. Their otyugh companion was about the size and bulk of a full-grown mastiff. Based on her size and behavior, Tess guessed she was a juvenile. She had three stumpy legs and yellow jaundice spots dotting her leathery green skin. Two short, spiky tentacles flanked a single eyestalk with three eyes that flicked back and forth between Anson and Baldric, watching their every move in case they happened to drop some food on the ground. A gaping mouth opened above her barrel-like chest, exposing rows of jagged teeth that could really use a good brushing, but honestly, even Tess wasn't brave enough to take on that job.

She hoped the time spent on these treasure chests would serve as a much-needed morale boost. It was only their first mission together as a party, but they'd been exploring the cold, dank ruins for two days now and were no closer to finding the spellbook they'd been hired to retrieve from its bowels.

It had taken some doing to find the place. The entrance to the hidden temple was located deep in a sea cave on the Sword Coast, several miles south of the city of Waterdeep. Time and tide had flooded many of the upper chambers, and Tess didn't think she'd ever get the seaweed smell out of her hair, but it finally looked like they were getting somewhere.

"Aren't you wizards supposed to know about these things?" Baldric said, addressing Cazrin. "Can't you just . . . I don't know . . . sense a mimic the way you sense magic?"

"Of course," Cazrin said dryly. She put two fingers to her temple and furrowed her brow. "Just let me stretch my awareness into the magical Weave so I can detect the presence of all mimics in the immediate vicinity." She hesitated. "Come to think of it, that would be a handy spell." Quickly, she reached into the small satchel riding at her hip and pulled out a spellbook with a pair of blue stones embedded in the cover that looked like eyes. "New entry, please, Keeper."

"Absolutely, Cazrin," the spellbook chirped, immediately falling open in her hand, pages fluttering until it landed on a blank section. Then it floated into the air, awaiting further commands.

"Save the note-taking for later," Tess said, just as Cazrin was about to take out her quill and ink. "If either of these chests really are mimics, we need the party wizard to be focused too."

"Right, excellent point!"

Tess went back to her work. She quickly located a pattern to the pressure plates. As long as they walked on just the green slate stones, they should be safe to cross the floor to the treasure chests. She relayed this information to the rest of the group, and before she'd even finished speaking, Lark plunged into the room, hopping from one green stone to the next, his lute thumping against his back on his way to the closest treasure chest.

"Wait for the rest of us!" Tess called after him.

"Find out which one's the mimic, new guy," Baldric said. He winked when Tess shot him a look. "He'll be fine."

Tess sighed again and began making her way carefully across the floor, motioning for the others to stay behind her. Anson scooped Uggie up with a grunt and carried the otyugh awkwardly in his arms.

If Lark would just stick to the plan, let her check the rooms thoroughly before barreling in, it would make everyone's life a lot easier.

"We're in!" cried the bard triumphantly.

Tess's head snapped up. "How is that possible?" she demanded as Lark tossed the first treasure chest's opened lock aside and reached for the lid. "Did you even *try* to check that thing for traps?"

"I did everything you taught me in that chest-cracking seminar you made me sit through," Lark said, his tail swishing back and forth smugly. Tess couldn't fathom how he managed to make a tail look smug, but somehow, he nailed it. "Also, the lock wasn't fastened." He shrugged.

"Lark!" Tess cried, quickening her pace as the tiefling lifted the chest lid. "If it's not locked, it might as well have a sign on it that reads, 'It's a trap, suckers!' Just wait a minute!"

Too late. The lid creaked open and clanged loudly against the floor as Lark opened it wide and peered inside. His angular features drooped into a frown. "Empty," he said. "Well, not quite. There's a weird little figurine that looks like a tankard, but nothing else." He reached into the chest and pulled out a small object, stuffing it into his shirt before Tess could get a good look. "Alas, I've nothing more to show for my heroic efforts—wait!" he shouted, making Tess jump. He reached both hands inside the chest, going elbows deep as he rooted around for something she couldn't see. "I knew it!" he said, swiveling his head to beam at them. "False bottom!"

"Hold up," Tess said, motioning the rest of the party to stop while she crouched on the floor. She'd found the spike trap's control mechanism, cleverly concealed to look like part of the stone. Once she could disable it, the rest of them could move freely through the room.

And she could tie up Lark and throw him into Anson's bag of holding.

As she worked, Lark yanked out the false bottom of the chest, tossing it across the room. It landed on a gray stone, and instantly a nest of sharpened spikes erupted from the floor, skewering the piece of flimsy, velvet-covered wood.

"There's another one disabled for you, Tess," Baldric said cheerfully.

Tess gritted her teeth and kept at it.

"What are you seeing, Lark?" Anson asked. The bard had fallen silent as he examined the inside of the chest. "Anything tasty?"

"It connects to a tunnel," Lark said. "Delves deep into the floor and then curves away, probably into another chamber." He leaned down, the upper half of his wiry body disappearing into the chest.

"Well?" Tess demanded. She was trying to hurry, and her fingers fumbled with the trap mechanism. "What's in there?"

"It just keeps going," Lark said, his voice muffled. "Tunnel's big enough for a person to fit, I'd wager. We can explore—" He stopped. Out of the corner of her eye, Tess saw Cazrin's fingers tighten on her staff. Silence reigned in the room except for the hiss and spark of the torches along the wall and the harsh wheeze of Uggie's breathing.

Then Tess heard it. A soft *tap tap tap tap* tapping sound coming from somewhere beneath their feet, like the quick patter of a hand drum.

"Lark?" Tess asked. "What is that?"

No response.

"Lark?" Anson said, an edge of concern in his voice. "Silverstring!"

Tap tap tap tap. The sounds were getting closer.

A terrible suspicion seized Tess. Fingers flying over the trap mechanism, she finally disabled it with a soft click. Abandoning her careful footing, she broke into a run toward Lark. "Get him out of there!" she ordered. "Baldric, help me!"

They reached the bard, who was now buried to the waist in the treasure chest. Wrapping her thick arms around his legs, Tess heaved Lark out of the chest while Baldric supported his torso.

A small, hideous creature that looked like a brain that had sprouted four overly large feet was attached to Lark's face by its front claws. Three others just like it poured out of the chest around him and moved spiderlike across the room, their claws scrabbling over the stone.

"Intellect devourers!" Cazrin cried, just as Lark let out an ear-piercing scream.

Tess dropped Lark's legs, leaving Baldric to hold him while she drew her daggers, all the while thinking, *Brains with legs, brains with legs, Lark is about to have his face ripped off by a brain with legs.* Luckily, Tess had learned the trick of aggressive internal panicking while at the same time being in complete control of a situation.

"Cover me!" she shouted, trusting the others to hold off the horde of intellect devourers that had spilled out of the false bottom of the treasure chest. If only it *had* been a mimic. She hacked at the disgusting creature attached to Lark's face with her dagger, causing the thing's slimy brain to jerk and quiver, but it refused to let go of the tiefling.

Cazrin's chanting voice drifted from across the room as she held up her staff to channel her magic. The purple stone at its tip flashed a fiery carnelian.

"Incoming!" Cazrin warned. "Tess, stay still!"

Tess braced herself as a bright sphere of flame blossomed on the floor just to her right, scattering the three intellect devourers that had been converging on Lark and singeing their wrinkled flesh. The smell of burning brain caught inside Tess's nostrils, and she gagged.

Anson came up on her left with his sword, a once fine blade that had been broken a foot or so above its cross guard, leaving a jagged end. Blue light sparked up and down its shortened length. While Cazrin chased intellect devourers around the room with her fiery sphere, Anson took a swipe at one of the creatures scuttling away from the fire toward him. The monster dodged the blow, leaping aside with surprising dexterity. The strike sent Anson off-balance, but he caught himself with one hand on the floor.

With the devourers distracted, Tess was able to focus on Lark. Clutching a dagger in each hand, she stabbed as hard and as deep as she could into opposite sides of the creature's brain. While Baldric held the tiefling steady, she ripped the monster off Lark's face and heaved it across the room, spraying the far wall with an arc of crimson. The creature landed in a heap, twitched once, and lay still.

One down, Tess thought, breathing heavily.

Lark reared back, blood running down his face and neck to stain his fur-lined coat. Luckily, the wounds were shallow. It looked like the creature hadn't had time to do any real damage. Slumped against Baldric, Lark saluted Tess weakly.

"My thanks," he muttered. "Let me just catch my breath and—"

"We're not out of this fight yet," Tess reminded him, turning to face the other devourers.

"But I'm injured!" Lark complained, just as a dozen tiny motes of golden light took form in the air in front of him, settling into the claw marks slashed on his face. The wounds glowed briefly in the light of the healing magic before fading. Lark's pinched face relaxed, and he shifted in Baldric's grip. "Ah, there's your sweet touch sent to restore me."

"Dust yourself off and kill those beasts, then," the cleric said dryly, hauling Lark upright.

A loud grating sound filled the chamber. A section of the torch-lined wall near Tess was sinking into the surrounding stone, sliding aside to reveal a hidden room. Tess could make out no other details, as there was currently a tall, robed figure looming in the doorway. It stepped forward into the torchlight, and Tess gasped in horrified recognition.

Their very first mission together, and they were facing—

"Mind flayer!" she cried. "Illithid! Heads up, everyone!"

Instantly, the party's attention swung to the figure that entered the room. It was at least six feet tall, dressed in dark robes stained black and stiff in places by old blood. The monster's lavender head vaguely resembled an octopus out of water, with deep-set, piercing eyes and four tentacles that writhed around its face. Tess suppressed a shudder at the sheer wrongness of its appearance.

"Rush it!" she cried. "Don't let it attack or—"

The mind flayer's head jerked in her direction, and all at once, the writhing tentacles stilled. Tess thought she caught a flash of something, an eldritch-purple light deep within the illithid's eyes, and then she felt the pulse of psionic energy sweep through the room, an invisible wave that struck her in the head.

The effect was immediate. Pain exploded behind Tess's eyes, as if someone had stabbed her with an ice pick. Lark and Anson cried out and went to their knees, Anson dropping his sword and clutching the sides of his head. Lark vomited into the open treasure chest. Tess's head throbbed, but she remained on her feet, though she felt dizzy and sick.

She looked around at the others. Luckily, the attack didn't seem to have affected Baldric or Cazrin very much. Tess could hear the cleric muttering some kind of prayer, although it sounded more like he was arguing with himself. His voice was low and gravelly, insistent, but then, suddenly, he thrust his hands out, and a bolt of golden light sprang from his outstretched palms, slamming into the mind flayer's chest. The monster staggered, the golden light lingering on its body like a second skin, its tentacles flailing in displeasure.

"Yes!" Cazrin shouted, whipping her staff in the air. Her flaming sphere rolled across the room, running right over the intellect devourer in its path and setting it on fire. It continued its path of destruction, catching the mind flayer at the legs and driving it back into the room it'd come from. She threw a glance at Baldric, and they exchanged brief, wild grins born of fear and panic as much as excitement.

Tess mentally shook herself, forcing her head to clear and her legs to move. She needed to protect Lark and Anson. But when she looked over to see how her companions were faring, her stomach clenched.

Lark had gotten back to his feet, though he was obviously dazed and unsteady. Anson was still on his knees, and an intellect devourer had scuttled up his back, digging its claws into his shoulder blades. Anson looked up, met Tess's gaze, and then his eyes went wide and vacant as some sort of magic took hold of him.

"Anson!" Tess threw her dagger at the creature, but at the last second, Anson's body jerked into the weapon's path, like a puppet with its strings pulled taut. The dagger sliced open his arm before clattering off the far wall.

"I've got him!" Lark fumbled with his lute as he swung it off his back. It was clear he was still reeling from the effects of the psionic attack from the mind flayer. There was a brief spark of light at his fingertips, but the magic fizzled and died.

Too slow, Tess thought. *Too slow. If I don't do something, we're all going to die.*

The illithid surged back into the room, bearing down on Tess. Instinctively, she lunged forward with her other dagger, stabbing it in the midsection through its thick robes. The mind flayer let out a wailing shriek that rang in Tess's ears. Behind her, Cazrin shouted some arcane phrase, and missiles of light were suddenly raining down on them, riddling the illithid's head and shoulders with wounds and disrupting whatever psionic attack it had been readying next.

"Thanks, Cazrin!" Tess shouted. "Great reaction!"

Cazrin's only reply was a distressed yelp. Tess whipped toward her, expecting a new threat, just in time to see a large mass pushing past Cazrin's legs, almost making her drop her staff.

It was Uggie. She must have been clearing the room of devourers with Cazrin. Head down, tongue lolling, tentacles snapping to attention, she charged toward Anson and the intellect devourer attached to him.

The creature never knew what hit it. It simply disappeared inside Uggie's cavernous maw, and the next thing a shocked Tess knew, there came the sound of intense chewing, like someone eating a fresh orange, peel and all. Anson collapsed to the floor, unmoving, with Uggie standing over him like the strangest, drooliest guard dog ever born.

"Great job, Uggie, that's the last of them!" Cazrin cried.

Tess lunged at the mind flayer again with her dagger, stabbing and moving, never giving the illithid a chance to get near her with its tentacles. A crossbow bolt whizzed over her shoulder, stirring her hair as it flew past her and stuck in the monster's neck. Tess twisted, moving around the mind flayer in time to see Lark reloading the crossbow. He'd abandoned his attempts at a spell and was just using his weapon, his brow furrowed in pain.

Tess darted in behind the mind flayer as it staggered, bleeding from multiple wounds, the breath wheezing in and out of its body. She brought her dagger up and stabbed it in the back with all the force she could muster.

The illithid howled in pain, a thin, reedy shriek that made Tess want to cover her ears, until she realized that the scream was echoing inside her head. She couldn't have blocked it out if she'd tried. The mind flayer sank to the ground, blood pooling on the stones as it slumped onto its side. Tess pulled out her dagger and stepped back, putting her body protectively between the mind flayer and Anson and Lark.

And then the monster spoke.

Tess shuddered as the hissing voice crept into her thoughts, like clawed fingers gently scraping the back of her skull. *I know why you've come,* the illithid crooned, angling its bulbous head in her direction. *You seek the Ruinous Child.*

The Ruinous Child? Tess was confused. They'd come only for the spellbook, not for a person. She opened her mouth to ask what the mind flayer meant, but then she cursed herself. It was probably a trick to draw her in. Before the illithid could speak again, Tess stabbed it in the chest, burying her dagger to the hilt.

"Wait!" Cazrin said. "It was saying something in my head!"

The others must have been hearing it too. It didn't matter. Tess wasn't going to take any chances with the monster. She gazed down at it dispassionately as the light faded from its eyes.

In her head, a last stray thought drifted hazily amid the monster's death throes. *I pass the bane to you, then. The Ruinous Child will be your doom.*

CHAPTER 2

"Anson," Tess said, holding the man's head gently in her lap. He was conscious—sort of—but staring up at her blankly. "Can you hear me?" She patted his cheek with her gloved hand. "I need you to wake up now, all right? You can sleep later."

Her tone was matter-of-fact, but Tess's heart was thundering in her chest. She'd never seen Anson like this before, like there was *nothing* behind his eyes. She hadn't done an in-depth study of intellect devourers, but she knew enough to know that they could seriously mess with your brain if given half a chance.

"I think he's drooling," Lark said, wrinkling his nose. His face was still covered in blood, matting his long dark hair in sticky strands. He'd removed his fur-lined coat and used it to cover Anson, for whatever good that was doing. Thankfully, he seemed to have mostly recovered from the mind flayer's psionic attack.

Uggie had scrunched up her body next to Tess, pressing against her hip and whining in distress. "It's all right, girl," Tess said, patting the otyugh with one hand while she discreetly wiped Anson's chin with the other. "He's going to be just fine." She raised her voice, deliberately keeping her tone calm and even. "Baldric, we need some help over here."

"Give him some space, and I'll be right there," Baldric ordered from across the room.

Tess glanced over to see the cleric searching the mind flayer's body. Baldric's long, sleeveless cloak gathered and draped around him as he stood and came over to them. Cazrin stood nearby, her staff clutched in one hand and worry pinching her face.

Lark obediently moved back, and Tess gently nudged and cooed at Uggie until she shifted behind her, her tentacles lashing the air restlessly.

Baldric crouched next to Anson and waved a hand in front of the man's eyes, snapping his fingers to try to get some reaction.

"He *is* drooling," Baldric said, amused.

"That's what I said!" Lark had moved away, trying to look nonchalant as he shuffled closer to the second treasure chest, which sat untouched in the opposite corner of the room.

"No." Tess snapped her fingers and pointed at him. "Wait for the rest of us."

"I'm not a dog." Lark's shoulders slumped, and he let out a dramatic sigh.

"You had your fun opening the deck of many intellect devourers," Tess said, "and while we're on the subject, you and I are going to have a discussion later about following directions and waiting for backup before you go treasure diving. The figurine in that chest was obviously bait for a trap, and you took it."

"*Fine,*" Lark groused. "I can wait."

"Can you help him?" Cazrin asked Baldric as she sat down on the floor near Anson and Tess.

"Of course," Baldric said. "It's just going to take a bit of coaxing and bargaining." He lifted one end of a ribbon of cloth tied at his belt, which was inscribed with the holy symbols of various gods.

"Bargaining with what?" Lark asked in alarm, putting his body between the cleric and the treasure chest that he'd somehow gotten even closer to in the last few seconds, despite Tess's warning.

"Relax," Baldric said, adjusting the helmet on his head, which had left subtle indentations on his dark brown skin. "I'm not going to offer up any of our loot. Oghma wouldn't be interested in coin anyway." He gave a resigned sigh. "I'm just going to increase my debt to the god of knowledge a bit more. As long as he shows me some grace, we should be fine."

Tess and the others fell silent so Baldric could concentrate, though Tess jerked her head in the direction of the exits from the room, silently bidding Lark to watch their backs. The tiefling nodded, and then all Tess could do was wait as Baldric closed his eyes and uttered a quiet prayer to the god of knowledge, making his offer and waiting to see if it was accepted.

As he finished his prayer, Baldric reached out, his eyes still closed, fingers falling on the open lock Lark had discarded from the first treasure chest. Baldric clutched it in his hand. There was a flash of radiant light, making Tess blink rapidly. When the spots of light in her vision faded, she saw that the lock had vanished. A second, softer burst of radiance illuminated Baldric's cloth, and when it too was gone, there was a new pattern woven onto it. It was a blank scroll—Oghma's symbol.

"You're right," Baldric murmured softly, and somehow Tess knew he wasn't speaking to any of them. He was still communing with the god. "Knowledge unlocked. It's a decent metaphor. We have a deal."

Baldric opened his eyes. His hands glowed golden, and the small blue gem in the center of his helmet pulsed like a heartbeat. He put his hands on Anson's chest, and the light spread over the man's body.

"Come on, Anson," Baldric coaxed, his voice strained from the power he channeled. "Time to wake up. We still have another treasure chest to open. You don't want to miss that. Oh, and you won the bet," he added. "It wasn't a mimic."

Tess leaned forward as Anson began to blink rapidly, awareness and intelligence slowly creeping back into his eyes. His chest expanded on a huge breath, and he sat up—or tried to, since Baldric's hands were still on his chest, pinning him to the floor.

"Easy now," Baldric said gently. "Take a few deep breaths before you try to sprint around the room."

"What happened?" Anson's hands were moving, instinctively

reaching for his sword. Tess had seen the gesture often enough to recognize it. Anson was never far from the broken blade, and he always knew where it was.

"You got mind-blanked by an oversized brain on legs," Lark said helpfully, "and you missed seeing Tess and I bravely facing down a mind flayer together, executing a deadly dance of death that tentacle face could never hope to withstand."

Cazrin grinned.

Tess rolled her eyes. Inside, she felt quivery with relief. That had been close. If Baldric hadn't been with them . . . no, there was no point thinking that way. There were always going to be unknown dangers on missions like this, but when the crisis came, everyone had stepped up and done their jobs—well, Lark had been more of a hindrance than a help, but she'd deal with that situation later.

"Here you go." Cazrin offered Anson his blade. Tess hadn't noticed that she'd picked it up off the floor. She smiled apologetically. "Uggie was trying to use the jagged end as a toothpick, so you might want to clean it later. And she and Baldric are the real reasons you're all right."

"Uggie executed an unplanned but extremely heroic rescue," Tess agreed, "and Baldric came through with the perfect spell to bring you back. I think they're destined to be great partners and friends."

"I'm never intentionally working with that creature," Baldric rumbled. He grinned at her. "I only agreed to travel in its company because I'm waiting for it to murder you in your sleep one night and eat your body so that I can say *I told you so.*"

Tess considered that. "But if I'm dead, how does that give you any satisfaction?" she asked. "Lark, so help me, if you take one more step toward that treasure chest . . ."

Anson eased into a sitting position and took his sword from Cazrin with a weak smile. "Thank you all," he said, and nodded to Baldric. "I mean it, thank you, and sorry for the trouble."

"No trouble," Baldric said, adjusting the cloth at his waist and removing his helmet. "Oghma, it turns out, was happy to help. He's pleased we're rediscovering his lost temple and ridding it of the monster that defiled it."

"Thanks to you too," Anson said, reaching out to give Uggie scritches on the back of her eyestalk, right where she liked it. Instantly, the otyugh bounded forward, heaved her two front legs into the air, and slapped them onto Anson's chest, licking his face ferociously. The fighter absorbed the impact with a faint grunt but didn't complain.

"All right, people, we need to collect loot, get what we came for, and get out of here," Tess said, taking charge once more.

"Does that mean it's finally treasure chest time?" Lark asked hopefully. He steepled his crimson fingers, tapping them restlessly.

"If there's a false bottom, I'm leaving." Anson stood up, handing Lark's coat back to him. "Are you all right?" he asked, gesturing to the blood drying on the tiefling's face, which gave his skin a mottled appearance.

"It's just a scratch." Lark flicked his hair back from his face and gave a careless shrug.

"It helped that Baldric healed him and that he also chugged his last healing potion as soon as the illithid went down," Tess pointed out as she went over to the other treasure chest. She checked it thoroughly for traps, then pulled a lockpick from a small slit concealed in her glove and made quick work of opening the lock. Tossing it aside, she carefully pushed back the lid.

"Finally," Lark said, crowding close to Tess to see what the chest contained.

It wasn't a mimic.

Tess's heart stuttered excitedly as she beheld the pile of gold and platinum coins heaped inside the chest. On top of the mound were two other intriguing items—a triangular-shaped lantern of polished brass and a finely crafted leather mask made to look like a cat's face, complete with two jade eyes.

Tess nodded to the items. "We'll need to check those later to see if there's any magic in them," she said. "And the figurine Lark thinks he's hiding in his coat."

Lark gave an indignant snort, but he reached into the chest pocket of his coat and pulled out the tiny figurine that had been in the other treasure chest.

"Adding this to the coin that Sefeerian Annil already promised us, we're looking at almost a thousand gold, plus whatever those items are worth," Anson calculated with a hum of appreciation. "Not bad at all."

Not to mention it would set people talking about the adventuring party that had successfully infiltrated a lost temple to the god of knowledge *and* killed a mind flayer in the process. Lark could spread the story once they returned to Waterdeep—so would Tess, but a bit more discreetly—and their next job would be even more high-profile than this one.

Everything was going exactly the way Tess had hoped.

"What do you think, Cazrin?" Tess asked, picking up the cat mask. "Any chance these trinkets are magical?" When there was no reply, Tess looked up, searching for her. "Cazrin?"

The wizard was standing in the doorway of the secret chamber from which the mind flayer had emerged, one hand on the wall as she looked inside. She glanced over her shoulder, and her eyes sparkled with excitement.

"I figured it out," she said, "the thoughts the illithid projected into my mind just before it died. It was talking about a Ruinous Child."

"The Ruinous Child will be your doom!" Lark said, in a cringingly accurate imitation of the illithid's telepathic warning. "Very creepy and apocalyptic, but the delivery needed work. What did it mean?"

"It's the spellbook we were hired to find," Cazrin said. She nodded toward the secret room. "The spellbook is the Ruinous Child, and it's *here*."

"Wait right there," Tess said. She and Baldric immediately got up and crossed the room to Cazrin, while Anson and Lark scooped the coins and treasures into Anson's bag of holding. Then they joined the others at the doorway to the illithid's inner sanctum.

Bookshelves lined two of the four walls, and there was a massive, scarred wood table along another wall that was covered in tools and specimen jars containing bones and some squishier-looking things that Tess didn't want to examine too closely.

In the center of the room was a tall, candlelit pedestal. A thick, ancient tome lay closed on top of it and, just as Cazrin had said, the title on the spine read, in Common, *The Ruinous Child*. There were other writings etched into the cover in what looked like multiple languages, none of which Tess could read.

Tess carefully examined the doorway and the floor for traps, but the area was clean. She motioned to the others to spread out and search the room, while she and Cazrin approached the tome situated on the pedestal.

"It matches the description Sefeerian gave us," Cazrin said, pointing out the features of the book. "Red ribbon, elegant silver lock on the cover, made from leather and bits of dragon hide." She ran one finger down the iridescent, purplish-blue scales that covered the lower half of the book. "It really is an impressive tome."

A tiny black thorn, no thicker than a sewing needle, speared from the cover and stabbed the pad of Cazrin's index finger.

"Ouch!" Cazrin jerked her hand back, sucking on the bleeding appendage. She gave the book a hurt look. "What was that for?"

"Guess it doesn't like to be touched," Lark said, turning from where he and Baldric had been searching the bookshelves to examine the tome with a frown. "Are you sure that's leather?"

"If the book has defense mechanisms built into it, maybe we should leave it alone until Sefeerian has a chance to look it over," Anson said from where he stood near the worktable. "Otherwise, we might accidentally unleash its magic and risk hurting ourselves and the book."

"Could jeopardize our reward too if the tome's been messed with," Baldric pointed out.

"They're right," Tess said, giving Cazrin a sympathetic look. "I know you were hoping to study the book, but we should wait until we're back in the city and Sefeerian's had a chance to look at it."

Cazrin's face fell, but she nodded. "Of course. I'll just put it away for safekeeping." Opening one of several satchels she carried, Cazrin carefully slid the tome inside and buckled it shut. "There," she said, still not quite able to hide the disappointment in her voice. "Safe and sound."

"All right," Tess said, "we've got what we came for, so let's strip this room of anything else of value, and then we need to get out of here. It'll take us a full day to get back to Waterdeep, and I don't know about you, but I'm ready for a bath and a drink, not necessarily in that order."

"Drink first," Lark declared, and Anson nodded vigorously in agreement.

Tess walked over to the fighter and pointed to where a patch of his black hair was sticking straight out from his head. "Um, I think Uggie left some intellect devourer parts behind when she licked you earlier," she said.

"She means there's bits of brain in your hair," Baldric said, slapping Anson on the back. "Bath first, maybe."

CHAPTER 3

When they emerged from the temple, it was after nightfall, and Selûne, the cloud-draped moon, shone faintly in the sky, so they made camp in a small wooded area a few miles to the north. The others had wanted to stop sooner, but Tess was determined to put some distance between them and the temple, just in case the illithid had friends that might come looking to avenge its death. She highly doubted it—more likely they would come for the spellbook and the coin they'd taken—but it always paid to be cautious.

When their campsite was secure and they were satisfied there were no monsters lurking in the woods, Baldric lit a small fire, and they gradually settled in for the night. Lark stripped off his blood-stained coat and brought it over to Cazrin with the most forlorn expression and sad puppy dog eyes.

"You have to help me," he begged. "I can't go another hour in this condition. It's unbearable."

Cazrin chuckled as she took the coat and began casting a spell. "You know this thing is completely impractical for adventuring," she said, running her hand over the garment and letting the magic pull out the blood and sweat and seal up the tears in the fabric as if they'd never been there at all. "It has *white* fur. It shows *all* the dirt."

"Yes, but I look amazing in it onstage," he said, taking the coat back from her.

"He really does," Anson said, walking past them with an armful of firewood. Baldric stopped him to examine the slash Tess's dagger had left in his arm. Tess had bandaged it for him before they left the dungeon, but the cleric lifted the stained cloth and moved his hand over the wound, casting a healing spell that made Anson close his eyes and sigh. "Thanks," he said. "That feels a lot better."

"No reason to suffer when I'm right here," Baldric said.

With a throaty whine, Uggie rolled over onto her back in front of Tess, exposing her belly for rubs. Chuckling, Tess complied, and Uggie's tentacles swished back and forth excitedly, kicking up bits of dirt and grass. Her three stumpy legs pawed the air in ecstasy.

"You're a menace, aren't you?" Tess said fondly. "Ever since the night Anson and I found you."

It had been a year ago on a job that had sent them on a grand tour of the Baldur's Gate sewer system in search of a nest of wererats and a stolen diamond necklace. Unfortunately, the otyugh had found the nest first, scattering most of the creatures and killing the rest. When Tess and Anson had arrived, they'd discovered the bloated otyugh covered in blood and mewling pitifully in a pile of unmentionable sludge and wererat parts.

Tess had to admit, her first instinct had been to let nature take its course, but Anson had insisted on healing the creature, since she had done most of their work for them and been hurt in the process. So, with only a little reluctance, Tess had fed the otyugh a healing potion, but it wasn't until several hours later that she and Anson realized the creature had been suffering from indigestion, not wererat bites. Eventually, the otyugh successfully . . . passed the diamond necklace back to them, and then had refused to leave their side. After some discussion, they'd determined the only logical thing to do was to adopt the creature and name her.

"That was a fun night, but I'll never go back to those sewers again," Anson said, dumping the firewood next to Cazrin. He accepted a mug of tea from her with a grateful smile. "Uggie, come here!" He slapped his leg, and Uggie sprang up and bounded across the camp to snuggle against his side.

"I'll take first watch," Tess said. "Everyone should try to get some rest. We're back on the road at dawn."

There were some groans and sighs, but everyone bedded down quickly enough, and soon there was snoring coming from all sides of the camp. Tess glanced over at Cazrin. The wizard was sleeping soundly, her satchels of books stacked up next to her bedroll.

Silent as a shadow, Tess stood up and crept across the camp. When she reached Cazrin's side, she bent down and unbuckled the satchel that held the Ruinous Child. Quick and quiet, she pulled out the tome and returned to the other side of the fire. Placing the book on her lap, she began a cursory examination of the lock holding it shut.

"Little light bedtime reading?"

To her credit, Tess didn't yell out, but she jumped so hard she got a crick in her neck. She looked up to see Anson standing over her, one hand on his hip and a faint smile on his face. He'd taken a quick dip in the sea when they'd emerged from the temple to get rid of the worst of the blood and intellect devourer bits, so his hair was still damp, and he smelled of salt water.

"You can move quietly when you want to," Tess commented with a scowl.

"Look who's talking," Anson said. "I thought a ghost was drifting through the camp just now."

"You're not supposed to be on watch yet," Tess admonished, but she patted the ground beside her anyway, and he took a seat.

"I couldn't sleep," he said, staring absently into the fire.

Tess heard the disquiet in his voice. She reached out and touched his shoulder. "Is it the intellect devourer? Are you feeling all right?"

"I'm fine," he said, but he didn't look at her. "Oh, I got my wits scrambled pretty good, but everything's back to normal." He grimaced. "That's part of the problem actually. Now that I can think straight, I'm remembering that I wasn't very useful in that fight with the mind flayer."

"There's a reason there are five of us in the group," Tess reminded him. "Six, if you count Uggie."

"I *always* count Uggie."

They shared a soft laugh, but the set of Anson's shoulders remained tense. "I keep replaying the fight in my head," he said. "I thought I had everything covered, but I didn't think about there being secret doors and passages in the room that could hide an ambush. When the threat came, I wasn't fast enough to get to it."

"Sounds like you know where you went wrong, so you know how to adjust for next time," Tess said. "That's all you can ask of yourself." She'd been thinking back to that fight herself, trying to see where they could improve. "Next time I'll take more steps to rein in Lark," she said, sighing. "That's on me as party leader. He needs to learn to respect authority."

"But you can't control the way everyone acts on a mission," Anson said. "At some point, you have to trust them to do their jobs, even if they don't do them the way you might like."

"I'm not trying to control Lark," Tess said, frowning at him. "I just want him to wait until I clear a room of traps before he goes waltzing in to make himself comfortable."

"Yes, that would be helpful," Anson admitted. He finally turned to face her, his expression serious. "For it being our first mission, I thought we really came together in that illithid fight. You picked a good group, Tess. Maybe Lark wasn't your first choice to round us out, but—"

"Whazzit?" Lark lifted his head from his pillow, his eyes still shut. "Who said my name? No autographs."

"Go back to sleep, Lark," Tess told him. "You're dreaming."

The tiefling flopped onto his stomach and was immediately unconscious again.

"I don't know," Anson resumed, "I just feel like . . . like we really might have something here with this party."

Pride stirred in Tess's chest. "Didn't I tell you this was going to work?" she said, prodding him in the ribs. "This is just the beginning,

Anson. Now that we've got this first mission under our belts, we've got great things ahead of us. Wait and see."

"I wouldn't dare doubt you. You know, this means we're going to have to pick a party name eventually. Make things official."

"You're right," Tess said. "I'll open it up to the group for suggestions. It'll be fun."

Anson nodded, but his lips were twitching. "That, and you're terrible at names."

"That's not true," Tess said. "I'm very creative."

"Says the woman who named her otyugh 'Uggie.'"

Tess punched him in the arm.

"Ouch. I take it back. You're a master."

They sat together for a while, listening to the sounds of the camp and watching the darkness for any sign of trouble. Cazrin mumbled something unintelligible in her sleep and rolled over, her mouth falling slack. Baldric was snoring softly, and Lark's tail was twitching in the throes of some dream. Uggie had spent the last half hour dragging her body slowly and silently around the fire and was now sleeping three inches away from Baldric.

Idly, Tess toyed with the ribbon sticking out of the spellbook. Even through her gloves, she could feel it was thick and rough, with a texture disturbingly like that of a tongue. And was it her imagination, or was the cover of the book warm to the touch? Cazrin's satchel must have been sitting closer to the fire than she'd thought.

"What's going on there?" Anson asked, nudging Tess's knee with his. "I thought we agreed we weren't going to open that book until we turned it over to Sefeerian."

"Oh, we did, but I have a feeling Cazrin might get itchy hands in the middle of her watch, if you know what I mean," Tess said, sighing, "so I thought I'd at least look over the book to make sure there were no traps that might take her hand off."

He eyed her with a raised brow. "You know these people pretty well already, don't you?"

"Like I said, I'm the party leader. It's my job to anticipate what the group needs and what they might do in any given situation," Tess said, lifting her chin. "You know I'm always prepared."

"I do," he said, "but remember what you just told me. There are five of us. Six, I mean. You don't have to try to do everything yourself. We're all capable, if you give us a chance."

"I understand, and thank you." She patted his arm. "But it *is* my watch right now, and you need to get some sleep."

"Whatever you say, fearless leader." Anson chuckled and moved off to his own bedroll. A few minutes later, he too was snoring in a soft counterpoint to Baldric.

Tess tipped her head back to look up at the stars, listening to the sounds of the night creatures in the woods, always alert for any noises that were out of the ordinary. But everything was as it should be, and it seemed no one was coming after them in the night.

She eyed the spellbook with suspicion. When Cazrin had tried to examine it, the tome had stabbed her with a thorn, so there was obviously some defensive magic built into the book. But it was sitting quietly enough now, so maybe the magic only activated when someone tried to open the book.

Tess wasn't intimidated by those sorts of dangers. In fact, with her training, she considered herself a connoisseur of complicated traps and mechanisms. The Ruinous Child was just a different kind of puzzle, and she was confident she could overcome the book's defenses and spring the lock.

Her mind made up, Tess removed her lockpicking tools from her gloves and spread them on the ground next to her. She tossed another log on the fire and scooted a little closer to the flames to soak up the heat. She focused part of her mind on the lock, checking it over carefully, while the rest of her attention was on her watch. When she was satisfied that there were no traps on the lock itself, she removed her gloves and selected a couple of her favorite lockpicks, fitting the familiar tools to the calluses on her fingers. She took a deep breath, centering herself.

"Now, let's see if we can't get you to spill your secrets," she whispered to the tome.

She inserted the lockpicks and went to work. At first, everything seemed normal. The lock was bigger than it had looked from the outside and deeper than she expected for something placed on a book, but it was nothing she wasn't prepared for. She wouldn't be surprised if the lock was magically altered to seem smaller than it actually was. She'd seen such tricks before, and her tools were more than enough to compensate for them.

Pressing the lockpicks in deeper, Tess concentrated, making tiny adjustments, miniscule movements, manipulating the core of the lock to do exactly what she wanted. Her world narrowed to that one small opening, while around her the forest sounds at night continued as normal. All was well.

Or so she thought. Suddenly, there was an audible *click,* a flash of silver, and both the lockpicks snapped in half. Cursing, Tess yanked out the picks and stared at the ruined ends in bewilderment.

"You've got to be kidding me," she murmured.

She bent closer to examine the lock. It took her a moment, but then she saw it. Twin rows of tiny silver teeth, filed to razor-sharp points, had clamped on to her lockpicks and broken them. Tess was certain they hadn't been there a moment ago when she'd checked the lock for traps. They'd appeared out of nowhere.

"Wait a minute," Tess whispered as a prickle of suspicion crawled up her spine. She blinked, turning the book this way and that in her hands, looking at the lock from different angles. In the wavering firelight, if she squinted just right, the lock almost looked like . . .

A mouth. The intricate silver lock that had appeared to be securing the Ruinous Child's secrets was not a lock at all. It was a mouth, with teeth.

The mind flayer's dying warning echoed in the back of Tess's mind. She pushed it away but couldn't quite suppress a shudder. All right, then, no more messing around with this spellbook. The sooner they handed the Ruinous Child over to Sefeerian, the better.

Then they could get on with the business of making a name for themselves as an adventuring party.

Tess laid the spellbook aside and built up the fire some more before the end of her watch. She still had concerns about the party, of course, especially about Lark. Tess could only hope she'd made the right decision in taking a chance on him. She gazed into the fire, thinking back to that day in Waterdeep.

CHAPTER 4

WATERDEEP—CITY OF SPLENDORS

ONE MONTH AGO

"I think we have to take a chance on him, Anson," Tess whispered, pointing to the stage. "We're running out of options."

"Which one?" Anson whispered back and smiled apologetically when the orc sitting in front of him turned around in her seat and glared. He lowered his voice even more. "There are five of them, and they're doing that tumbling routine so fast I can barely tell them apart. Maybe we should recruit the whole group."

"What?" Tess scowled at him, though he probably couldn't see it in the darkened theater. "Not the *acrobats*—although, yes, I can see where that might come in handy. But I'm talking about the bard waiting offstage." She pointed to the wings. "The one with the lute. His name—well, his stage name—is Lark Silverstring."

"Oh, I see him," Anson said, leaning forward slightly in his seat. "Wait, I thought we were here to look at that flautist from Baldur's Gate. The gnome. What was his name?"

"Doesn't matter," Tess said. "He told me no, and he went back to Baldur's Gate. Lark's our focus now."

"All right, what makes you think *Lark* could be an adventurer?"

"Just watch," Tess said as the acrobats cleared the stage to a rousing burst of applause.

Before the cheers and clapping had died down, the tiefling bard swaggered to center stage. He was dressed in a long white coat with fur trim, and he held a beautiful polished lute carved with small glyphs. He acknowledged the audience with an elegant bow and a charming, crooked smile that sent murmurs of appreciation through the crowd.

The audience hushed as he began to play, and the bard's voice ripped through the air in a song about lost love that was an angry tirade, an accusation, and a plea, all at the same time. He tipped his head back, throat bared, giving everything to the performance. As the song went on, Tess watched the bard's hands closely. His be-ringed fingers made little flourishes as he played, and in response, the music grew louder, richer, seeming to echo from every corner of the theater. A flashing spotlight shone down from somewhere above the bard, where no light had been before. On certain verses, he turned his head so the shadows fell just right on the planes of his face, making him appear devilish and compelling. If you weren't paying attention, you'd miss the subtle changes, the small magics that the bard snuck in through sleight of hand.

Anson noticed it too. "Wow," he said with a low whistle, which earned him another dirty look from the orc. "He's good."

"Right?" The bard's magical effects, and the way he made a connection with each member of the audience, demanding their attention with the power of that magic and the magnetism in his voice—Tess could only imagine what he could do when he focused that power on a monster in battle.

"His magic is impressive," Anson said, slouching down in his seat and pulling Tess with him, probably so he wouldn't have to endure another dagger stare from the orc in front of them. "But weren't you more excited about that halfling druid you were trying to recruit through your contact at the Emerald Enclave? What happened to him?"

"He also said no." Tess waved a hand dismissively. "Trust me, he wasn't a good fit for us."

He'd demanded 20 percent more of the reward for every job in exchange for healing magic, and he'd wanted to share leadership of the party with Tess on account of her *inexperience*. Tess had declined and ended the meeting before she could impale his big toe with a dagger.

No, Lark wasn't her first choice. Or her second. In truth, he hadn't been on her list at all. Asking around about him, Tess had heard a common refrain of "overdramatic," "smug," "devil-may-care," "headache-inducing," and "actually extremely fun at parties." They also agreed that Lark was a hugely talented performer, and Tess had seen that for herself. But if he was so talented, she couldn't help but wonder why he wasn't headlining at an evening show in North Ward, instead of doing an afternoon slot down by the docks in a theater that smelled like fish.

Tess wasn't just gathering up strays to make some quick coin. She was trying to build something here—a group that she hoped to mold into the best adventuring party in Faerûn. On the surface, Lark didn't seem to be an ideal candidate for that, but he was undeniably charismatic. He had the audience eating out of his hand with his confident smiles and easygoing charm as he chatted with them between songs. All of it was calculated, yet it looked effortless. He invited the audience in, but only so far. Tess was the leader of the party, but every group needed that thread of charm and affability. Anson had it too, but his was altogether genuine. Tess didn't believe he was capable of using it to manipulate someone, but she was willing to bet that Lark did so often.

Her mentor had always told her to trust her instincts. Tess's instincts were singing to her that this bard was going to be trouble, but from what she'd seen, he could do the job. He was just going to require a firm hand and some guidance. Given enough time, she could mold him into the adventurer they needed to complete their party.

Anson turned to her. "So, how do you want to approach him?"

Tess sat up in her seat and watched the tiefling finish his last song. The crowd surged to their feet for a standing ovation. True, it was an afternoon show at a dockside theater that seated only a few dozen patrons, but the audience had been rapt through the whole thing.

"Let's head backstage," Tess said. She stood up and carefully inched her way down the narrow aisle, effortlessly hopping over people's boots and the tankards of ale they'd smuggled into the theater from the tavern next door because the drinks were cheaper. Anson followed behind her more slowly, grunting and apologizing as he stepped on some toes.

Off to one side of the stage, there was a small door leading to a dimly lit hall. Tess held the door for Anson and then closed it firmly behind her, cutting off the sound of the applause, which showed no signs of slowing, even though the bard had already left the stage.

There was a door on either side of the dingy hall. Like the rest of the theater, this area had obviously seen better days. The paint was peeling off the walls, and the smell of old sweat was cloying. "His dressing room should be one of these two," Tess said, knocking on the door to her right.

A familiar, smoky voice called out, "Come in."

Tess had been expecting a dressing room, with mirrors and a changing screen and maybe a couch or some comfortable chairs, so she was surprised to find herself stepping into a glorified storage room. Crates overflowing with props lined one wall, and racks of costumes filled most of the remaining space. In the corner farthest from the door, someone had hung a plain mirror on the wall with a jagged crack running down the center. There was a small table and stool positioned in front of it. Lark sat on the stool, facing away from them. A pair of candles in iron holders flanked the mirror, providing some meager, uneven light. The only other illumination came from the small, dirty windows high above them on the wall.

"Glorious, isn't it?" Lark said, watching Tess in the mirror with a sardonic smile. He had a damp towel around his shoulders that he was using to wipe the sweat off his face. "The flowers should be arriving shortly. They do a lot to brighten up the place."

"I'll bet," Tess said. "You deserve them. It was a great performance."

The tiefling's face lit with pleasure as he swiveled on the stool to face them. "Guests who come bearing flattery are always welcome too," he said.

"That first song you did was a knockout," Anson said. "What's it about?"

"Bad breakup, among other things," Lark said easily, leaning back to rest his elbows on the table.

"Oh, well, I'm sorry to hear that," Anson said. "Must be hard to write about lost love."

"You misunderstand, friend." The bard's shoulders shook with silent laughter, his eyes dancing merrily. "I was in a *band,* and we broke up. A regrettable but common tale in the world of musicians. Two of the members were skimming extra coin from our shows. Trust was broken, and that's hard to recover from," he said, sobering. "But it made amazing fodder for songs, as you witnessed."

"I'm glad things worked out for you in the end," Tess said. She strode across the room and stuck out her hand. Lark took it in a firm grip. "Tessalynde Halendria," she said, "but you can call me Tess. My friend's name is Anson Iro. We're professional infiltrators."

"Really?" Lark asked, clasping Anson's hand in turn. "I love it— sounds absolutely nefarious."

"Thanks, but it's mostly just a technical term," Anson said, leaning against the wall.

"But an accurate one," Tess said. "We do engage in infiltration missions, even dipping into the occasional burglary when called for, but it's all ethical."

"How intriguing," Lark said, his smile widening. "And how do you go about this 'ethical burglary'?"

"I can't speak to specific missions or clients," Tess said, neatly sidestepping the question, "but I can tell you we recover lost items, find missing persons, and, yes, sometimes we steal back that which has been stolen from others, especially when the authorities fail to recover said items for the victims."

"You're right, it all sounds very ethical and aboveboard," Lark said, pressing a hand to his chest. "So, what can a humble musician and thespian like myself do for master infiltrators like you?"

There was nothing humble about the tiefling, and Tess returned his grin to make sure he knew she wasn't fooled.

"Anson and I are putting together an adventuring party," Tess said, "led by me, with work for a party of five—"

"Six," Anson interjected.

"Possibly six," Tess said, stepping on the toe of his boot. She wasn't ready to discuss Uggie yet. Uggie was . . . a lot.

Luckily, she was saved from elaborating when Anson picked up a theater program from a box by the door. "They misspelled your name here."

"Let me see that." Lark snatched the program and stared indignantly at the caption below a passable sketch of his face. "Lerk? *Lerk?*" He threw the program down on the dressing table with an affronted sigh. "How hard can it be? It's *four* letters!"

"A travesty," Anson agreed. "Can I have it back, though? There's a coupon in there—two-for-one fish plate at Neera's next door."

"I should've never signed on for a dockside show," Lark muttered. He caught Tess watching him. "One does what one must for coin, especially when one is trying to make up for being swindled by one's former friends."

"You know who'll never misspell, mispronounce, or otherwise disrespect your name?" Tess asked, seizing the opening Lark had inadvertently given her. "Who'll never cheat you? A dedicated party of adventuring companions assembled from all corners of Faerûn with more than three hundred years' combined experience going for them."

"You want me to join your ethical burglary band?" Lark looked up from where he'd been ripping the coupon out of the program to give to Anson.

"For a trial run, at least, with an eye toward a long-term arrangement. We already have a talented wizard and cleric," Tess said. Baldric Goodhand had done some healing for them in the past, and Anson had found Cazrin Varaith through a mutual contact when he was looking to have some magic items identified, so they'd worked together before. "The first job is for the wizard Sefeerian Annil. He wants us to recover a spellbook he lost long ago in some underground ruins just south of the city, near the coast."

Lark's expression had turned bored, which didn't bode well. "Poking around in old ruins for hours on end sounds thrilling, but what exactly is in this for us city dwellers, storytellers, and lovers of finer things?" he asked.

Tess had been hoping he would ask that question. It meant she still had his interest. Now to seal the deal.

"The reward is any treasure we recover in the ruins"—Tess paused for effect—"plus five hundred gold pieces for successfully delivering the lost spellbook intact."

Lark didn't immediately reply, but Tess noticed the tiefling's tail, which had been absently curling and uncurling around the leg of the stool, went still. There was a flash of something avaricious in his eyes, so quickly smothered that Tess almost thought she'd imagined the tell. But no, the bard had inadvertently betrayed himself.

He needed money—which stood to reason, considering his past and where he was performing—and he was much more interested in this job offer than he wanted to let on. Tess resisted the urge to rub her hands together in excitement. No doubt about it. She had him.

Now she just had to hope she wouldn't come to regret it.

CHAPTER 5

WATERDEEP—CITY OF SPLENDORS

PRESENT DAY

The party arrived back in the city late the following day. Every time she returned to Waterdeep, Cazrin felt her heart flutter with excitement, as if she were visiting the place for the first time. Maybe it was a trick of the City of Splendors, some unknown magic that made the city show her a new face each time she passed through its gates.

It was a city of endless possibilities. The people who lived and worked here had come from the far corners of Faerûn and everywhere in between. It was a place where you could disappear and be anonymous your whole life if that was what you wanted. A city where you could make your fortune and hear your name sung in ballads in taverns in every ward. You could stride onto the docks and take ship to the Moonshae Isles or to the far north, to Luskan and the borders of the Sea of Moving Ice. Or you could sail and sail to lands unknown, places where few folk had walked—and lived to tell their tales.

Waterdeep was a city where your past didn't have to define you, and your future was a story unwritten. Cazrin smiled dreamily up at the towering buildings. She hoped she never lost that fluttery feeling when she returned to the city.

"Are we getting drinks or what?" Lark threw a companionable arm around Cazrin's shoulders as they dodged out of the path of a loaded wagon that was approaching with some speed on the narrow lane.

Cazrin coughed on the dust cloud that rose in the wagon's wake, wiping her streaming eyes. There were other, less romantic parts to the city too, she allowed. "A drink would be nice," she admitted, coughing again, "but we should really get Sefeerian's spellbook delivered to him, shouldn't we?"

"And collect our reward!" Tess said brightly from the front of the group.

Cazrin's hand went automatically to her satchel, where the Ruinous Child was still safely tucked away. She'd kept her word and hadn't tried to get into the locked tome. Not that she'd been thinking about it. Much. And anyway, Tess had reiterated when she'd woken Cazrin for her watch that the book was not to be trusted, and that it was probably best to leave the thing alone until they talked to Sefeerian. Still, it was so tempting. If she could just spend some time with it, conduct some experiments and take notes, maybe examine the lock for magical properties . . .

Cazrin shook her head. No, she would wait. She could do this.

Sefeerian Annil's townhouse was situated on a quiet street at the edge of North Ward, one of the more residential and well-to-do wards of the city, though not as flashy as some. Eventually they left the worst of the traffic and road dust behind them, but when Cazrin and the others stopped in to request a meeting, Sefeerian's housekeeper briskly informed them that the wizard was out visiting a friend and wouldn't be back until later that evening.

Cazrin couldn't help being disappointed at the delay. She'd hoped to have an in-depth discussion with Sefeerian about the Ruinous Child. But her stomach was growling too, reminding her she'd had an apple for breakfast and nothing else.

Lark was bouncing on the balls of his feet. "Drink now?" he asked plaintively.

Tess rolled her eyes, but she was grinning. "Drinks and food," she agreed. "We'll come back this evening, but for now: to the Yawning Portal!"

The others nodded their assent, and Anson said, "It's probably the most Uggie-friendly of all the taverns."

He had a point. Cazrin glanced down at Uggie, who was ambling along behind the group, wearing a custom-fitted cloak and hood designed to hide her tentacles and intimidating mouthful of teeth. It worked well enough on a crowded street when no one was looking too closely. People just assumed she was a large, pampered dog. When they went inside inns and taverns, Cazrin had offered to cast an illusion over her to make her look like an actual dog. But the Yawning Portal, with its open passage to the famed Undermountain right in the middle of the tavern, saw more than its fair share of monsters coming up from the depths. So, if Cazrin's illusion broke, most people in the tavern probably wouldn't think twice about it.

"Or we could just have her wait for us in the alley," Baldric pointed out.

"You don't mean that," Cazrin said, smiling at him. "I caught you feeding her a strip of bacon this morning before we broke camp."

Baldric looked aghast. "It was a moment of weakness! You swore you wouldn't tell!"

WHEN THEY ARRIVED at the tavern, the crowd was sparse, and the party was able to grab drinks at the bar and find a table on the second level near the balcony, in full view of the large, open well in the common room below—the entrance to Undermountain. Tess took a spot near the balcony railing, and Cazrin noticed she scooted her chair closer to the edge so she could look down, as if she were waiting for the curtain to rise on an evening show.

To be fair, the Yawning Portal did get more than its fair share of excitement. If it wasn't monsters crawling up from the depths to menace the drinkers and diners, it was adventuring parties descending the same dark tunnel to try their luck in the dungeons of the famed Undermountain.

The subterranean maze of caverns and monster lairs, traps and treasure hoards, and everything in between was overseen by the mad mage Halaster Blackcloak. Only the very skilled or the truly fool-hardy—or both—ventured into its depths to seek their fortunes and delve the dungeon's mysteries.

"Someday, it's going to be us going down there," Tess murmured, as if she could read Cazrin's thoughts. Her eyes were bright from the wine she'd been drinking. She rested her arms on the balcony rail and propped her chin on them, staring dreamily down into the dark well.

It was the first time Cazrin had seen the elf relax. Maybe it was just the wine and the thrill of returning from a successful mission that had her lowering her guard. Either way, Cazrin found she liked seeing a glimpse of the less professional, buttoned-up side of their party leader.

The others were ordering more drinks and food for the table and weren't paying any attention to them. Cazrin leaned on the balcony rail next to Tess and followed her gaze. "There must be an awful lot of magic hidden down there," she said, with a wistful sigh. "Imagine all the spells just waiting to be discovered."

"That's what I'm saying!" Tess's eyes lit with excitement. "Every-one in this group is passionate about something. We have ambitions. We *want* things. Just like you with your magic. We need to harness that, use it to become the best adventuring party that Faerûn has ever seen."

"Is that what you want?" Cazrin asked curiously. "To be the best?"

"I . . ." Tess's voice trailed off as she considered the question, her gaze going unfocused for a moment.

"You think Undermountain is the way to become a legend?" Bal-dric drawled, pushing in between them. "Isn't that just where they send all the obnoxious new adventurers when they need to cull the ranks a little? It's like pruning the garden to get rid of the weeds."

"You're terrible," Cazrin said with a giggle. "That's not what Un-dermountain is for."

"Prove me wrong," Baldric challenged, gesturing over the bal-cony with his glass. "This place is a huge, multilevel tavern with a gigantic hole in the center. Dangerous enough for the common drunk and surely goes against several municipal codes, but that"—he pointed at the dark void—"doughnut hole of disaster is just begging for adventurers to wander up, get drunk on ale or their own arrogance, whichever they have the most of, and then scuttle over and jump into the hole, never to be seen again."

Cazrin cocked her head, considering. "You do make some compelling points," she allowed.

"Don't encourage him," Tess said in exasperation. "Baldric, are you really saying you wouldn't jump at the chance to become a legend?"

Baldric snorted. "You'd be surprised at how little that title gets you."

"*I* want to be a legend," Lark butted in. "For a song and a dance, for a good story and a romance," the tiefling sang, his voice carrying the impromptu tune perfectly. Abruptly, he dropped the song. "But I'm with Baldric. I've no desire to launch myself into a deep, dark, doughnut-hole dungeon ruled by a mad wizard in order to be unceremoniously slaughtered and forgotten."

Lark beckoned Cazrin closer, whispering in her ear so Tess wouldn't overhear, but the elf had already turned away to say something else to Baldric. "If I'm being completely honest, I'm a bit salty about this tavern because my former bandmates are going to be playing here next month," he explained, "and this was also the place we were playing the night I left them. It's probably not fair to blame the venue, but the band broke up under intense circumstances."

"What happened?" Cazrin asked. She felt the tiniest bit guilty for prying, but she couldn't help her curiosity.

The bard leaned in closer. "Well, you see, there was a woman I . . . cared about. We'd been together for six months before our harp player, Gustan, met her and the two of them . . . well . . ." A spasm of pain crossed Lark's face. "The rest, as they say, is history. I just couldn't stay with them any longer after that betrayal."

"Oh, I'm . . . sorry," Cazrin said, feeling awkward. Hadn't Tess said something about Lark's band breaking up over money? Maybe she'd misheard. "Of course you couldn't stay with them." She looked around the room. "Should we go somewhere that's more comfortable for you?"

Lark gave her a tremulous smile. "We all have to face our pasts eventually, don't we? But thank you for understanding, Cazrin. I . . . appreciate that."

She was saved from replying when their server returned and placed a platter of steaming bread with honey and butter in the center of the table, followed by a large block of orange cheese. More wine and fresh tankards of ale joined these, all of which drew Lark's attention away from his painful memories.

Cazrin put a slice of thick cheese on her bread and took a generous bite before reaching into one of her satchels. "I examined those items we recovered from the temple," she said, removing the small figurine, the lantern, and the cat mask and placing them on the table.

The party immediately crowded closer. "Are any of them magical?" Anson asked. He'd picked up the figurine and was comparing its general shape to the tankard in his other hand. They were surprisingly similar, though the figurine had been made up to look like an adorable miniature house.

"They all are," Cazrin confirmed. She nodded to the lantern. "I think Baldric might get the most use out of that," she said. "It'll channel his healing magic to anyone standing in its light, disbursing his power more widely."

"How poetic," Lark said, "not to mention useful. I will bask in its glow whenever possible."

"I bet you will." Baldric grinned as he took the lantern.

Cazrin picked up the cat mask and handed it to Tess. "This helps locate things that are hidden, specifically trap mechanisms," she said.

"Really?" The elf's brows rose in curiosity as she turned the mask over in her hands. She held it up in front of her face so the others could see the effect. As she pressed the leather against her cheeks, the mask slowly conformed to the contours of her face so that it fit her perfectly. The green gems flashed with a brief magical light. Tess removed the mask, and a slow smile spread across her face. "Oh, I'm going to like this," she said. Then, as if sensing the others watching her, she cleared her throat hastily. "That is, it'll be a valuable asset for the party. What about the figurine?"

Cazrin took the small tankard from Anson. "This one we'd better test out when we're alone and have plenty of space," she cautioned.

"Why?" Anson asked. "Does it produce endless amounts of ale? Because that would be the dream."

Lark raised his wineglass. "I'll drink to that."

"I'm afraid it's not that," Cazrin said. "Well, maybe . . . let's just say, the magic summons an extradimensional space."

"And what's inside this space?" Tess asked warily.

Cazrin lifted her shoulder in a shrug. "I'm not sure," she said. "We'll have to find out."

The server returned just then with their meals, so Cazrin took the figurine and slipped it into her pouch. Bowls of stew were passed around the table, and Tess took one of them and set it on the floor beside her, where Uggie was waiting to be fed. Her tentacles slapped impatiently against Cazrin's and Tess's chairs, but luckily, with the illusion spell firmly in place, the otyugh just looked like a big drooly sheepdog wearing a cloak.

Uggie sniffed the contents of the bowl and gave the soup an unenthusiastic lick. She looked up at them with forlorn eyes and whined.

"What's wrong, girl?" Cazrin asked, patting her head. "You don't like your stew?"

"It's probably too bland," Anson said. He raised a finger at a passing server, a halfling boy who was carrying a tray loaded with drinks. He stopped by their table, brown curls falling into his eyes, looking harried.

"Can I get you something?" he asked, puffing his cheeks and blowing the hair out of his face.

"Yes, please," Anson said, flashing him an affable grin. "Can you bring me a bucket of bacon grease?"

The halfling blinked dark brown eyes. "Pardon?"

"There's probably one sitting in the alley out behind the kitchen," Anson said. "Bring that in, and if there's any refuse scattered around the alley—apple cores, rusty nails, cat vomit—feel free to scoop that in there too. Add some vinegar, throw a cloth over the bucket, and bring it to the table." Anson dropped a silver shard coin on the halfling's tray. "We'd be so grateful."

When the boy continued to stare at Anson with his mouth open, Tess chimed in. "It's for our dog," she explained, pointing to Uggie. "She has . . . unusual dietary needs."

"Iron deficiency," Anson said.

The halfling caught sight of Uggie, and his face split in a grin.

"Oh, what a cute doggy. And look at her little doggy cloak! Oh, if I wasn't carrying this tray, I'd give you so many belly rubs! Yes, I would!"

Uggie thumped her sheepdog's tail—tentacle—against the floor and wiggled her entire body in excitement.

"I do believe it's love," Lark said, as the halfling left the table with promises to bring back Uggie's special meal.

"The feeling is mutual, I think," Cazrin said, keeping a hand on Uggie's back to stop her from trotting off after the halfling.

"We should discuss party names," Tess said, changing the subject. "Now that we've got our first mission as a group behind us, we should consider the long term. We need people to be able to put a name to our reputations. I'm thinking Tess's Treasure Seekers, but I'm open to suggestions."

Lark made a face. "How about anything but that one?"

"What, you think you can do better?"

"The League of Loot," Anson said, thumping his tankard on the table.

"Fortune's Fools," Lark countered. "I enjoy the tragicomedy of it."

"The Mighty Mercs," Baldric suggested.

"It'll come to us," Lark said. "You can't rush these things." He finished his wine and reached for his lute. He began to play softly, humming along with a song he'd been working on during their trek to and from the temple. Cazrin had asked him its title, but, much like the name of their adventuring band, inspiration had eluded him so far.

The silver pendant around his neck glinted in the light as he played, and Cazrin sat back in her chair, comfortably warm and sleepy from the food and wine. She was just contemplating getting out her spellbook to take some notes on their adventure when Anson leaned across the table, catching the party's attention with an intent look.

"We're being watched," he said, keeping his voice low. He leaned back and took a casual swig from his tankard while surreptitiously tilting his head in the direction of a table off in the corner of the tavern.

Lark gave a nod but kept playing so as not to arouse suspicion.

Cazrin made a show of adjusting the satchel strapped to her belt while glancing in the direction he'd indicated.

Three cloaked and hooded figures sat at a nearby table, huddled together in the shadows, so it was difficult to make out anything about their appearance. But their attention was on the party.

"Maybe they're just music lovers," Baldric observed dryly. "Followers of yours, Lark?"

"They would have already come over to shake hands and buy me a drink, if that was the case," Lark said. His hat was tipped low on his head, but he peeked out from under the brim to get a look at the figures. "They do seem to be awfully fixated on us."

"They don't look very friendly to me," Tess said. "Let's slip out the back. No need to make a scene." She pointed to Lark and Baldric. "You two go first. Pretend you need the outhouse or something."

Lark stood up from the table with an exaggerated stretch. "Ah, that wine went right through me," he said, slurring his words slightly as he fell into the performance.

"Me too," Baldric said, also rising. Cazrin noticed that he angled his body in such a way as to make sure his large and intimidating-looking mace was visible to the figures skulking at the back table. "Time to be getting on with our night anyway."

They slipped away from the table. Tess rose next, leaning across the table to snag a last hunk of cheese, which put her in position to whisper to Anson and Cazrin. "Let's have Uggie do a little distraction. I'm going to cover Lark and Baldric." Anson gave a nod of acknowledgment, but he appeared distracted, fiddling with an empty sheath at his belt.

"What's wrong?" Cazrin asked him.

"Nothing," Anson said. "I just realized one of my daggers is missing—the black one that I liked. I must have dropped it sometime during the illithid fight."

"We'll get you another one later," Tess promised him, and with that, she moved away from the table, vanishing into the shadows with astonishing ease.

"She's impressive," Cazrin whispered to Anson.

"It's unnerving sometimes," Anson whispered back.

They lingered at the table, chatting, until the cloaked figures also left their table, heading for the stairs. Then Cazrin gave Anson a nod. He bent and patted Uggie's head.

"Go say hello, girl," he told her, nodding in the direction of the three figures. "I think they might have bacon."

Uggie needed no extra encouragement. She bounded across the room and jumped up to put her front paws on the smallest figure's back. There was a muffled *oof* as the figure stumbled, cursing.

"Get that dog away from us," they snapped in Common.

"Oh, I'm so sorry," Anson said, hurrying over to pull his "dog" away. Cazrin tried to get a closer look at the three as he did so, but the low light and hoods kept the figures' features stubbornly in shadow. "She just loves people, you see. She won't bite. She's just the sweetest."

Cazrin hid her smile behind her hand. Using the distraction, she too rose from the table and melted into the crowd heading to the bar. When she was relatively sure she wasn't being watched, she headed downstairs and out the back exit to join up with the others.

INTERLUDE

"We're ready to move," the Zhentarim soldier said from the doorway. "Just give the word."

Lorthrannan looked up from the document he'd been reading and snared the human's gaze. The Zhent was short and on the scrawny side, a man who'd never eaten quite enough as a child, and it showed as an adult. Lorthrannan remembered, in an abstract sort of way, when things like eating and drinking had been concerns that occupied his thoughts. When day-to-day survival had been a tenuous thing.

It had been a very long time ago.

He felt the gulf of time most keenly when others looked at him, as the Zhent was doing now. To his credit, the man didn't cower in fear. His face was a mask of neutrality, but it was a brittle thing. He stayed firmly on the opposite side of the room, in the safety of the doorway, poised to run if it came to that. They were always poised to run.

They never got far, but there was no reason to let the man know that.

"See it done," Lorthrannan said. His voice had changed over the long years. He remembered that he used to love to sing, and he'd been skilled at it. Had he ever sung a song that made people weep? It felt like he had, but that had been a long time ago too. Now when he spoke it was a husk of sound, deep and unpleasant, but still somehow resonant enough that it made people turn and give heed.

He enjoyed that too, trading one sort of power for another.

The man in the doorway nodded and turned to leave, his expression losing some of its rigidity. He couldn't quite hide his relief at being dismissed from Lorthrannan's sight.

Maybe that was what made Lorthrannan call out to the man right before he made his escape, snaring him again with a question.

"Did you see *him* with the others?" Lorthrannan asked. "The one who was looking for you? *Anson*, was it?"

The man stiffened, and Lorthrannan heard his soft intake of breath. But his voice was calm enough when he answered. "You honor me by remembering, Lorthrannan. My troubles are nothing you need concern yourself with. I have everything under control."

"I don't think it's your place to tell me what my concerns should be," Lorthrannan said, and was gratified to feel the wave of fear that rolled off the man. "Is it, Valen?"

The man's eyes widened when he heard his name, and the fear intensified. Lorthrannan felt a stab of irritation. Really, did his servants imagine that he wouldn't learn every intimate detail of their lives? Their pasts, their family connections, debts, joys, and deepest fears? Knowledge was how he exercised control.

Especially with names. Names were Lorthrannan's favorite form of power. Show a person you know their real name, and you show them that you know all about the past they've tried to leave behind.

"Forgive me," Valen said. "I shouldn't presume to tell you your business. I only meant that *he* won't be a problem."

"Good," Lorthrannan said. He was appeased, and now he was tired of the man's presence. "Proceed, and report back as soon as it's done."

The man bowed and quickly left the room. This time, Lorthrannan didn't call him back.

It wouldn't be long now.

Lorthrannan stood and walked to the full-length mirror that hung on the back wall of the chamber. There was no reflection in the silver-bordered glass, but he'd enchanted it to show other scenes. At the moment, the mirror displayed a sweeping view of the Lake of Dragons on approach to Marsember. Lorthrannan extended a hand and touched the glass with his fingertips. His finger bones stood out prominently against pale, papery flesh.

The mirror rippled at his touch. The pewter lake darkened to inky black, the scene shifting to a firelit study, a partial view of a leather armchair where a feminine figure sat with a book open on her lap. Her head was bent over the text, just the pointed tips of her ears showing through her long, pale blond hair. Her hand, as it moved to turn the page, was a webwork of rotting flesh.

"I trust you have a compelling reason for disturbing me," Valindra Shadowmantle said without looking up from the book.

"Forgive me." Lorthrannan smiled, feeling the skin pull against his hollow cheeks. "I wouldn't dare intrude upon your privacy, but I have a proposition for you that I believe you'll want to hear. You see, I've located the Ruinous Child."

CHAPTER 6

Evening had turned to night by the time the party regrouped and made their way to Sefeerian's home to keep the appointment they'd made earlier. Tess led the group along a winding route through the back streets of Castle Ward, ducking into warehouses and other taverns, keeping to the shadows so they wouldn't bring trouble to their employer's doorstep. By the time they crossed over into North Ward, there was no sign of the figures who'd been watching them in the tavern. The party was tired, slightly drunk, but still buzzing with excitement.

With one last look around to make sure they weren't being followed, Anson nodded to Tess, and she strode up to Sefeerian's door to knock. When she put her fist against the wood, the door swung open a few inches with a soft squeaking sound.

"Someone left the door open?" Cazrin asked, as a prickle of unease swept across the back of Tess's neck.

"I don't like this." Tess frowned as she bent to examine the latch and lock. "There's blood on the doorframe here. It's fresh." She turned to Anson. "Watch our backs. I'm going in. I'll signal the rest of you when it's clear."

Anson nodded and drew his broken sword, watching the quiet street. Lark joined him, and Baldric walked up to the door to stand next to Tess. "Don't go too far alone," he cautioned. "We don't know what we're walking into."

Tess gave a nod and eased the door open with her gloved hands, careful to avoid the blood, which she could see now was dripping down the doorframe. She slipped inside the house, her stomach tightening with foreboding as she made her way into the small foyer. Magical driftglobes lit the space in a soft, welcoming glow, and the air smelled of fresh flowers and furniture polish, but with a jarring undercurrent of copper. A vase was overturned on a side table, and a mixture of water and blood had been ground into the carpet nearby, as if someone had slipped, tried to catch themselves on the table, and fallen.

More blood formed a trail to the foot of a marble staircase.

Tess stood silently, listening for any sounds of movement and life in the house. A soft thump echoed above her head, followed soon after by a faint moan.

Someone was upstairs.

Tess hurried back to the door and peeked her head out. "There's a lot of blood, but there's also at least one person alive in here," she said. "You'd better come." She pulled back into the house, and the others filed into the foyer behind her.

"Don't touch anything until I've looked at it first," Tess warned as Lark drifted over to examine the overturned vase. She pulled her newly acquired cat mask over her eyes, hoping it would help in her search. For a second before the magic activated, the room was all shades of green seen through the tiny eyeholes, restricting her field of vision. But then, it was as if a film had been lifted, and her vision sharpened and expanded all at once, setting her momentarily off-balance. When she'd recovered her equilibrium, she discovered that everything in the foyer was in hyperfocus, allowing her to see fine details without having to get too close.

Tess wished she could have taken some time to tinker and play with the mask, but they needed to get moving. "I'll check out the staircase before we go up," she said. "Everyone, watch yourselves. We don't know what kind of defenses Sefeerian might have guarding his home."

"Or what kind of messes he leaves behind for his housekeeper," Lark commented, bending over to scoop up a small glass vial that had rolled under the table. A pinkish residue swirled in the bottom. He tossed it to Baldric, who caught it in one large hand. "Healing potion, do you think?" Lark asked.

Baldric sniffed the vial, then tipped the last bit of liquid onto his fingertip. He touched his tongue to the liquid for a quick taste. "Healing potion," he confirmed. "Looks like someone was hurt, downed the potion, and then took off in a hurry."

"What if that had been poison?" Anson asked with a raised eyebrow. He was holding on to one of Uggie's tentacles so she didn't wander. The illusion that Cazrin had cast on her earlier had faded, and she was back to looking like herself again.

"Then you'd be down one cleric," Baldric said with a grin. "Don't worry, I can smell a healing potion a mile away."

"Let's check out the second floor," Tess said, moving slowly up the staircase. She motioned to the group to follow behind her. She heard Cazrin's soft tread and the swish of her overskirt coming up first, sticking close to Tess as she chanted the words of a spell softly under her breath. Tess didn't have to ask what it was. She recognized the chant, if not the words, that Cazrin had used down in the temple when she was looking for hidden magic.

Baldric came up behind Cazrin, his heavier footfall and the soft swish of his cloak easily recognizable. Lark was next, and though his was a lighter tread, the restless flick of his tail gave him away. Uggie was easy. Her walk was more of a hop, punctuated by the occasional tentacle slapping wetly against the floor. Anson came last, and Tess recognized his footsteps because of the pause between each one—not because Anson was cowardly or unsure, but because he was always poised to act, readying himself to charge in when he was needed.

Despite the tense situation, Tess couldn't help but be pleased with herself. The more time they spent together, the more the group seemed to fit just a little bit more securely, like pieces of a puzzle slowly slotting together. Cazrin knew to check for dangerous magic without Tess having to ask. Anson would always be there watching their backs when there was trouble, and Baldric knew the tools of his trade enough to recognize a healing potion from just one drop. And Lark—well, he was a work in progress, but at least he knew to be quiet now and let Tess work.

Sefeerian's house wasn't ostentatious, but everything in it was old, finely crafted, and well cared for. And, though he hadn't made a show of it when she'd first met him, Tess had gotten the impression that the wizard guarded his home well, so to see it broken into like this was shocking.

"There's no defensive magic here or on the ground floor, from what I can see," Cazrin whispered when Tess paused at the top of the stairs.

"Is that good or bad?" Tess asked, noting the confusion in Cazrin's voice.

"It's good for us," Cazrin said. "I don't think we would have gotten very far if all of Sefeerian's defensive magic was in place. I sensed there was a great deal of it here when we visited to accept the job."

"But it's gone now," Tess said, understanding. "Did someone dispel it?"

"They must have," Cazrin said, "but it would have taken an awful lot of magic to do it."

"Great," Lark muttered. "Remind me, why are we so eager to confront burglars in a house that isn't even ours?"

Baldric cleared his throat. "We haven't gotten paid yet," he reminded Lark. "Those burglars might be stealing our reward right now."

Hands on her hips, Tess waited for Baldric's point to sink in. Lark rubbed the back of his neck, considering, then he nodded. "You're absolutely right, we need to confront the dastardly villains who broke into our employer's home," he said, gesturing up the stairs. "Onward, Tess."

"Thanks," Tess said dryly.

At the top of the stairs, a hallway curved off to the left and right, though it was fairly obvious where they needed to go. Down the left hall, the blood trail continued, and the still-smoking remains of a magical glyph was burned into the carpet in front of a door.

"There's one bit of magic the burglars didn't find," Anson said. "Gods, the *smell*."

He was right. The air reeked of burned flesh. Whoever had triggered the glyph had gotten a nasty surprise.

They moved cautiously down the hall, avoiding the blood as much as possible. Tess stepped aside to let Cazrin examine the glyph. The wizard crouched and ran her hands over the burn marks in the floor, her brow furrowed.

"This was triggered very recently," she confirmed. "Within the last thirty minutes or so. It's safe to walk on now, though. There's no lingering magic." She stood up and walked onto the glyph to demonstrate. Tess's heart seized for an instant, but, of course, Cazrin was right. Nothing happened as she walked onto the spent glyph. She knew the ins and outs of magic the same way Tess knew a trap mechanism.

Tess moved to the door and listened. There was no thump or moan or any sign of life from the other side of the door, and that sense of unease gripped her again. She tried the brass handle, which had been worked into the shape of a griffon.

The door swung open, and Tess's heart sank.

The room was obviously a private study. Dark wood paneling and thick crimson curtains over the windows gave the room a somber look, brightened only by the bookshelves covering one wall and the comfortable chairs arranged near the stone fireplace at the back of the room.

But the once fine study had been destroyed. Many of the books had been pulled off the shelves, pages ripped out and discarded, and several of the shelves had been smashed, as if the burglars had been looking for hidden compartments or rooms behind them. The chairs were overturned and slashed, their stuffing littering the floor. Even the fireplace had been searched, the cold coals and ash scraped out and ground into the carpet along with the rest of the debris.

In the far corner of the room, near the bookshelves, Sefeerian Annil lay on his back in a thick pool of blood, a black-handled dagger sticking out of his chest.

Baldric rushed to the wizard's side, but after a quick examination, he looked up and shook his head sadly. "He's dead."

"Anson," Tess said, "is that . . ."

"It's my missing dagger, yes," Anson said tightly.

Tess did a quick sweep of the room, then pulled off her mask and hurried to the elf's side with the others. Sefeerian's pale, waxy skin was still warm to the touch. His long white hair lay spread over his shoulder, soaked in blood and half obscuring his face.

Gently, Baldric pushed the hair back, careful to avoid touching the black dagger's hilt. "He hasn't been dead long," he said "If we'd gotten here just a bit sooner . . ."

"It must have been him I heard moaning when I first came in downstairs," Tess said. "But let's check the room to be sure."

Anson stood up, gestured for Uggie to stay put next to Tess, and began making a methodical search of the room, checking to see if any other bodies or burglars were lurking out of sight. Lark joined him, while Baldric nodded to the bookshelves, drawing Tess's and Cazrin's attention to the ruined books.

"Whoever did this seemed awfully interested in the wizard's library," he said.

"And not so interested in money," Lark called from across the room. The tiefling was crouched by a section of floor near the fireplace where the carpet had been ripped back, exposing the wood floor beneath. "There's an open trapdoor over here and a lockbox that's been broken into, but it looks like all the coin is still here. Must be at least two hundred gold."

"There's really no way to know what was taken from here," Cazrin said, moving over to the bookshelves. She gave a gasp of dismay at the torn pages and damaged covers. "Sefeerian's collection—there are so many rare books here, and they just destroyed them!" She picked up one of the ruined books, cradling it in her hands like a wounded creature. "Why would they do this?"

"Maybe they weren't looking for coin or valuables they could fence," Tess said, exchanging a glance with Baldric. She could tell he was thinking the same thing. "Maybe they were looking for a very specific book."

Cazrin's hand went to the satchel that held the spellbook. "You think they were after the Ruinous Child?"

"Makes sense if you think about it," Baldric said. "We were hired to recover the spellbook, and we came to Sefeerian's house earlier in the day and spoke to the housekeeper. We were inside just long enough that if someone was watching the place, they might have assumed we'd already turned over the book. They could have been the ones watching us in the tavern too."

"They were just waiting for nightfall to come and retrieve it," Tess said. Her own party had returned almost in time to—what? Prevent Sefeerian's death? The wizard was powerful and well protected in his home. Whoever did this had known that and come prepared. They'd caught the wizard unawares and murdered him in his own study.

With Anson's dagger.

The Ruinous Child will be your doom.

The illithid's warning still echoed in Tess's head, raising gooseflesh on her arms.

"Did Sefeerian ever give any indication that there were others searching for the Ruinous Child?" Cazrin asked, pulling Tess out of her thoughts.

Tess shook her head. "All he said was that the spellbook had been lost long ago, and he'd only recently learned that it had ended up in the ruins of one of Oghma's temples. I don't think he knew that an illithid had taken up residence there either."

"Maybe it was the illithid who destroyed the temple in the first place," Anson spoke up. He was standing to one side of the window, looking down at the street outside through a slit in the curtains. "Maybe it was after the Ruinous Child too."

"I need to get that book open," Cazrin said, frustration evident in her voice. "There's obviously some valuable knowledge inside if people are willing to kill for it."

"Hang on," Lark said, holding up a hand. He was still standing by the lockbox of gold. "The wizard's dead, and even if we take this gold—which we absolutely are, to be clear—it won't amount to half the reward we were promised, so I'm failing to see how any of this is our problem anymore."

Baldric crossed his arms. "I'm all for taking what coin we can and cutting our losses, but we've still got one big problem."

They all turned to look at Anson's dagger protruding from Sefeerian's chest.

And Cazrin had the Ruinous Child, which was a strong contender for the motive for the wizard's murder, in her satchel.

CHAPTER 7

Baldric had to hand it to Tess, she kept up a convincing mask of calm, but he could see by her pursed lips and the way her hand clenched into a fist on top of her thigh that she realized just how much trouble they'd unwittingly stepped into.

Anson spoke first. "Obviously, we're innocent," he said, but he spoke rapidly, belying his panic. "The housekeeper can testify that we had an appointment with Sefeerian this evening to deliver the spellbook. Why would we then murder him and take it for ourselves?"

"We can get rid of the dagger so there's no frame-up, but where is this housekeeper who's going to be our salvation?" Baldric asked, gesturing around the room. "Do you see her or any other servants around here?"

"We haven't searched the whole house," Anson pointed out. "They could be hiding, or they could have run when the murderers broke in."

"Or they could be dead," Lark said. He was scooping up handfuls of gold coins from the wizard's lockbox. Cradling them against his chest, he carried them over to the bag of holding Anson had tied to his belt. "Open up," he said, prodding the bag at Anson's hip with his knuckle. "We need to hurry and get out of here."

"Taking this loot is going to make us look even more guilty," Anson said, pulling the satchel out of reach. "And I'm not robbing our murdered employer."

"We're not robbing anyone of anything," Lark said firmly. "This is money we're *owed*. I'm just taking what we were promised. Really, we're the ones who've been cheated here. Obviously, this Sefeerian never intended to pay us our full reward if he didn't have the coin on hand." He paused. "I wonder if we should check the rest of the house for hidden stashes."

"Or we could just keep the Ruinous Child," Cazrin said, her hand clutching the satchel with the spellbook possessively. "That would make things even."

"Focus, everyone." Tess snapped her fingers, dragging their attention back to her. "There's no need to worry, because I have a plan. Yes, the City Watch is obviously going to be looking for us for questioning after this, but like Anson said, we're innocent, and it's only a matter of time before they figure that out. We'll just get rid of the dagger and lie low until the situation blows over."

"Sounds right to me," Baldric said. "But there's no reason we can't also point the Watch in the right direction, which is to say, *away* from us."

"What are you thinking?" Tess asked.

"Honestly, since we couldn't save him, I wish we could take Sefeerian's body to the nearest temple and have him brought back by one of the clerics there," Baldric said. "It would solve everything, but it would also cost a fortune that none of us have. But even if we can't bring him back, we can still talk to him." He glanced down at Sefeerian's corpse and then up at Tess. "I have a spell that can contact the dead. We could get some valuable information while we're here."

"Do we have time for that?" Anson interjected. "The longer we stay here, the worse it's going to look for us, and if we're caught, none of these plans will matter." He looked down and batted Lark's hands away from the bag of holding. "Have you been slipping coins in there this whole time?" he demanded.

"I told you, it's *our* gold," Lark argued.

"Lark, stop looting the house," Tess said, rubbing her forehead with a sigh. "Baldric, what do you think?" she said. "Can we get this done and get out of here in the next few minutes?"

"I can be quick," Baldric said, stroking his beard thoughtfully. "Let's be thinking about the most pressing questions you have for the wizard, because you won't get very many."

"All right," Tess said. "Give Baldric some space to work. Cazrin, help him out if you can."

"Do something about this while you're at it." Baldric pointed at Uggie. The otyugh had wrapped one of her tentacles around his ankle and was chewing nervously on the toe of his boot, as if the creature could sense the tension in the air.

"Uggie, come here." Tess pulled the beast away as Baldric knelt next to Sefeerian's body. Cazrin arranged herself opposite him. Gently, she took one of the wizard's hands in her own and said in a low voice, "We're so sorry to have to do this, Sefeerian. You deserve to rest, but we want to find answers and hopefully bring you justice."

"We'll do our best," Baldric murmured, but his thoughts were only half on the dead wizard. He ran a finger absently down the cloth at his belt.

Each time he had to cast a powerful spell, one that would normally be beyond his means, he appealed to the god he thought most likely to respond and offered the god an honest exchange of favors. He didn't consider himself a cleric in the traditional sense, but he reveled in the challenge of imagining what would attract a god's attention, and he had his own tricks and strategies to give himself the best chance of success.

In this case, Baldric's first instinct was to appeal to Kelemvor, god of the dead, but he wondered if the god would appreciate their group disturbing Sefeerian's remains. Their motives for doing this were to clear their names, and surely if they obtained justice for the murdered wizard, Kelemvor would be pleased.

But some instinct made him hesitate. His hand went to his mace, enchanted by the will of Tyr, the god of justice. Baldric often fell in and out of favor with that deity. Speaking of complicated relationships, theirs was . . . well, they had a history. Still, Baldric thought this cause might appeal to him.

He drew his mace and laid it on the floor next to him, touching the symbol of Tyr on the cloth he wore. He closed his eyes and made his case. With the god of justice, it wasn't flowery words or cajoling. He simply pictured Sefeerian's body, the dagger protruding from his chest, his home ransacked and his rare books defiled. His servants had been scared away or killed. He deserved justice for what had happened to him, and Baldric was offering to get that. All he needed was to be able to ask Sefeerian a few questions. Surely, that was worth disturbing the wizard's remains and borrowing a little bit of Tyr's divine power to make it happen.

The sounds of the rest of the party talking and moving around the room slowly quieted as Baldric slipped into a meditative state. He was aware only of the soft carpet beneath his knees, the smell of old books and blood in the air. Gradually, even those faded, until Baldric was alone in a dark void, calling out to Tyr.

No, not alone.

A chill crept over his body as two familiar eyes opened in the void, at once near and far away, like some otherworldly presence slowly turning its attention to him. Baldric would have liked to have believed it was Tyr answering his call, but those eyes, unsettling as they were, lacked the immensity of Tyr's presence. When the god of justice turned his attention to you, you felt it like a father's heavy hand on the back of a child's neck.

These eyes that watched him felt cold, calculating.

Hungry.

Who are you? he demanded, trying to tamp down the creeping fear as those unblinking eyes continued to watch him. *Why do you keep answering when I didn't call you?*

But you did call me. I haven't forgotten.

Baldric immediately wished he hadn't asked the question. The voice in the dark was low, full of amusement, with a rumbling undercurrent like hot coals stirred in a fire. It was not a pleasant sound.

Instinctively, Baldric retreated from the unknown entity, but he wasn't willing to give up yet. He called out to Tyr again, more insistently this time. Through the darkness, he focused on the mace, feeling the weapon's contours in his hand, the heat of its magic warming his palm. He took a deep breath, centering himself, drawing away from the eyes staring at him.

I don't need you anymore, he insisted. *Go away.*

Slowly, the ravenous gaze receded, and Baldric felt the cleansing presence of the god of justice. It was like coming up for air, like splashing cold water on his face after waking from a nightmare. Power flooded Baldric, the spell he needed tingling in his hands and through the mace. Tyr had heard his petition after all, and he'd accepted.

Before the god could change his mind, Baldric cast the spell and opened his eyes.

Sefeerian's study looked just the same, with the party restlessly milling about the room, but it took Baldric a few seconds to reorient himself and shrug off the chill darkness of the void.

It was all right. He had everything under control.

Cazrin still held the wizard's hand, and as they watched, Sefeerian's eyelids twitched and opened to slits. Baldric didn't think the wizard could see him, or anything else for that matter, but he sensed an awareness. A spark of life had returned to the corpse, bolstered by Tyr and willing to linger just long enough to answer his questions.

"Let's make these good," he said, nodding to Cazrin and Tess, who'd returned to crouch next to him. "We don't have long."

Tess nodded to Cazrin, letting her take the lead, no doubt because of her interest in the spellbook.

"Sefeerian," Cazrin said, "it's Cazrin Varaith. You remember me—we talked about your rare book collection the last time we met." She smiled faintly. "You told me you had a hidden collection of signed first-edition travel journals written by Volothamp Geddarm. You said you'd never sell them." Her expression clouded. "I'm so sorry this happened to you." She squeezed his hand. "Please tell us who killed you?"

Sefeerian's mouth opened, and a soft, faint voice, barely an echo of how the wizard had sounded in life, issued forth. "A black knife. Pain like fire in my chest." His gaze sharpened suddenly, and Baldric swore the corpse was actually looking at them all. "You did it. I used a sending . . . to warn the Watch. I told them it was you."

Baldric broke out in a cold sweat. Lark stood with his mouth hanging open in shock. Anson cursed, backing into one of the overturned chairs and nearly falling.

"It wasn't us!" Anson looked at Cazrin. "What are you waiting for? Tell him he's wrong!"

"It doesn't work like that," Baldric said calmly. "He's only repeating what he saw."

"Baldric's right," Cazrin said. "Whoever did this probably used magic to disguise themselves as us. It would explain why that group in the tavern was watching us: so they could recreate an illusion to fool Sefeerian and his staff. They didn't know they were being tricked."

"And I bet they made sure there were witnesses who saw them enter and leave the house as us," Tess said, her voice tight with anger. "So, it doesn't matter if we get rid of the murder weapon or lie low. We're in this now."

"Yes, it looks that way." Cazrin glanced at Tess helplessly.

Tess nodded at her. "It's all right. Keep going," she encouraged. "Ask him about the Ruinous Child. We need all the information we can get."

"We found the spellbook you sent us to find," Cazrin said, turning her attention back to Sefeerian. "We think that's why you were killed. Are we right about that?"

"Yes," Sefeerian responded, the word a soft hiss.

Cazrin nodded, exchanging another look with Tess. "What's in the Ruinous Child that would cause people to kill for it, Sefeerian?"

A rattling breath pushed the wizard's chest up, raising the hairs on Baldric's arms. "A terrible power. A threat that should never have been brought back to the world. Should have been . . . left in the depths and forgotten. Forgive me. I was only doing . . . what was asked of me."

Baldric sensed that the wizard wasn't asking their forgiveness. Perhaps he was making his own peace with the gods before he moved on.

"*Who* asked it of you?" Tess put in, leaning forward to hear the answer.

The sightless gaze shifted ever so slightly in Tess's direction, as if following the sound of her voice. Baldric could see Tess suppressing a shudder. Only Cazrin seemed unaffected by the scene. She still held the wizard's hand in a gentle grip.

"The seekers . . . of the collection." Sefeerian's voice was very faint. "They'd already taken the others."

"One more question," Baldric cautioned them. He could feel the spell slipping away, that brief spark of life fading from the corpse.

Tess looked at Cazrin again, but the wizard seemed torn. Baldric didn't blame her. Every answer the dead man gave led to more questions. Who were these seekers, and what *others* was Sefeerian referring to?

"Hurry up," Baldric said. The spell was almost gone.

"What were you going to do with the Ruinous Child?" Tess asked.

The body of Sefeerian stirred one final time, the last of the breath hissing out of him as the wizard answered Tess's question. "Keep it from *him*—Lorthrannan. He discovered its existence, and now he will not rest until it is in his hands. I thought I could protect it. I was . . . wrong." The last word was little more than a wisp of air between cracked lips. The spark of life was gone, and Baldric felt the divine presence of Tyr depart as well.

"Well, at least we got a name to put with this mess, but the rest of that was disappointingly cryptic," Lark said. He was leaning against the fireplace. "And you could have at least asked him if he had any more coin hidden in the house."

Cazrin carefully released Sefeerian's hand and touched the wizard's forehead briefly. "Thank you," she whispered. "Rest now."

Baldric stood up, his knees creaking in protest. "So, all this time, the wizard knew someone was after that spellbook, and he knew it was dangerous." He turned to Tess. "It would have been helpful to have this information before we accepted the job. Sefeerian was obviously holding out on us."

"I agree we should have been told more, but I've never heard of a wizard who didn't have a dragon's hoard worth of secrets," Tess said. "Did you really think Sefeerian was going to spill his to a group of adventurers he didn't know?"

"At least we got our answers in the end." Anson had collected himself, though he still looked rattled. He twitched aside the curtain to look outside again. "They just weren't what we were expecting. Good job coming through with the spell, Baldric. Otherwise, we wouldn't have known how much trouble we were in."

Baldric nodded but didn't answer. The spell had faded, but he couldn't shake the feeling of those eyes watching, boring into the back of his neck.

"All right, let's clear out," Tess said. "We don't want to be here when—"

Anson cursed again and whirled from the window to face them. "We've got trouble," he said. "Lantern light coming up the street, raised voices, and they're all wearing green-and-gold doublets. It's the Watch."

CHAPTER 8

"Damn it." Tess jumped to her feet. "I thought we'd have more time before they showed up."

"Now the Watch can catch the murderers red-handed," Anson said as they hurried for the study door.

"Do we really look like murderers?" Lark demanded. He gestured up and down his body. "Does this outfit scream 'murderer' to you? Because if it does, we need to have a conversation about fashion."

"There are still some bloodstains on your sleeve," Tess said, grabbing Lark's arm and towing him out into the hall.

"But it's *my* blood! Cazrin just missed a spot!"

"Let's try to hurry, everyone," Anson said, his voice tense.

"Servants' stair, over there," Tess said, feeling perfectly calm. Talking to dead bodies was not part of her expertise. In fact, it gave her the creeps, but she was in her element now. "We'll go out the back and slip away. Who's got Uggie?"

"I do," Baldric said wearily as the otyugh thumped along eagerly at his side, her eyestalk whipping in all directions, like this was a great game they were playing.

Tess led the way down the dusty back staircase and into the kitchen. The floors and counters had been swept clean, but a couple of dirty pots beside the stove served as evidence that a meal had been prepared recently, and the smell of onions and garlic lingered in the air. But there was no sign of any servants, and no blood here, so they had either fled or had already left for the evening when the murder took place.

Tess opened the door to the narrow alley running behind the house and peeked out, looking in both directions. She heard the sound of voices in the distance and a shrill whistle, like one group signaling to another.

Frowning, Tess glanced back at the party. Five people and an otyugh in a narrow alley were not conducive to moving stealthily or leaving the city unnoticed.

And they were going to have to leave the city. Sefeerian had accused them by name as he lay dying. It wasn't safe here.

"We need to split up," Tess decided.

"Is that really a good idea?" Cazrin asked, coming up behind her.

"Check the alley!" shouted a voice, and there came another whistle. "Close off the side streets and make ready if we need robes. Get those people back inside. I want everyone to stay in their homes."

"We don't have time for a better plan," Tess said. "Meet outside the city gates, near the coast. Remember that abandoned wagon we passed on our way back to the city, the one with its wheel sunk in the mud? That's where we meet."

"And if they catch us?" Lark asked.

"They won't," Tess insisted. "We'll get out of the city, and then we're going to clear our names and find the real murderers."

"We're doing what now?" Baldric asked from the back of the group. "Because it sounded like you said we're going to catch the real murderers."

"It's all part of my fallback plan." Tess turned to Cazrin. "You and I will take Uggie and go out the River Gate. Anson, Baldric, and Lark will be able to move faster without an otyugh, so they'll go the longer way, lose themselves in the city, and head out the South Gate. Got it?"

Even if they'd wanted to, there was no time for anyone to argue.

The voices and footsteps were getting closer. Anson's group took off down the alley away from the Watch while Tess pulled Cazrin across the street to a nearby garden gate. The lock was as basic as they came. It took Tess all of ten seconds to pick it, and the pair slipped inside, with Uggie thumping along behind them.

"We'll cut through here and go over the back wall," Tess whispered as they moved carefully in the dark, Cazrin keeping close behind her. The smell of roses and lilacs heavily perfumed the air. "That should get us far enough away from where they're searching."

"That sounds smart, but—" Behind her, Cazrin stumbled and gave a muffled yelp.

"Are you all right?" Tess stopped and turned to the wizard. "I forgot you can't see in the dark the way I can. You can hold on to me if you need to."

"It's not that, although it is a little hard to see with just the moonlight and the garden lanterns," Cazrin said. She had her satchel open, and Tess was surprised to see she held the Ruinous Child by the spine between her thumb and forefinger. "It's the book. It keeps setting things on fire."

"It—*what?*" Tess stepped closer to get a better look. Sure enough, the inside of Cazrin's satchel was blackened, and Tess could feel the heat radiating off the book. "What is going on with that thing?"

"I don't know," Cazrin said, sounding concerned but also slightly giddy. "It's a *fascinating* puzzle. I can't wait to study it more. Do you know, I felt the book growing warmer and warmer the farther we got from Sefeerian's house?" She gasped. "You don't suppose it misses Sefeerian, do you? I was nursing a theory that the book might have some form of sentience, and I think I might have been right. Maybe it didn't want to be separated from its owner, or—"

Tess raised a hand to cut her off as voices echoed over the stone garden wall. Taking Cazrin's arm, Tess pulled her deeper into the garden, ducking beneath the low-hanging branches of a cluster of apple trees. Uggie squeezed in beside them, chewing on strips of tree bark until Tess pulled her away and shushed her.

"We'll wait here a minute until they pass," Tess whispered, silently hoping the Watch didn't come into the garden. She glanced down at the Ruinous Child, which Cazrin was still holding between her fingertips. "Is it burning you? Do you want me to hold it for a while?"

"Actually, it's getting cooler now," Cazrin said. "I think I can put it away." She opened her satchel and grimaced at the ruined interior. "This was my favorite," she said sadly. Then, brightening, "But it doesn't matter. I'll just get a new one with a fireproof lining. That's something I should have anyway, to protect against fire magic."

"Well, at least you found a bright side," Tess said. "You know, once we get out of the city, I think we should take the Ruinous Child to Candlekeep. They might be able to tell us more about it and how to open it. We're going to need all the information we can get if we're going to solve Sefeerian's murder."

Cazrin practically vibrated off the grass. "Candlekeep!" she squealed softly. "Oh, I've always wanted to go there. I've dreamt about it since I was a child, but my family . . ." She cleared her throat. "That is, it's difficult to gain entry."

"I know," Tess said. To get inside, they would have to present the Avowed, the keepers of the library, with a book that was new to Candlekeep's collection. "We'll figure something out." She cocked her head, listening. "I don't hear the Watch anymore. We should try to move while we have the chance."

They made their way out from beneath the apple trees to the ivy-covered back wall, which was about six feet tall, with plenty of hand-holds for Cazrin and Tess. Uggie was another story.

"Do you have some magic that can lift Uggie over the wall?" Tess asked hopefully.

"Oh yes," Cazrin said, waving a hand, as if she made otyughs fly on a regular basis. "I could get her all the way to that rooftop if you wanted." She pointed to the townhouse bordering the garden.

Tess followed her gaze. "You know, that's not a bad idea," she said. "We don't know how many streets they're closing off, and the houses here are packed pretty close together. We could travel by rooftop until we get out of the area."

She waited while Cazrin cast the spell. When she'd finished, Uggie gently floated up as if she were being lifted on a cloud, her tentacles waving and stumpy feet running on air. Uggie let out an excited little bleat, and Tess put a finger to her lips.

"Quiet, Uggie," she whispered. "I know it's fun, but we're trying to be stealthy."

"Yes, if someone were to lean out their window and see a floating otyugh, we might have trouble," Cazrin said. "It's not something you see every day."

It was a good point. Tess probably should have thought this plan through a bit more. "If we move quickly, I'm sure no one will notice," she said, projecting as much confidence as she could.

Cazrin secured her staff to her back through a small harness, while Tess scrambled up the ivy-covered wall, Uggie floating along beside her. When she reached the top, Tess looked down to see Cazrin gaping at her in the darkness.

"How did you get up there so fast?" Cazrin demanded.

Tess grinned. "I do this a lot," she said, reaching a hand down to help Cazrin as she climbed the wall. When they were standing side by side at the top, Tess steadied Cazrin while she adjusted her overskirt so it wouldn't trip her.

Cazrin looked doubtfully up at the looming wall of the townhouse. There was a three-foot gap between it and the garden wall. "I think I can get across, but I'm not sure I'm up for *that* climb," she said. "Maybe I can hold on to Uggie, and the spell can lift us both, although I know there's a particular weight limit because I tested it once on a full rain barrel, and the results were less than promising, so it might not work."

"It's all right," Tess said. "Once we cross the gap, I'll have you get behind me and put your arms around my neck, and then I can get us both up to the roof. It's not a problem."

Cazrin looked relieved. "Well, as long as you're sure I won't be too heavy."

Tess scrutinized the wizard. "I doubt you're heavier than a sack of stones. We should be fine."

"Do you, er, have much experience climbing with sacks of stones?" Cazrin asked.

"Of course. Come on." Tess leaped from the garden wall to the closest window ledge of the townhouse, easily finding small handholds in the surrounding bricks. Fortunately, all the windows on this side of the building were covered by heavy curtains, and there were no lights on in the townhouse that she could see. Either the occupants had retired for the night or, if they were lucky, no one was home, so no one would accidentally open their window for some fresh air and instead get a front-row seat to the floating Uggie show.

She stretched out a hand across the gap to Cazrin. "It's all right," she repeated calmly when Cazrin hesitated. "It's not as far as it looks. My hand's right there—just take it."

Cazrin glanced up and met Tess's gaze, and then she nodded, as if reassured by whatever she saw in Tess's face. She reached out, tilting her body almost too far—but then Tess had her hand and tugged. Cazrin jumped, landing next to her on the window ledge. Tess steadied her with an arm across her back like a bar.

"That was . . . exhilarating!" Cazrin said. "If we weren't being chased by the Watch, this would be the perfect night."

Tess snorted in amusement as she turned to find more handholds on the bricks to pull them up. She gestured for Cazrin to get behind her and felt the wizard's arms encircle her shoulders. "Hold on," Tess said.

And up they went. Thankfully, the darkness and the late hour went a long way toward hiding their strange procession: Tess crawling carefully up the wall with Cazrin on her back, Uggie floating beside them. It felt like it took forever, but finally they reached the rooftop of the townhouse, and no shouts of alarm went up at their presence. Tess breathed a quiet sigh of relief.

She took a moment to get her bearings on the roof. Mount Waterdeep rose in the west, topped by the famous walking statue known as the Griffon, near Peaktop Aerie. From there, as she pivoted, it was easy to find the soaring Castle Waterdeep. "All right," Tess said. "I think I know where we need to go. If we move from rooftop to rooftop, we should be able to—"

"Would you look at that view?"

Tess turned to see Cazrin gazing wistfully out over the city skyline, her elbows resting on a stone chimney protruding from the roof. Twinkling lights shone from hundreds of houses. The sounds of the city were muted up here but still present, a soft hum of activity and life, even as people gradually settled down for the night. The moon was waxing toward full, the little asteroids known as the Tears of Selûne draping behind it like a starry cloak, illuminating wisps of broken clouds that wound around one another like silver ribbons across the horizon.

"Don't you just love it?" Cazrin said when Tess came to stand beside her. "The city, the possibilities—the great unknowns just waiting out there?" Her gaze turned inward. "I know some people never want to leave their homes, and I understand that, but on nights like this, doesn't it all feel so . . . so . . ." She gestured helplessly at the view, as if searching for the right words.

Tess knew what she meant. She felt something similar herself when she considered the city—and also what lay beyond in the wider world. The bigness of it, the all-encompassing longing of everything she wanted to achieve, the things she wanted to discover, so close that she could practically taste them. She'd worked hard to get where she was, but it still filled her up, that longing. She wanted all of it, and she thought she could never get enough.

"It feels like everything happening out there matches everything going on inside me," Tess murmured. Then she realized what she'd said and felt a flush of embarrassment creep up her neck. She hadn't meant to confess that.

"We should get moving," Tess said, turning away from the view and squaring her shoulders to reassert a professional demeanor. "We need to get to the gate before the Watch sends word to seal it off."

"Tess," Cazrin said, "I—"

"What's this? Who is that over there? Show yourselves!"

Tess jerked around just in time to see a human in familiar green-and-gold livery step out from behind a chimney on the rooftop next to theirs. She cursed under her breath. The Watch in this city were too damned efficient. They'd even sent scouts to the roof.

"Time to go," Tess said. She pointed to the rooftop opposite theirs. The gap between them was only a couple of feet, though from this distance it looked wider. "We're going to jump. Get ready!"

"Jump?" Cazrin kept pace beside her, with Uggie loping along behind. "Can we all make that?"

"Absolutely," Tess said. "All part of my fallback plan!"

She hit the edge of the roof first and jumped, easily clearing the gap to land on the opposite side. The Watchman was shouting after them and calling down to alert his companions below.

Turning, Tess held out her hands as Cazrin jumped. Despite her overskirt and slower speed, she easily cleared the gap, landing on the roof tiles beside Tess, who gripped the woman's arms to keep her on her feet. Tess turned back just in time to see Uggie launch her body into the air like a misshapen boulder from a trebuchet. The force of the jump carried her almost but not quite into Tess's arms. She hit the side of the roof and started to slip, legs flailing, but Tess grabbed her upper body and hauled her to safety.

Then they were running. Across the rooftops, under the waxing moon, they jumped from building to building with the Watchman doggedly chasing after them. Luckily, Tess was on familiar ground. She'd spent her entire childhood trying to get into places she wasn't supposed to be. She was just as at home on the rooftops of Waterdeep as she was running along any of the roads of Faerûn. With the night wind in her hair and the moonlight shining down, she guided Cazrin and Uggie unerringly around protruding chimneys, loose tiles, rooftop gardens, and trysting nooks, gradually widening the gap between them and the Watchman.

Unfortunately, in the exhilaration of the moment, she forgot that her companions were not used to running for long lengths of time over uneven surfaces. Her only warning was the sound of Cazrin's harsh breathing before the wizard stumbled with a sharp cry.

Tess looked back in time to see Cazrin fall to her knees on the slanted rooftop and start to tumble toward the edge.

"Hold on!" Tess jumped, using her momentum to slide down the roof toward Cazrin. She caught herself with one hand on a protruding rainspout, reaching out with the other to snag the back of Cazrin's shirt and bring her to a stop.

Uggie hurtled past her in the darkness, tentacles waving behind her like banners. Tess had no free hand to reach out and stop the otyugh as she went flying over the edge of the roof.

"No!" Cazrin cried. She reached back and made a fumbling grab for her staff, which by some miracle she'd managed to keep strapped to her back while she went sliding down the roof. She spoke a word, and a flash of purple light streaked down to surround Uggie, halting her in midair. The light faded, and the otyugh drifted serenely to the street below.

Tess lay back on the slanted roof and released a breath, staring up at the stars as her chest rose and fell. Disaster averted. They were all right.

Her relief was short-lived. Shouts echoed in the distance, and as she rolled over onto her stomach to get a look down at the street, she saw approaching lantern lights. The Watch were still tailing them and closing fast.

"Uggie, go!" Tess called down to the otyugh. "Find the others! Find Baldric! He needs you. And whatever you do, stay out of sight!"

Uggie bounced on her two front legs, making a sound that was something between a bark and a screech, before she took off down an alley, burrowing through a pile of garbage and out of sight.

"Do you think she actually understands what you're saying?" Cazrin asked, glancing uneasily in the direction Uggie had gone. "Or will we read a broadsheet tomorrow that there was an otyugh terrorizing the citizenry while a group of wanted murderers stalked the streets?"

"If everything goes according to plan, we'll have escaped the city and won't be reading *any* news tomorrow," Tess said optimistically. "Are you all right?" She crouched by Cazrin, who was rubbing her ankle and grimacing. "Can you still run?"

"I think so," Cazrin said. "Sorry, my foot caught one of the tiles sticking up back there."

"It's all right," Tess said. The voices below were getting closer. "But we need to keep moving. We're not far from the gate."

"I'm ready." Resolutely, Cazrin got to her feet, taking one last look across the rooftops. "It's still a great view," she said.

CHAPTER 9

Uggie had a mission.

Uggie had to find her person.

Baldric.

Baldric person needed her.

It was very important that Uggie find him. Her Tess person said so, and Tess was always—

Look at this pile of treasure food: apple cores, peach skins, gristle, potatoes, parchment soaked in ink and cat urine, more gristle, crunchy gravel, rust-filled water, straw laced with horse dung, ale, soiled rags, soiled bandages, rancid pork, a hair ball—no, *two* hair balls; it was a feast, and Uggie could fit it all into her mouth at once in an explosion of flavors—

Baldric.

Uggie crunched, swallowed, and lifted her eyestalk, turning it this way and that to get her bearings. The world was awash in smells and sounds and hidden delights around every corner. Uggie wanted to savor all of it, this city that was a pleasure palace for the senses and the hunt.

One more bite of straw, and some yellow puddle water.

Such sweet nectar.

Now, time to go.

Carefully, Uggie sorted through the scents lacing the air, narrowing down to the familiar scent of her Baldric person's sweat, his wonderful beard that smelled of mint and sometimes bits of cheese. Uggie wished she had a beard to store her treasure food this way. The two-footed creatures were truly fortunate.

There it was. Uggie pulled out the thread of her Baldric person from the thousands of wanderers that called the city home, and she followed it down the dark street, making a concerted effort to ignore the siren calls of food that lined the alley.

Baldric was more important right now.

Uggie loved all her people, especially her Tess person and her Anson person. They were the first friends she'd ever had, and they'd given her a name. Anson had insisted she needed one, and so Tess had given her one. She was Uggie now, and she quite liked the name.

So, she would never let on to them that her Baldric person was her favorite. Uggie was very discreet. But Baldric had the wonderful beard that smelled of food. Uggie couldn't help herself.

Uggie paused at the mouth of the alley. Footsteps were coming this way. Scrunching her body as close to the wall as she possibly could, she burrowed into a pile of rags and crumbling crates, tucking her tentacles in close to disguise them. Just to be safe, she sent a tiny mind picture to whoever was coming, nudging them away from her hiding spot and on down the street to chase an imagined shadow.

She waited in the dark, trying not to breathe too loudly as the footsteps passed by. Tess person was always warning her about this. Voices talked about a chase on the rooftop. Uggie hoped that her Tess person and Cazrin, her sparkly person, had escaped, but she wasn't too worried. Tess person would make sure everything was all right. And Tess person had given her a mission. She wasn't going to fail.

The sound of the footsteps receded, and Uggie crawled out of her garbage heap and continued, following the smell of Baldric person.

Uggie had never thought she'd have this many people all to herself. She'd never minded being alone before, but now that she wasn't, she realized this was better. This was what she wanted—to eat, and to be with her people.

Wasn't that all anyone really wanted?

Uggie considered this as she stopped to lap at another puddle. She was young, but hers was a good life.

Or it would be again as soon as she found her Baldric person.

She licked her lips and trotted off into the night.

CHAPTER 10

Anson, Lark, and Baldric turned down yet another alley as Anson guided them in what he hoped was the direction of the South Gate. In the distance, he could hear the shouts of the City Watch, but they were too far away for him to make out what instructions were being relayed. Anson thought they'd managed to evade the closing of the streets around Sefeerian's townhouse, but he wasn't slowing his pace in case they were being followed.

"I've always wanted to do the Waterdeep After Dark tour," Lark commented as he splashed through a puddle of garbage and other questionable substances. "It's just as picturesque as I was expecting."

"Some tour guide we've got, though," Baldric said, snickering as he ran alongside Anson. "He's not even showing us the points of interest."

"We're paralleling the Way of the Dragon," Anson said without missing a beat. "Syretta's Sweets is closed for the night, but behind it, there's a dead-end street where I lost a tooth trying to help a merchant who'd been jumped by a couple of thieves. Turns out it was a trap. The merchant was part of the act, and the three of them got me up against a wall to try to beat me unconscious. Broke my nose too, but I eventually got the best of them." He smiled wistfully at the memory.

"Right, so we'll check that one off as the alley where Anson was nearly beaten to death," Lark said dryly. "I can't wait to see what taverns you recommend."

Anson paused to peek around a corner, checking the street signs to see where they were. He breathed a quick sigh of relief. There it was: the Way of the Dragon, exactly where he'd thought it would be.

He hadn't grown up in Waterdeep, but when you lived on the streets of any city, the back alleys, nooks, and crannies all started to look the same after a while, and it wasn't hard to fall back into his old habits of navigating them, finding places where a child could hide, doorways to block the wind, trash bins where the food had just been thrown out, steam still rising off the meat . . .

"You all right?" Baldric rumbled from beside him.

Anson wrenched himself out of the memory, his hand going automatically to his sword hilt to center himself. "I'm fine," he said, meeting Baldric's keen-eyed gaze. "I'm just wondering if we should get back on the main road here. We're getting close to the gate and—"

"Who's back there?" a voice barked from behind them.

"Wonderful," Lark muttered.

The trio turned to see two City Watch members step into the alley from the narrow street a few steps behind them. Anson had been sure when they'd passed that street that it had been clear. Bad luck—sometimes that was the story, whether you were an innocent party fleeing a murder scene or a child taking a wrong turn with his brother on the docks . . .

Stop, he told himself sternly. He couldn't afford to be distracted now.

One of the Watch members was a human woman, tall and well muscled, her graying hair pulled back from her face, carrying a lantern in one hand and a mace in the other. The orc walking next to her was shorter and wiry, with pale blond hair cut very short. He had a sword but hadn't yet drawn it. He was the one who had called them out.

"S-sorry," Lark said to the pair, his face slackening into a lazy smile. "We were tavern-hopping, and this one took us down the wrong street." He jerked his thumb at Baldric and put his other hand against the alley wall as if to steady himself. "I'm composing a drinking song to mark the occasion. Do you want to hear it?" Without waiting for a reply, he tipped his head back like a wolf howling at the moon and launched into a rapid-fire rhyme.

Oh, I drank an ale
in Westgate
was going by an alias

But wait!

Took a chug
from the jug
of Spider Queen cider

Went straight!
To my vision
With precision
Can't fight it

"Oh, cheers to that!" Anson bellowed, clapping enthusiastically while Lark took an unsteady bow. Truly, he was impressed at how effortlessly the bard slipped into the performance. Lark didn't need a stage to put him in the mindset of an actor. It came to him naturally.

"We took a wrong turn back at Syretta's," Baldric was saying to the Watch, pitching his voice just a little too loud. "Isn't the Tipsy Whistler supposed to be around here somewhere?"

"Oh, you're way off for that, friend," said the orc with the sword. He seemed much more relaxed than his companion. He pointed over his shoulder. "That's two streets back and turn left. Look for the whistle and grapes painted on the door."

"Good of you to help," Anson said. He crossed to Lark and slung his arm around the tiefling's shoulders. "Ready for another round and another verse?"

The woman with the lantern was eyeing them suspiciously. "For a group that's been having so much fun, you don't smell like you've had much to drink."

"It's the perfume," Lark said, waggling his eyebrows and pulling Anson back a few shuffling steps. "I make it myself. Smells of lemons and—"

"Hold!" she commanded. "Stay where you are."

Anson froze. He felt the muscles in Lark's shoulder shift as the tiefling subtly reached behind himself, hand going for his lute. Anson let his own hand trail slowly down Lark's back, shifting the instrument so it was within easy reach.

"Aw, whatsa matter?" Baldric whined, holding up the cloth at his waist in such a way so the symbol of Tyr was the only one visible. "I'm a simple holy man on a quest for the best red blend in Waterdeep. Surely, you won't deny me my life's work?"

The human and the orc exchanged glances. Then the woman sighed and turned, her lantern swinging, casting dancing shadows on the alley wall. "I'll go talk to Delton," she said. "He just came from North Ward about some commotion. If it's nothing serious, we'll let them go."

Anson tensed, but he could feel Lark already moving, coaxing a soft bit of music from his lute. The tiefling hummed the words of a spell and gestured toward the two Watch members.

"My friend isn't wearing any undergarments," the bard called out to them.

"What?" Then Anson saw the magic hit them. They stiffened, the woman's lantern jiggling in her hand. The corners of her mouth twitched, and then a wide grin spread across her face. She giggled—an unnerving sound in the tense silence. The orc began to laugh too, his eyes widening as he pointed at the woman, as if they were sharing the same private joke.

"What did you do to them?" Anson murmured. "You're not hurting them, are you?"

"Quite the opposite," Lark said, a self-satisfied smirk crossing his face. "I'm just giving them a chance to share in the carefree mirth of the evening. A little laughter never hurt anyone."

Or a lot of laughter, in this case. The woman's shoulders were shaking as the fit of giggles continued. She leaned against the wall to catch her breath. The orc had doubled over, clutching his belly as loud guffaws echoed down the alley.

Baldric crossed his arms and glanced at Lark. "You couldn't have chosen a quieter way to subdue them?" he asked, his words muffled by the rising laughter.

Lark winced. "In retrospect, yes, I should have thought ahead, but you have to admit, this is pretty entertaining."

"Let's move," Anson said. He ran to the mouth of the alley and looked out at the Way of the Dragon. "We'll cut across the road here and go back into the alleys. We should—look out!"

A large object hurtled out of the shadows toward them. Anson just managed to pull back out of its path, but Baldric wasn't so lucky. The otyugh slammed into the cleric's chest, driving him back against the stone wall with a solid *thud* as she put her front legs on his chest, her tongue lolling out the side of her mouth.

"Uggie," Anson said, bewildered by the otyugh's sudden appearance. "How did you find us?" His heart gave a lurch. "Are Cazrin and Tess all right? You were supposed to stay with them!"

"Sit," Baldric commanded, his words carrying the weight of magic. Instantly, Uggie dropped to all threes, staring up at Baldric adoringly.

Baldric pointed at the otyugh, and then at Lark. "Tell *him* how happy you are to see us," he suggested, and Uggie launched herself at the bard instead.

Anson watched the scene with a strange sense of detachment, his thoughts racing. It had been a mistake to split up. He'd had a feeling back at Sefeerian's house that this was a bad idea. Tess and Cazrin could be in trouble. They could have been caught and were probably even now sitting in a cell waiting to be questioned. He had no way to find them. They'd think he abandoned them . . .

Anson felt someone shake his shoulder. He blinked, glancing over to meet Baldric's calm gaze. "Take a breath," the cleric said. "You're looking a little pale."

Anson didn't know how he looked, but he knew his skin was clammy, and it felt like there was a vise clamped around his rib cage. He forced air into his lungs, and the tightness gradually eased.

"Don't you dare," Lark wheezed, struggling under the massive weight pushing against his chest as Uggie strained toward him, trying to lick his face. "I just had this coat cleaned! Get off! Baldric, I hate you!"

With a reluctant whine, Uggie pushed off Lark's chest and thumped to the ground, where she proceeded to dance around the three of them excitedly.

"Don't worry," Baldric said, patting Anson on the shoulder. "She's not hurt, and she's obviously happy. She probably just wandered away from Tess and Cazrin. That's all." He cocked his head. "Besides, she's not going to answer your questions on account of she doesn't speak any of our languages, so we may as well get moving."

"Good point." Anson ran his hand through his hair sheepishly. He still felt the dregs of panic swirling in his chest like a sour soup, but the worst of it had passed, and he felt calmer. "I think she understands us, though, at least a little bit," he said, as the others fell into step beside him. They made their way furtively across the road and into the shadows of the alley on the opposite side of the street, leaving the sounds of the laughing Watch officers behind them.

"Of course she does," Baldric said, smiling indulgently. "Anyway, at least we aren't walking into a trap, like that night in Dock Ward."

CHAPTER 11

WATERDEEP—CITY OF SPLENDORS

ONE MONTH AGO

"When you said to come by the docks at nightfall, I assumed you meant you were taking me to a tavern you knew," Anson commented as he and Baldric made their way stealthily along the narrow pier toward the derelict ship bobbing in the harbor.

Actually, the wreck barely deserved to be called a ship. Her main mast was broken, her sails shredded, flapping like listless ghosts in the night breeze. The deck had been stripped of anything of value long ago. Even the figurehead had been torn away or rotted off the bow of the ship. It appeared to be abandoned, which made Anson wonder why they were bothering to sneak up on the thing.

The cleric glanced back at him distractedly. "Did we need to be at a tavern for you to give your recruitment speech?" He gestured to the ship. "I thought we could just do it along the way."

Anson considered that change of plans. Tess had instructed him to charm the dwarf over drinks, but Anson was getting the sense that Baldric might appreciate just a touch more directness. "Are we in danger right now?" he asked.

"Well, we're in Dock Ward, so in a general sense, yes, but if you mean immediate danger, then no." The dwarf shrugged. "Things could take a turn later. Will that be a problem for you?"

Anson relaxed, finding himself back on familiar footing. "I'll be fine," he said. "About this adventuring party we're forming . . ."

"You need a cleric," Baldric said, stopping in front of a rotting gangplank that gave Anson serious doubts as to whether it would bear the weight of a child, let alone a grown human and a dwarf. "You should know up front that I'm a bit of a non-traditionalist." He started up the gangplank, the wood bowing dangerously.

"What does that mean?" Anson followed him. Luckily, the plank held together, and the two of them were soon standing on the deck of the ship.

"Just that I have a different sort of arrangement with the gods," Baldric explained, drawing a mace from his belt. He headed for a ladder that disappeared into the shadowy bowels of the ruined ship. "You don't happen to have a weapon on you, do you?" He lowered his voice. "We're getting closer to that immediate danger I was hinting at."

Anson drew his sword, its jagged edge gleaming in the moon-light.

Baldric looked at it skeptically. "Fine, but where's the other half?"

"If there were any justice in the world, it would be resting among the bones of a blue dragon somewhere in the High Forest," Anson said softly. "But I doubt that's the case."

Baldric raised a curious eyebrow. "Is that why you're forming an adventuring party? You have a grudge against a blue dragon? Because I don't think you have enough coin to pay me for that task."

Anson shook his head. "It was a long time ago. My father broke off the sword in the dragon's body, just before it crushed him. It gave the rest of my family a chance to escape."

"Sorry to hear that." A crackle of energy passed along the broken sword, casting soft blue glows over Baldric's face. "Looks like there's still life in the blade yet," the dwarf observed.

"It's been that way ever since its breaking," Anson said. "I think it had something to do with the sword's innate magic mixed with the dragon's blood. It's not always reliable, or safe, but it's valuable.

I've had more than one person offer to buy it over the years—or try to take it."

Anson didn't usually talk this much about his past, and most people didn't ask. But Baldric deserved to know more about the people he'd be travelling with, assuming he accepted the invitation to join the party.

They slowly descended the ladder, Anson using the erratic blue light from his sword to guide his steps. Broken crates and smashed barrels indicated a cargo that was long gone. The air was thick and hot and reeked of rotting fish.

Baldric gestured to a door about ten feet away. "Captain's cabin," he said. "That's where they'll be."

"Who?" Anson asked. "Who are you hunting?"

Baldric sighed. "Well, you see, it all started because I had a long-term arrangement with Moradin."

"The dwarven god of creation," Anson said. "That's who you worship?"

Baldric shook his head. "No, I told you, I'm a non-traditionalist. We just have an agreement where I tutor some of his younger clergy a few times a year, and in exchange, he gives me power over the undead."

"All right," Anson said slowly, "but what does that have to do with this ship and why we're here?"

"I'm getting to that." Baldric was whispering now as he approached the door. "Anyway, a couple of these young hotheads decided it was time for their rebellious phase, so they defaced a local shrine to Sune, covered it with symbols of the cult of the Dead Three—Bhaal, Bane, and Myrkul—just to be shits."

"You're telling me this is about Moradin, plus the goddess of beauty, *and* the gods of murder, tyranny, and death?" Anson whispered back. "Are there always this many deities involved in your life?"

Baldric rolled his eyes. "You have no idea. So, Moradin got a little huffy and was of the opinion that I wasn't upholding my end of the bargain by keeping the dwarven youths out of trouble. I promised to set things right, and at the same time, since Sune was now involved, I figured it couldn't hurt to appeal to her rather passionate nature and offer to make the youths pay for their crimes by forging some elegant weapons for the defense of her shrines. In exchange, I'd get a death ward to use on a job that I was planning for—"

"Baldric," Anson interrupted. He was starting to get a headache behind his eyes. "Why are we here?"

"You wanted to ask me to join your adventuring party," Baldric reminded him, unnecessarily. "It sounds intriguing, especially what you said about this dungeon being a lost temple to Oghma. I have some debts to pay to the god of knowledge, but we have to take care of this first. The miscreant youths, I mean. I tracked them to this ship. It's their little hideout." He snorted. "Isn't that adorable? We're going to go put the fear of Moradin in them, so to speak. That way I can keep my powers over the undead *and* get my death ward."

Anson felt a twinge of disappointment. He'd been hoping for some real danger, but he supposed he could put on a good show to scare the youths back to the path of righteousness.

He wasn't sure how to untangle Baldric's complicated web of favors curried among different deities. But surely Tess wouldn't mind a nontraditional cleric in the party? As long as he got the job done?

He didn't have time to speculate, because Baldric kicked in the door to the captain's cabin and led with his mace, calling out, "Playtime's over, children. No more defacing holy . . . shrines . . ." He trailed off. "Well, this is unexpected."

Anson looked over Baldric's shoulder to see two young dwarves with scraggly red chin beards sitting at a stained table, surrounded by two men and three women in dark robes.

"You didn't expect them to actually be working *with* the cultists?" Anson asked.

"Nope," Baldric said with a chuckle. "Didn't think they'd be smart enough to lay a trap for us either. Oh, this is too good. I'm going to parlay this into some sweet spirit guardians from Tyr. Just watch me."

"Kill them!" shrieked the nearest cultist.

Anson raised his sword to intercept an axe blade wielded by a human man with bulging muscles and foul breath. He deflected the clumsy strike and sent a bolt of lightning through the axe and into the cultist's body. The man dropped to the floor in front of the dwarves, body rigid and convulsing under the force of the magic.

"See!" Baldric cried, his voice booming through the cabin as he swung his mace at another cultist. "This is what befalls those who stray from Moradin's benevolence!" He shot a wink at Anson. "Keep it up. You're doing great!"

And to think, Anson had been nervous going into this meeting. It had turned into just his kind of night.

CHAPTER 12

SOMEWHERE ALONG THE SWORD COAST
PRESENT DAY

Tess leaned against the old rotting wagon, its front two wheels half-sunk in mud that had dried and hardened and now refused to release them. Its owner had never come back for it, which made Tess wonder what had happened to them. She fidgeted, tossing a dagger from hand to hand and fiddling with the gold earrings dangling from her ears.

Cazrin was sitting on the ground nearby, examining the Ruinous Child's lock. When she looked up, Tess stopped fidgeting. She didn't want to give the other woman the impression she was worried.

She wasn't worried. Not really. The others would be here soon. She'd just hoped they would already be here waiting for them. But she was sure they'd gotten out of the city safely. Everything was going to be fine.

"Any luck getting that thing open?" Tess asked, to distract herself from her fretting.

Cazrin shook her head. "I tried a spell, but the cover just rippled and stabbed my fingers with a patch of thorns, and then I heard this noise that—well, it sounded suspiciously like laughter." She looked up at Tess with an expression of bewildered hurt. "Do you think this book is actually *laughing* at me?"

Tess shrugged. "A few days ago, I would have said no, but we've already seen the trouble that book attracts, and you said yourself it might be sentient. I wouldn't be surprised if you're right."

Cazrin's brow furrowed as she picked up the book. She was wearing gloves to protect her hands from any more hidden thorns that might decide to pop out, and the book didn't seem to be giving off heat right now. Tess had been half-afraid it was going to light itself on fire out of spite just as they'd been approaching the city gate. *That* certainly would have attracted suspicion.

"If it is sentient, I wish I could get it to understand that I just want to be friends," Cazrin said. She fingered the silver lock absently. "You know, I'm starting to wonder if this is even a real lock?"

Tess coughed and looked away guiltily. She hadn't told Cazrin about her failed attempts to open the book that night at the camp. "Just looking at it from here, I think you might be right about that too," she said.

Tess's ears perked up at a sound from down the road. Crouching by the wagon, she motioned for Cazrin to hide in a cluster of nearby trees. Tess looked around the wheel to see three—no, four—familiar figures heading toward them. A weight lifted as she stood up and waved to her party. "Over here!"

Anson's face broke into a smile as he and the others jogged over. Uggie rubbed against Tess's legs and then bounded over to nuzzle Cazrin.

"Glad you all made it out safely," Tess said, "though I never had any doubts at all."

"At least one of us was confident," Baldric said. He spread his hands. "Well, here we are, wanted fugitives, driven from the city, with our coin purses disappointingly light." He eyed Tess expectantly. "What now?"

Tess felt the sudden tension in the air, chasing away the relief at the party's reunion. She didn't blame them. It had been a long night for everyone, and it wasn't over yet. They needed to get on the road and put some more distance between themselves and the city before they could sleep.

"What happened tonight is just a temporary setback," Tess assured them. "I told you that we're going to find Sefeerian's murderer so that we can clear our names."

They didn't have a choice at this point. They certainly weren't turning themselves in to the mercy of the City Watch, and Tess wasn't ready to leave Waterdeep behind for good. She'd worked too hard to establish her reputation there to have it permanently tarnished.

Tess led the group off the road and gathered them around the broken-down wagon. "The key to all of this is the Ruinous Child," she continued. "I think we can agree on that?"

Cazrin nodded eagerly. "We also know there's someone named Lorthrannan who's after the book. We need to find out why," she said, "but we can't get the thing open."

"Which is why we need to take it to Candlekeep," Tess said. "The Avowed know more about the books of this world, magical and otherwise, than anyone. Surely, someone there would be able to help us."

Baldric stroked his beard. "It's not a bad plan," he said. "I wouldn't mind seeing inside the place myself. My mothers used to tell me stories about the great library a long time ago. They claimed that some of the rooms were so cavernous it was like being inside a mountain, but instead of stone it was words, books surrounding and protecting you just like the mountain would."

Cazrin's gaze went dreamy at this description. "I've always wanted to see it too," she said, sharing a look with the dwarf.

"That's all wonderful," Lark said, leaning against the wagon, "but I've heard these Avowed don't let just anyone browse the stacks like in a normal library. How are we getting in?"

"The Ruinous Child might be enough to get us in on its own," Anson put in, gazing at the book. "I'm sure they'd be interested in it for their collection."

Cazrin's hands tightened possessively on the book. "They can look," she said firmly, "but we're not giving it to them."

Anson raised his hands. "Just a suggestion," he said. "We won't know anything until we ask for admission." He nodded at Tess. "We should keep moving. It's a long way to the library."

The others nodded in agreement, and after a quick rest and a check of the supplies they were carrying to make sure they had enough food and water, they headed back to the road and turned south, away from Waterdeep.

"We should have bought horses," Lark complained as they set off. "I was counting on a few days to rest my poor feet, but now here we are, back on the road again. Horses would have at least made up for that."

"No horses," Tess said from the front of the group. "They're never a good investment."

"Maybe our group name should be No Horses," Baldric joked, elbowing Lark in the ribs.

"The Walkers of Waterdeep," Anson offered.

"Future Acquitted Murderers of Waterdeep." Lark hummed in his throat. "You know, that's not half bad. Even when we clear our names, that hint of scandal will still be there. I think it can only help our reputations."

Tess considered that. Lark could be right—not about the party name, that one was terrible. But provided she spun the story in just the right way, put some whispers in the right ears, it could end up being a boon to their reputations.

The night wore on, and they kept walking. After a couple of hours, Tess started looking for a good place to camp, especially when the complaints started to filter in from the back of the group, a slow swell of grumbling that got louder and louder the longer they trekked down the road.

"We're almost ready to stop, children," Tess said in exasperation a few minutes later, after Baldric began complaining that he was going to have permanent loss of feeling in his toes.

Ahead of them, the land swept up on either side of the road, and the trees grew dense along the embankment, roots protruding from the eroded soil even as their branches arched together over the road and blocked out the brightness of the moon. Tess instinctively slowed her pace as she examined the terrain with a frown.

Anson drifted up from the back of the group and touched her arm. "You see it too?" he asked quietly.

Tess nodded. "Somewhere in those trees would be a great spot to camp once we make sure there's no ambush waiting for us," she said. She glanced sidelong at him. "You up for some light scouting in the trees?"

He gave her a crooked grin. "Always."

"Take Cazrin with you, one of you on each side of the road."

He nodded and faded back to speak to Cazrin in a whisper. Baldric and Lark must have heard some or most of their conversation, because they'd fallen quiet. Even Uggie was subdued, as if sensing there was something amiss. The night was very still, but there came the sound of restless animals from the trees ahead, and somewhere farther off, an owl hooted. Its call was answered by a second owl closer to them.

Tess glanced over her shoulder to see Anson and Cazrin fade off to either side of the road. Cazrin murmured something that Tess couldn't hear. Her staff gave a faint pulse of purple light, and the wizard vanished.

"Let's keep moving," Tess said to Baldric and Lark, who were right behind her, with Uggie bringing up the rear. "We'll be camping soon, don't worry. I'm sure this is nothing."

Neither of them replied, but Tess heard the swish of fabric as Baldric adjusted his cloak, probably for better access to his mace. She glanced over her shoulder to see Lark take his lute off his back and make a little show of tuning it casually.

The land rose around them as they continued on, and the back-and-forth calls of the owls faded. The only sound was the soft crunch of their footsteps on the road.

No, not the only sound. Tess's ears strained, and she watched the sloping embankments on either side of the road.

There.

A small spray of pebbles and loose dirt skittered down the hill among the tree roots. Sometimes that was all it took to give you away. Without hesitating, Tess drew a dagger, but before she could call out a warning to the others, a storm of crossbow bolts erupted from the trees.

The party scattered. Tess cursed as she took a bolt to the calf. She hurled her dagger at the spot where she'd first seen movement. There was a high-pitched cry as the dagger hit a dark shape hiding among the trees.

From the opposite embankment, two figures jumped from the trees on the sloping hill and landed in the road. A scraggly-mustached, stocky human and a lithe dwarf with a braided brown beard were dressed in black and had swords out. Neither of them was bothering to hide the symbol on their clothing—a winged serpent in flight.

"Zhentarim," Tess said.

CHAPTER 13

Tess's dagger was still sticking out of the figure hiding in the trees on the left side of the road. From this distance, they looked like a halfling. Another Zhent, she presumed. Normally, they operated as a criminal network of spies, thieves, and smugglers, among other illicit dealings. She hadn't expected to encounter them lying in ambush here. How many were there?

"Uggie, go up the road and scout," she instructed the otyugh. "Make some noise if there are more coming from that direction."

With a squawk, Uggie took off, veering wide to avoid the Zhents that had sprung from the hill and were now advancing toward the party. They had weapons out, and their expressions said they weren't here to talk.

Baldric and Lark regrouped at Tess's back. Tess considered the battlefield and made a quick decision. "You got these two?" she said to them.

"Go," Baldric said simply.

"Time to have some fun," Lark said.

Tess scowled. "Lark, stay with Baldric. Follow his lead, and don't do anything reckless."

"We'll be fine," Lark snapped. "Weren't you going somewhere?"

Sighing, Tess gripped her dagger, activated the magic that would make it teleport to its twin, taking her along for the ride, and vanished.

She reappeared on the sloping embankment, off-balance from the sudden shift in terrain. Luckily, there was a small tree growing from the side of the hill in front of her. She wrapped her free hand around one of its branches and leaned forward, backstabbing the Zhent who'd taken her first dagger to the shoulder. The halfling had been in the process of aiming a crossbow, but she dropped it on a cry and slumped forward. The sleeping toxin Tess had applied to the dagger took effect, and the halfling didn't move again.

Tess retrieved her other dagger from the Zhent's back as shouts echoed from the road. Baldric and Lark, now alone, had squared off with the two Zhentarim there. Baldric drew his mace, brandishing it in front of him as golden fire raced along its length, lighting up the forest around them and casting long shadows from the spindly trees near the road. He swung the weapon, the golden light reflecting off his helm. The mace met the sword of the nearest Zhent, clanging loudly. Baldric reared back and struck again, breaking through the human's guard and digging into the gap in his shoulder plates with a meaty *thwack* that sent the man staggering back. The light pulsed into flame, and the Zhent cried out in pained surprise.

Seeing that light, the other Zhent dropped back a few paces, coming around to take a swing at Lark's flank, his blade whistling through the air. Lark dodged. The sword ripped a gash in his coat, narrowly missing his flesh.

"*That's my favorite coat!*" Lark's voice rose in fury, magically amplified to carry across the battlefield. "You're going to pay for that, you slime-sucking piece of bilge filth! Come here, you wart on a diseased sewer rat!"

"Oh, you got him riled up now," Baldric tutted. The dwarf shuffled to one side to get his body in front of the tiefling, offering some cover as the bard worked his vicious mockery spell.

"You leaking pustule on a politician's lip!"

From Tess's left, a storm of light erupted from the trees as a set of glowing missiles streaked unerringly to tag the Zhent who'd attacked Baldric. The human raised a shield in his other hand to try to defend himself, but the missiles whizzed around it and found him anyway, and he fell to his knees under the onslaught.

Cazrin appeared on the embankment, taking advantage of both the high ground and the cover of the trees to fire the missiles from her staff. There was a soft glow of magical radiance outlining her narrow shoulders, shielding her from any ranged attacks the Zhentarim might make.

"You scum in a bucket of rotting mudfish!" Lark roared as the dwarf who'd slashed his coat staggered and clutched his head as if in pain. "You toe fungus on a night hag's corpse!"

Where was Anson? Tess spared a thought to worry that her friend might have walked into a second ambush within the trees just as she heard shouts and grunts from the other side of the road.

Anson and another human man burst out of a cluster of trees and rolled down the hill. The Zhent was reaching for Anson's throat, but Anson shoved his arms between the man's hands and broke the grip. He rolled them over, pinning the man beneath him as they struggled in the dirt.

Tess reached for her hand crossbow and darts. She uncorked one of the vials of poison she kept ready in a belt loop and dipped one of the darts in the viscous green liquid, careful not to drip it on her fingers as she loaded the crossbow.

Lark's voice rose again over the din of battle, but this time he wasn't hurling insults. He played his lute behind Baldric, still using the cleric for cover as his magic swirled in the air. The trees around him rustled, the leaves seeming to hiss and sing along with the music coming from the lute. Tess felt the magic sink into her, buoying her actions in a way that she couldn't have explained but that she nevertheless felt deep inside her. She aimed her hand crossbow at the dwarf who'd been trying to strike at Lark. Of the pair of Zhents, he seemed the least hurt, and she was afraid to fire into the midst of Anson's wrestling match with the other human.

Taking aim, she pulled the trigger. The dart went wide of the mark she'd been aiming for, but it still grazed the dwarf's throat, slicking poison neatly into the wound as blood dripped down his neck to stain his braided beard.

Using the tree in front of her, Tess swung around and down the embankment to the road, loading and dipping another dart as she went. Anson and his opponent rolled into her path, forcing her to break stride and dodge. The Zhent viciously shoved Anson off him. Tess skittered to the side, aimed, and fired again at the dwarf with the throat wound. This time the dart sank deep into the back of his neck, applying a second dose of poison. The Zhent stumbled and bent double, giving Baldric an opening to hit him with his mace. That put him on the ground.

Besides Anson's opponent, only the human with the scraggly mustache was still standing.

"Tess, watch out!" Cazrin cried.

Instinctively, Tess dropped to her belly and felt something hiss by her ear, nicking her jaw and leaving behind a fiery trail of pain. Blood trickled down the side of her face. She rolled over and looked behind her.

The Zhent she'd backstabbed with the sleeping poison hadn't been quite as unconscious as she'd thought, and the halfling was quickly reloading her crossbow for another shot.

Cursing, Tess realized she was in a deadly triangle between the Zhents and her companions. Putting aside her crossbow and gripping her teleporting daggers in one hand, she put two fingers of her free hand into her mouth and whistled. It wasn't a perfect imitation of a lark's call—all right, it was far from a birdcall of any kind—but the tiefling got the message because he groaned loudly. "I'm in the middle of—if you maim me, I will expect lifetime compensation!" Then he took one hand off his lute and held it up in the air.

She didn't know why the bard should complain. They'd rehearsed this maneuver a few times before going down into the temple, and Tess had only nicked Lark once—maybe twice.

Tess surged up and threw one of her daggers to him, timing the spin and momentum so the hilt would strike his palm. It worked. Lark snatched the weapon from the air and Tess teleported behind the tiefling, grabbing it out of his hand in one smooth movement. She angled around Lark's body and threw the dagger at the not-quite-unconscious Zhent with the crossbow. The blade caught the halfling in the chest, and this time, Tess could tell she was dead before she hit the ground. With her other dagger, she took a swipe at the Zhent with the mustache but missed.

Wavering light blossomed in the clearing, coming from the direction of Anson and his opponent. The smell of lightning and burnt flesh filled the air, and the Zhent cried out and rolled away.

Tess glanced in their direction, but she already knew what had happened. Anson was on his knees, his broken sword in his hand. Sparks danced along the blade, flashes of lightning that arced outward to strike the Zhent, leaving him twitching in the dirt.

Tess felt a prickle of unease. Something wasn't right. Anson never waited so long to draw his blade. She'd assumed he'd lost it in his fight with the Zhent in the trees, but it seemed he'd had it all along. Why was he just now using it?

She didn't have time to puzzle it out. The Zhent with the mustache was coming at them again with murder in his eyes. Tess started to move in for another dagger slash, but Lark thrust out a hand to keep her back.

"Help's coming," he said with a wry smile and a nod toward the trees.

Tess turned to look just as Cazrin pointed her staff at the Zhent. "Baldric, please move!" Cazrin called out.

Baldric didn't need to be told twice. He backed away, taking a slice to his ribs from the Zhent as he retreated. The man's lips curled in a sneer as he pursued, then suddenly, a shard of ice slammed into his back, finding the cracks in his armor and driving deep. The missile exploded, sending small, lethal shards spraying all over him. The man cried out and dropped heavily to the ground, unmoving.

That left only Anson and the Zhent he was fighting. The Zhent had taken significant wounds from the lightning burst from Anson's sword, and the man had his own blade out now, the two of them fighting in the shadow of the hill.

Tess ran over to retrieve her dagger from the halfling's body, but when she turned, looking for an opening to plant it in the remaining Zhent's back, Anson called out to her.

"Don't!" he said sharply. "I've got this."

"Then stop playing with him and finish it," Baldric said in irritation as he cast healing magic over the wounds to Tess's jaw and calf.

"Just stay back," Anson growled, absorbing a blow from the man's longsword against the guard of his blade.

Cazrin came down from the embankment and joined Tess. "Is everyone all right?" she asked.

"Fine," Tess said, shooting her a grateful smile. "Thanks for the timely magic."

"My pleasure." Cazrin nodded at Anson, her brow furrowed in concern. "Is it just me, or is there something extra fearsome about the way Anson's fighting that man?"

She was right. Anson had a stormy look in his eyes as he fought. The Zhent wasn't a particularly skilled swordsman, yet Anson wasn't taking advantage of any of the openings the man was giving him. As Tess watched, the man presented obvious gaps in his defense that Anson could have exploited with his blade, but each time, he held back.

"Anson!" Tess called. "We don't have time for this. What are you doing?"

Anson didn't reply. His chest rose and fell, then he drove forward, parrying a strike from the Zhent and pushing the blade aside. He twisted the broken sword, and at the same time he brought his foot down on the man's boot with bruising force. The man grunted, his grip on his blade slackening. Anson twisted again and wrenched the blade out of the man's hand, sending it clattering onto the road.

Before the man could reach for a dagger on his belt, Anson grabbed him one-handed by the front of his shirt and shook him like a rag doll. "Enough," he said, in a tone of cold anger Tess had rarely heard from him. "If you want to live, tell me how you know Valen."

"Valen?" Lark repeated in confusion, putting away his lute. "Anson, do you *know* these Zhents?"

Anson shook his head grimly as the man went slack in his grip. He raised his arms in surrender, but there was an insolent smile on his face.

"Don't mind him," the Zhent said. "He's just upset 'cause I said I know his little brother."

CHAPTER 14

"Everyone off the road right now," Tess said into the charged silence following the Zhent's revelation. "I want some cover in case there are more of them out there. Hide the bodies in the woods. Let's move!" She whistled for Uggie, hoping the otyugh hadn't gone too far in her search for more enemies.

Lark and Baldric were already collecting the dead Zhents from the road and dragging their bodies up the hill. Tess went to take care of the halfling while Cazrin kept watch, her staff at the ready in case any other surprise attacks came.

Anson and the Zhent he'd captured were still standing in the middle of the road. Anson had sheathed his broken sword but hadn't loosened his grip on the man's shirt. He was holding him almost on his toes, his muscles straining, that fearsome expression still fixed on his face like a mask.

"Anson," Tess said, her voice calm but firm, "we'll figure this out, but we need you to move now." When he still didn't take his eyes off the Zhent, Tess walked over and laid a hand on his arm, tugging until he turned his head to look at her. "I mean it, Anson," she said quietly.

"Yes, come to heel, Anson," the Zhent said in a mocking tone. "Don't make her tell you twice."

Between one breath and the next, Tess's dagger was in her hand and digging into the delicate skin of the man's throat. "Did I invite you to contribute?" she asked conversationally.

The man swallowed and fell silent.

"We need to make sure everyone's all right," Tess went on, keeping the dagger in place and her attention on Anson. "Baldric's probably used most of his healing magic, and none of us are up for another fight tonight. We need to get to safety."

Mentioning everyone else's exhaustion got through to him, just as Tess had known it would. Slowly, Anson nodded, and without a word, he hauled the Zhent off the road and into the trees. Tess followed. She didn't know what the story was between Anson and his little brother—she hadn't even known he had a brother—but she sensed this conversation was not going to go well.

"Here's Uggie," Cazrin called, seconds before the otyugh came bounding back down the road toward them. A tattered, bloodsoaked squirrel tail dangled out of the left side of her mouth.

"I told you to scout, not hunt," Tess said, pointing at the remains of the unfortunate animal.

Uggie worked her mouth, sucking up the rest of the squirrel like a noodle from a bowl, and belched. Tess just groaned.

When they'd finished searching and concealing the bodies, they regrouped in the small wood, well out of sight of the road. Anson had his Zhent prisoner pressed up against a thick oak tree, his forearm across the other man's chest to restrain him. Up close, he was younger than Tess had initially taken him for, with long, stringy brown hair, light olive skin, and a thin goatee, but there was a malicious glint in his eyes as he looked at them all.

Anson didn't appear impressed by the bravado. "If you have any interest in seeing the sunrise, you'll answer our questions quickly and truthfully," he said. "Where is my brother?"

"And why did you attack us?" Tess added. "If you're holding him hostage, we can negotiate—"

The Zhent interrupted her with a barking laugh. "Hostage?" he said. "His brother's the one been helping us find you all."

"That's not true," Anson said at once. "Valen's not . . ." He trailed off, a haunted expression coming into his eyes.

"Easy enough to settle this," Baldric put in. "I've got a spell that will make it impossible for the Zhent to lie."

"No," Anson said. "We don't need to coerce him that way. He's just trying to get under my skin."

"Can't help it if your brother got a better offer from the Zhentarim than his own family," the Zhent said, shrugging as much as he was able to under the pressure of Anson's forearm. "Been following you since it came to light that we were after the same prize."

"The same prize?" Cazrin's hand strayed to her satchel where she'd stored the Ruinous Child. The Zhent tracked the movement. Tess made a mental note to take Cazrin aside later to warn her about her tells.

"You came for the Ruinous Child," Anson said, and some of the color drained from his face. "Were you involved in Sefeerian's murder?"

"Don't know what you mean," the Zhent said, flashing that insolent smile again.

Baldric took a step closer, his mace back in his hand. There was a bit of blood drying along its edge. "Why do the Zhentarim want this book so bad, then? This seems a bit specialized for their dealings."

"It's true. We were contracted by a . . . third party, you could say." The Zhent leaned back against the tree. "Once we have the Ruinous Child, there are great things ahead for the Zhentarim."

"Sounds amazing, pup," Baldric drawled, rolling his eyes. "Come try to impress me when you get a little older."

The Zhent's cheeks darkened with color, and there was an ugly look in his eyes. "Scoff if you want," he said, straining against Anson's arm. "I serve powers greater than you can possibly imagine!"

"You're getting awfully worked up over someone who isn't even here to help you out now," Lark spoke up. He'd been sitting with his back against a tree near Cazrin, his arms crossed. "Are you referring to Lorthrannan?"

A wariness came into the Zhent's eyes. "How do you know about him?"

"Never mind that," Tess said breezily, but her thoughts were racing, making connections. It didn't sound like Lorthrannan was a member of the Zhentarim, so he'd most likely hired the group to secure the Ruinous Child. Which meant that even if he hadn't killed Sefeerian himself, he had probably orchestrated the murder.

"We're more interested in how badly Lorthrannan would like to have the Ruinous Child," Baldric interjected, a gleam in his eyes. "Maybe there's a deal to be made."

Cazrin started to speak, but Tess gave her a quelling glance, at the same time covering her own surprise. She hoped Baldric knew what he was doing. She looked back at the Zhent with a raised eyebrow. "Well, what do you say?"

The man shook his head slowly, incredulous. "Who do you think you are? You don't make a deal with a lich. You just give him what he wants and *hope* he lets you survive."

Tess stilled. Cazrin gave a soft gasp, and the others exchanged tense looks.

"You're lying," Tess said automatically, and at the same time her skittering thoughts pleaded, *Oh Gods, please let him be lying.*

The Zhent read their faces clearly. "Oh, this is too good," he said. "You all have no idea how far in over your heads you are, do you?" He turned his attention to Anson, looking positively gleeful. "Your brother's come up in the world since you saw him last. Lorthrannan has given us all things we could never have dreamed of."

"Stop it," Anson said, biting off the words. "Valen's a fool if he's thrown in with a *lich*, and so are you. Do you know how dangerous a position you've put yourself in? This Lorthrannan is an undead monstrosity that will get you all killed."

"You're warning *me*?" the Zhent said, sniffing in derision. "You're the ones who stole a lich's rightful property and went on the run with it." He looked at all of them in turn while his words sank in. "That's right, the Ruinous Child belongs to Lorthrannan, and he's coming for it. If you all want to live a bit longer, you'll be smart and hand the book over to me to take to him."

"Absolutely not," Cazrin said. Her voice was shaky, but her expression was determined. "We're not handing the book over to anyone."

"Then you're going to die," the Zhent said bluntly. "Don't say I didn't try to warn you."

The Zhent's words hung ominously in the air. Uggie paced around their feet, as if sensing the fear and tension. Tess was trying to wrap her mind around the fact that just a few hours ago, they'd all been celebrating a successful mission together, drinking, laughing, and looking forward to collecting their reward from Sefeerian.

Since then, the elf had been murdered, and the party were fugitives from both the City Watch of Waterdeep and a lich named Lorthrannan who wanted them all dead.

Baldric had let the head of his mace fall to the dirt, the weapon slack in his hands. Lark fingered the pendant around his neck as if it were a talisman to ward off evil. Cazrin was staring down at her satchel with a shocked expression, as if only just now realizing that she might be carrying something with evil intent. Even Anson had torn his gaze from the Zhent's smug face to look imploringly at Tess for guidance.

She glanced over at Anson, trying to summon something encouraging to say. A tingle of warning ran down her spine, the sense that something wasn't right. Belatedly, she realized that in shifting toward her, Anson's grip on the Zhent's chest had slackened. Tess opened her mouth to tell him, but she was too late.

The Zhent brought his knee up between them and kicked Anson viciously in the chest. The breath left Anson's body in a rush, and he staggered back, catching himself against a nearby tree. Before the others could react, the Zhent turned and lunged at Cazrin in a flying tackle.

"Cazrin!" Tess cried, but she was too far away. She could only watch as Cazrin looked up, eyes widening. She clutched her staff and muttered a word, vanishing just as the Zhent landed on the ground in the spot where she'd been standing. She reappeared next to Tess, stumbling in a tangle of underbrush. Baldric pivoted toward the Zhent, using his momentum to swing his mace, a dark look in his eyes.

The Zhent took the blow to his shoulder with a cry of pain, but he had just enough strength to twist a silver band he wore on his smallest finger.

"No!" Tess drew a dagger and flung it, but it passed right through the Zhent's now insubstantial form as he vanished. Tess looked around wildly, waiting for him to reappear nearby like Cazrin had. But the seconds stretched, and there was no trace of the man.

"It must have been a teleportation spell," Cazrin said, glancing at the spot where the Zhent had been. "He could be hundreds of miles from here."

"You almost were too," Baldric said to Cazrin. "Good reflexes there."

"Yes, too bad none of the rest of us managed to be as quick," Lark said. He tipped his hat to Cazrin, its feathered quill stirring in the night breeze. "You narrowly avoided becoming a lich's prisoner." He grimaced. "A fate that still awaits us all."

Tess found her voice. "I'm calling a party meeting," she said, trying her best for an authoritative tone. On a burst of inspiration, she reached into her pouch and pulled out the magical tankard figurine. "Time to see what this thing can do."

"Here?" Cazrin looked dubiously at the densely packed trees surrounding them. "There's not much room."

"Then we'll find a clearing," Tess said, "ideally deeper in the woods. If this figurine really does create an extradimensional space, it could provide us with somewhere more defensible to stay for the night, in case there are more Zhents nearby looking for us."

Or a lich. She didn't need to say it. She knew they were all thinking the same thing.

She turned to Anson, who was patting Uggie absently, though he was staring at the spot where the Zhent had been. "Are you all right?" she asked. "That was all . . . unexpected. I understand if you need a minute—"

"I'm fine," Anson said curtly. "Don't worry about me."

Tess didn't push him, though sooner or later, they were going to need answers about Anson's brother and his involvement in all this.

CHAPTER 15

They found a good spot to test out the tankard about a mile into the woods. It was a small clearing, and within it, scorched grasses and leafless trees indicated a fire had swept through the area some time ago. The blackened remains of the trees stood like eerie sentinels guarding a clearing that Tess hoped was big enough to accommodate the magic of the figurine.

Feeling unaccountably nervous, Tess walked into the center of the clearing and placed the figurine on the ground. Stepping back, she recalled the arcane activation phrase that Cazrin had found inscribed on the bottom of the figurine.

"Take us to The Wander Inn," she said.

Nothing happened, and Tess wondered if the whole thing was just someone's idea of a joke. Then, light blossomed from the tankard's tiny windows, swirling into a colorful vortex that quickly filled the clearing. The kaleidoscope of color grew and grew, reaching almost as high as the surrounding trees. Tess raised her arm to shield her eyes against the brightness.

Seconds later, the light faded, and when Tess could see again, she gasped. In place of the figurine, a full-sized tavern took up the clearing. The wood-and-stone structure was roughly circular, fashioned to mimic the shape of a tankard of ale, just like the figurine. Small triangular windows dotted its front, and a large bay window jutted off one side of the place. A ramp led up to the door, which had another triangular window in its center.

Lark whistled softly in appreciation. "Well, that is certainly a handy piece of magic to carry around," he murmured.

"No kidding," Anson said. He pointed to a soft golden glow shining from the tavern's windows. "There's a light on. Think that means someone's home?"

"Let's hope not, since it's *our* home now," Tess said, leading the way up the ramp to the door. It was closed but unlocked, and it swung open with the loud creak of unoiled hinges, leading them into a cramped common room. The light they'd seen from outside came from four magical driftglobes floating in iron sconces on the walls. To their left was a crescent-shaped bar carved of birchwood, with racks of empty bottles and a few casks situated behind it. Everything was covered in a thick layer of dust. There was a battered table in the center of the room with mismatched chairs stacked upside down on top of it, as if the place had been closed up for some time. At the back of the common room was a large stone fireplace, with a basket of firewood sitting nearby. A hallway curved off the room into darkness.

"It's an actual tavern," Anson said, looking around. "I thought the figurine was just decorative, but it depicts just what the space is." He shook his head in wonder. "Imagine that."

"Bit of a fixer-upper," Baldric commented, tapping one knuckle against the cracked doorframe. "Good bones, though."

As they trooped inside the small common room, Lark immediately went exploring behind the bar. Anson and Cazrin began pulling the chairs off the table so there would be places to sit, although one of the chairs came apart in Anson's hands. Baldric made his way to the fireplace to see about lighting a fire, Uggie trailing behind him.

Tess approached the hall leading off the common room and peered into the darkness. Immediately, more driftglobes lit themselves along the walls, illuminating a hallway that seemed to stretch much farther than the tankard-shaped tavern could accommodate.

As she watched, mouth agape, two doors sprang into being along the hallway, swinging open to reveal a pair of bedrooms with multiple beds squeezed into each room, enough for all of them.

"It's as if the place is making room for our group," Tess said. She glanced over at Cazrin. "Have you ever seen anything like this before?"

"Only in books I've read," Cazrin said. "But these sorts of extradimensional spaces often do conform to the needs of their owners. We can probably make tweaks and requests, within reason."

"How about we each get our own bedroom?" Tess directed her question at the empty air, feeling slightly foolish, but it was worth a try.

They waited, but nothing happened. The two bedrooms remained as they were, and no other doors appeared along the hallway.

"We may need to spend more time in the space," Cazrin suggested. "Attune ourselves to the magic of the tavern gradually."

"All I care about right now is that there's still some ale back here," Lark said cheerfully. He was grabbing tankards from the shelves beneath the bar and laying them out in a row. "Who needs a drink?"

They all did. Leaving the hallway and bedrooms to be explored later, Tess went to the bar and began distributing drinks as Lark filled tankards from one of the tapped casks. Anson and Cazrin took seats at the table, and Baldric sat on the edge of the hearth while he worked on building up a fire, Uggie settling in at his feet. He shot her a dubious glance, but then he sighed and let her make herself comfortable.

Tess pulled out a chair and joined Cazrin and Anson at the table. She cleared her throat before speaking. "Obviously, this day didn't go the way we hoped it would." She adopted a businesslike tone, as if this were just any other party meeting. "However, my plan remains the same."

Lark paused with his tankard halfway to his mouth. "Except now we're being hunted by a lich, a wizard who offered his soul and Gods alone know what else in exchange for power—"

"How do you know so much about liches?" Cazrin interrupted, raising an eyebrow at Lark.

The bard took a long drink from his tankard and turned to get a refill. "I don't, actually, but I've heard all the tavern stories." He glanced over his shoulder at Cazrin. "Why, am I close?"

"In a general sense," Cazrin said. "Liches and their goals are as complex and varied as any person you might meet. What most of them have in common is an obsessive pursuit of knowledge and power. That's why they seek to live as long as possible. They sacrifice their bodies to give themselves more time to amass as much of both as they can. What they choose to do with them is often why they are feared." She reached into her satchel and pulled out the Ruinous Child, laying it on the table. Tess noticed Anson subtly scoot his chair away from the book. "No matter what else we decide to do, we have to get the spellbook open," Cazrin said, a determined set to her mouth. "We have to know what's in here that Lorthrannan wants."

"Isn't it obvious?" Anson spoke up, his voice rusty. He stared at the tome in distaste. "That Zhent said it was Lorthrannan's book in the first place. He wants it back."

Tess shook her head. "I'm not inclined to take anything that man said at face value. We need to consider that he may have been lying, trying to intimidate us into giving up the book."

Baldric didn't look convinced. "The Zhent's excitement seemed genuine," he said. "Sounded to me like they're all thrilled by this alliance with a lich and where it might lead."

"Well, I'm certainly glad someone's happy," Lark muttered.

"If that's the case," Tess said, "then Cazrin's right, and we need to deal with this spellbook. That's step one. We'll take it to Candlekeep and give it to the Avowed. They love books like this, and they obviously have the resources and people to handle it properly, so let's make the book their problem. Then the lich will have no more reason to hunt us, and we can shift our focus back to clearing our names."

"No," Cazrin burst out, causing the others to turn to her in surprise. Flustered, Cazrin ran her gloved hands over the book's cover, dodging another thorn patch that shot up from the leathery scales. "That is, I'm all in favor of taking the book to Candlekeep to learn more about it." She looked at Tess accusingly. "But you never said we'd *give* them the book."

Tess squirmed in her chair. She didn't like the way Cazrin was looking at her. "That was before I knew a lich might be involved," she pointed out.

"True, but that doesn't mean we aren't capable of handling this book and discovering its secrets," Cazrin said, "and we're going to need it in order to help clear our names. I'm sorry, Tess, but dumping it off on the Avowed isn't going to solve our problems the way you hope it will."

"Do you really believe that," Anson asked gently, "or do you just want the secrets of the book for yourself?"

Cazrin bristled. "What's that supposed to mean?"

Anson didn't back down. "Admit it, you've wanted to get your hands on this book ever since you heard it was the focus of the job. The rest of us aren't as blinded to the risks."

Cazrin's face flushed. "I have far more experience in arcane studies than you do, and I know better than anyone what the risks are. But I don't think we solve our problems by just casting the book aside and running away."

"No one is running away," Tess said, trying to intervene and get the conversation back on track before either Cazrin or Anson said something they'd regret. She walked over to the wizard, looking down at the book. "After everything that's happened, you really think the best thing to do is keep the book?" she asked.

Cazrin nodded. She looked apologetic, but there was a defiant light in her eyes as she regarded Tess. "I know we're in danger." Her hand hovered over the book's cover, not quite touching it. "But I think learning about this book is important, and it might help us take on this lich if we know what he wants. Having more knowledge is always better than none, even if you don't always like what you learn."

"That's fair," Tess said slowly. "Though I hope, for our sakes, it doesn't come down to a fight with the lich. But in the meantime, you're right. We should find out as much as possible about the book, then decide what to do with it."

"If you think so, Tess. I trust your judgment," Anson said, though he was clearly unhappy.

In truth, the last thing Tess wanted to do was keep the tome, but she knew that Cazrin, for all her sunny optimism, was also single-minded about what she wanted, and she wasn't giving up her quest to understand the Ruinous Child and its secrets.

"All right, if everyone is on board, we'll continue to Candlekeep," Tess said. "We won't give over the tome to the Avowed, but we'll seek their help in unlocking its secrets, and we'll act based on what we find out. Agreed?" She glanced at Cazrin to see if she was satisfied.

"Agreed." The wizard looked relieved.

"Good. Now let's talk about Valen." Tess turned to Anson, who met her gaze with a pleading look.

"You said yourself we can't trust what that Zhent was saying." Anson gripped his tankard tightly between his palms. "There's no way my brother's involved in this. It was a lie to get under my skin. That's all." He spoke with an air of finality.

Tess could have pointed out several flaws in his reasoning. She also could have asked why, if Anson was so convinced the Zhent was lying, he had reacted with such rage and pain during the battle. Out of the corner of her eye, she noticed Baldric and Lark exchanging glances, as if they were thinking the same thing.

But Anson wore such a look of repressed anguish that Tess let it go for now. She knew him well enough to know that he would talk about his brother when he was ready.

Or at least, she hoped so. The last few hours had left her wavering on many of her certainties.

"We should get some rest, then." Determined to end the meeting on a lighter note, Tess moved to the center of the room and lifted her tankard. "Let's have a toast first. Here's to new adventures with the . . ." She lost the thread as she suddenly remembered they still didn't have a party name. "Whatever we end up calling ourselves."

"The Tavern Keepers," Baldric suggested.

"The Tankard Takers," Lark put in.

"The Company of the Tavern," Cazrin said.

Anson didn't say anything.

"We'll keep working on it," Tess said.

CHAPTER 16

Lark awoke in the middle of the night and couldn't remember where he was. It wasn't the first time this had happened, so he wasn't overly worried. He put his hands behind his head and stared up at the dark beams of the unfamiliar ceiling, the cracks and whorls in the wood illuminated by the single candle burning by his bedside. It would come to him in a moment.

Anson shifted in the bed across the room, and Lark remembered.

Ah, yes, Tessalynde's lovely portable tavern.

Lark had never expected this to be one of the side perks of joining up with the ambitious elf's adventuring party. The day he'd met with Tess and Anson in that cramped changing room in the back of that hovel someone had the nerve to call a theater, he'd been attracted by the amount of coin being offered and the opportunity to work his experiences into his repertoire of songs and storytelling onstage. He was really a simple tiefling with simple needs.

Well, perhaps not simple, but at least he was straightforward about his goals. He wanted to perform. He wanted to have even a fraction of the fame and fortune his former bandmates now enjoyed—and then he wanted to surpass them. But he didn't want the kind of attention that would attract the unsavory individuals hunting him.

So here he was, pursuing fame—or infamy—and fortune through a different route. One that included a portable tavern that turned out to have bedrooms, although they were a bit plain, and a strange, long hallway that Cazrin had advised them all not to explore just yet.

It's probably nothing, just that you might get lost in a pocket dimension and not be able to find your way back out again.

And then she'd handed out balls of string to everyone, advising them to keep one end tied to their bedpost so they wouldn't get lost when they got up to relieve themselves in the middle of the night. Or if the rooms suddenly disappeared or relocated themselves. Though, in that case, they were probably going to need more than string to help them.

What had he gotten himself into?

With sleep eluding him, Lark rose from the bed, grabbed the ball of string, and stepped quietly out into the hall. He had half a mind to defy Cazrin's advice and go on a midnight stroll just to see what would happen, but the sound of a poker being thrust into the fireplace and the crackle and scrape of logs drew Lark back to the common room.

Baldric was the one wielding the poker. He was seated on the edge of the hearth, stabbing the logs and muttering under his breath. He'd taken off his heavy cloak and had laid his cloth of holy symbols out beside the fire so the light caught the colors and flourishes on the designs.

"Couldn't sleep either?" Lark asked, coming to sit at the table. He put down his ball of string and turned his legs and tail so they were best positioned to soak up the heat from the fire. "You know, I never pictured you having trouble sleeping. I always thought you'd be exhausted praying to all those gods of yours at night, and that you'd fall asleep mid-supplication." He grinned. "Dearest Tyr, grant me the power of an ox and the grace of a wolf so that I may smite mine enemies . . ." He trailed off into snoring noises.

Baldric poked the fire one final time and turned to Lark. He combed his fingers through his beard, taming some of the wild strands. "Yes, that's exactly how it goes," he said mildly, laying the poker aside. "What kept you awake, then? Thinking up more of those funny jokes?"

"An artist's workday never ends." Lark stretched, draping one arm over the back of his chair. His gaze grew serious. "Actually, I half expected to see you slip out in the middle of the night. Is that what's happening? Am I interrupting?"

Baldric chuckled. "Don't worry, you're not thwarting an escape attempt. If I wanted to leave the party—and I'm not saying I haven't considered it—I wouldn't skulk away in the middle of the night. I'm not afraid to tell the others to their faces if I want to go."

Leaving the uncomfortable implication that Lark might be the type to do the skulking. Or maybe he was just being paranoid, and Baldric meant no such thing.

"I don't have the best history of making long-term arrangements work, myself," Lark admitted. He hadn't even been able to stay in a band of musicians, let alone adventurers risking life and limb together. "The others were right, but it's obvious they have secrets."

"You mean Anson," Baldric said.

"I mean all of them, but particularly Anson." It rankled that Tess spent so much time lecturing and mistrusting Lark but gave the fighter a pass when it came to a situation that might prove dangerous for the whole group.

What did he expect? If she'd had a better option, Tess probably would have replaced Lark by now.

And why did he care what Tess or anyone else thought anyway? It wasn't as if he owed them any loyalty. The whole situation was making his head hurt. It was too complicated.

"I suppose it doesn't matter what secrets everyone's keeping, since we probably won't survive long being hunted by a lich," Lark muttered.

"Well, aren't you full of optimism," Baldric said. "I don't know that I would count us out just yet. There have been some bumps, and I don't agree with all of Tess's decisions, but we've worked well together so far." He turned his gaze to the fire. "Don't know if it'll last, but if it doesn't, I can always go back to being on my own." He ran his fingers absently over his cloth as he spoke.

"There are far fewer expectations placed on you when you're alone," Lark said, but he found he couldn't summon any of his usual humor to go with it.

"And far fewer disappointments when it all goes wrong," Baldric agreed. He gave a humorless laugh. "So why does it feel so depressing when we put it like that?"

"Speak for yourself," Lark said. "I am the picture of good cheer and happiness. You know, this reminds me of the story of how I left my old band. Did I ever tell you about that? Now there's a tale of perseverance in the face of disappointment. I had written an amazing song, a ballad of love and death to make the angels weep. I showed it to my best friend, Gustan, the one who started the band with me." Lark sighed. "They took it and said they were going to 'make some tweaks' to really shine it up before we showed it to the others. I had no idea they were going to steal my song. It was the worst—" He stopped short at Baldric's snort of laughter. "What?" he demanded.

Baldric shook his head. "I can't fathom why the others see you as such a mystery. You've got a story ready for everything, but you're the easiest one of us all to figure out."

"Really?" Lark drawled, whipping his tail back and forth. "Do tell. Bare my soul for all to see." He struck a dramatic pose in his chair, head thrown back, throat exposed.

Baldric sighed. "I'm not going to rip you open, Lark. I was only going to say that it's clear to anyone who wants to look closely that you're scared. All the time. Makes it easier to play the part of the charming liar. Now, I can maybe guess at some of the things you're afraid of, but I don't know your whole story, and it isn't my place to judge. But the more you try to hide who you are—especially from yourself—the worse the fear will get."

So much for not ripping him open. Lark sat up straight, abandoning his ridiculous pose. He hadn't noticed his heart beating faster, but he felt it now, thudding against his ribs, each beat bringing a spike of unexplained anxiousness. He took a few deep breaths to try to calm it, looking away from Baldric's steady gaze.

"You and Tess could both give lessons on motivational lectures," he said. He'd meant it to sound like a joke, but his voice wasn't quite steady enough to pull it off. Damn them all.

No, he wasn't going to slip out in the middle of the night, but that didn't mean he was going to stay for good either. In the end, it wouldn't matter. He'd disappointed enough people in his life that adding a few more to the list wouldn't make much of a difference.

"I'm going back to bed," he announced, standing and grabbing his ball of string. He walked breezily back down the hall to his bedroom, waving at the dwarf over his shoulder. "Don't stay up too late, dear. The gods and all the rest of us need you fresh in the morning."

"Sweet dreams, songbird." Baldric's knowing chuckle followed him back to his room.

Lark tossed and turned for hours after that, but he fell asleep wondering if the reason Baldric was so astute at identifying Lark's fears was that the dwarf carried a fair share of his own fears that he was simply better at hiding.

In the morning, they set off for Candlekeep. Lark had never been there before, and neither had any of the others, but Cazrin had apparently done extensive research on the place at one time and had spent half the night "brushing up" so she was prepared when they arrived.

Lark thought she was being a bit premature, considering it was a journey of hundreds of miles and just thinking about it made his feet throb.

Fortunately, Tess, in her infinite capacity for planning, had accounted for the lengthy journey as well, because by their second day of travel, she'd negotiated the group a spot guarding a caravan travelling the Trade Way, along with some heavy cloaks and hoods to help hide their identities. Blending in with the caravan folk had kept the Zhentarim off their backs, and they'd settled into an uneventful, if tedious, daily routine on the slow journey south.

They reached Baldur's Gate without being discovered and spent a fruitful day in the city, spreading the word that they were adventurers looking for paying work and that they were going to be staying in the city for at least a tenday. Tess even arranged several meetings with prospective clients—and then the party left the city under cover of darkness with yet another caravan, never to be heard from by those clients again. It was a shame, and Lark could see it was difficult for the elf, who prided herself on her professionalism, to build and burn so many bridges in a single day.

But if it led Lorthrannan and the Zhentarim to waste a few days following the party's trail in Baldur's Gate while Tess and the group got a head start on the Coast Way toward Candlekeep, then it was worth it.

Cazrin's excitement only grew the closer they got to the great library. As they walked, the wizard's spellbook floated in front of her, and occasionally, Cazrin would read from her notes some tidbit or other about the place. She carried a bottle of ink and a quill that she used to make notes in the margins. All of this she accomplished mostly without tripping and falling. Lark was impressed—and also slightly irritated—at the constant stream of commentary.

"There's the Hearth, and of course the House of the Binder, which is a great temple to Oghma," Cazrin was saying just then, stopping to make another note. Her foot caught on a rock as she started walking again, and she stumbled.

Anson, who'd been walking just ahead of her, shot out a hand and gripped her arm to steady her. This had happened several times already.

To pass the time, Lark retreated into his own head, composing song lyrics and plotting out future performances, until something Baldric said pricked at his attention.

"That intellect devourer–filled dungeon was also once a temple to Oghma," he reminded them. "Is it possible the god of knowledge or some of his followers had the Ruinous Child before the illithid came in and took over? Could they have been hiding it from this lich?"

"I wondered the same thing!" Cazrin said excitedly. She dropped back to walk beside Baldric, her spellbook floating along as if on an invisible leash. "Keeper, flip back to that set of notes I made about Oghma's temple in the dungeon. It's on the page that got soaked in salt water."

The spellbook's pages fluttered and snapped, lying flat again on one of the earlier sections. It floated up under Cazrin's nose so she could read the small scribbles. Baldric reached out and gently guided Cazrin around a dip in the ground that would have sent her sprawling. She nodded her thanks absently as she read. After a moment, she looked over at him.

"But if that's the case, did the clerics of Oghma get the tome from Sefeerian? He said he lost it long ago, so maybe they found it in the meantime?"

Baldric raised an eyebrow at her. "That would be putting the best possible face on it, yes, but we already established that Sefeerian didn't tell us everything about his connection with the tome."

"You're saying you think it wasn't his book either?" Anson asked from ahead of them. "You think he lied about it?"

"I don't have any proof either way," Baldric said, shrugging, "but there was obviously more to the story of the spellbook than the elf ever intended for us to know. Just something to keep in mind."

Cazrin made another note in her book, her quill scratching over the page. Lark wrinkled his nose at a sudden smell and tapped the wizard on the shoulder. Cazrin looked up distractedly. "What is it?" she asked. "Do I have ink on my chin again?"

"Yes," Lark said, pointing to the tiny dot, "but that wasn't what I was looking at." He nodded to her satchel. "Is that smoke, by any chance?"

Cazrin's eyes widened. "Not again!" Quickly, she pulled off her belt and dropped the satchel on the ground. Using her gloves, she undid the clasp and yanked out the Ruinous Child.

It was on fire.

"So, this happens often?" Lark asked, as Cazrin frantically smothered the flames with her gloved hands while the others gathered around and Anson stooped to help her.

"Never this bad," Cazrin said, snatching her hand back as a gout of flame surged from the spine of the book.

Tess came over with her waterskin in her hands, pulling out the cork. "Stand back," she said.

"Oh, Tess, I don't think water will be good for the ink—"

"I'm betting it'll survive," Tess said, and dumped a stream of water on the flames. There was a loud hiss as steam rose from the book, filling the air with the foulest stench Lark had ever experienced. It burned the insides of his nostrils and made his eyes stream.

"That thing is wretched," Baldric said, holding his nose and backing away. "I thought nothing could smell worse than Uggie, but I was wrong."

It took half the contents of Tess's waterskin, but the fire finally went out. When the steam cleared, Lark noted that there didn't appear to be so much as a scorch mark or water stain on the book.

"To think that Sefeerian actually *wanted* this back in his library," Anson said.

"It's a spiteful little thing," Tess agreed, frowning. "Don't worry, Cazrin, we'll get you a new satchel. Er, another one."

Uggie, who'd been standing outside their loose ring around the book, suddenly surged forward, snatching up the book in her jaws.

"Uggie, no!" Cazrin cried, horrified. "Uggie, drop it! *Drop* it!" she warned, as Uggie backed away with the book clenched tightly between her teeth.

"I say let the beast destroy it," Baldric said. "We'll all be better off."

"I don't think a powerful, ancient spellbook is going to be taken down by an otyugh, even if she does have a cast-iron stomach," Tess said.

Uggie seemed determined to try anyway. Ignoring Cazrin's cry of dismay, she sucked the book into her mouth with a loud slurp and began to chew. Sort of. The sound reminded Lark of a cat with a hair ball, only in this case the hair ball was more like a limestone slab. Uggie grunted and choked, her throat bulging with the outline of the book. The eyes on her eyestalk widened, and she tossed her head from side to side.

"It's not going to happen, girl," Anson said, reaching out to pat the otyugh on the head. "You'd better quit while you have all your teeth."

Uggie let out a mournful wail, shook her head one more time, like a dog fighting with some invisible prey, and then vomited the Ruinous Child onto the grass in a stream of gooey saliva. Every inch of the book was covered in jagged black thorns that dripped green poison, mixing with the saliva in a disgusting soup.

"Gods," Tess said, wrinkling her nose. "Uggie, that is foul."

"That *book* is foul," Lark said. "And the otyugh is probably poisoned." He glanced at Baldric with a mischievous smile. "You may have to come to the rescue."

Baldric opened his mouth to protest, but then he saw the expectant look on Tess's face and just sighed. "Fine, I'll heal the beast."

Lark noticed that Baldric gave the otyugh a couple of reluctant pats before he gruffly muttered the words of a healing spell and called for one of the benevolent deities to take pity on the creature and heal her without any strings attached. And at least one of the goodly gods must have been looking down on them fondly, because the next minute, Uggie was rolling around happily in the grass and snuffling at everyone's boots, looking for attention or food or both. Not even Cazrin could be annoyed with her for trying to eat the book. Uggie nudged her hip and whined while Cazrin attempted to clean up the Ruinous Child and coax it to retract its thorns.

Lark watched her work with the strange, malevolent thing, talking to it as if it were just a sullen child rather than something that looked like it had been ejected from the Nine Hells.

Anson must have noticed it too. "Is anyone else worried if the book is this dangerous when it's safely locked, what exactly is going to happen once we're able to open and read it?"

Everyone fell quiet as the implications of that sank in. "It's natural to worry, but this isn't the first time I've dealt with dangerous magic," Cazrin said firmly. "This is my job."

"Hopefully the Avowed will also be able to help," Tess said. "I'm sure they've seen lots of sentient magical tomes. They probably have an entire protocol for dealing with them."

Lark hoped they were right. He eyed the Ruinous Child with distaste. The gleaming dragon scales that had once made the cover appear attractive were now a dull gray-black, and there were raised ridges where the thorns had been, changing the shape of the thing and making it look less like a book and more like a half-melted pile of sludge. Was that Uggie's doing or the tome itself? Every time he looked at the thing, its appearance seemed to change slightly, as if it was never quite the same book twice.

"What kind of person would create such a monstrosity?" he murmured.

But the others were already preparing to move on. Only Tess heard him. In a rare moment of accord, they shared an uneasy glance. "And would Cazrin ever agree to give it up?" she asked.

CHAPTER 17

WATERDEEP—CITY OF SPLENDORS

ONE MONTH AGO

Tess stood in front of the abandoned warehouse, wondering if she was in the right place. The building hunched like a sullen gray troll between a pawn shop and a seedy-looking tavern in the middle of the Southern Ward. The windows had been boarded over, though several of the wood planks had come loose and were banging loudly in the wind.

Tess tucked her cloak closer around herself and glanced up at the sky. The clouds had thickened and darkened to dull pewter, and the scent of petrichor in the air mingled with the stench of mildew and garbage on the street.

She checked the scribbled directions from Anson one more time, just to be sure this really was where the wizard was supposed to be staying, then she strode up to the door and knocked.

It swung open under her hand. Besides not being locked, it was barely latched. The rusted knob hung off the door. Tess stepped cautiously into the dark warehouse, giving her vision a moment to readjust to the sallow light coming in from around the boards over the windows. She could see well enough in the dark that she wasn't too worried, but it was nice to have the extra light anyway.

"Hello?" Tess called out into the gloom. All around her were stacks of crates, weathered and slowly rotting from what looked like decades of moisture seeping into the wood. The smell was abhorrent, a combination of mold and rat urine and who knew what else. Tess wrinkled her nose and pushed farther into the room.

"Is anyone here? Miss Varaith?" she tried again and heard a muffled reply from the back of the warehouse. Tess sighed and headed in that direction, weaving through the crates and dodging more than one rat along the way.

Maybe she should have brought Anson along to help on this one, or at least to make the introductions. But Tess had wanted to talk to the wizard alone, to take her measure without any outside bias.

"Miss Varaith?" she tried again. "It's Tessalynde—Tess—Anson's friend. We had an appointment."

This time the reply was clearer. "Tess! That's right, I'd forgotten that was today. Come on back—er, just follow the sound of my voice. And please call me Cazrin. Sorry about the mess!"

Rounding a particularly high tower of crates, Tess came upon a scene that made her mouth fall open in surprise.

Seven crates pushed up against the back wall of the warehouse had been completely emptied, the mildewed straw they'd been packed in strewn all over the floor. Where there wasn't straw, there were books—hundreds of them, in various stages of decay. A rangy, dark-haired woman who had to be Cazrin Varaith was meticulously stacking them in towers, organizing them by some method Tess couldn't follow. Three spheres of golden light floated above the wizard's head, illuminating an open spellbook that hovered at her elbow.

The rest of the space had been devoted to what looked like a small camp. There was a bedroll spread over a pile of straw, the remains of a half-eaten breakfast, and more books lying open to different pages as if for quick reference.

"Watch your step. There are so many obstacles here," Cazrin said without looking up. She spoke loudly, and Tess realized that the wizard hadn't heard her approach. It was habit on Tess's part, to move stealthily, especially over uncertain terrain. "I'm sorry I didn't prepare any tea. I woke up this morning and found the collected lecture notes on Tarance Filinore and his study of thaumaturgical variations across magical disciplines, and then I looked up and it was past lunch and I hadn't even gotten through the introductory section."

Tess coughed politely.

Cazrin spun around, saw her standing just a few feet away, and blinked several times. A bit of a flush crept into her cheeks, and she offered Tess a smile.

"Hello," she said. "Have you been there long?"

"Not long at all," Tess assured her.

Cazrin chuckled. "Sorry, I do tend to go on a bit, but this collection is the most amazing treasure trove, and it was just sitting here, rotting away! So many valuable texts!"

"I'll take your word for it," Tess said, eyeing the water-stained pages and ripped covers of the books. "So, do you, um, *live* here?"

"What?" Cazrin had gone back to organizing the stacks. She looked up, and rich laughter filled the dreary space. "Gods no! What made you think I—" She glanced at the bedroll and breakfast remains and hummed in her throat. "Yes, I guess I can see how you'd get that impression. No, I have a rented room on the other side of the city, but it was just easier to sleep here while I sort the collection. I bought it—at a steep discount, I might add—on the condition that I clean out the warehouse of anything of value before it gets demolished next month. The building, I mean."

Tess looked at their surroundings skeptically. Working on her own, at the rate she was going, it would take Cazrin a solid year to clean the place out, but she kept that thought to herself.

"My friend Anson said he spoke to you and that you might be interested in joining the adventuring party we're putting together," Tess said. Selecting one of the smaller, cleaner crates nearby, she sat down and watched Cazrin buzz from one stack of books to another. "He mentioned that you were particularly interested in the spellbook we're being sent to retrieve."

"Oh yes!" Cazrin beamed at her as she flipped through a small leather-bound book with most of its pages stuck together. Turning, she pulled a quill from behind her ear and made a quick note in the spellbook floating next to her. "I'm always interested in acquiring new spells, so I was hoping we could negotiate that as part of the reward from this Sefeerian Annil you mentioned. I'd be more than willing to relinquish part of my share of the monetary reward in exchange for the privilege."

"We can try to arrange that," Tess said. "Our cleric is also interested in acquiring any tomes we might find in the ruins of Oghma's temple. Are you all right sharing that bounty with him?" Tess wanted to head off any potential intraparty conflicts before they began.

"Not to worry," Cazrin said brightly, adding the book in her hands to a stack near her bedroll. "I can get absorbed in my work sometimes, but I'm perfectly capable of sharing. Knowledge should be accessible to everyone, not hoarded away by dragons or left to rot in dreary warehouses." She turned her attention to the spellbook floating in front of her. "I think that's all for now. Thank you, Keeper."

"Very good, Cazrin," a cheerful voice from the spellbook intoned. "Please do let me know if you require anything else."

"Keeper?" Tess repeated as the spellbook obediently closed itself and floated down to rest on top of Cazrin's pile of blankets. The cover had a pair of blue beryl stones embedded in it that looked a bit like eyes, along with a few other embellishments that suggested a face when viewed from the right angle.

Cazrin flashed an impish grin. "I guarded my diaries and journals so fiercely when I was a child that my family used to call them my little secret keepers. Maybe it's not terribly clever, but I've always liked the name."

"Is Keeper . . . alive?" Tess asked. She'd heard of such things, but she'd never seen that kind of powerful magical item up close.

"I'm afraid not," Cazrin said, and she must have seen Tess's confusion, because she added, "I've just put a great deal of my own magic into the book's design so that it can easily access and repeat all the knowledge it contains. I also added a few flairs here and there to make it seem more like a friend and research partner." She hesitated, biting her lip. "Does that sound odd? To have a book for a friend?"

"Not at all." Tess had read some books in her time that had become lifelong friends. It was always a comfort to revisit them. But this wasn't the time or the place to share a story like that. This was an interview, and Cazrin no doubt expected professionalism. "I imagine Keeper is an invaluable research tool," she clarified.

"Exactly," Cazrin said. She reached for a cloth draped across one of the crates and used it to wipe the dirt from her face. Her warm brown skin was slightly flushed. "So, when do we head out on this mission?" she asked, tossing the cloth aside when she was finished.

Tess blinked. "Just like that? I thought you'd have more questions for me."

"I probably should, shouldn't I?" Cazrin said thoughtfully. "But to be honest, you had me at 'lost spellbook.' I couldn't resist."

"But are you interested in joining up with us full-time?" Tess pressed. "This wouldn't be just a onetime mission, or at least, I'm hoping it isn't. I'm hoping, if we're successful, to turn this into a more permanent arrangement."

Cazrin considered. "I'm not opposed to the idea," she said. "I haven't travelled with a group in some time, and I've missed it— being around people, I mean." She gestured at the dim surroundings. "Research is all well and good, but it can be daunting when tackled alone." She smiled at Tess. "And what about you?"

Tess blinked. "What about me?"

"What made you decide to put together an adventuring party?"

That brought Tess up short, although it really shouldn't have. It was a perfectly reasonable question. It's just that none of the other interviewees had asked her that. "Well, there's the job I mentioned," she said. "I knew from the beginning it was going to take more than just Anson and me. And if we wanted to continue to take on bigger missions and build our reputations, it seemed like the logical next step to get a skilled group together. That was the start of it."

"Ah, all right, then," Cazrin said, but Tess thought she heard a disappointed note in the other woman's voice.

"Why, is that not a good enough reason?" Tess asked, feeling suddenly defensive.

"Oh, I didn't mean that," Cazrin said quickly, holding up her hands. "And I've never put together an adventuring party myself, so what do I know? I was just wondering if there was a story behind it, that's all. In any case, I'd love to join the mission. Just as soon as I get this collection sorted, I should be able to—"

Out of the corner of her eye, Tess noticed a particularly large rat jump from one tower of crates to another. The weight of its body was just enough to make the precariously stacked pile teeter dangerously from side to side.

Cazrin looked up, following Tess's gaze. "Oh dear," she said, just as the tower started to tip in her direction.

"Watch out!" Tess was across the room in seconds, one hand on the wizard's shoulder, ready to push her out of the path of the falling crates. But before she could act, Cazrin sketched a quick pattern in the air and muttered some arcane phrase that Tess didn't understand.

A thunderous *boom* echoed through the warehouse, sweeping the tower of crates back in the other direction—whereupon they slammed into another tower of crates, and another, and another, until the whole mass fell over and smashed against the opposite wall of the warehouse. The already flimsy vessels burst apart, showering a small storm of antiques, furniture, and other bits of junk all over the floor.

When the thunder and crashing noises had ceased, the two women were left standing in a thick cloud of dust. Tess coughed and waved her hand in front of her face to clear it. "That was . . . impressive," she decided was the best way to put it.

Cazrin winced. "Probably a bit of overkill, but don't worry! I'd already gone through those crates, and there were no books inside."

"That's a relief," Tess said, coughing again to cover her chuckle.

"You moved like one of those displacer beasts I've read about," Cazrin said, looking at Tess in admiration. "I barely had time to react before—*poof*—there you were." She smiled. "Thank you for coming to help."

"Not that you needed it, but you're welcome," Tess said. She looked at the disastrously large pile of debris before them. "Now what?"

Cazrin ran a hand through her mussed hair and glanced at Tess with a hopeful expression. "Do you think I could also negotiate some help cleaning this place out as part of my share of the reward?"

Tess looked at the mess with a slightly pained smile. "I'm sure I can think of something."

CHAPTER 18

THE SWORD COAST

PRESENT DAY

Once the party left Baldur's Gate, they travelled mostly under cover of darkness. It slowed their pace but kept the Zhentarim off their trail, and they reached Beregost without any signs that they were being followed. From there, they took the Way of the Lion out of town, as it was the only road extending across the narrow peninsula to Candlekeep.

Cazrin noted all of this in the journal portion of her spellbook as dawn cast its first deep pink streaks across the pale threads of cloud in the eastern sky. When she looked up, her breath hitched.

There it was. After all her dreams and imaginings, there should have been fanfare—trumpets and banners and song—but no, Cazrin simply looked up, rubbing the stiffness from her neck, and caught her first glimpse of the massive library of Candlekeep in the distance.

It was still too dark to make out much detail, but the sight of the library's many towers rising from a volcanic crag of rock overlooking the sea was breathtaking. Golden light flickered behind a scattering of windows all throughout the fortress, signaling that someone was awake and studying at all hours.

Cazrin's spellbook was still open and waiting at her elbow. She took her quill in hand to chronicle her first impressions of the place. She'd waited so long for this moment, but for once, she found she didn't have any words to write. Her quill hung slack, and she just stood there and stared, moisture gathering in her eyes.

At the front of the group, Tess called the party's attention to the library, glancing over her shoulder to locate Cazrin. Tess must have recognized the state she was in, because the elf dropped back to wait for her while the others went on ahead. Cazrin gave her a tremulous smile as she swallowed the ball of emotions churning inside her.

"I had no idea it would make me feel like this," Cazrin whispered as Tess drew near. She wiped the wetness from her eyes and gave a trembly laugh. "It's silly, isn't it? We're not even there yet and I'm just . . ." She gestured helplessly at the immense structure.

"It *is* impressive, and it's not every day a person who loves knowledge as much as you do comes face-to-face with the biggest collection of it in the world," Tess said. "Of course you're going to be a bit overwhelmed." She cocked her head. "I'm actually surprised you've never been here before. I would have thought you'd have begged your parents to take you since you first learned to walk."

"Begged, pleaded, cajoled, threw temper tantrums—you name it," Cazrin said. Her face clouded. "My family . . . well, not all of them approve of my studying magic."

"Really?" Tess looked surprised. "But you're so talented at it."

Cazrin winced, fiddling with her quill until the vanes were ragged. That was part of the problem. She'd been *too* talented at it, even from a young age. Sometimes she wondered: If she hadn't proven adept at magic and learned so quickly, would her family have been so afraid for her?

Would they have been so angry when she'd left?

"My ancestors once had an affinity for magic," Cazrin said. She had no desire to dredge up these memories, but she wanted to give Tess an explanation. "The problem was, not all of them used it for good. One, in particular, used it to cause a lot of harm, and even though she's been gone for a long time now, my family is afraid others might someday follow in her footsteps. They decided they would be better off if they discouraged their children from using magic altogether, rather than risk them doing something awful with it."

She knew the rest of the party, particularly Anson, had their own concerns about her dabbling with the Ruinous Child. Cazrin couldn't blame them, but it still hurt. It brought back memories of her mother's pinched, disappointed face when Cazrin had confided in her that Keeper was more than just a book, of her sister's tearful name-calling when Cazrin accidentally set one of her potted plants on fire.

"It seems like an extreme solution, assuming everyone will handle magic the same way," Tess said, pulling Cazrin from her thoughts. "That can't have been easy for you. I don't know what I would have done if my parents had told me I couldn't do the things that came naturally to me as a child. I would have run wild."

Cazrin smiled at the thought of little Tess tearing through the green forests, leaves and twigs caught in her golden hair. "Something tells me you were wild anyway," she said.

Tess chuckled and ducked her head. "Guilty," she said.

It was midmorning, the sun high and warm in the sky by the time they reached the imposing double gates proudly displaying the castle-and-flame sigil of Candlekeep. Cazrin drew a quick sketch of the gates in the margins of her spellbook, noting the strange black metal that was said to be immune to certain magical effects and divinations.

Only one of the gates currently stood open, and it was guarded by several monks in purple vestments. As the party approached, Cazrin put away her spellbook and quill and went to join Tess at the front of the party. She kept her hand on her battered satchel but didn't remove the Ruinous Child from it yet. Her heart was pounding so loudly in her chest, she expected the gate guards to hear it. Maybe they could, judging by the suspicious looks being cast their way.

A halfling woman with pale skin and red-gold hair layered in braids atop her head stepped forward to greet them. Her smile was polite but aloof, as if she had had many such interactions with travelers before. Her posture was neither threatening nor particularly welcoming.

"Well met," she said to Cazrin and Tess. "How can I help you today?"

Tess took the lead, as they'd planned. They'd rehearsed this conversation and any variations they could think of for several hours the previous night. Tess didn't like leaving anything to chance, and in this case, Cazrin was in full agreement. She couldn't help thinking the monks were going to snatch the Ruinous Child from her and lock it away in the vast fortress before she could learn its secrets.

Knowledge locked away, out of reach—not for you. It was Cazrin's worst fear, the refrain she'd heard so often in her childhood and hated. *Don't touch. Don't ask. Don't look. Some things are not meant to be known.*

No. Cazrin refused to believe that was true. All knowledge had a purpose, dangerous or not. She'd spent her life stubbornly holding on to that belief.

Maybe the people here would understand that.

Tess was introducing herself and Cazrin to the halfling woman, who hadn't given a name in reply. Cazrin focused her attention back on the conversation.

"My companions and I have come to request the assistance of the Avowed," Tess was saying. "We need their wisdom to unlock a tome that came into our possession recently—a singular book named the Ruinous Child, which we believe to be sentient and malevolent. We need guidance to discover how best to handle such a tome, and we knew there was no better place to seek it than here."

Tess spoke confidently, with no hint of nervousness, as she stood before the halfling woman and the four other monks gathered by the gate. She was as comfortable in the spotlight as Cazrin was in a research library.

The halfling woman gave a nod of acknowledgment of Tess's petition, but she offered no sign that she either recognized the name of the spellbook or was concerned about its nature. Cazrin wouldn't have enjoyed playing poker with the woman.

"What is it that you offer the library in exchange for the services you require?" the halfling asked. "Have you brought a tome to donate to the collection?"

At this, Cazrin opened the satchel and removed the Ruinous Child, offering it up for inspection only. She did not hand it to the woman. Once again, she was gripped by the irrational fear that she would snatch it away and run.

"We were hoping—" Cazrin started, but she stopped when she felt Tess elbow her gently in the ribs. Right. This was transactional. She needed to be confident and assured. "The Ruinous Child is, as my friend stated, a singular work, and while we regret that we cannot make it a permanent addition to the library's collection, we are more than willing to lend it for study, with the common goal of understanding its secrets and unlocking the knowledge within. I'm sure this would be of significant interest to the Avowed."

The halfling woman was not looking at Cazrin as she spoke. Her gaze was fixed with a scowl upon the Ruinous Child. She turned her head, exchanging the briefest of glances with one of her fellow monks. Then she turned back to Tess and Cazrin and cleared her throat. Some of the flintiness was gone from her face, replaced by genuine concern.

"I assume you know that you carry something of great evil," she said, looking at Cazrin intently as she spoke.

Cazrin nodded, resisting the urge to squirm under that gaze. "We understand that and the risks involved, which is why we came here."

"You were right to do so, but you ask a great deal of the Avowed with no donation for the permanent collection," the woman said, shaking her head. "I'm afraid it's not enough."

Cazrin swallowed. If only she'd had time to pack some of the books that she'd recovered from that warehouse before the party left Waterdeep. She could think of at least three from the collection that would have sufficed as a donation.

She'd hoped it wouldn't come to this, but she had to get that book open. She couldn't lose this chance.

Slowly, her hands shaking slightly, she reached into a separate satchel and pulled out her spellbook. "I know that the Avowed will at times accept offerings in the form of journals and accounts of a person's life," she said. "I have—"

Tess spoke over her. "We would also be willing to perform a service for the Avowed in exchange for their aid," she said smoothly. "We are very capable, with a wide array of talents and magic in our group. I'm sure we have something to offer you."

The halfling glanced between them with a curious arch to her brow. "Perhaps," she said. "Wait here a moment. I will return."

She turned and walked away, presumably to consult with the monks and perhaps others unseen inside the library.

Tess turned to Cazrin with an incredulous look. "Were you really about to offer *your own spellbook* to the Avowed?" she demanded. "That wasn't part of the plan."

"I was only going to offer them my journal pages," Cazrin said. "Which you would have known if you hadn't interrupted."

Tess raised her eyebrows, but she looked more amused than offended. "Are you angry? I didn't think you ever got annoyed about anything."

"Well, you cut me out of the conversation." Cazrin crossed her arms over her chest. "I'm just saying, I might have gotten us in immediately if you hadn't butted in."

"I'm the party leader," Tess reminded her. "It's my job to 'butt in,' as you put it, especially when one of my party members is going off-script and not following our plan."

"We don't have time to perform a service for the Avowed," Cazrin said, throwing up her hands. "This way is faster."

Tess shook her head, her gaze softening. "I've seen you writing in that journal. Pages and pages. It's a part of you, Cazrin. You don't have to give that up when we have something else to offer." She leaned in closer. "The Ruinous Child isn't worth that. You need to trust me."

Cazrin blinked at her in surprise. "I do," she said. She trusted the whole party more than she had anyone else in a long time, in fact. They *saw* her.

And just now, Tess had refused to let Cazrin sacrifice an important part of herself to this mission. She understood how much Cazrin's magic meant to her.

It's a part of you.

She held on to the elf's words, savoring them like a secret and a treasure, that small, unexpected burst of being seen.

Before she could say anything else, the halfling woman returned. She offered them a smile that was more genuine this time and beckoned the entire group forward. "Your offer has been considered and accepted," she said. "Welcome, Seekers. The gates of Candlekeep are open to you."

CHAPTER 19

The next few minutes for Cazrin were little more than a blur as she accompanied the party inside the gates of the great library and into the Court of Air. Here was the House of the Binder, a temple dedicated to the god of knowledge, as well as the Baths, the House of Rest, and the Hearth, all places for visitors to gather, rest, and refresh themselves after a long journey.

On any other occasion, Cazrin's weary feet would have drawn her to the promise of a hot meal and an even hotter bath after all their days spent on the road. But she couldn't have rested now if she'd wanted to. Energy zinged through her body as she looked across the cobblestone courtyard to the western wall, where the Emerald Door—the famed gateway to the Inner Ward that she'd read about in countless books—gleamed at her in the sunshine.

The gateway to knowledge.

It was too much. A lump rose in Cazrin's throat, and her vision blurred again.

Baldric stopped beside her, pressing something soft into her hand. She looked down and saw that it was a handkerchief.

Cazrin shook her head. "I can't take this," she said, sniffling. "I'll ruin it."

"For the love of the gods, keep it," Lark said wearily as he came up on her other side. Uggie stood next to him. Cazrin had once again disguised her as a sheepdog, but she wasn't sure how effective that would be under the scrutiny of Candlekeep's magic. "You're probably going to need it," Lark went on, "and you're making the rest of us all weepy just looking at you."

Baldric cleared his throat loudly. "Except me, of course. I'm beyond such things." He gave her a tiny wink.

Cazrin laughed and used the handkerchief to blow her nose and wipe her eyes. Ahead of them, Tess and Anson were speaking to the Keeper of the Emerald Door, who greeted them and led them into the towers to a reading room, where they were instructed to wait for one of the Avowed to join them.

"Couldn't we have stopped for a meal first?" Lark complained as he threw himself into one of the chairs arranged around the long cherrywood table that dominated the room. "There were such lovely smells drifting out of the Hearth, and I would do murder for a drink."

"We're *all* tired," Tess said, taking a seat herself. She lifted her shirt and sniffed. "And we could all use a bath too, but we need some answers first."

"You don't have to stay," Cazrin said, as she carefully removed the Ruinous Child from her satchel and placed it on the table in front of her. "Please, go and rest. I can speak to the Avowed and tell you what I learn later."

Lark was already half out of his chair, Uggie following, but the door opened and a stocky dragonborn strode into the room. They were dressed in the vestments of the Avowed, their copper scales shimmering in the light. They nodded to each of the party, an unmistakable gleam of interest in their deep-set eyes.

"Well met," the dragonborn said, their voice a warm rumble. "My name is Breskid Rodoll. I was asked to assist you . . ." Their voice trailed off as their gaze fell on the Ruinous Child. "Is that actually a book, or is it a pile of dung?"

Cazrin blinked. That was not an auspicious start and not at all how she'd pictured her first interaction with the Avowed. But when she glanced down at the book, she gasped.

The Ruinous Child had once again changed its appearance. The glittering scales on the cover had shifted to look like folds of lumpy flesh the color of cold oatmeal. Thorns and dark, wiry hairs sprouted liberally from the spine, and Cazrin heard what sounded like a faint growling noise coming from the book.

"I'm sorry," she said, addressing Breskid. "It usually doesn't look like this, but I think it might be a defense mechanism. My theory is that the book will react with hostility when it feels threatened."

"Or when it's just in a bad mood," Lark said, inching toward the door.

"The seal on it's still intact," Anson said, pointing to the silver binding. "We were hoping you could help us open it."

"It doesn't respond to lockpicking," Tess said, ignoring Cazrin's cocked eyebrow. "We tried that already."

Breskid nodded thoughtfully and came around the table to stand at Cazrin's elbow. "May I examine the book?" they asked.

Once again, Cazrin hesitated, but they didn't press, only waited patiently while she wrestled back that feeling that someone was going to take the book away from her.

The dragonborn gave a nod, as if they knew exactly what she was thinking. "I promise not to remove it from your sight," they said.

Cazrin suddenly felt silly. She scooted her chair over to make space for Breskid. "Please," she said, gesturing to the book. "I'd welcome your expertise."

The rest of the party leaned a bit closer to watch. Even Lark lingered by the door to see what was about to happen, but Breskid didn't touch the book right away. Breskid bent over the table and examined the spine and cover, taking out a pair of spectacles and two white archival gloves, which they pulled over their taloned hands. The spectacles nestled into a groove on their snout to look at some details around the lock. They picked up the book, and almost at once a large black thorn, thicker than all the rest, sprang from the spine and impaled their gloved hand.

"I'm so sorry!" Cazrin said to Breskid. "Be nice," she scolded the book, slapping the table as if she were a parent trying to get an errant child's attention.

But the scribe only chuckled and pulled their hand back, showing her the glove was unmarked. "It's all right," they said, "and I apologize. I should have told you before that my area of expertise is in hostile tomes. I came prepared."

Baldric gave a booming laugh. "There's a whole field of study dedicated to books with a temper? I'm going to have to reexamine everything I thought I knew about librarians."

"I imagine there's a field of study for everything in a place like this," Anson commented. He was perched on the edge of the table near Baldric, eyeing the Ruinous Child warily.

"What about the lock?" Tess asked. She'd jumped up when the thorn stabbed Breskid, and now she had her hands on the table, leaning forward. "Can you open it?"

"Eventually." Breskid continued to examine the tome for several moments. Tess tapped her fingers on the table. Lark started to fidget, and even Baldric, interested as he was in the proceedings, was looking toward the door.

"I might visit the temple of Oghma," Baldric said when Cazrin caught his eye. "Then go have a drink. Lark?"

Lark was halfway out the door before he'd finished speaking, pulling Uggie along with him. "Call us if you need anything," he threw back over his shoulder.

Anson reached across the table, giving Tess an expectant look. Tess slapped a gold coin into his hand. "You win," she said with a sigh.

"Told you they wouldn't make it half an hour."

Come to think of it, Baldric had seemed more and more interested in the god of knowledge. Cazrin wondered if he was settling on one god to petition to or if there was something else he was seeking. Before she could think further on that topic, Breskid whistled under their breath.

"What is it?" Cazrin asked eagerly. "Did you find something?"

"There's writing on the front and back covers of the book," Breskid said. "As fast as I can read it, it conceals itself, like the book's trying to tease and bait me. Did you notice any of this before?" they asked Cazrin.

Cazrin shook her head, feeling disappointed in herself. She'd looked at the book dozens of times and hadn't seen anything like that. "Can you read it?"

"Some of it," they said. "Enough to know that the lock on the book is a blood binding." They glanced at Tess. "You can use a lockpick to serve as a key, but it has to be properly treated first."

"With someone's blood," Anson said, looking at the Ruinous Child in disgust. "Are we absolutely sure we want to open this thing?"

"I'll do it," Cazrin said, already rolling up her sleeve. "I'm the one who wants to study the book the most, so it should be me." She glanced up at Tess, who looked like she was ready to launch an argument. "It's what we came for," she reminded the rogue. "I'm not afraid to do this."

"We didn't think you would be," Anson said, looking at Cazrin in concern. "Just be careful. We're right here if you need us."

Cazrin gave him a reassuring smile and turned to Breskid. "Let's do it." She furrowed her brow. "Wait, we'll need something—"

Tess stepped forward with one of her daggers. "It's clean," she said, and looked at Cazrin. "If you'll let me do it, it'll be quick and—almost—painless."

Cazrin nodded. "Thank you," she said, and held out her arm.

Faster than her eye could follow, Tess sliced a shallow cut on her arm. Cazrin felt the heat of it and the lightest pressure before the blood welled and the sting followed. She marveled again at Tess's skill. She could be as gentle with a blade as she was deadly, and her enemies rarely saw her coming—

Gods, but that does sting! Cazrin thought as Tess took a lockpick and covered it in the blood dripping from Cazrin's wound. When she was done, she nodded to Anson, who stepped in and wrapped Cazrin's arm in a quick, expertly done bandage.

"I'll go find Baldric and bring him back," he said, but Cazrin laid a hand on his arm.

"I'm fine," she said. "It can wait." She nodded at the bloody lockpick in Tess's hands. "Let's see if this works."

Breskid laid the book in front of Tess. Without hesitating, Tess plunged the lockpick into the silver mouth. She'd barely given it a twist before there was a loud *click*, and with a heavy *thunk* against the table, the binding opened.

A rush of fetid air blew through the room. Cazrin wrinkled her nose, but that wasn't the worst of it. As she reached over and opened the cover of the book, a wave of something else washed through her, a shuddery feeling as if someone had walked over her grave. It swelled into a malevolence, a presence that filled the small room, and Cazrin could have sworn she heard a soft, breathy laugh.

At her hip, she felt Keeper move, restlessly pushing against the straps that held its satchel shut, as if it were trying to get out.

Or to get away.

Her spellbook had never done that before. Cazrin had a strong sense of foreboding, a feeling that she'd opened the cage door of a predator and was now watching it stretch its legs.

Anson and Tess had taken instinctive steps back from the table. Breskid was frowning at the book in consternation. Cazrin noticed they were staring at the inscription on the inside cover. It was written in Common, in the Thorass script.

> Within these pages is the life's work of
> Alagesheth the Wise
> The pieces of my soul live on
> Though my body turns to dust
> Those who survive the wrath
> Of the Ruinous Child
> Have earned the knowledge here
> To them I bequeath my legacy
> Do with it what you will
> And be prepared to pay the price

"Well, that's not ominous at all," Anson said dryly, reading over Cazrin's shoulder.

"More ominous than you know," Breskid said.

"Why?" Cazrin asked. "Do you know who Alagesheth the Wise is?"

"I know who he *was*," Breskid corrected. "A lich who lived in the time of Netheril. He was destroyed centuries ago, but his research lived on and was well known and respected in certain circles. It's said that the lich Valindra Shadowmantle was a follower of his work and collected some of the rarer volumes he wrote on ritual magic and history. These were later stolen, and eventually, all accounts of Alagesheth's life and work found their way to be safely contained within this library." Breskid's eyes darkened. "Or so I thought. Obviously, I was wrong."

"The 'seekers of the collection,'" Tess said thoughtfully. "Sefeerian said they were the ones who asked him to find the Ruinous Child." She looked at Breskid. "He was talking about you. About Candlekeep, I mean. You wanted to gather all of Alagesheth's collection for safekeeping here. But you say you knew nothing of the Ruinous Child?"

"That's correct," Breskid said. "Sefeerian Annil sent us all the known volumes of the lich's collection as he gathered them, but he must have discovered the existence of the Ruinous Child much later, because we hadn't heard from him in decades."

"Why is it called the 'Ruinous Child'?" Tess asked. "Seems like an odd choice for someone's life's work."

"From the inscription, my best guess is that Alagesheth, having no heirs of his own, always intended to pass on the wealth of his accumulated knowledge and power to worthy successors," Breskid said. "The Ruinous Child is his legacy, but he would have ensured that those who sought it had to pay a high price for the privilege."

"He succeeded, because other liches have learned about the book as well," Cazrin said. Her chest tightened. She worked to school her expression in front of Breskid, but she caught Tess's and Anson's eye and saw her concern mirrored in their faces.

Lorthrannan. Alagesheth the Wise. Valindra Shadowmantle.

They weren't dealing with just one lich, but *three* of them.

CHAPTER 20

"You said we were going for a drink," Lark whined. The bard had managed to remain silent as they'd lingered outside of Breskid's makeshift study, but now that they were out of earshot, he seemed determined to make himself heard. "Instead, you made me eavesdrop on our own party, when we could have just stayed in the room with them the whole time, and now you're dragging us through these boring, dusty archives, and there's no tavern in sight." But even as he complained, he followed Baldric through the maze of towering shelves, Uggie trailing behind them. "Do you even know where you're going?"

"It's a library, Lark," Baldric said, pointing to a sign on the archway before them. The arch itself had been composed entirely of magically suspended books, aligned so that the gilded pages of each tome created a bow of gold leaf. "They're fairly good at marking where everything is so visitors don't get lost."

Lark glanced at the sign, then back at Baldric, his eyes narrowed. "I can't help but notice that sign—and the last two that we passed—mentions that this section of the library is restricted to select personnel. Did we obtain a special pass I didn't know about?"

"We did," Baldric said, turning down another aisle, scanning the shelves of ancient tomes stacked like intimidating sentinels before them. "I had a quick chat with the goddess Tymora, promised that I'd help another soul who was down on their luck if she would in turn help point us in the direction of more information about this Alagesheth you heard Cazrin and the others talking about."

"Fine, but again, why didn't you just stay in the room with the esteemed librarian and listen to their fascinating lecture on Alagesheth's exploits through the centuries?" Lark asked. "I'm sure it would have been riveting." He reached down and pulled Uggie away from the bookshelves before she could snatch one of the tomes and eat it.

Baldric shook his head. "Cazrin, Tess, and Anson will get all the answers they can from the Candlekeep folk," he said. "They don't need us there for that. I'm more interested in what they're not willing to tell us."

He'd been in the game long enough to know that even in the fairest negotiations, you'd be a fool to think the other party wasn't holding something back. Candlekeep guarded its knowledge well, but one of its best security measures, as far as Baldric was concerned, was the vastness of the place. You could hide the deepest, darkest secrets of the world behind a tattered cover, on a dusty shelf, in a forgotten room deep in the bowels of this grand library, simply by surrounding it with thousands of other similar-looking volumes.

That's why, sometimes, you needed a little help to tip the scales of fortune in your favor.

Baldric took out the platinum sun coin he'd used to seal his deal with Tymora, flipping and catching it one-handed as he strolled past the shelves, waiting to feel some inkling from the coin that he was moving in the right direction.

Lark watched him, although the tiefling did his best to seem uninterested. "You don't need to stay," Baldric pointed out. "You can take Uggie and go get that drink. I'll meet up with you later."

"Why do they listen to you?" Lark asked, nodding at the coin as it sailed through the air. "These gods you dally with—why do they care to give you so much of their attention?"

"You don't think it's my natural charm and sense of style?"

"I think if that were the case, we both know they'd be fawning over me instead," Lark said. "Come on, tell me. Is it a family gift, passed down from your ancestors? Do the gods owe your line a debt?"

"My clan has no idea, the things I can do."

Baldric ran his thumb over the griffon rider and dragon engraved on one side of the coin. He'd expected it to grow warm in his hand or glow with silver light when he was close to where he needed to be, but so far, it hadn't led him to any divine inspiration. Maybe Tymora was just playing with him to see how he'd react. The trickster gods were fickle and strange, but they were still as fallible as the other deities.

"Ah, so it's a shameful secret you keep from them," Lark said, deftly snatching the coin out of the air when Baldric tossed it again.

He knew the bard was baiting him, probably in retribution for the way Baldric had spoken to him that night in the party's new tavern. Maybe he even deserved it.

"It's not shame that keeps me quiet," he said. He leaned down and absently petted the otyugh as she twined a tentacle around his knee. "If my clan knew about this gift I have, they'd never let me leave their hall again."

He loved his family—well, some of them—but he'd given them enough of himself over the years. He'd needed to forge a path on his own, and he'd done that. But if they ever discovered the level he was negotiating at these days, they'd convince him to come back—for the good of the clan, of course—using and exploiting his gift in their mercantile empire until there was nothing left of him.

His first taste of freedom had been intoxicating. He'd reveled in being alone, no one to answer to but himself. He'd thought he would live that way forever, no attachments, no commitments but the ones he made through his deals with the gods.

Except here he was, travelling with a group, making deals on their behalf, and enjoying it. Maybe he hadn't changed as much as he'd thought.

At least this time, if and when he decided to leave, it would be easier to cut ties. These people weren't his family. He would feel no guilt about walking away.

None at all.

Lark's humor faded as he watched him, and he flipped the coin in Baldric's direction without a word. It arced through the air, spinning, spinning—and then it slowed, coming to rest on the edge of a nearby shelf, touching a large tome with a faded blue cover.

The needle in the haystack, Baldric thought, taking the book off the shelf. Knowledge hiding in plain sight.

"What's in it?" Lark asked a moment later, as Baldric paged through the book. He couldn't quite keep the impatience out of his voice.

"I don't recognize the language, so I'm not sure," Baldric said. He balanced the open book on his palms, indicating a folded bit of parchment that had been tucked into the pages. He felt a tingling in his scalp, like a tiny prod from Tymora. "I think this is what we're looking for."

Lark gingerly removed the parchment from the book and unfolded it. It was so old that it should have crumbled to dust, but it remained whole, leading Baldric to believe there was some preservative abjuration magic at work.

"It looks like a map, maybe of some underground complex," Lark said, pointing to the small, crude drawings of tunnels and rooms. "There's writing here too, but it's so small and . . ." He trailed off. "Wait, is it . . . moving?"

"What?" Baldric squinted doubtfully at the map, but then he realized the bard was right. The tunnels and rooms changed locations before their eyes, the ink on the parchment blurring, fading, and reappearing in a different configuration, so they were never looking at the same map for more than a few seconds at a time. It made his eyes water staring at it too closely. "Well, that's helpful, Tymora," he said, as he put the book back on the shelf where he'd found it. "Should have known you'd never be straightforward with me."

Lark slowly turned the map in his hands. "When you want to both remember and protect the location of something valuable, you make a map that's magically encoded like this. You have to spend a certain amount of time studying it in order to imprint the true map in your thoughts. I've never actually used one before, though. Cazrin might know more."

"Good enough for me," Baldric said. He took the map from Lark, folded it up, and stuffed it down his shirt. "They'll never miss it," he said. He winked at the bard. "How about that drink now?"

"You're just going to casually sneak a magical map out of Candlekeep?" Lark asked, grabbing the platinum coin off the shelf and pocketing it.

As Baldric began to retrace their steps to the exit, Uggie trotted up happily beside them, a red ribbon sticking out of her mouth like a tiny second tongue. Baldric let it go. He wasn't going to fight the beast over one dusty book.

"We'll find a way to create a distraction so I can smuggle it out," Baldric said. "I'll think of something."

"Nefarious," Lark said with a dreamy sigh. "Baldric, you might just be my new hero."

Uggie spat out the ribbon and belched.

CHAPTER 21

Anson stared at the Ruinous Child lying open on the table, the inscription laid bare like a curse. *This* was what his brother was involved in—a chain of liches going back to the time of Netheril? How was he supposed to begin to untangle Valen from all of that?

Should he even try?

It was clear his brother had made his choice, and, advertent or not, that choice had set him against Anson. The pain of that burned in him like a poison, yet it was still so easy to slip into the memory of his little brother as a helpless child, before everything had gone wrong. Valen had needed Anson once.

Anson shook those thoughts away. The past was set. It couldn't be changed. He had to focus on the here and now. His party was in danger, and Anson felt like that danger had increased exponentially now that the Ruinous Child was open.

Cazrin pulled the book toward her and began gingerly turning the pages, the expression on her face like that of a child given a key to a sweets shop. Even the wizard's good nature and her tendency to see the best in everything couldn't quell Anson's fears that she was blinded to the book's evil. A tangible sense of malice bled from the book's pages, filling the small reading room.

Did either Tess or Cazrin sense it too? Breskid had left the room to consult with a colleague, giving them a few minutes alone.

"What do you make of it?" he asked Cazrin, snaring the woman's attention as she paged through the book.

"It's . . . overwhelming," Cazrin said, and there was a reverent note in her voice. "The combination of languages, the dates of these earliest entries—there are even wards over some of the *paragraphs*. Imagine, abjuration magic at the sentence level!" She shook her head. "It's going to take me months, if not years, to unravel all these secrets."

Tess made an unhappy noise as she sat back down at the table. "We don't have that kind of time," she said. "We need to find out what Lorthrannan wants with the Ruinous Child."

"What *doesn't* he want?" Anson said, pointing to the book. "Breskid said this was written by an even more ancient lich. Lorthrannan could find any number of uses for it."

"It could also have something to do with this Valindra Shadowmantle," Cazrin suggested. "Her exploits are famed and dark, and if she's a collector of Alagesheth's work, Lorthrannan could be trying to acquire the book for her."

"Or use it against her," Tess mused.

And Valen and the Zhentarim obviously hoped to profit off of whatever Lorthrannan gained from the book, Anson thought.

"Just give me some time, and I'm sure I'll be able to tell you more," Cazrin said, with a pointed, hopeful glance at the door.

Anson got the hint and sighed. "I don't think it's a good idea to leave you alone with that thing," he said. "Now that it's open, we don't know what it might do."

"I don't like the feel of the thing anyway," Tess said, and Anson was glad to have confirmation that he wasn't the only one sensing the wrongness of the book.

"I'll be fine," Cazrin assured them. "Stay if you want to, but you have to be quiet and let me think—not that the two of you are loud," she added hastily, "but you can be, um . . ."

"Distracting?" Anson said with a chuckle. "Fair enough." He

glanced at Tess. "Maybe you should stay here, and I'll go check on Baldric and Lark."

Tess nodded. "I want Baldric to look at Cazrin's wound too," she said, "and then we can—"

The door to the reading room burst open, and Breskid stormed in. "We have a problem," they said. "There's danger in the library, and we need to call upon your offer of service." They glanced down at the Ruinous Child. "Bring the book with you. We suspect it may be involved."

"Involved?" Anson repeated incredulously. "It hasn't left this room. How could it be responsible for trouble in the rest of the library?"

"You'll see," Breskid said grimly. "Please, hurry." The scribe left without another word.

Tess was on her feet. "Let's go," she said. "Cazrin, lock the book and put it back in its satchel, just to be safe. Then go and grab Baldric and Lark. We'll need them."

Cazrin nodded, closing the book and reaching for the silver clasp. Anson followed Tess out of the reading room, hurrying to catch up with Breskid.

It was chaos in the courtyard. High-pitched magical alarms sounded, and visiting seekers were pouring out of the Hearth to see what the commotion was about. Above, there were screams and cries of distress coming from the towers.

Breskid led them into one of those towers, past a pair of guards, who stepped aside with terse nods. All around them, monks were sealing off the various rooms, casting powerful protections on the doors. The air crackled with arcane energy and the chants of the spellcasters, the protectors of the library all mobilizing at once to combat the unseen threat.

They rounded a corner, and Anson stopped short. An open gallery spread before them, filled with tables and reading nooks, all lit by soft magical light. Curving around the back wall was a series of floor-to-ceiling bookshelves, with sliding metal ladders at either end of the room to reach the upper shelves.

Dozens of books floated in midair in the center of the gallery, swirling in a vortex of fluttering pages and rushing wind. High-pitched shrieks and wails filled the air, making Anson wince. He looked around for the source of the distress, until he realized that what he'd taken for the screams of people actually seemed to be coming from the books themselves.

He could see why.

Beneath the vortex, a large tome lay open on the floor. Thick green vines and leafy branches were swiftly growing out of the pages, thickening and shooting across the floor at alarming speed to wrap around the reading tables and chairs, creating a junglelike fort in the middle of the room.

That wasn't all. Anson drew his sword as a clawlike, vine-covered appendage burst from the book, impossibly large, pushing and contorting itself to rip free from the tome. Moss and pond-green lichen made up its large, lumbering frame. A set of bony jaws cracked open in the place where a face might be, and as it heaved itself out of the book, the smell of rotting vegetation filled the air.

And then a second creature began to claw its way out of the book behind the first.

Tess yelled, "Kill it and seal that book!"

Anson didn't know what the creature was, but Cazrin would, and she was bringing Lark and Baldric as backup. That was all he needed to know. He plunged into the strange library-turned-jungle, stumbling as the vines, leaves, and moss shifted under his feet, a living carpet that seemed determined to slow him down however it could.

Tess fared a little better, leaping out of reach of the grasping, heaving vines, firing her hand crossbow at the plant creatures. Anson forced his way forward until he was within reach of one of the creatures' unnaturally long arms. He focused on his breath, drawing a surge of strength from each inhale and exhale, falling into a trance-like state. His sword became an extension of his body. He was in complete control as he launched his attack, tearing and severing vines with a precision born of long years of practice.

The creature roared in pain and swept its arm around, trying to knock him down. Anson jumped straight into the air, lifting his knees to clear the thick vines as they swung beneath him. He landed on the soft, mossy vegetation and stabbed his blade into the crea-

ture's torso—or at least where he imagined that part of the shambling body might be.

There was another earsplitting shriek as the plants convulsed and
withered away around the jagged end of the sword. Anson yanked
the blade out and stabbed again, and this time, he felt the telltale
energy of the sword's erratic magic tingling under his hands. Blue
sparks sputtered from the blade's hilt, and the smell of ozone filled
the air, briefly overwhelming the scent of swamp.

"Anson, stop!"

Baldric's voice. Anson looked over his shoulder in time to see
him and Lark burst into the gallery, Uggie trotting behind them.
Baldric had his hand outstretched toward Anson, his eyes wide.

Whatever he was trying to warn Anson about, it was too late.
The electrical energy travelled up Anson's blade and into the plant
creature in a blue-white arc that temporarily blinded Anson. He
staggered back, arms aching from the blast, blinking his vision clear.

When he could see again, the plant creature had surged forward,
bearing down on him with its vine arms outstretched. Anson had
expected to see a smoking crater where the lightning had struck it,
but instead the leaves and plant matter seemed to be re-forming
before his eyes, covering the wound with renewed vitality.

Anson cursed, dodged another sweeping strike from the vine
arm, and shouted over his shoulder, "What are these things?"

"Shambling mounds!" Baldric yelled back. "Whatever you do,
don't hit them with lightning again! And get down!"

Anson dropped to his knees as Lark's crossbow bolt whistled
above him, striking the creature. It roared in pain and shuffled back,
vines writhing. Jagged teeth gnashed, and dark spittle flew from its
mouth.

Taking advantage of the distraction, Anson shifted around the
creature, dodging a parting strike from the vine arm, and darted to
the back of the room. He sheathed his sword—he couldn't always
control when the lightning magic would activate, so it wasn't safe to
use—and climbed the closest metal ladder to get an aerial view of
the battlefield.

Lark reloaded his crossbow and was firing at the other shambling mound, which had grabbed Tess and wrapped her in its vine arms, dragging her toward its body. Baldric had his mace out and was wading into the jungle to help her. Uggie had engaged the creature Anson had attacked, and it looked like she was trying to eat her way through the plant matter as it tried to snare her and wrap itself around her tentacles.

There was no sign of Cazrin at all.

Trying not to panic at the thought that the wizard might have been smothered by the vines, Anson opened the bag of holding and pulled out a polished longbow, one of his most prized possessions. He reached back into the bag and grabbed a quiver of arrows on a leather strap, which he slung over his shoulder. Bracing his feet on the metal ladder, he nocked an arrow to the bow, took a deep breath to will himself back into a state of calm, and released. The first arrow struck the creature holding Tess in the back. The shambling mound shrieked again, its mouth gaping, and tried to shuffle sideways to get behind one of the tables. But it was slow, and Anson fired again before it could find cover, this time impaling the creature in the jaw. His arms fell into the familiar movements without his mind consciously following what he was doing, and he released arrow after arrow into the creature.

At the same time, Tess managed to wrench one of her arms free. She hurled a dagger at the bookshelf next to him, and almost as soon as the blade buried itself in the wood, she vanished, appearing beside him with the hilt in her hands and clinging to the shelf like a spider.

"Thanks," Tess said breathlessly, putting away her dagger and reaching for her hand crossbow again, all the while balancing on the narrow ledge of the bookshelf.

"Where is Cazrin?" Anson demanded, as one of the shrieking books hurtled past him. They were still swirling in the vortex, the writing on their pages twisting and crawling as if the ink were being ripped from them. "Did one of the mounds grab her?"

"I don't know!" Tess was slathering her darts in poison before turning to aim at the closest mound. "I haven't seen her since we separated!"

Anson had a bad feeling in his gut. He couldn't have explained it, but the memory of that foul stench and the wrongness of the Ru-inous Child was still fresh in his mind. "We have to find her," he said. "We have to make sure that damn book is secure."

"No argument," Tess said, loading the dart, "but we're a little busy at the moment!"

"Cursed beasts are slimier than the otyugh!" Baldric shouted as vines wrapped around his arms. His mace slipped from his grasp and was quickly buried under a carpet of moss and crimson-capped toadstools, which continued to sprout from the book in the center of the room. "Going to need a little help here!" He shot a pointed glance at Lark, who was still firing his large crossbow from the safety of the doorway.

"Lark, Baldric needs backup," Tess commanded.

"Seriously? Last Resort was just getting warmed up!" Lark cried, referring to the crossbow. He gave a dramatic sigh and tossed aside the weapon. "Do you know how hard it is to get grass stains out of this coat?"

"Just help him!" Tess snapped as she leaped from the bookshelf to the ladder Anson was standing on. "We've almost got the other one down!"

Anson kept burying arrows into the other mound. Tess was right. The creature was starting to unravel, its vines twitching and tangling with one another as it tried to slink away but could find no good place to hide its large bulk from the hail of missiles.

Out of the corner of his eye, he watched Lark reluctantly grasp his pendant and the rings arrayed on his fingers. A flash of bright, multicolored light erupted around the creature, followed by a thun-derous *boom* that reverberated in the chamber and made Anson's ears pop.

The shambling mound didn't react.

Lark cursed but kept moving, finding the smallest opening to wade through the vines to Baldric's side. He put his hands on the dwarf's shoulders and muttered the words of a spell. Then the vines came between him and Baldric, yanking them apart as the mound pulled the dwarf fully into its body.

Tess gasped. "Lark, get out of there!"

"You think?" Lark leaped backward, barely avoiding being wrapped in the vines as he skittered to the side, but he slipped on the mossy ground and fell to one knee.

Anson buried another arrow in the second creature and breathed a sigh of relief as it writhed and shrieked but then lay still. Tess threw her dagger at the remaining mound, scoring a direct hit in the back of what was probably its head. Anson grabbed her arm before she could teleport into the fray after it.

"Wait," he said, pointing to the spot where Baldric had disappeared. "I think Lark did his job."

As they watched, the vines peeled back, and Baldric's head emerged. With his face covered in sweat and moss, Baldric sucked in a breath and then let out a mighty shout as he punched his way out of the mass of vines, muscles bulging with a bull's strength under the effects of the spell Lark had cast. He pressed forward, head down, every muscle in his body straining, until he could reach his arms across his body, gripping handfuls of greenery in each fist. Shouting, he ripped them free and shoved his way out of the creature's grasp.

The shambling mound screeched in agony, but it couldn't reform itself around the wound. The vines shriveled and retreated toward the book, leaving trails of slime and moss in their wake. The mound gave one last feeble attempt to put itself together before collapsing into a heap of plant matter that browned and shrank before their eyes.

When it was over, there was nothing left in the room of the strange jungle except for a mass of green stains everywhere, some dead flowers and vines, and the faint smell of swamp water. The books that had been swirling in the air all snapped shut at once and fell to the floor with a loud *boom*.

Anson jumped off the ladder and ran to the large book from which the shambling mounds had emerged. He slammed the tome shut, revealing the title: *The Busy Gardener's Illustrated Guide to Gentle Magical Enhancements.*

Gentle.

Anson snorted and put his boot on the tome just to be sure it stayed shut. He scanned the room quickly.

"Where's Cazrin?" he demanded again, directing the question at

Lark and Baldric, who were stripping vines off themselves with disgusted looks.

"How should we know?" Baldric said. "She was with you two when we left."

"We sent her to get you when all the Hells broke loose," Tess said, frowning. "Didn't she find you?"

Lark shook his head. "We were . . . occupied, but we came when we heard the screaming—against my better judgment, I might add."

Which meant Cazrin hadn't even made it to the battle. Anson's relief that she hadn't been absorbed and suffocated by the shambling mounds was short-lived, as Breskid burst back into the gallery, calling their names.

"Please tell me there's not another monster," Tess said, wiping green moss and slime off her dagger. "We just finished killing two of them. Surely, that's service enough for the library."

"Service?" Breskid said faintly, looking around at the scattered books, their pages torn out and drifting down to lie in piles in the wake of the vortex. The dragonborn took in the destroyed furniture and the remains of the shambling mounds, which had left a coating of green slime and dead plant matter on every inch of the floor. They cringed hardest at the sight of Anson's boot planted squarely on the large book in the middle of the room, but Anson didn't remove it. He didn't want to risk more monsters coming out of there.

"I know this doesn't look great," Anson said, "but trust us, you didn't want those shambling things getting out of this room to do even more damage."

"It's not a monster doing damage out there," Breskid said, their eyes narrowing. "It's your friend."

CHAPTER 22

Cazrin was lost in the library.

Her older sister used to tease her about that fate when she was a child.

One day, little Cazrin's going to wander into a library and never come out again. And then something gruesome about how, years later, they'd find her bones clutching some esoteric tome. At the time, Cazrin had pretended to be horrified by the notion, but secretly, she'd thought it would probably be the best way to go.

Except in those daydreams, there hadn't been a massive shadow following her, dogging her steps as she ran down row after row of shelves, searching for an exit from the endless labyrinth of books.

Was she even still at Candlekeep? Nothing around her looked familiar.

She rounded a corner, and the smell of rot and decay filled her nostrils. Skidding to a stop, she watched as shadows bled from the books on the surrounding shelves, coalescing into a massive, vaguely humanoid shape that rose in front of her, blocking her path.

Cazrin.

The voice was a hiss in her ears, a whisper in the dark. She backed away instinctively. Her shoulders collided with a wall. She turned and found herself hemmed in by endless shelves of books. They stretched and curved above her head into a prison of tomes.

"You're not being very original," Cazrin said, trying to keep her voice steady as the shadow advanced on her. "Making a cage out of books isn't going to frighten me."

Oh, Cazrin. Cazrin. The voice made her name into a caress. Cazrin shuddered. *It's not a cage. It's a gift. All for you. Everything you've ever wanted. Why would you run from such a treasure?*

"Because it's a trap," Cazrin said. "I'm not accepting anything from you."

Curious. The shadow dipped toward her, the body seeming to expand, filling the space between the shelves. The smell of decay intensified, making Cazrin gag. *You should know better than anyone that magic is simply a tool. It can be used for great evil or overwhelming good. Isn't that what you've always told your family? Isn't that why you've spent so much time trying to uncover my secrets?*

Cazrin stared.

"You're the Ruinous Child," she said, "or, the spirit of it . . . The heart?"

She remembered now. She'd been on her way to get Baldric, Lark, and Uggie, but something had happened. Everything had twisted, and now she was . . .

Lost.

Instinctively, Cazrin reached for her spellbook, needing Keeper's familiar comfort.

Her satchel was empty.

Frantic, Cazrin searched the other pouches on her belt, even though she knew none of them was big enough to contain the book. The shadow laughed as she grew more and more panicked.

"What did you do with it?" Cazrin demanded. "Where is my spellbook?"

You don't need it anymore. It cowers and snivels and wails, just like all the souls of the books that come within my presence. They are not worthy. Everything you've ever wanted to know is right here, Cazrin, the voice said invitingly. *All you have to do is tell me what you want.*

"Why?" Cazrin asked, stalling for time as she tried to puzzle a way out of this mess. The Ruinous Child was in her head. Well, of course. She'd given the book her blood. She should have known that would come with . . . complications. Hadn't Anson tried to warn her about the book's dangers? "Why are you so eager to give up your secrets now, after you worked so hard to keep me out before?"

Knowledge comes to those willing to sacrifice for it, the voice said. *Blood, bone, love, safety. The more you give, the more worthy you are to carry on my legacy.*

A chill crept up Cazrin's neck. "*Your* legacy," she said. "You're Alagesheth the Wise, then? Or what's left of him." She thought about that. Maybe the book wasn't so different from her own spell-book, in the end. If the lich had poured enough of his own magic and essence into the book over the centuries, might it have taken on a will and personality all its own? A shadowy reflection of its creator, the closest thing the lich would ever have to a child. "Do you know how long it's been since you—well, the rest of you—have been gone? Do you even know where you are?"

Time has no meaning in the pages of a book, the shadow said dismissively. *The wider world may see war and famine, ages coming and crumbling to dust, and there will still be inner worlds like these, waiting for the right hands and minds.*

So, there were limits to the Ruinous Child's sphere of influence. The thought comforted Cazrin a bit. If she couldn't get herself untangled from the book's magic, there was a chance her friends could do so from the outside. But she was going to do her best to make that unnecessary.

"Show me, then," she said, taking a single, defiant step forward. "I gave you my blood, so show me your secrets. What's so special about your legacy?"

The book could detect her thoughts at the surface level, that much was clear; she strained to hide her reasons for asking the question, and hoped. She didn't even want to consider the book's reaction to finding out there were other liches interested in acquiring the Ruinous Child.

Oh, not yet, not yet, the book teased. *All will be revealed, but I must know what you desire. What are your dreams, Cazrin? To make your family respect you? It would be better, in the end, than seeking acceptance.*

The latter is such a tenuous thing, easily snatched away when things are difficult.

"Get out of my head," Cazrin said, pressing back against the bookcases. *This isn't real,* she told herself. *None of this is real.*

Peals of mocking laughter filled the space. *Of course it's real,* the Ruinous Child said. *This isn't a dream you can wake from. You've always wanted to be here, Cazrin. If you didn't, you'd have freed yourself long ago.* The voice became a low, menacing growl. *Stop playing games and tell me what you want.*

CHAPTER 23

Tess ran. The others were close behind her as she followed Breskid back toward the reading room. Turning down the hall, Tess nearly tripped over a body lying sprawled across her path.

It was one of the guards from the courtyard. He was alive—Tess could see his chest rising and falling—but he and three of his comrades were on the ground, while at the other end of the hall, standing in the doorway to the reading room, was Cazrin.

Her eyes had gone completely black, and her mouth was set in a grim line. The Ruinous Child floated before her. Cazrin's hand hovered above the tome, fingers stretching and contorted into a clawlike pose. The bandage Anson had wrapped around her arm was gone. Blood dripped from her open wound onto the pages of the book, sinking into the ink and turning it a glistening red. She didn't appear to be aware of their presence, but when one of the guards picked herself up and tried to approach, an invisible force blasted her back against the wall.

"Cazrin!" Tess called to her. "Stop!"

"Well, that's new," Lark commented. "Since when can she throw people through the air without touching them?"

"It's the book," Tess said tersely, motioning them all back. "Let's make some space. We're already beat up, and I don't want a fight with our own party member."

Beside her, Uggie began to whine. Anson stroked the back of the otyugh's head. "I know, girl, don't worry. We're going to fix this."

Tess hoped that was true. Her heart beat loud in her ears as she beheld what was very likely Cazrin being possessed by the Ruinous Child. They should never have left her alone and unguarded with the book. They should never have opened it. Tess couldn't believe she'd been so stupid.

"Baldric, can you . . . I don't know . . . clear her mind, the way you did with Anson when he got attacked by the intellect devourers?" Tess asked. She began to inch toward Cazrin, trying her best to appear nonthreatening.

"Hard to do that if she won't let me get close enough to touch her," Baldric said. "Unless the rest of you want to rush her and try to rip that book away from her first."

"Normally, I'd be all for that," Anson said, "but we can't be sure what that thing is doing to her head."

"Well, it can't be anything good," Lark said sharply. "The longer we stand around arguing, the more chance it has to hollow her out."

"Would everyone shut up a minute and let me get a plan together?" Tess snapped.

Uggie whined again, and Tess forced herself to take a calming breath. Panicking now wouldn't help anyone, least of all Cazrin.

"I'm going to try talking to her first," Tess said. She didn't wait for the others' opinions but took a cautious step forward. "Cazrin?" she tried. "Are you all right?"

Cazrin's eyes flickered, and her head jerked in Tess's direction, like a doll being manipulated by a child's hand. Gooseflesh erupted on Tess's arms.

"Hello, *Tess*," Cazrin said, drawing out the *s*'s in her name, her usual cheerful tone undercut by something dark and mocking. "Where have you all been? I was worried."

Lark shuddered and wrinkled his nose. "All right, that's seriously creepy. I liked the cheerful wizard better."

Tess elbowed the tiefling in the ribs. "We were worried about you too, Cazrin," she said. "It's been a long day. What say we all go get a drink and call it a night? You can study the book some more in the morning."

Cazrin laughed, and it sent a chill skating up Tess's spine. "Oh, Tess, you're no fun. Cazrin and I aren't done playing yet."

"Yes, you are," Baldric growled, striding forward past Tess.

"Baldric, don't!" Anson said, reaching out to grab the dwarf's arm.

Cazrin's head snapped in Baldric's direction, and her eyes flashed again as she cast a spell.

TELL ME WHAT you want.

"Fine," Cazrin said, biting off the word. What would a lich want to know most? What might Lorthrannan have in common with Alagesheth? She pursed her lips for a moment, and then she had it. "How can I be like you?" she asked. "You've seen inside my head. You know how my family feels about me and my magic. How can I create my own legacy, one as vast and complete as yours?"

The shadowy form laughed at her again. *Sweet child, do you really have it in you to be as I am? To seek a vessel for your soul that will give you true immortality? I think even you would shrink from that knowledge, you who prize it above all.*

Cazrin didn't know everything about liches, but she understood enough to know what the Ruinous Child was referring to. In addition to the rituals that gave them unnatural longevity, they consigned their souls to a vessel to protect themselves against being killed.

"That's not true immortality," Cazrin said. "If your vessel is destroyed, so are you. And that's exactly what happened, leaving only this . . . echo of you left," she said, gesturing to the shadowy mass drifting between the shelves. "All that's left of you is knowledge."

Ah, but I had learned the secret, the shadow said. *I learned how to make the vessel a force indestructible. I was brought low before I could implement the process, but the knowledge exists, Cazrin. It is in these pages for you to take, if that is what you truly desire.*

The book could have been lying. How many times had Cazrin been drawn in by the Ruinous Child, only to have the book scorch her fingers or stab her with a thorn? Was that what this was, only on a grander scale?

Or was the knowledge real, and that was why Lorthrannan wanted the book so badly? Any lich would pay dearly for the knowledge of how to make themselves indestructible. Whether it was Lorthrannan or this Valindra Shadowmantle or some other, unknown threat—if any of them got their hands on the book, they could finally achieve immortality beyond limitation. If the Child was being honest, it also explained why the Zhentarim had allied with Lorthrannan. With the might of an indestructible lich behind them, they would become a force capable of toppling even the most powerful leaders in Faerûn.

That would mean nothing good for the rest of the world.

I'm waiting for your answer, Cazrin, the book taunted. *I can be patient, but how long can you resist? All this knowledge, waiting at your fingertips. Choose. Just choose any book.* At the shadow's words, books floated down from the shelves, one after another, parading themselves in front of Cazrin. Wine-red leather and gold-leaf shine. The smell of aged paper. The sound of fluttering pages in a quiet room on a rainy afternoon. Cazrin was right back in her childhood, and it was at once a comfort and a thorn digging into her heart.

The Ruinous Child sensed her wavering. *I'll give you the answer to one of your most burning questions for free, because you gave me your blood. Then we can discuss the price for the rest.*

It was so tempting. Even though, rationally, she knew how much danger she was in, Cazrin couldn't help how her gaze was drawn to the spines of the books floating past her. Spells she'd never heard of, magical theories she'd not considered possible, historical accounts of Netheril written by people who'd actually been present—the possibilities were making her lightheaded. In a daze, she stretched out her hand, and one of the books danced toward her.

"Cazrin!"

Cazrin snatched her hand back like she'd been stung.

Was that Tess's voice?

Ignore it, the Ruinous Child urged her. *I lay the world at your feet—anything you ask for, the first question free!*

Cazrin shook her head, feeling some of the cobwebs lift from her thoughts. "You wouldn't offer me anything freely," she said. "I know there's a price."

"Are you all right?"

The voice was nearer now, and it was definitely Tess's. Relief flooded Cazrin. Her friends were nearby. She could feel it. They would show her the way out of here.

You will regret losing this chance. The shadow billowed before her, scattering the floating books and casting the rest of the phantom library into darkness. *If you reject me now, you will lie awake at night for the rest of your days wondering what might have been.*

Cazrin felt a chill creep over her skin again. "Maybe I will," she said softly. "But I won't give myself away piece by piece like you have. That's not my path." She thought of Tess, calling to her. Baldric giving her his handkerchief. Anson looking at her in concern in the reading room. Lark with his music and his jokes. As the memories played out, Cazrin felt something cool and smooth against her palm, like a comforting touch from a friend.

She looked down. There was a silver key in her hand, the triangular bow inscribed with a swirl of magic. It reminded her of the triangular windows in their tavern, lit with a golden glow to welcome her home.

Not fully understanding what it meant, Cazrin nevertheless sensed it was good, an anchor in this realm of shadows. "I have something else to sustain me now," she said, holding the key tightly in her hand.

Nothing you have now will last. It will wither and fade, like all mortal things. The Ruinous Child sounded sullen, the shadow hunching in frustration.

"That's why they're the most important things," Cazrin said. She closed her eyes, holding the key and focusing on the voices of her friends, pushing toward them in the dark.

Baldric raised his hands, crossing his arms, and threads of golden light shimmered over his body, protecting him from the impact of whatever spell Cazrin had hurled at him. He staggered but somehow managed to stay on his feet.

"That all you've got?" Baldric taunted with a smirk. He squared his shoulders, and the golden radiance spilled like a waterfall down his cloak, making him seem larger, his presence filling the hallway with a holy aura as his voice boomed, "Begone, undead filth! Leave her alone!"

Cazrin shrank from the light, her lips twisted in a snarl, but before she could retaliate with another spell, Tess darted forward and knocked the Ruinous Child from Cazrin's arcane grasp. A bolt of white-hot pain shot up her arm as she severed the connection between wizard and spellbook.

As soon as the book hit the floor, Anson and Lark were on it, slamming the cover shut and fastening the lock. Cazrin crumpled, but Tess caught her and kept her head from hitting the stone floor.

"Get that book out of here," Tess barked. "I don't want it anywhere near her right now."

Anson nodded and scooped up the book, which was bleeding black smoke from its pages, the cover rippling weirdly and thrusting thorns at Anson's fingers. He juggled it in his hands, ignoring the magical tantrum. He tossed the book inside the empty reading room and slammed the door shut.

Tess lowered Cazrin gently to the floor as Baldric crouched beside her. He muttered the words of a spell and ran his hands over his cloth. Tess wondered if there was a bargain being made, and what Baldric might be offering. At the moment, she was willing to offer up her own bargain to any of the benevolent gods who might be listening if it helped Cazrin.

She held the wizard's hand. It was cold, but Tess refused to panic. Cazrin's chest rose and fell with steady breaths. She wasn't dead, just unconscious.

Golden light engulfed Baldric's hand as he touched Cazrin's shoulder and finished the spell. For a second, nothing happened, and Tess's breath caught in her chest. But then Cazrin's eyes flickered open, and she looked up at Tess and the others, who'd all gathered around them in the hallway. She raised her other hand, the one Tess wasn't holding. A silver key gleamed on her palm.

"Well," Cazrin said in a shaky voice. "That didn't quite go as I'd planned."

"I CAN'T BELIEVE they're throwing us out," Tess said, stomping around the courtyard in a huff. She could feel the gazes of the guards at the Emerald Door boring into her back, as if they expected their group to try to break back into the library. "It was Candlekeep who wanted Alagesheth's collection in the first place, and now they're just going to send us away?"

"We did make a mess of that gallery," Anson pointed out.

"Killing the shambling mounds before they did any more damage," Lark said dryly. "For which we were never thanked, I might add. But don't worry, I'm at least going to get an amazing song out of this. 'Terror in the Library.'" He mimed making a banner of the words in the air. "Or maybe, 'The Green Menace.' I'll work with it."

Breskid, who had come to see them off, bowed their head apologetically. "I'm sorry it had to come to this," they said. "I wanted to make a more thorough examination of the Ruinous Child to help you, but we simply can't risk keeping it inside these walls for long."

"We understand." Cazrin wore her usual smile, but it was more subdued, and there were dark smudges beneath her eyes that hadn't been there this morning. Baldric had healed the wound on her arm, but she still rubbed absently at the spot where it had been. "You can't have a book in the library that causes other magic books to go mad."

"Are you sure that's what happened?" Tess demanded. "How can you be certain the Ruinous Child was responsible for the monsters in the gallery? Couldn't it have been a coincidence?"

Cazrin shook her head sadly. "The Ruinous Child as much as admitted it when I was . . . connected to the book," she said. "Its presence affects the functioning of other magical tomes." She put her hand on her spellbook in a comforting gesture as she spoke.

"It's true," Breskid said. "There were even books in the collection we had no idea contained any degree of sentience until they became animated by the Ruinous Child's influence."

"I should have seen this coming, considering how Keeper reacted in the Ruinous Child's presence," Cazrin said.

"I don't know if anyone could have seen that coming," Baldric said, "or your possession."

Cazrin shuddered. "Don't remind me," she said, running her hands up and down her arms as if to ward off a chill. "No, this is my fault. I was so fixated on studying the book, I left myself vulnerable." She glanced over at Anson. "You were right to be worried."

"We're all responsible for this," Tess said firmly. She turned to Breskid. "Can we at least stay the night? Powerful and dangerous people are after this book, and they don't much mind killing us to get to it."

And now they didn't even have the option of dumping the Ruinous Child on the scholars of Candlekeep, which, after the events of the day, Tess would have been more than glad to do.

Breskid shook their head. "I'm afraid we can't risk another incident," they said, gesturing to the courtyard, where a small crowd of the visiting seekers had gathered, along with more members of the Avowed. "Many of our visitors have had their own studies disrupted, and it will take some time to clean and fix the damage done by the books."

Tess sighed, but she sensed there was nothing she could say to change their mind. In the eyes of the Avowed, the Ruinous Child and, by extension, their party were a threat to the library's safety. They wouldn't risk letting them stay.

"What do you suggest we do with the tome, then?" Anson asked. "If it's not welcome at Candlekeep, where can we take it?"

Breskid hesitated, glancing at Cazrin. "You could try taking it to the great libraries of Silverymoon," they suggested. "Outside Candlekeep, their scholars are some of the most renowned in Faerûn." They glanced away with a guilty expression. "But you may find their reception unwelcoming."

Catching the look, Baldric snorted. "Let me guess—they'll know what the book's capable of because you'll tell them, won't you? You'll send messages to all the major libraries that there's an evil spellbook on the loose, and whatever they do, they shouldn't let in the adventurers who are carrying it. Just leave them out in the cold."

Breskid didn't confirm his suspicion, but they didn't have to. Tess could see it in their face. "What you do with the Ruinous Child is up to you," Breskid said, and again they looked at Cazrin, "but sometimes the price paid for knowledge is too high. You have to decide when that's the case and act accordingly."

Breskid left them then, and Tess could tell by the shifting stances of the guards that if they didn't start to make their way to the gates soon, they'd be given an escort.

"Let's go," Tess said grimly. "Back to the road." She glanced over at Cazrin and noticed her examining that strange key she'd had in her hand earlier. "Where did you get that?"

Cazrin pointed to the triangular bow. "I can't be certain, but I think it will unlock the door to our tavern." She ran her fingers over the smooth metal. "The magic of it feels the same. I'm not sure why it's just appearing now, but I saw it in my vision, and I had it when I woke up."

"More mysteries," Tess murmured. "Well, at least we know we'll always have a warm place to sleep."

After that, she wasn't sure where they were headed.

INTERLUDE

"You let them enter Candlekeep. With the Ruinous Child."

The figure at the top of the hill stood in the shadow of a white birch tree, her back to him, but Lorthrannan had no trouble hearing the fury in Valindra Shadowmantle's voice. Rain poured from the sky as he moved toward her, but the magic of his robes kept him perfectly dry. Lightning rendered the night in flickering silver flashes, herald of the storm that travelled the coast and swept inland like a dark curtain.

"I left too much in the hands of the Zhentarim," Lorthrannan said, bowing his head as he came closer. "I overestimated their competence. I won't repeat that mistake."

"You won't have the opportunity."

For an instant, as Lorthrannan climbed the hill, he considered turning back. He'd known when he started this that he walked a dangerous road. Allying with the Zhentarim had given him a greater reach and expanded his network of information, but he hadn't yet amassed enough power or influence to be taken seriously by his peers.

He craved knowledge, the experience of those who'd walked this path before him. Valindra Shadowmantle could give him those things. A partnership with someone like her would assure his safety as he started his own ascendancy. Eventually, he would supplant her, but for now, he needed her strength and connections. He needed to learn from her, much as it galled him to ask for help.

When he learned of the existence of the Ruinous Child, he knew the book was the way to attract the elder lich's attention. The rest of Alagesheth's collection had slipped through her fingers, but the Ruinous Child was the centerpiece, the crowning achievement of Alagesheth's existence. She would do anything to possess it.

Sefeerian, you decrepit fool. Did you think that you would be able to keep the book from me? Did you think our long-ago friendship would mean anything in the face of that kind of power?

He reached the top of the hill, and Lady Shadowmantle swung to face him. She was wrapped in a hooded cloak that also magically kept the weather at bay, and her eyes bored into him with barely concealed rage. "Tell me why I shouldn't burn you down where you stand, reduce you to a column of ash."

Lorthrannan spread his hands in a placating gesture. "The Ruinous Child will not stay at Candlekeep," he assured her. "The Zhent spy I sent inside assures me that the group is leaving with the book. You'll have what you seek very soon. You have my word."

"Oh, I know that I will, Lorthrannan," Valindra said, managing to make his name sound like something sour on her tongue. "Because I no longer intend to wait for it."

Lorthrannan was careful not to betray the sudden flash of fear that twisted inside him. That was why she'd come in person. If she'd sent servants, he could have dealt with those. But for her to come here herself . . .

"I will put my forces in place for another ambush, but this time I'll see to the book's retrieval personally," Lorthrannan said. "By sunrise, we'll be studying Alagesheth's legacy together. We'll be the first of our kind to make our souls indestructible. Think about that, Valindra. Nothing will be out of our reach. With the Zhentarim behind us, we could take Candlekeep apart piece by piece if it pleased us to do so. We could strip the great libraries of Silverymoon of all the knowledge they've kept so well guarded for centuries. Even the most powerful wizards of Faerûn won't be able to stand in our way. Have patience, and let me see this through. Everything is still proceeding according to plan."

"You think I don't know all the possibilities ahead?" The ancient elf stared at him with a mixture of amusement and pity. "This is not a game where you get second chances, upstart," she said. "You've already made me regret what little faith I put in you."

Rage overtook Lorthrannan's fear. How dare she! How dare anyone, after all that he'd been through, all he'd sacrificed to climb to this height. His family. His body. His human dreams. He'd killed them all, and she dared to call him an *upstart*? As if he knew nothing of the sacrifices required to get to this place.

"I haven't failed you yet," Lorthrannan insisted, rotting teeth gritted as he bit back all the things he wanted to say. "We *will* have the book."

"Forgive me, have I made you angry?" Valindra laughed. Her face was pale and gaunt, eyes sunk deep in her skull. She was old and capricious, and Lorthrannan realized too late he had overplayed his own confidence with her. "Did you really think I would risk letting the book slip out of time again, lost for centuries? I was never going to leave this to chance, Lorthrannan, and I had no reason in the world to trust you." She folded her arms and took a step toward him. "I'll be retrieving the book myself, since you can't seem to accomplish that simple task. Afterward, I expect never to hear from you again."

She started to walk away, dismissing him as if he were nothing. Lorthrannan could barely see through the red haze of fury that descended over him. Before he could think better of it, he was stepping in front of the lich, blocking her path.

"We do this together," he said harshly. "I won't be shunted aside like a child you've grown tired of, and I am not so weak as you believe."

Valindra tilted her head, still looking amused, but there was something dangerous and hungry in her expression. "Think carefully," she warned him. "Are you truly ready to test yourself? Do you want to make an enemy of me, Lorthrannan? Because you will. If the dust settles and that book is not in my hands, I will see that you are destroyed." She lifted a shoulder in a careless shrug. "It should not take up much of my time."

She was baiting him. He shouldn't have lowered himself to being swayed by petty taunts, but maybe he was still more human than he wanted to admit. Because all of Lorthrannan's rage, frustration, and disappointment exploded out of him in that instant. He raised his hands, the words of a spell ripping from him, and the hill was suddenly alight with an explosion of magic that filled the night with crackling energy.

Valindra had already taken to the sky, flying above him with her dark cloak spread out around her like billowing wings, her hair stirring amid the magical energies.

"Come on, then," she said, beckoning him with one spindly finger, her face lit with malicious glee. "Let's see how good you really are."

CHAPTER 24

They'd been on the road most of the day when the storm moved in and the downpour came. Because of course they needed one more thing to worry about, Tess thought. The rain slanted sideways, blinding them as they bent their heads and pressed forward, but the path quickly turned to mud beneath their feet, and when lightning struck a tree just off the road, splitting it in half, Tess called a halt.

She led them off the road toward a series of small farmsteads. Night came early with the arrival of the storm, and under cover of darkness, Tess found a small wood where they could conceal the tavern.

The door had changed. Where only a knob had been before, there was now a lock and keyhole. As Cazrin had predicted, the wizard's new key unlocked the door, and the group filed inside.

The common room had been repaired and cleaned. Tess could smell the soap and polish, as if an invisible crew had just swept through and tidied the place while the party had been away. The bar was freshly stocked with wine and ale casks, and there were two cold chests, one with fruit and vegetables and one with meat. An iron rack had appeared on the wall near the fireplace, with pots, pans, and utensils hanging from the hooks. A fire was already roaring in the hearth, as if the tavern had known the party would be soaked to the skin when they came in.

Tess glanced down the hall and noticed that there was now a third door, on the left-hand wall. When she opened it, she discovered another bedroom, this one with bookshelves lining one wall. A quill, ink, and parchment sat on the bedside table, and a midnight-blue quilt covered the bed.

"I think this is meant for you, Cazrin," Tess said.

Cazrin joined her, peering into the room. "Oh, it's lovely," she said, laying a hand on the doorframe, as if addressing the tavern itself. "Thank you so much." She hesitated. "And thank you for the key. It came just when I needed it."

They returned to the common room, and Tess stared at the space. Was it her imagination, or was the room bigger than she remembered it? "You were right, the tavern is changing to meet our needs," she said.

"The sky is a strange color in the east," Anson said. He stood at the window and didn't seem to be paying attention to the changes in their surroundings. "It's burnt orange, like there's a fire somewhere, but it's . . . purplish around the edges."

"Let me see." Tess came up beside him, and he moved to let her look.

He was right. The sky was the color of a bruise, and there was a faint charge in the air, like lightning tickling the back of her throat. "It looks like spell traces," she said. "A lot of magic released all at once, left behind like a signature in the air."

"What does that mean?" Lark asked. He was sitting at the bar, opening a bottle of wine.

"Wizards fighting," Baldric said shortly. He'd taken a seat at the newly cleaned table. "I've seen it before. Powerful folk in an uproar with each other, not caring who might be in their path."

Wizards. Or maybe liches. Tess didn't say it, but when she turned away from the window, the rest of the party were exchanging uneasy glances.

"It's nothing to do with us," Tess said firmly. "You heard Baldric. Wizards fight. Folk carry on with their lives, and so should we."

"By doing what?" Baldric asked. "What's the plan now, Tess? We've been thrown out of Candlekeep, we still have an evil book and a lich to deal with, and we're no closer to clearing our names."

"Those are all extremely good questions," Lark said, lifting his wineglass to toast the cleric. He turned to Tess. "You know, when I signed up for this job, it was with the expectation of working with powerful and capable people and making a lot of coin in a short amount of time. So far, none of those expectations have been met."

Tess's face heated. "Now, wait a minute—"

"Still," Lark said, cutting her off, "I hung in there after Sefeerian's murder, thinking we could salvage something out of this job." He paused, and a muscle in his jaw worked. "But it isn't a job anymore. It's a *hunt*. We're being hunted, and it's only a matter of time before the Zhents or this lich catch up to us. So, I have to ask myself, what is this all for?" His voice had risen as he spoke, fingers clutching his glass. "Especially since you didn't even want me in the group in the first place."

"What?" Caught off guard, Tess stared at him. Then everything fell into place. "That night at the camp, after we left Oghma's temple—you weren't really asleep, were you?" she said. "You heard Anson and me talking."

Lark flicked his wet hair back from his face and pointed to his ears. "These aren't just decorative," he said irritably. "Fine, you didn't want me in the party. I figured I could prove myself to you, make you warm up to me eventually, but you wouldn't let me do that either. You just move me around like a pawn on the chessboard whenever we get into a fight. You never trust me to do things my own way. So why should I trust you to get us out of this now?" He turned his back on her to refill his glass.

"You're not being fair, Lark," Tess said stubbornly. "I wouldn't have brought you into the group if I didn't want you, but yes, I admit, I do have concerns." She ticked them off on her fingers. "You don't listen, you rush in when I tell you not to, you keep secrets from the group, and you focus on yourself to the exclusion of . . . well . . . pretty much everything else."

"Any one of those things can endanger the rest of the group," Anson agreed.

"Says the man whose brother is working for a lich," Baldric muttered.

Anson stiffened. "If you have something to say to me, Baldric, just say it," he snapped.

"You can't still deny that your brother's involved in this hunt for the book," Baldric said. "You know it's true. It's been written all over your face ever since you wouldn't let me cast that truth spell on the Zhent we interrogated. I've kept my thoughts to myself up until now, but I don't care for hypocrites. We've all speculated about what the bard's story is"—he jerked a thumb at Lark—"but he's not the only one keeping secrets and endangering the party. I'd just like us all to remember that."

"I'm not keeping my brother a secret," Anson said defensively. He swiped at the circles of moisture left behind by his tankard. "I just didn't want to believe what that Zhent said. I've been trying to find Valen because I haven't had any word from him in months." A spasm of pain crossed Anson's face. "We've never seen eye to eye on anything, and he has reasons to hate me, but I swear, I never thought he'd end up in the company of the Zhentarim working for a lich." He looked over at Tess, his gaze imploring. "You have to believe me, I didn't know about that."

Tess nodded. "I believe you," she said. "It's a terrible thing to learn that your own brother has betrayed you."

Anson sighed, rubbing his face with both hands. "Yes, well, family is complicated, or at least mine is. What's left of it," he added under his breath.

Baldric said nothing.

"It's all right," Cazrin put in, filling the silence. "Everyone here has things they'd rather not share. We still don't know one another that well, but we'll get there."

"Is there a good reason we should?" Lark challenged her.

"I'm wondering that myself," Baldric said. He raised his hands when Tess frowned at him. "Before you rake me over the coals, hear me out." He gestured to her and Anson. "You two obviously trust each other, and you helped put the group together, so maybe you think you owe each other something. And the wizard has a stake in this too, for her own reasons. But I don't know what's in it for Lark and me, so I can't help but wonder if it would be better if we agreed to go our separate ways."

For a moment, Tess was too stunned to speak. Of all the outcomes she'd anticipated after leaving Candlekeep, splitting the party for good had never even occurred to her.

Maybe it should have, though. As much as she hated to admit it, Baldric had a point. The party had come together for a job that, instead of cementing their bond as a group, had led to them running for their lives.

Tess took a moment to observe everyone. Lark was leaning against the bar, cradling his wineglass, shoulders slumped like a kicked dog. Baldric was also nursing his drink, but his free hand kept going to his cloth with its array of holy symbols, and he looked distracted in the wake of his suggestion that the party split. Anson and Cazrin were staring at the fire. It was hard to tell what they might be thinking, but neither of them looked happy. Uggie was passed out by the hearth, blissfully unaffected by the tension and unease in the room.

Tess's thoughts raced. She had to make everyone see how important the group was, that this was an opportunity they couldn't afford to pass up. She scooted her chair back in agitation, stood, and began to pace before the fire. "I know we're all at a low point here," she said, "but remember when we were in that treasure room in Oghma's temple, swarmed by intellect devourers, and then that mind flayer stepped out of the secret door?"

"We were all there," Lark said dryly, without looking up from his drink.

"None of us knew what was going to happen," Tess said, "but the way we came together, the way we helped each other when it counted, it was like we'd been doing it for years." She shook her head. "I'd never seen a group mesh so well, and I've been putting together jobs for a while now. My mentor's been doing it even longer, and if she were here, she would say that we've got something special. We shouldn't waste it by splitting up now, not when we're just getting started."

Baldric looked at her skeptically. "Pretty words, but who's to say you're not using us and our skills to make yourself look good? What happens when that ambition gets one of us killed by this lich? Not a very appealing employment opportunity."

"That's not what I'm doing!" Tess snapped, trying to tamp down her frustration. She looked to Anson and Cazrin for support but found them both carefully avoiding her gaze.

Tess stopped pacing and gripped the back of her chair, a heavy weight settling in her stomach. Was Baldric right? *Was* she just using the group for their talents and telling herself otherwise? It was true that she'd always wanted to build a party of expert adventurers. She'd made no secret of that.

But it was more than just making a name for herself that drove her. She'd tried to tell Cazrin as much, that night in the Yawning Portal tavern, but she'd lost her nerve. Even as a child, Tess had felt that she was different from other people. She was always trying to explore places she wasn't supposed to go, to climb the trees the other children were afraid to touch, just to see what she could see from the topmost branches. Her parents had been amazing, and they'd tried to support her, but they also hadn't known exactly what to make of the precocious child who was forever being dragged home by neighbors and strangers for being found someplace she wasn't supposed to be.

When she'd set out to gather a group of adventurers, she'd wanted people who felt like she did. People who didn't quite fit but who were amazing at what they did and just needed someone else to see it. Tess saw it in Cazrin's thirst for knowledge, her excitement at every new discovery. She saw it in Anson with the way he never gave up, either on a broken sword or on the people around him.

Even Baldric and Lark had that hunger in them—wanting more for themselves and more from the world. Lark wanted his name and songs to be known, to distinguish himself from his past with his old band and from whatever other demons were haunting him. Baldric was a strategist after her own heart, and he'd worked himself to a place where he negotiated with the gods themselves. With his experience and her planning skills, they could be a formidable duo when it came to working all the angles of a job and seeking the best outcome for the party.

Tess had gathered them together for all those reasons, but she'd wanted especially, if she was being honest with herself, to surround herself with people like her so she wouldn't feel so alone.

As Tess stared into the fire, it occurred to her that she'd never shared any of this—even with Anson, whom she was closest to of all her companions. She told herself it was because she'd been trying to maintain a professional distance, to be a more effective leader, but maybe that was all dung and bluster. Maybe she'd just been afraid to share the truth. And since her companions didn't know any of that, maybe they had a right to feel as if they were just being used for their abilities.

Tess gathered her wits and stood up straight. She had always dreamed of leading. Now she had to be brave enough to do it.

"Lark," she said, looking over at the tiefling, waiting for him to meet her eyes. "It's true that you weren't my first choice for this party. I was worried you were going to be trouble, but I let those worries overshadow everything, and I didn't give you a proper chance to prove yourself or to carve your own space in the party. I'm sorry. I should have handled everything better."

She turned to the others. "I know that I'm not always the best leader." She shook her head minutely at Anson when he started to protest. "I'm still learning, and I'm always looking ahead, always wanting that horizon, and I wanted to pull you all with me, whether you wanted to go or not. I know that's what I'm doing now, and I'm sorry for that too." She looked at each member of the party in turn. "The truth is, we all fit so well as a group, I didn't think much beyond what I knew we could accomplish. I knew we could make a lot of coin and a name for ourselves in Faerûn. I should have known you'd have your own reasons for doing what you're doing, and that you're not obligated to trust us with your secrets." She hesitated, then plunged ahead. "But I wasn't lying when I said I think we can do great things together if we give this group a chance. It won't always be easy—it definitely isn't right now—but I truly believe we're stronger together, and we can help each other if we give each other a little bit of trust." She looked away. "Besides, if we disbanded now, I'd worry about all of you. I'd probably sneak around watching over each of you to make sure you were all right, and that would be exhausting, having to keep track of everyone."

"Well, we wouldn't want that," Cazrin said, smiling a little at the joke.

Tess felt a surge of hope. "I don't just want you for your skills," she said, willing them to believe her. "I was thinking . . ." Tess searched for the right words. *Well, might as well go for it. Cards on the table.* "I thought we were all becoming friends. I thought we could stay together because of that too." Her voice faltered as she ran out of words, and embarrassment flooded Tess at how much she'd revealed. Quickly, she sat back down at the table and crossed her arms over her chest, trying to gather up her shreds of professionalism.

A log shifted in the fire. Anson sat up straight in his chair and leaned across the table toward Tess, stretching out a hand. "Thanks for saying that." He offered her a crooked smile, the first one he'd cracked since Candlekeep. "I've always known you and I were friends, but it's nice to hear you say it." His smile dropped away. "For what it's worth, to the rest of you, I'm sorry for my brother being involved in this. I do want to find Valen, now that I know he's tangled up in this, but if you're worried that I'll put him or my own interests before the group, I promise I won't." He looked at Baldric as he spoke.

The dwarf nodded slowly. "I can accept that," he rumbled. "Just be careful making those promises. Believe me, I'm an expert on owing debts that are difficult to pay. As you said, family is complicated. Whether it's out of love, guilt, or obligation—sometimes all three—family can make you do things you wouldn't otherwise consider doing. Good thing is, you've got the rest of us to keep you mindful of that." He raised a forestalling hand at Tess. "That doesn't mean I'm staying, it just means—"

"I'll stay," Lark interrupted. "Hey, Tess, you think this food is safe to eat?"

Baldric blinked at the sudden turnaround in the tiefling's demeanor. Tess was a little confused herself. "Just like that?" she asked. "What about—"

"Oh, I know I was bent out of shape before, but you made a good apology." He winced. "If I'm being brutally honest, I probably wouldn't be my first choice for an adventuring party either. And you're right," he added, "this group, despite what I said earlier, is the most capable I've found in my travels. And you all have far more secrets and drama than I could have ever predicted. Imagine the songs I'll get out of this!"

"Well, that's . . . something," Tess said. "A start, at least."

She regarded the bard for a moment. He seemed sincere, but he was hard to read, and of all the party members, she still suspected Lark would be the least likely to stick around if things continued to get rough. But she'd committed to giving him a chance, and if she was going to ask the party to trust her, she had to try to trust them too.

Tess went over to Lark and clapped him on the shoulder. "To a fresh start," she said, and grabbed her tankard off the table, lifting it to clink against his wineglass. Then she turned her attention to Baldric. "Well?" she asked, trying not to let too much of her hope and enthusiasm show.

Baldric gave a low chuckle. "You'd be a terrible Three-Dragon Ante player, Tess," he said. "Don't take up the cards, ever." He sighed and shrugged. "All right, I'm willing to give this a chance and see how it goes. Beyond that, no promises."

It was more than Tess had expected, and she nodded. "I understand."

Her excitement faded when she glanced over at Cazrin, who was staring down at the table, lost in thought. Tess walked over and sat down next to the wizard. "We need you too, Caz," she said, "though nobody here would blame you if you didn't want to have anything more to do with the Ruinous Child."

"You know, I never had a nickname growing up," Cazrin said. She looked up from the table, offering Tess and the others a watery smile. "I like it. I like having friends. When I was alone with that *thing*, somehow, I knew that you all would come to help me. Even though I did exactly what I shouldn't have and got too deeply involved with the book. You came anyway."

"Everyone gets in over their head sometimes," Anson said. "That doesn't mean we're going to abandon you."

"I know. Thank you." Cazrin sat up straighter in her chair. "Now that we've committed to this party, we need to plan our next steps. That means I need to tell you what happened at Candlekeep."

CHAPTER 25

Cazrin could feel her friends watching her, though some of them tried to be casual about it. Baldric had stripped off his cloak and cloth of symbols and hung them over the bar to dry, and he kept asking Cazrin if she needed anything. Lark was plucking his lute strings softly, working on a song to immortalize their Candlekeep adventure, but he kept shooting glances at Cazrin and losing the tune.

As for Tess and Anson . . . well, they weren't really trying to hide their concern at all, bless them. They had arranged themselves on either side of her at the table, and Anson had brought her the blue quilt from her new bedroom, which she'd wrapped around her shoulders. Even sitting close to the fire, she was shivering, her hair hanging in wet ringlets down her back. She knew the sensation wasn't entirely from the cold.

Tess didn't say anything, but she didn't need to. After everything she'd just said about the party, Cazrin would have given her the moon if she could.

Anson refilled everyone's drinks, while Uggie moved over to sleep next to Cazrin's chair, draping herself across the wizard's feet.

Between the otyugh's body heat and the wine, Cazrin was starting to feel almost like herself again.

Almost.

By unspoken agreement, Tess had taken over carrying the Ruinous Child in a fireproof satchel the Avowed had given them before they left Candlekeep. But even though it was packed away in the satchel with its lock in place, Cazrin could feel it. Ever since she'd put her blood on the thing, it had come awake. She could feel the pulse and thrum of power like a heartbeat, like something waiting and watching them.

That hungry presence.

It weighed on her, and she thought it weighed on the others too, though they might not be as aware of it as Cazrin was.

Wrapping her hands more tightly around her glass, Cazrin gathered herself to tell them what she needed to tell them.

"I think that we have to find a way to destroy the book," she said softly, half afraid the Ruinous Child would hear her. She knew from her conversation with the shadowy entity that the book wasn't aware of what was going on in the outside world, not in the way the rest of them were, but still, she wondered what the book might be thinking now that she'd freed herself. Would it still try to tempt her, or would it target one of the others? The instinct to discover and research warred with the part of her that wanted to hurl the book into the sea.

Tess was the first to speak. "I have to admit, that wasn't something I ever thought I'd hear from you," she said.

"I'm shocked myself," Cazrin said with a hollow laugh. It went against everything she believed in. She sipped her wine. "Do you disagree?"

They all spoke at once.

"Absolutely not," Tess said.

"Light it on fire," Anson suggested.

"We'll find a sea serpent to feed it to," Baldric assured her.

"I'd feed it to Uggie if we hadn't already tried that," Lark added.

Cazrin found herself laughing helplessly as a tear rolled down her face. She felt Anson's hand come to rest on her shoulder. She resisted the sudden, ridiculous urge to tuck her head against his shoulder like a child.

"Do you want to tell us what happened when you were under its control?" he asked. "You don't have to if you don't want to, but it might help."

Cazrin nodded, wiping her eyes and taking another sip of wine. "I don't remember how it started," she said. "Just that one minute, I was walking out of the reading room, and I had the Ruinous Child in my hands. The next minute, I was . . . somewhere else."

Somewhere cold that smelled like death and decay, a perversion of the libraries she'd known and loved as a child.

"I think the Ruinous Child is imbued with some of the soul, or at least the personality, of Alagesheth the Wise," Cazrin said. "I think that's what he meant in the inscription when he talked about passing on his legacy. He wanted to pass on all the knowledge he'd gained, but he wanted to make whoever possessed the book pay as high a price as they could in exchange for that knowledge."

"You mean like surrendering their soul?" Anson asked, his lip curling in distaste.

"Very likely," Cazrin said. "A devil's bargain if ever there was one—all the knowledge you could desire, if you're willing to sacrifice everything that makes you a person."

"There are ways around that," Baldric interjected. "The oldest tales speak of clever folk outsmarting creatures that tried to claim them."

"In the end, I refused the bargain, but I *was* tempted." Cazrin shuddered at how close she'd come to losing herself. She'd never dreamed until that moment that she could become corrupted like her ancestress. "There's more."

She told them about the research Alagesheth had done into making the vessel for his soul indestructible as a bid for immortality, and how the knowledge was there in the book for the taking.

"And these liches that are after us won't care about the sacrifices that have to be made," Baldric said with a sigh. "It's an easy choice for them."

"So that settles it," Lark said, draining his wineglass and plunking it down on the bar. "We light it on fire. Let's do it now."

Cazrin and Baldric both shook their heads. "It's not going to be that easy," Baldric said. "This is a powerful magical artifact we're talking about. It's not going to succumb to a campfire."

"Then what?" Lark demanded. "Should we set the whole Sword Coast ablaze? I'd be willing to go that route too." He waggled his eyebrows at her, and Cazrin couldn't help grinning at him.

"You're impossible," she said.

"Well, you were worrying me," Lark said. "You're always so cheerful and upbeat. When you're not, it feels like the world's ending, and, worse, it takes the spotlight off of me."

"Not quite world-ending, but if we let Lorthrannan get the Ruinous Child, and he becomes effectively unstoppable, it's certainly not looking rosy for the rest of Faerûn," Tess said.

"And now I'm back to being worried again," Lark muttered. "Why is it *we* have to be the ones to take responsibility for this potentially world-affecting problem? Wasn't this why we went to Candlekeep in the first place? To get help? And they threw us out! Why shouldn't we just toss the book in the sea and hope it gets lost forever?"

"Even if we did, we're still wanted on suspicion of murder in Waterdeep," Anson said. "We can't toss that problem away."

"We have to destroy the book," Cazrin insisted. "That's the most important thing right now."

"But again, why *us*?" Lark demanded. "We're not powerful enough for either this book or a pack of liches. Shouldn't there be someone more qualified than a group of adventurers who've barely been together a season?"

"Yes, there absolutely should!" Tess interrupted, running her hand through her hair. "But do you see anyone like that here?" The elf blazed on without waiting for an answer. "It's just *us*, the wrongly accused, wanted murderers, who have to fix this. I don't know how, because this isn't something I've ever had to plan for, and frankly, it's messing with my head a little to try, but if we don't do it, I don't think anyone else is going to."

In the wake of her outburst, Cazrin found herself patting Tess's arm in comfort. It was the least she could do.

"It's been a long time since I've seen you ruffled," Anson commented, nudging the elf's shoulder with his own and smiling at her.

"I kind of enjoyed it, to be honest," Lark said.

"Well, don't get used to it," Tess said. "It's just a temporary condition. An impermanent ruffling."

"You're right, you know," Baldric said, sighing. "It's like taking out the trash. No one wants that job, but if someone doesn't do it, everything starts to rot, and the place smells and no one wants to visit anymore."

"Yes, that's exactly what it's like," Lark said, rolling his eyes. "You should write a song about that, Baldric. You've hidden depths we never knew about."

"I could make a song about the bard who slept in a magical tavern and woke up with his lute shoved up his—"

"So, we're all in agreement," Tess said. "We're now destroying the Ruinous Child so no liches can get their hands on it, and after that, provided we're still alive, we'll clear our names and go back to the normal dangers of adventuring."

Cazrin nodded. "But if we're going to destroy the book," she said, "we *do* need help."

"I have an idea there," Baldric spoke up. When the others turned to him expectantly, he shrugged. "Visiting the largest library in Faerûn was helpful in more ways than just unlocking the Ruinous Child." He reached into his shirt and pulled out a piece of folded parchment. "Lark and I took a . . . let's call it an informational detour, and we found a magical map. I think it's related to Alagesheth, but it's also encoded." He glanced at Cazrin. "I was hoping you'd be able to crack the code with your magic."

Cazrin examined the map, her brow furrowed in concentration. After a moment, she sighed and shook her head. "The map is magically imprinted with hundreds of different variations to keep the true one secret. You'd have to study it for months to determine the correct one."

"Are you sure there's not a shortcut?" Tess asked, staring at the map. "We don't have months to spend on a lead that we're not even sure will amount to anything."

"Maybe we just need some help," Baldric said. He looked down at the cloth at his belt with a pensive expression. "What could it hurt," he murmured, half to himself. "Not like things can get worse."

He looked up at the group. "The goddess of magic will probably have some idea how to read a map like that. If there's a shortcut to be had, we could ask her for it."

"Will she want us to?" Tess asked. "Mystra *promotes* magic in all its forms. She might not like the idea of destroying the Ruinous Child, and that's our ultimate goal here."

"What about Oghma?" Anson asked Baldric. "Might he have any insight?"

Baldric winced. "He might, but I've already asked him for too many favors of my own. Mystra's the surer bet." He turned to Cazrin. "You should join me in the request. It might help to have someone steeped in the arcane arts present, and you can make a better case for why we need this information. You don't have to state directly that destroying the book is what we're after. Focus on the map first, and I'll guide the negotiation from there."

Cazrin nodded. "Just tell me what I need to do."

"Whatever you do or say, be prepared to back up your words with actions," Baldric advised, "and don't make any promises that you're going to regret later."

CHAPTER 26

As Baldric settled himself across from Cazrin in front of the fire, he meticulously prepared the things he'd need for the ritual to commune with the goddess of magic. Though he projected the aura of confidence and care he'd cultivated over a long series of bargains with deities, inside his own head was the notion that this was all going to go horribly wrong.

It wasn't just the idea of confronting those eyes in the dark again. He was going to attempt to strike a hefty bargain with the goddess of magic, and who knew what Mystra might demand of him and the others in return?

His life used to be simpler. He'd spent his days in high-stakes negotiations on behalf of his clan's mercantile empire and his nights taking in a show at the Sea Maidens Faire or trying his luck at any of the other gambling dens across Faerûn. He'd loved the satisfaction of closing a favorable deal and relished the blade's-edge thrill that came with sliding a pile of coins across the table when he was holding a nothing hand of cards. The thought that he could sway a person to act a certain way just by what he showed or didn't show on his face—he loved walking that edge.

That thrill had intensified a hundredfold when the gods had gotten involved.

But so had the risk, and Baldric had gotten in deeper than he'd intended. He owed so many favors to the gods now, but he needed more time to uphold his part of their bargains. He'd tried to communicate that he was working on it. He'd cleansed Oghma's lost temple, but that hadn't fully cleared his debt. And he hadn't yet had time to address Tyr's demand that he obtain justice for Sefeerian. Now he owed Tymora for her guidance with the coin. He could feel them all nudging at his spirit, each deity wanting their due.

He took a calming breath and forced himself to focus. Mystra was surely a reasonable deity. She would see their need and take that into consideration when deciding if she would help them. He would worry about the price for that help later.

And if that *thing* showed up in his head again, he would just ignore it. Cazrin had survived a possession by the Ruinous Child. Surely, he could shrug off a phantom that showed up in his prayers.

"Are you all right?" Cazrin asked softly, the words meant for him alone.

Baldric glanced around. Tess and Anson had taken Uggie and gone to scout the area around the tavern to make sure they hadn't been followed from Candlekeep, and also to keep an eye on the magical storm in the distance. Lark was keeping watch in the common room to make sure nothing went wrong with the ritual.

Cazrin's spell lights were arranged on the floor between them as a kind of soft focus to light their way and give comfort. Or at least that was how Cazrin had described it. She had a soft heart, that one, and her eyes as she looked at him were full of concern. She knew something was wrong. Far too discerning for Baldric's comfort.

"I'm fine," he said, trying to sound reassuring. "Just preparing myself. I've not had many dealings with the goddess of magic, so I'm glad you're here to help smooth the way."

"I'll do whatever I can," Cazrin said, though something in her gaze said she didn't entirely believe Baldric's excuse.

No more stalling. It was time.

Baldric adjusted his helm, reached out, and took Cazrin's waiting hand. Her grip was warm and firm and did more than words to reassure him. When had that started happening? When had he started feeling safer with these people than he had alone? It wasn't an altogether comforting thought, the idea that he might have come to rely on the others. All of this was so new. What if Tess's promises that the group was stronger together were just that—empty promises? What if Lark, still skittish, took off in the night? How long would the rest of them last?

Those doubts would only hinder him. For now, he had to focus on the fact that everyone was still here. He could do what he needed to do, same as he'd always done with his bargains.

Closing his eyes, listening to the sleepy silence in the common room, and feeling Cazrin's restful presence, Baldric let the tension flow out of his body as he opened himself up and began his request to Mystra.

Lady of Mysteries, if you're out there and you can spare a thought for a bunch of people who got in over their heads with magic . . .

He couldn't help smiling at that. How many times must the goddess have heard a plea that started out like that?

More often than you know.

For a second, he thought it was Mystra answering him, and something like hope sprang up in his chest. This would be a bargain like any other, with no interference, no sense of doom hanging over him.

But then he realized he could no longer sense Cazrin's presence near him or feel her hand gripping his. Instead, his fingers felt cold, like he'd plunged his hand into an icy pond. He opened his eyes, or tried to, but there was only darkness, except for two pinpricks of light that appeared several feet away.

Two glowing eyes staring at him from the dark.

Baldric's breath quickened, but he refused to panic. He'd faced this before. He could do it again.

What do you want? he demanded. *Can't you see I'm busy petitioning an actual god, not some toad that hides in dark corners?*

Soft, cackling laughter answered him. Baldric clenched his jaw.

I'm here because I have the answer you want, the entity said in a soothing voice. *I've been watching over you, Baldric. I know you want a way to destroy the Ruinous Child. I don't blame you—wretched thing, full of petulance and sullen pride. Like a ghost that refuses to acknowledge its own irrelevance.*

And you're so much better, is that it? Baldric sneered. *Offering me the world. Sounds a lot like the devil's bargain Cazrin refused. Why should I treat you any different?*

Because you know if you don't find a way to stop it, that book will be her doom. All of you will come to ruin through it, just as you've been warned. That's why you're here, the entity said.

Trust the strange, malevolent presence to have a point, just when he'd rather dismiss it completely. Baldric cursed himself for a fool, but he plunged in anyway.

Fine, I'm listening. Since you won't let me speak to Mystra, or she's not answering, tell me your offer.

I know the place where the Ruinous Child was composed, where its bindings were made and its enchantments sealed into the pages one by one, the entity said. *Take it back to Alagesheth's laboratory in the depths of Undermountain, and you'll find the tools to break it down again and destroy it forever.*

Oh, it's that easy, is it? Baldric scoffed. *Search the whole of Undermountain, try not to die at the hands of a thousand different monsters along the way, all to find a lich's centuries-old laboratory, which may not even exist anymore.*

The eyes flared so bright that Baldric had to work hard not to flinch. *Don't fret, child,* the entity cooed. *It exists. You've already found the paths. I can show you which one is true.*

The map, Baldric realized with a start. That's what it was protecting—the way to Alagesheth's laboratory. The entity was offering the shortcut Baldric and the others needed.

If you show us the way, Baldric said, *what will you ask in return?*

This was usually the thrilling part—the negotiation, walking a tightrope with a deity. People stood in such awe of the gods, but in Baldric's experience, they really weren't all that different from people, in the end. Full of joy and vindictiveness, flush with their own pride and struggling with their weaknesses, same as all the folk in the world. But they were undeniably powerful, whether they deserved to be or not, and they brought that power to the negotiation.

Baldric didn't even know if this entity *was* a god. And when you didn't know who was sitting at the bargaining table with you, it put you on the back foot from the start. Baldric was in over his head and he knew it, but he refused to be cowed.

All that I ask, the entity said, *is a bit of your own power and vitality. A small trade, for giving you this chance to clear your name and have your life back.*

Assuming you're telling the truth, Baldric said, *you really expect us to stroll into Undermountain on your instructions? You could be leading us into a trap.*

Oh, but you don't really believe that, the entity said in a mocking tone. *I came to you when you were in need. You called me, and I showed you what I could do. I asked nothing then in return. I've never lied to you, Baldric. I can do many things, for the right price. You've always known that. That's why you can't fully escape me. You can't bring yourself to renounce the possibilities I offer.*

Baldric gritted his teeth. He didn't want the entity's words to be true, but he knew himself and he knew his flaws. Yes, the entity had proven it had power. And if Baldric gave the word now, he would have everything he desired.

A path forward to destroy the Ruinous Child and get a lich off their backs, and maybe even a way to clear their names. It was more than they'd been offered so far. Candlekeep was supposed to have been a sanctuary, but instead, they'd been turned away at the first sign of trouble. Now they had nowhere else to go to get help. Yet help was being offered here.

A bit of power and vitality. Of course, when phrased that way, it didn't sound so bad. Baldric had been half expecting to be asked to fork over his soul—and if he wouldn't commit to one god, he sure as Hells wouldn't pledge himself as some patron's warlock. But it was still a slippery slope. A bit of power here and there, giving away pieces of himself . . . just like the book.

No, it didn't have to be that way. Just this one more time, because he was desperate, he could give this small thing.

Or he could leave. The option was still on the table. Cut and run, before things got too complicated.

Damn it if Tess's words didn't still ring in his head. There *was* something different about this party. They were good together, and they worked well together, but it wasn't just that. He'd been worried about being used for this gift he had with the gods, but in truth, these people hadn't ever asked more of him than he was willing to give, and they didn't try to put a price on their help when they offered it.

Now he had to consider just how much he was willing to give up for these people that he *might* want to call friends.

He looked at the entity, those hungry eyes watching him, and steeled himself. He was tired of being afraid of the unknown. Whatever happened, whatever came of this deal, he could handle it. He bargained with the gods—he could bargain with this entity.

You have a deal, but just this once. I don't serve the gods, and I'm not pledging anything to you. Baldric stretched out his hand.

He had a brief impression of the shadows surging, lengthening into something that was more claw than hand, reaching for him. Then there was only cold, a lance of pain straight into his chest that made Baldric recoil. He fell, head banging against the floor, stars exploding in his vision as he tried to draw breath around the chill that clutched his heart.

Stepped in it this time, didn't you, he thought, but then he had no more room for rational thought. Images crowded his mind, driving out even the memory of the pain. A series of cold, dark tunnels, some natural and others man-made, cutting deep into the caverns of Undermountain. Iron-handled doors, secret passages. The ground shook, and centuries passed in an eyeblink. Hidden places were buried and terrible secrets entombed with them. An entire legacy gone.

But not forgotten.

Paths still existed to reach the ritual chamber, but they went deep, and nothing about them was safe. It was a terrible place to exist, but then there were also terrible things that called the place home.

Baldric saw no hint of what these monsters might be, only sensed them waiting, the way he'd sensed the entity watching him in the darkness. And at the end of it all, he saw a flash of the chamber they needed, a yawning cavern cracked and broken like an egg, fissures in the earth that dropped away to an endless abyss. By luck or, more likely, magic, the chamber had survived the ravages of time, and it still had what they needed.

If they could reach it.

Faster and faster the images flew behind his eyes, the trail repeating over and over, the true path of the map burning into his memory until Baldric shouted for the entity to stop or his mind would become trapped in that endless loop.

A soft chuckle came out of the darkness, and the images mercifully slowed and stopped. *Forgive me,* said the entity, in a tone that clearly communicated its delight in Baldric's pain, *I forget how fragile the minds of lesser creatures really are. Go now, and when you discover that what I've told you is true, maybe you'll consider there is more I could offer you. Much, much more than you could ever dream.*

Not likely, Baldric wanted to say, but he was still too focused on drawing breath into his lungs. Every inhalation felt like icy shards coming up his throat. He would never be warm again. But he had the path. He could call it up effortlessly in his mind, and he had the grim suspicion that were his mind to wither and rot with age, on his deathbed he could still recall the way to the hidden laboratory in Undermountain.

CHAPTER 27

"Get him another blanket," Tess ordered, standing over Baldric while the others retrieved blankets from the bedrooms, warmed water over the fire for tea, and generally fussed around the dwarf while he watched them with a bemused expression on his exhausted face.

"I'm really fine," he said, which annoyed Tess because, clearly, he was not *fine* and hadn't been fine since his communing ritual started.

But maybe that was the problem. Maybe he was in shock and didn't fully grasp the gravity of the situation. "Cazrin, do you have a mirror?" Tess asked. "Lark, what about you? Anyone carrying a mirror?"

Cazrin hesitated in the act of pouring Baldric some tea. She, at least, seemed none the worse for wear after the ritual ended. "It's in there," she said, nodding to another of her satchels.

"Thank you." Tess rooted around until she came up with a small, bronze-backed mirror with dusty glass and the initials M. V. carved into the handle. Tess scrubbed the glass as clean as she could with her sleeve and then turned it in Baldric's direction so he could get a look at himself.

"Ah" was all Baldric said when he laid eyes on the new streaks of white in his dark beard and the deepened wrinkles around his eyes, highlighting the exhaustion in his face. "Does it at least look distinguished?" he added with an attempt at a grin.

"You look as handsome as always, but I don't think that's our fearless leader's point," Lark said, tossing another blanket to Baldric, which he caught with a steady hand and whipped over his shoulders. Tess watched the movement and nodded in approval. That was an improvement from when he'd first woken up shaking, cold, and disoriented.

"What happened?" Tess demanded. The magical map lay forgotten on the floor in front of Baldric. It was nothing but a blank sheet of crumbling parchment now, its magic spent. Tess had vowed to give Baldric some time and space to recover before asking for an explanation, but her impatience was getting the better of her, and the sight of Baldric obviously drained of his life essence on her watch had shaken her. "This was supposed to be a simple prayer to commune with Mystra." She looked to Cazrin. "Did you see what did that to him?"

Cazrin shook her head. "I felt the presence of the goddess very briefly," she said. "It was a comforting touch, like she knew everything I was going through and wanted to reassure me, but then the connection was gone, and I opened my eyes and saw Baldric convulsing on the floor."

"Good to know the goddess was listening, at least for a little while," Baldric said. He held up a hand when Tess started to speak. "I know you want answers, and I'll give them to you, just . . . give me a moment." He took a sip of his tea and tucked the blankets more tightly around himself as the wind howled outside the tavern and lightning periodically lit up the night. Whether it was lightning from a normal storm or part of the magical one going on to the east, Tess couldn't have said. She just hoped it wasn't coming this way.

"Are you really praying to the gods at all when you ask for your powers, or is there something else going on?" Tess pressed, unable to contain herself.

"I make deals with them," Baldric corrected her. "It's a fair exchange, and everyone benefits. It's served me well for a long time."

He hesitated. "Only recently has that started to change. It happened one night when I got myself into some trouble at the gaming tables. I was on a hot streak, and the mercenaries I was playing cards with didn't take kindly to having all their wages stripped. They jumped me in the back alley, and there were six of them. I panicked and called out to Tyr for help, but I'd forgotten we were on the outs at the time, and there was no answer."

"Getting the silent treatment after a petty spat with the god of justice." Lark laid a hand over his heart and sang, "Baldric, sweet Baldric, you're everything I aspire to be."

"Fawn over him later," Tess said, rolling her eyes. "What happened?"

Baldric's shoulders hunched beneath the blanket, and he looked sheepish. "Like I said, there were six of them, and I'm pretty sure they meant to kill me. I got scared, and the fear made me vindictive. I thought, 'Well, I'll show him.' Tyr, I mean. So, I called out to anyone or anything that would listen. An open invitation. That's when the entity first showed itself."

"Since you're here with us now, I'm guessing it helped you defeat the mercenaries," Cazrin said.

Baldric nodded, his expression haunted. "With a vengeance," he said. "Afterward, the entity was much more . . . present in my negotiations with the deities. It kept offering me things."

"Like a devil might?" Lark said before Tess could. "Because it sounds to me like you're dealing with a devil. In fact, this has devil written all over it."

"Thanks, Lark," Baldric said dryly. "That thought never occurred to me before now."

"Then why didn't you say something?" Tess asked. "All this time, you've been making deals on our behalf, and you had this thing hanging over your head."

Baldric shrugged, but that sheepish look remained. "I thought I had it under control," he said. "When you came to me with the offer to explore the ruins of Oghma's temple, I knew that would help repay my debt to the god of knowledge, but I also thought I might get some answers there. I've been chasing down leads, trying to figure out why this entity has latched on to me, but I haven't gotten anywhere. And I couldn't very well agree to be the party's cleric and not use my abilities on your behalf, could I? I wouldn't be doing my job."

"But if you'd told us what was happening, we might have been able to help you," Cazrin pointed out. "At least you wouldn't have had to carry the burden alone."

"I—" Baldric shifted, looking uncomfortable. "It's not that I didn't trust you," he said. "Well, maybe it was a little bit that. You said yourself that we don't know one another that well, and we're all carrying secrets. But I also haven't had people to rely on in a long time, not since I was still at home. And even then, usually it was my clan relying on *me* to get things done. It's hard to shake that role." He looked up at Tess. "But I wanted to believe what you said," he told her, and there was an earnestness in his face that Tess couldn't remember ever seeing before. "When you told us what the group could be, I wanted to see that too, even if we were a long shot. That's why I made the deal. No matter how it came about, I think the information is good. I think it was worth the price to transfer the map into my head."

Tess nodded slowly. She hadn't expected to hear this from the dwarf, that he might actually believe in the party as much as she did. She felt a warmth spread through her chest, but she also felt the weight of responsibility.

I have to care for this group. I have to make sure that I'm the leader they deserve.

Tess glanced over her shoulder as Anson slipped quietly into the tavern, Uggie following. He'd been scouting the area again and gave her a subtle signal that yes, all was well. She nodded in thanks and gestured for the two of them to come over to the fire.

When they'd joined and been filled in on everything Baldric had shared, Tess said, "If Baldric believes the information from this entity is good, then we should use it. The Zhentarim aren't going to stop searching for us, and we're a target on the road. A moving target, yes, but we can't keep running forever. We're going to have to go on the offensive."

"I like the sound of that," Anson said. "I'm tired of looking over my shoulder."

"It's all well and good to turn and fight," Lark said. "Believe me, I wish every problem could be solved that way, but if we really mean to take this road into Undermountain, it means we have to go right back to where all the trouble started."

"Back to Waterdeep, where we're wanted fugitives," Tess said, nodding. "I haven't forgotten."

"Oh, good, so you have a plan for waltzing back into the city unnoticed," Baldric said. "Because that's a trick I'd like to see."

"I have a plan for everything," Tess said. "I'm back on my game." She turned to Lark. "That night we celebrated at the Yawning Portal, you said your old band was going to be performing there soon, didn't you?"

"I told Cazrin that in confidence," Lark said indignantly. "You were eavesdropping!"

Tess shrugged, unrepentant, and pointed to her ears. "These aren't just decorative," she said, mimicking his tone. "Was it true, or was it just another of your tales, like the one about how you left your band?"

Lark ignored the jab, counting off the days on his fingers. "Not that I keep close track of their movements, but they just started a short run in Daggerford, so they should be returning to the city in about—" He froze, and his head snapped up, a look of slow-dawning horror on his face. "You can't. Be serious."

"I always have a plan," Tess repeated, hands on her hips. "Don't worry, you have the starring role in it. You'll love it."

"No."

"Come on, Lark."

"I'd sooner be dead and my body strung up on the God Catcher's sphere for all to see than go to my old bandmates." He ran both hands through his long hair, tugging sharply at the strands as he rocked back and forth next to Anson. Uggie nudged him with one of her tentacles, but he ignored her. "Do you have *any idea* how incredibly awkward and off-putting it would be for me to approach them, hat in hand, and ask for their help?"

Tess raised an eyebrow. "You're giving me some idea, yes, but it will be just fine for the rest of us."

"It's true," Cazrin said, but she gave him a sympathetic smile.

"Sometimes you have to make sacrifices for the good of the group, Lark."

"Cut out my heart while you're at it," he said with a gusty sigh.

"We'll settle for your dignity." Anson was unable to hide his grin. "Did you really part on such bad terms?"

"We were *civil*," Lark said, "but it wasn't a good time for anyone. I was ready to go solo, take my talents to greater heights, and the rest of them just didn't want to let go." He shrugged. "These things happen in the music world."

"Really?" Tess said skeptically. "Or did they just kick you out?"

"Tess, you have a deeply suspicious mind, and while I admire that most times, I don't appreciate it turned in my direction," Lark said, making a shooing motion toward her. At the same time, his tail twitched restlessly.

Tess narrowed her eyes at him. "You're just dying to tell us what's really going on with you, aren't you? You can barely contain yourself."

Lark opened his mouth, presumably with a rebuttal, then closed it again and scrubbed a hand over his face. "You have *no* idea," he said.

Tess chuckled. "Someday, we're going to need to have a conversation where you don't dodge every question. Agreed?"

Lark wouldn't meet her eyes, but he gave a nod. "Agreed." He added, his voice full of reluctance, "And if we manage to intercept my old friends on the road back to Waterdeep, I'll do what I can to convince them to help us."

Well, that was one thing settled, at least. Tess turned to Baldric next. Some of the exhaustion and pain had left his face, which she was glad to see, although he was still shivering.

"And you," Tess told him. "No more making deals with this entity. No more talking to this entity, no more looking in its direction until we know more about what we're dealing with. When this is all over, the lich is dealt with, and we've cleared our names, we'll figure out what this entity wants and find a way to get rid of it."

Baldric shook his head. "This isn't your problem," he said. "It's my responsibility."

"Nonsense," Cazrin said matter-of-factly. "I've already got plans to start researching when we get back to Waterdeep. We'll figure this out together."

"It's no use arguing," Anson said when Baldric started to reply. "We've got your back, just like you've had ours. Like you had mine when you got the intellect devourers out of my head." He shuddered at the memory. "I know what it's like to have something foul creeping around in your thoughts. We're going to take care of this."

Baldric stared at them all in bemusement. Finally, his gaze landed on Tess. "So, you really meant what you said." He spoke quietly. "You want to do this."

"I do," Tess said. She glanced at the others, smiling fondly at Uggie, who was pushing her way around Cazrin to get closer to Baldric. "We all need this group for our own reasons. We need people we can trust. Am I wrong?"

"You're not wrong," Cazrin said. "We've all got things we're struggling with. Why not struggle together and make the burden a little lighter?"

Baldric gave a wan smile. "You're killing me with that optimism, wizard," he said, then swallowed, his throat bobbing. "But it's better than being killed by shadows."

Cazrin squeezed his hand. "I know exactly what you mean." She started to pull away, then looked down at Baldric's open palm and gasped. "Look," she urged him.

Baldric looked down at his hand, and Tess and the others crowded closer to see.

It was a silver key with the same triangular bow as the one that had appeared to Cazrin.

"Looks like you have your own key now too," Tess said, as Lark went to look down the hallway. "Is there another bedroom?" she called after the tiefling.

"Of course there is," Lark said sullenly. "When do the rest of us get our own private place to sleep? Do we have to make a soul-crushing deal with a mysterious entity too?"

"I think it might have something to do with all of us growing closer," Cazrin said thoughtfully. "Baldric did just do something amazing and selfless for the group. And when I was trapped in that vision with the Ruinous Child, what I wanted most was to find my way back to all of you. Maybe the tavern senses that we're committing to this party, to our friends, and it's handing out keys accordingly."

Tess shifted uncomfortably. If that was the case, why hadn't she been given a key yet? She was the one who'd had the idea to form the party in the first place. She cared about everyone, and she'd done her best to keep them together.

What did she have left to prove?

Wrestling with these thoughts, Tess offered to take the first watch, and gradually, they all settled down. Tess went outside just to assure herself again that no one had found the tavern's hiding place. She kept alert for any sounds that seemed out of place, wary of more Zhentarim on the prowl. The strange magical storm had ended, but a light, misty rain continued to fall, pattering softly on the leaves of the surrounding trees.

They would get on the move before dawn, returning north to Waterdeep. It would be a long series of days spent dodging their pursuers, but Tess knew they could manage it. The hardest part would be getting into the city and what lay beyond that.

Undermountain.

Tess stared into the darkness, her cloak tucked around her. How many nights had she dreamed of leading a group into its depths, adventurers on the path to glory? To confront the wonders and dangers of that place and come back with tales to tell her grandchildren one day.

It had all seemed very abstract and enticing, and even now, it was hard not to feel a giddiness in her chest when she contemplated the possibilities before them.

Except it wasn't abstract anymore. And the adventurers she'd imagined leading were not just concepts. They were people with real problems, secrets, and fears, and they were relying on her.

Once again, Tess felt the weight of her responsibility. Could she really do this? Could she protect them all and bring them back safely? There were still many things she didn't know about this group. Baldric had his entity. Lark had his secrets. Cazrin was grappling with the effects of the Ruinous Child. Even Anson, arguably the most solid member of the group, struggled with the knowledge that his brother was somewhere out there, working for a lich. Tess would have to have a fallback plan for everyone, for whatever happened. It felt as if all of their plans since forming the group had been fallbacks.

Tess started like she'd been lightning-struck. "That's it! That's our party name—the Fallbacks. It's perfect!"

No one answered her outburst. The forest was quiet except for the distant hooting of an owl, and the party was fast asleep inside the tavern. Tess headed back up the ramp to join them, and despite everything, her lips curved in a small, satisfied smile. "We can talk about it in the morning."

She wasn't going to be able to solve all their problems in one night. This group was bigger and more complicated than anything she'd ever handled before, but Tess had meant what she'd said. She was in this for the long haul, and she was going to do whatever it took to prove to the rest of the group that she could be the leader they deserved.

INTERLUDE

Lorthrannan ended the scrying spell, and the image of Tess on the grass outside blurred and faded in his mind's eye.

When he came back to himself, he was greeted with the sight of the ruined hilltop, the grass blackened, trees blasted away by his spell battle with Valindra Shadow-mantle.

He shouldn't have lost his temper. He'd known from the beginning he couldn't best her in a fight, but he'd needed to prove that he was more than an upstart, that he was worthy of the knowledge and power he sought.

He hadn't won the fight, but he had surprised her. There had been a moment during their duel when real fear had entered her eyes. Instead of continuing, she'd retreated under the guise of offering him one more chance to retrieve the Ruinous Child.

Fortunately for him, she hadn't seen how close she'd come to destroying his physical form. If the battle had gone on any longer, he would have lost.

Lorthrannan adjusted his dark robes, assessing the damage his body had taken in the fight. He didn't feel pain in the same way he once did, but the grind of shattered bones and scorched flesh was impossible to ignore completely. He needed to regenerate, to recover his power.

But there was no time. The adventurers were taking the Ruinous Child back to Waterdeep. They'd found the location of Alagesheth's laboratory, and now they were going to destroy the book.

He couldn't allow that to happen.

One of the Zhent soldiers was coming up the hill toward him. Lorthrannan observed him as if he were an annoying fly. When he was within earshot, Lorthrannan said, "Bring me the other one." What was his name? "Valen. I want to speak to him."

The Zhent paused, as if about to argue, but then he thought better of it and turned, hurrying back down the hill.

A plan was forming in Lorthrannan's mind. It was a risk, but if he succeeded, he would not only obtain the Ruinous Child, he would also have access to Alagesheth's lost laboratory. It was an unexpected and valuable prize to present to Valindra, an offering of peace to cement their alliance.

But it meant he'd have to allow the adventurers to live, for now. He'd have to continue to scry on them, following their trail back to Waterdeep and down into Undermountain. Oh, but he wouldn't leave them unscathed. He'd harry them, snap at their heels, keep them afraid, but allow them to believe they were one step ahead of him. Once they led him to Alagesheth's laboratory, he could finally kill them and be done with this whole business.

He would have to be cautious, and not expend more of his power than he had to. Undermountain was not a place to be taken lightly, and he'd already been weakened by the spell duel.

Valen climbed the hill and dutifully came to stand before Lorthrannan, inclining his head. "You asked for me, Sir."

"I want you to tell me everything you know about your brother and his companions." Lorthrannan said. "Leave nothing out. I need to know their weaknesses if I am to kill them."

Valen's gaze flicked to Lorthrannan's face, but he schooled his expression before he betrayed any emotion. "I can tell you my brother's weaknesses," he said slowly, "but I don't know his companions." He hesitated. "You should consider letting Anson and the others live. They could be valuable assets."

"Really?" Lorthrannan took a step toward him. "Explain. I'm afraid you'll have to be terribly convincing. I've imagined killing each one of them, slowly and painfully, far too often to give up that pleasure easily." He stared the man down. "And I hope this suggestion doesn't indicate a change of heart on your part. That would be very disappointing, Valen."

The Zhent swallowed, but he held his ground. "I'm committed to the Zhentarim and to you," he insisted. "This would be yet another way to expand your reach and gather more loyal followers. Think about it," he continued. "You've already made fugitives of them. Now they have limited options. The groundwork has been laid to show them that joining you is the only way to ensure their survival."

"You are a shrewd one, aren't you?" Lorthrannan said, amused. "Not a cowering dog like some of the others. No, you have ambitions, don't you? You want more than this world has seen fit to give you. I like that." It reminded Lorthrannan of himself. He gestured for Valen to come closer.

Yes, he would have to be patient and careful, moving all the pieces on the board in just the right way to get what he wanted. But he'd come this far in his long life by taking many such risks. He wasn't afraid, and whether they joined his cause or not, he didn't believe for a moment that five adventurers would have the ability to thwart him.

CHAPTER 28

Tess lay on her right shoulder inside a large crate that smelled like fresh-cut duskwood and sweat—mostly her own, although Anson shared the coffin-like space with her. They were hidden under thick blankets stacked with various musical instruments and stage props, the weight of which only served to enhance the feeling of being entombed alive. Tess breathed shallowly, imagining a dwindling air supply, even though they'd made sure to put plenty of holes in the crate.

Nearly a tenday had passed since the party had started their journey back to Waterdeep. They'd made decent time on the road, keeping their heads down and their pace quick. They slept in the tavern at night when they could find a place to hide it, and camped in caves or dense woods when they couldn't. On their third day of travel, they woke to the smell of rain again, and high winds sweeping in another storm. This one, at least, didn't appear to have any magic with it, though they'd all been worried about it slowing their progress. But in the end, the storm helped them more than Tess would have thought possible.

Well, the storm and the Ruinous Child.

During their journey, Cazrin had enacted protections against the book so that it would be much more difficult for the Ruinous Child to invade her mind. Tess didn't know exactly what form those protections had taken, but she saw Cazrin cast a spell every time she went to handle the book.

And then she'd started to read and research.

Tess was not against this, exactly. Cazrin had made a good case that the Ruinous Child might have spells or other information she could take advantage of for the party's protection, without delving into its darker rituals and secrets. She'd also confessed that she needed to face the book, to prove that it had no power over her any longer. Tess understood that too, but she'd made it clear to the wizard that no one in the party expected her to do anything with the book that she wasn't comfortable with, no matter what helpful magic she might find within its pages.

Tess knew she needed to trust her party members. She'd told Baldric as much the night he'd made the deal with his entity. They all needed to learn to trust more. Cazrin was experienced in magic, and she was no fool. She'd learned her lesson after her last encounter with the book.

Still, Tess wasn't perfect. Every night when she would look over at Cazrin to see her flipping through the book's pages, a feeling of disquiet stirred in her chest. After what had happened to her last time, Tess wanted nothing more than to march over, snatch the book, and hurl it into the sea.

But she couldn't deny the Ruinous Child had proved useful. In it, Cazrin had found a spell to shield the party from the effects of the elements for a time. Even better, it had given her more information about liches and about Alagesheth, specifically how he'd come to establish a secret lab in Undermountain, hiding from the infamous Halaster Blackcloak. The stories had fascinated Cazrin, but Tess had kept a sharp eye out in case the book's magic turned on them and led them into the sea. Thankfully, it hadn't. Perhaps it was trying to get back in Cazrin's good graces after having invaded her mind. Maybe it had no agenda at all except to protect itself, and that meant protecting its keepers for the time being.

Whatever the reason, the storm and the Ruinous Child got them back up the coast in good time, and then Cazrin was able to use her own magic to help Lark contact his former bandmates. Tess wasn't privy to the message or the reply, but when all was said and done, Lark had come stomping back into camp with his tail lashing, a stormy expression on his face.

"They'll help, but we need to pay them," he'd said curtly. "Gustan will wait for us by the South Gate with a wagon to sneak us in with the equipment for their show. On a side note, I hate all of you, and I'm never speaking to you again."

Then he'd gone to sit by the fire and get sloppy drunk before he fell asleep with his hat over his face.

Tess had devised a plan that required a trio of crates large enough to fit all of them except Lark, who'd be adopting a disguise and riding in the wagon with Gustan. None of them had wanted to pin all their hopes on someone they'd never met, so Lark would be the face of this operation, just as Tess had promised him.

They'd spent a day at a small village north of Daggerford, going from merchant to merchant until they'd been able to purchase a set of new crates—for an exorbitant price, in Tess's opinion, but the tabaxi woman who'd sold them to her seemed to sense her desperation and took full advantage. Tess had no one to blame but herself for her poor bargaining skills.

And here they were—Tess and Anson in one crate, Baldric in another, and Cazrin and Uggie in the third—rolling along in the wagon toward the Waterdeep city gates.

"Everything's going to be all right," Anson whispered. His back was to Tess, which created a wall of heat behind her and did nothing at all to help her feelings of claustrophobia.

"I know it is," Tess hissed back. "I'm fine."

Anson's soft chuckle reverberated through her shoulders. "You're stiff as a board, Tess."

He knew her too well. "I'm having a grand time," Tess drawled. "Who wouldn't want to ride in a mini coffin back into the city where they're a wanted fugitive? I am the picture of serenity."

"Cazrin's the real hero in this scenario," Anson said. "She's putting up with Uggie's body odor in these cramped crates. Can you imagine?"

Tess shuddered. She could, actually, and a wave of guilt washed over her that Cazrin had drawn the short straw when they'd been deciding who would hide with whom.

"I'll think of a way to make it up to her when this is over," Tess said.

"Here we go," rumbled a voice from the front of the wagon. It was Gustan, a curvy tiefling with dark backswept horns. "Guards passing by."

Tess immediately went still, listening for sounds of movement. There were murmuring voices and shouts mingled with the creak of the wagons passing through the city gates and the faint neighing of horses. It sounded like there was quite a crowd lined up to enter the city, most likely merchants and other travelers. Tess prayed they wouldn't be held up too long. Sweat made her shirt stick to her neck, and she felt like she hadn't had a breath of fresh air in days.

Footsteps approached, and a pair of voices addressed Gustan and Lark.

They'd crafted Lark's disguise using a combination of stage makeup and his own magic, so that the guards would see a blue-skinned tiefling with short, curly white hair and horns that had been lengthened and twisted into spirals.

"Well met, Gustan," one of the guards said. "Heard you were coming back to play the Yawning Portal." There was a pause. "Who's this? The rest of your band got here this morning."

Now came the real test. Tess tried not to squirm in the crate. She'd vowed to trust Lark with the job of talking their way into the city without arousing suspicion, at the same time keeping an eye on Gustan in case they tried to change their mind about helping them. But if there were any hard feelings between Lark and his old band-mate, they'd all know it soon enough.

"Torien's my name," Lark's voice rang out. He sounded younger and cockier, if such a thing was possible. "You're going to want to remember that. I'm Gustan's new flautist. You can say you met me the day before my big debut."

Both guards chuckled. "Where'd you pluck this sprout from, Gustan? I like him."

"Daggerford," Gustan said, the lie rolling easily off their tongue. "He's a handful, to be sure, but he's got talent."

"Is that so?" the other guard said, sounding amused. "Go on, let's hear you, then. So I can tell my grandchildren that I heard the great Torien before he became a legend."

Tess immediately tensed up again. *Why* had Lark bragged about being a flautist? Did he even own a flute? Or know how to play one?

As if confirming her worst fears, a discordant whistle pierced the expectant silence, and the guards cursed and one exclaimed, "Ho, now, stop that! My ears are bleeding!"

This was a disaster. They were going to be discovered. Before they put her in irons, Tess was going to make sure she took the time to wring the bard's neck.

"Relax, Torien," Gustan said. "You're just having a bit of stage fright."

"Listen, you—" Lark said in a strangled voice, but then he seemed to remember his part and mumbled, "Yes, Gustan. I'm . . . sorry. Let me try again."

Tess held her breath.

Suddenly, bright, cheerful music filled the air, and the wagon rocked back and forth gently, as if Lark was dancing in his seat. Voices murmured in appreciation, and there was the clink of coins landing on the crate. Even Tess forgot her anxiety for a moment while she listened to the music. When the song trailed off, the guards clapped enthusiastically and showered young "Torien" with compliments.

"Have a good show, Gustan," a guard said, "and best of luck to your new prodigy!"

The murmur of voices faded as the guards moved on, and the wagon rolled forward again. Tess sagged back against Anson in relief.

"Lark really pulled that one out in the end," Anson whispered.

"I know," Tess said, smiling to herself. "Don't tell him I said it, but I think he really is going to be a legend someday."

Gustan and Lark let them out of the crates in an alley in the Southern Ward that smelled like rotting fruit. It was not the fresh air that Tess had craved, but she sucked in a deep breath anyway as she sprang out of the crate and got her feet on solid ground again.

Anson and Baldric were no worse for wear, but Cazrin looked distinctly green as she scrambled out of the crate and trotted several feet away from Uggie, who lumbered out behind her.

"You all right there, Cazrin?" Baldric asked.

"I'm . . . fine," Cazrin said, taking shallow breaths and bracing one arm against the alley wall for support. "It's just . . . it was . . . like breathing the inside of a corpse. But truly . . . I'm fine."

Anson offered her his waterskin as Lark shared a quiet word with Gustan. He handed the other tiefling a pouch containing most of the coin they'd recovered from Sefeerian's home. "Like we agreed," he said curtly.

"My thanks." Gustan took the pouch, their dark eyes fixing Lark with an inscrutable look. Their purple skin was dull with road dust, but they had a laid-back charm that was a sharp contrast to Lark's restless energy. They would have been good together in a band, Tess thought. Like fire and ice, standing back-to-back onstage, belting out a bawdy tune to a packed house.

At the moment, there was nothing but tension between the two of them. The money exchanged, both seemed to be waiting for the other one to say something.

Tess stepped in, offering her hand to Gustan. "We truly appreciate your help," she said. "Lark does too. He's just being sullen."

A smile tugged at Gustan's lips. "I have to admit, when Lark said he was travelling with a new pack, I didn't believe it, but you've obviously been together awhile. You've got him pegged pretty well." The smile faded. "Take some advice—don't count on it lasting. Whatever he's promised you, I mean." They shot a glance at Lark. "He tends to disappear when things get rough, leaving others to clean up the mess."

A muscle in Lark's jaw ticked. "At least I contributed something while I was with you," he said. "You certainly took it and ran." He scowled at the writing on the side of the wagon. "Changed the band name, I see. Destiny's Discordance. So *deep*. Really makes you think."

Gustan shook their head and sighed. "You'll never change, will you?" They turned away, dismissing Lark and addressing Tess. "If you ever want to come and see a show, just tell the man at the door that you're here for a lark. They'll let you in for free the first time."

Lark's mouth dropped open, but he didn't have time for a reply before Gustan strode back to the wagon and jumped up onto the driver's seat. Tossing the party a wave, they guided the horses back to the street and were soon gone, off to meet up with the rest of the band.

"Well, that wasn't as awkward as it could have been," Baldric said, slapping Lark on the back. "They seemed like a decent sort of person."

"They're a showboating twit who resents playing second fiddle to anyone and wouldn't know a good song if it marched up and punched them in the face," Lark said in an even tone.

"Ah, well, I can see why the two of you like each other so much," Baldric said, grinning.

"Smelled like old vomit in an infected wound," Cazrin was muttering to herself as she took another swig from Anson's waterskin.

"All right, we need to get Cazrin some fresh air and find somewhere to lie low until nightfall," Tess said, as Anson walked over to the wizard and gently peeled her off the wall, keeping one arm around her waist to support her.

"I'm fine," Cazrin said, straightening. "Really, I'm—"

She stopped, her eyes going wide. Tess thought she was getting ready to throw up, then she realized Cazrin was staring at something at the mouth of the alley. Tess followed the woman's gaze and froze.

A merchant wagon had been left parked at the mouth of the alley near an old warehouse. Where the driver was, Tess had no idea, but the horse that was tied to the wagon was trembling in its harness. Tess could see the white of the beast's eye as it swiveled its head away from something just out of her sight.

Then, a blast of cold, fetid air blew through the alley, stirring Tess's hair and making her arms break out in gooseflesh. The horse began to buck and snort, neighing loudly in terror as a cloaked and hooded figure glided into view at the mouth of the alley. A gloved hand came up and touched the beast on the side of its neck before it could jerk out of the way. The horse went quiet and crumpled to the ground, hanging limp from its harness.

The cloaked figure turned and looked down the alley. Two pin-pricks of red light glowing from the depths of the hood met Tess's gaze. A violent shudder ran through her entire body.

"Run," Cazrin said, her voice little more than a whisper. "We need to run."

Yes, run, Tess thought, except her body wouldn't move. Her boots felt rooted to the ground, even as her mind screamed at her to get away from the hooded figure that was staring right through her with a burning gaze more terrifying than any nightmare she'd ever had.

The others were similarly affected. No one moved or spoke a word, other than Cazrin.

The cloaked figure began gliding toward them. Or maybe they were being drawn toward it. Tess couldn't tell. The alley walls seemed to warp and twist, bricks blurring into one gray mass.

Lorthrannan. The lich had found them. He'd found them, and he wasn't alone either. Four figures stepped into the alley behind him, keeping a healthy amount of space between themselves and the lich. Tess recognized the Zhentarim symbol on the clasps of their cloaks, and it was that, that small bit of normalcy—an enemy she recognized, a threat she could fight—that broke her paralysis.

"Run!"

Anson and Lark were closest to her. Grabbing their shoulders, Tess spun them around, breaking their gazes with the lich. Baldric was already moving, taking Cazrin's arm and hauling her along with him as the group turned and took off toward the other end of the alley, with Uggie loping as fast as she could at their heels.

Soft, hollow laughter echoed from behind them, and then a whisper of arcane phrases, accompanied by a sudden rush of heat. Tess cursed and risked a glance over her shoulder.

Lorthrannan had his hand raised, gloved fingers hooked into claws, as a ball of flame began to form above his palm. Stirred by the arcane power, the cloak's hood fell back, revealing the lich in all his terrible glory.

Tess's stomach lurched. She could see hints that Lorthrannan had once been a handsome man. Patchy strands of long, silky dark hair still clung to his skull, but the flesh that remained was thin and bluish, almost translucent, with white bone showing through at the forehead and brow line. His cheeks were sunken and withered, and more of the flesh had rotted away around his mouth, exposing teeth and gums that had turned black. His eyes—those burning, red eyes—were too big in his thin face. They engulfed everything, sucking the life out of all that gaze touched.

Tess tore her attention away only when the fireball exploded from Lorthrannan's hand, barreling impossibly fast down the alley toward the group.

"Duck!" Cazrin screamed.

Tess dropped to her belly at the opposite end of the alley from the lich. She looked back to make sure the rest of the group had followed suit, and her heart seized in her chest at the sight of Cazrin standing in the middle of the alley, clutching the Ruinous Child in her hands.

The book bled shadows that swirled and clung to Cazrin's form like a living cloak, billowing behind her in a smoky, sinuous wave and carrying the stench of brimstone. She shouted some arcane phrase as the fireball bore down on her.

Tess leaped to her feet, but before she could get to the wizard, the Ruinous Child flared to life, its shadows taking the shape of a shield. The fireball impacted the darkness as if it were solid instead of smoke, and deflected high into the air. It struck one of the buildings flanking the alley with an explosion that drove Tess into the opposite wall.

When she looked back, eyes watering, it was to see the roof tiles had peeled back, and the wooden portion of the building was ablaze, lighting up the evening sky in an orange conflagration that must have been seen by half the ward.

"Fire!" Lark shouted as he and the others got up and resumed running. "We need help, there's a fire!"

"Fire in the ward!" Baldric bellowed, and Anson added his own voice to the call for help.

"Call the Watch!" Tess waved her arms to get the attention of a gnome woman who'd stepped out into the street, a child perched on her hip. More people were pouring out of their homes and businesses to see what had caused the explosion. "Someone's throwing fireballs in the street." She put on a panicked expression—not difficult at all under the circumstances—as they turned a corner and pelted down the next street and the next, weaving between buildings and doing their best to put as much distance as possible between themselves and the lich and his Zhent escort.

With a bit of luck, the misdirected spell would summon every member of the City Watch in the immediate vicinity, who would in turn call in Magisters of the Watchful Order and force Lorthrannan to go to ground. If his presence in the city were exposed, it might even draw the attention of more powerful figures like the Blackstaff. Tess thought that even a lich of Lorthrannan's power wouldn't want that force brought down upon his head. But that would take days, if not longer.

The Fallbacks only had now.

The breath burned in her lungs, but Tess didn't dare slow down as they made their way through the warren-like streets of the city in the direction of the Yawning Portal. They had to get to Undermountain as soon as possible. They were running out of time.

Cazrin ran up alongside her, the Ruinous Child clutched in her hand. Luckily, the spellbook was making no effort to shoot out thorns or other impediments, but Tess could feel the usual cloud of gloom radiating off the book.

She glanced at Cazrin in concern. The wizard seemed fine, but Tess hated that the book had had a grip on her, even for a moment. "You saved us back there," she said. "Are you all right?"

Cazrin gave her an abstracted glance. "I will be," she said, with a wan smile, "if we can get rid of this thing."

"We will," Tess promised her. She wasn't going to let anything shake Cazrin's natural optimism, especially not the Ruinous Child.

They would destroy the book. They just needed to stay alive long enough to do it.

CHAPTER 29

WATERDEEP—CITY OF SPLENDORS

YEARS EARLIER

Tess hoisted the backpack onto her shoulders and eyed the rickety wooden stairs. Outside, the sun was just coming up. Pale orange light spilled through the broken windows on the ground floor of the abandoned building. Tess's footsteps echoed in the empty room as she got into position. The muscles in her back were already tense from the heavy load she carried: four flights to the top with the backpack full of stones.

And that was the easy part.

Tess planted her feet, took a deep breath, and broke into a run, boots pounding up the stairs. She did her best to listen for any sound that would betray her mentor's presence somewhere within the building.

Today, she was going to make it to the top. She was going to pass Mel's test and snatch the emerald-green scarf tied to a pole on the roof. Fringed in gold, the scarf was embroidered with oak leaves and holly berries, and it was a thing of beauty.

Tess had been unable to take her eyes off the scarf the first time she'd met her mentor—mostly because she'd been too intimidated to meet the halfling's piercing gaze, so she'd stared at her neck instead.

At the time, she'd thought she was being punished, banished to the woman's care after taking one too many trinkets from around her small town. Tess had tried to explain. It wasn't really theft. She didn't want to *keep* the items, and she'd always returned them. It was about the thrill and challenge of passing unseen, going where others didn't dare, and accomplishing something that most people couldn't. She hadn't expected Mel to understand.

She'd been wrong.

Tess's foot plunged through a rotting stair. Pain shot up her leg, and she came down hard on her other knee. The stones dug into her back, the weight of them pressing her to the stairs. She tensed her muscles, ignoring the pain, and pushed herself up.

Breathe, she told herself. *Focus. You've got this.*

She yanked her foot free of the rotting stair just as an apple dropped out of nowhere, bouncing off her head. On instinct, Tess reached out and snatched it out of the air.

"Ow," she said, rubbing her head with her free hand before taking a bite of the juicy red fruit. "No fair! There are no apple trees here."

"What does fair have to do with it?" Mel's words drifted down to her from somewhere at the top of the stairs, but no matter how hard Tess tried, she couldn't pinpoint where her voice had come from. It was one of Mel's many talents, the ability to make it seem like her voice came from everywhere and nowhere. She might as well have been a ghost haunting the old building. "Things aren't always going to go the way you hope they will, Tessalynde. The world isn't here to accommodate you, so you must be prepared to adapt to changing circumstances."

"That's what I'm doing," Tess said stubbornly. She tested her weight on her ankle to make sure it wasn't sprained, then resumed her run up the stairs. She jumped onto the rail at the next landing, deftly avoiding a patch of greasy substance that would have coated her boots and made it impossible to keep her feet. It was a trick Mel had used before, and Tess wasn't falling for it this time.

She tucked the apple into her pouch and adjusted the backpack. Her muscles burned, but not as badly as the first time she'd done this. Or the second. One day, Tess vowed, she'd be able to make the climb at a sprint without feeling the weight of the stones at all.

She leaped off the railing and kept going. Her heart thudded with excitement. This was it. She was getting closer.

But Mel was still somewhere above her, lying in wait. Tess had never seen someone who could move as fast or as quietly as the retired rogue. Mel was everything Tess aspired to be.

Her ankle was starting to throb. Maybe it really was sprained after all. Tess didn't dare slow down. She couldn't give Mel the opportunity to get the jump on her. She was almost to the next landing when she detected the faint scrape of a boot directly above her.

Got you.

Tess pulled out the apple and prepared to throw it. Before she could, a veil of darkness descended over her, and her world went black.

She froze, her excitement melting into panic. Mel was making her move.

Another boot scrape, right behind her. Tess whirled, but before she could react, deft fingers plucked the apple out of her grasp. A second later, it bounced off her head again. Blinded, Tess wasn't able to grab it, and she heard it plummet to the ground below.

"Ow!" she said again.

Tess swiped at the air around her, instinctively going into a crouch to protect herself. "You're using magical darkness now?" she demanded of her teacher. She opened her mouth to say that it wasn't fair, but she caught herself just in time.

Mel was right. Fair had nothing to do with it.

Tess reoriented herself, reaching out a hand to find the stair railing. Tracing her fingers lightly over the wood, she felt her way up the steps. She was moving at a snail's pace now, but she didn't dare try to run. She tested each step with her weight, and more than once she had to jump over another rotting stair and pray that the next one held her. Gradually, she fell into a rhythm, climbing higher and higher until she finally broke free of the magical darkness in time to see a plain wooden door looming in front of her. Tess examined it quickly and carefully, aware that at any moment, the magical darkness could return, along with any number of other obstacles.

There were no traps on the door, but the lock was complex. Sweat poured down Tess's back as she tried to concentrate, her muscles aching from the weight of the stones. Finally, the lock gave, and she swung open the door, stepping out onto the roof of the building in time to see a blazing orange sunrise greeting her in the east. Tess skidded to a halt, caught by the sight after the darkness and gloom of the stairwell.

"Beautiful, isn't it?"

The voice came from right behind her.

Tess flinched and spun, but fatigue and the stones made her too slow. Mel stood before her. Strands of her graying hair had come loose from her bun to flutter around her face, and she held a dagger at the level of Tess's stomach. Behind the halfling, across the roof, Tess could see the coveted scarf blowing in the breeze like a sail, gold thread winking in the sunlight.

Tess's shoulders slumped. "I surrender," she said. "I was distracted."

Mel's eyes twinkled. "You won't be next time. In truth, I'd be disappointed if you weren't affected by that sunrise." The wrinkles around her eyes deepened as she smiled. "It's my secret weapon, you know. All the students fall for it the first time they get up here."

It was cold comfort, but Tess would take it. "I'm not always going to fail," she said vehemently. "Someday, I'll earn that scarf."

"My dear, failure is part of the training," Mel said, her smile fading. "Haven't I made that clear yet?"

"But I let myself lose focus, and I didn't anticipate having to work in the dark," Tess said. "I won't make those mistakes again."

"Good," Mel said. "You do that, and in the meantime, I'll come up with a dozen other ways to trip you and slow you down—just like life."

Tess scowled, feeling frustration welling up inside her. "Am I never meant to succeed, then? Is that the point of the test?" What more did her teacher want from her?

Mel strode across the roof to retrieve her scarf, wrapping it around her neck. She turned back to Tess and threw her another apple, which Tess caught without looking.

"You couldn't do that when we first met, could you?" Mel said with a satisfied cackle. "Couldn't heft a bag of stones either, let alone prance up the stairs with them. What are those, if not successes?" She put her hands on her wide hips. "The point of the test is to make you understand that life is full of these sorts of lessons"—her face clouded—"and more disappointments than you think you can bear. How you handle them will tell you who you really are."

CHAPTER 30

WATERDEEP—CITY OF SPLENDORS

PRESENT DAY

This was not how Tess had pictured her first venture into Undermountain.

She'd daydreamed about turning the heads of all the patrons as she and her fearless companions approached the massive hole in the center of the common room, descending with calm resolution into the dark to face whatever dangers lay ahead.

The reality was that it was sunset when they arrived, sweating and panting for breath, at the Yawning Portal, and there were no crowds yet to speak of, so their only audience as they descended into the dark well was an elderly dragonborn couple having an early dinner and a pair of bored-looking servers throwing dice at the bar to pass the time before the evening rush.

But Tess discovered that instead of being disappointed at the lack of fanfare, she was simply grateful to go unnoticed. Lorthrannan had lost their trail, at least for now.

"How far do we have to go before we see signs of the lich's hidey-hole?" Lark asked as Cazrin's spell lights drifted around them, lighting up the tunnel shaft in a soft golden glow. He looked over at Baldric expectantly, but the dwarf shook his head.

"Nothing looks familiar yet," he said, "but the entire route's running on a loop in my head, so you'll all be the first to know when something changes."

Anson, with Uggie tied to his back, reached the bottom of the shaft first. Tess dropped down second and pulled her cat mask over her eyes so she could scout ahead for traps. Not far from where they stood, the passage split off in several directions, and those passages diverged in several others, and so on. For the first time, it struck home with Tess what an endless maze this place could be. How were they ever going to narrow down the chambers to Alagesheth's laboratory? The entity in Baldric's vision could be leading them anywhere.

She was just about to turn back to regroup with the others when she heard footsteps behind her. She turned to see Baldric coming up beside her. There was a strange, blank expression on his face, as if he were in a trance.

"Baldric?" Tess asked, laying a hand on his arm. "You all right?"

"He just walked away in the middle of a sentence," Anson said, as he and the others came down the tunnel to join them.

"It's this way," Baldric said, pointing down one of the side tunnels toward what Tess thought was east. He spoke in a dull monotone that sent a chill up her spine, and without warning, began to march toward the tunnel. Tess grabbed his arm instinctively, holding him in place.

Lark waved a hand in front of Baldric's face, but he didn't react. He was tugging against Tess's grip—not hard, but insistently—trying to lead them into the dark.

"I don't like this," Anson said. "We're putting way too much faith in this entity, and now it's openly affecting Baldric outside of his making a bargain. We can't trust this."

Tess wholeheartedly agreed. They were pawns in a maze, and they had a lich on their heels. But Baldric had insisted the entity's information was good.

She took a deep breath and released the dwarf's arm, letting him set off down the tunnel. "We can't trust this entity, but I trust Baldric," she said, following at the cleric's side and motioning the others to fall in behind her. "We knew what we were getting into, and with

Lorthrannan right behind us with the Zhents, we're committed now."

She glanced back at Anson, half expecting an argument, but he simply gave her a nod and faded in at the back of the party. Lark and Cazrin stayed in the middle of the group with Uggie.

They walked for hours. The tunnel's low ceiling and perpetual quiet were unnerving, and the farther they descended, the more Tess felt as if they were walking to the center of the world. How did someone like Halaster Blackcloak exist in a place like this? Would he sense the party's presence, or the Ruinous Child's, for that matter? Had he allowed Alagesheth to establish a lab here, or had he simply never noticed the lich in the sprawling complex of dungeons? It boggled her mind at times, contemplating the machinations of beings so powerful.

She'd imagined monsters around every corner on this journey, and though at first they heard only soft, distant cries, eventually Tess picked up the sound of scuffling and scraping much closer. She held up a hand to slow the party as she peered around the next curve in the tunnel.

A trio of rust monsters moved along the passage about thirty feet ahead of them, crowding into a hole in the wall where they must have made a burrow. Tess waited until the monsters had disappeared, then motioned to the party to move as quietly as possible past the hole. The last thing she wanted was a fight that would slow them down, with monsters who could destroy all the nonmagical metal they were carrying.

Luck was on their side, and they passed by the burrow without a sound, continuing the long, dark walk, gradually descending deeper and deeper into the ground.

Abruptly, Baldric stopped at a dead end in the tunnel. Tess had been so focused on the ground in front of them, searching for traps and pitfalls, that she hadn't noticed that the tunnel simply ended at a wall.

"Did we take a wrong turn?" Tess asked. She glanced over and a jolt of relief went through her to see Baldric shaking his head and blinking. His eyes had lost that unfocused, trancelike glaze.

"No, it's just . . . I think we're here," he said. "Sorry, the tunnels were all looking the same earlier. I couldn't figure out where we were, but then suddenly, it was like I locked in on the route, and then I couldn't focus on anything else. And I have the worst headache now!" He scrubbed both hands over his face and shook himself. He pointed to the wall. "There's a hidden mechanism that opens a door or something."

Finally, something she could control. While Baldric recovered, Tess crouched at the base of the wall, working her way up and scanning for hidden latches or concealed levers. The rest of the group waited behind them. Tess could feel their tension as they listened for signs of pursuit.

"They can't have followed us through the tavern entrance, can they?" Lark asked. "A lich striding into the Yawning Portal is going to cause a bit of a stir among the city's elite."

"There might be other entrances to Undermountain in the city that we don't know about," Cazrin pointed out. "The Zhentarim probably control several that Lorthrannan and his group could make use of."

"Yes, but they still have to *find* us once they're down here with us," Lark pressed, seeming to need reassurance. "What are the chances they'll be able to find the right tunnel to lead them here?"

"You're probably right, it's just . . ." Cazrin trailed off.

"Oh, I don't like that face," Baldric said. "What does that face mean?"

Cazrin sighed unhappily. "It means they might have other ways to magically track us. Everything I've read in the Ruinous Child suggests that liches have unimaginable powers. I might be wrong, but I don't think we should lower our guard."

"Terrific," Lark muttered. "Hurry every chance you get, Tess."

"I'm working on it," Tess said dryly, without taking her eyes from the wall. "You know, we haven't had a chance to discuss the party name I told you about," she added, to distract everyone. "The Fallbacks. What do you think?"

"We do keep changing plans on the fly," Anson said, nodding. "I like it."

"The Fallbacks," Cazrin said, a smile in her voice. "Has a nice ring to it."

"It's not bad," Lark allowed. "I would have preferred something a bit grander, like Mythic Mayhem or Sonorous Fury. What about the Discordant Note?"

Tess looked up from her examination of the wall to scowl at him, though he wouldn't be able to see it behind her mask. "Most of those are very musically themed. You aren't just giving us rejected band names, are you?"

Lark coughed and looked away. "You know, I think Fallbacks might be the way to go," he said.

Baldric chuckled. "Agreed," he said.

"That settles it, then," Tess said, just as a small metal thorn stabbed at her from the wall. If she hadn't seen a similar defense mechanism on the Ruinous Child, she probably wouldn't have yanked her hand back in time. She leaned in to get a closer look, but as soon as she did, four more thorns stabbed at her face, as if trying to keep her from getting too close. "Well, this is annoying."

Whatever defensive trap she'd triggered, it was now affecting the entire wall, transforming it into a giant pincushion. Thorns stabbed from the stone at irregular intervals, then retracted seamlessly into the wall, making it impossible to examine the area or predict where the next patch would appear.

"Let me look," Cazrin said, when Tess let out a growl of frustration. "There might be a magical element to this puzzle."

"I think I've almost got it, I—" Tess stopped when she saw Cazrin looking at the wall, her face creased in determination. She was right, Tess realized. If these traps were magical in nature, or related in some way to the Ruinous Child, Cazrin would have more insight than any of them.

Tess stepped back to give the wizard more space. Cazrin approached the wall, watching the thorns appear and disappear, as if looking for patterns. She held up her staff and cast a spell to detect any magic that might be hidden in the wall.

"There," she said after a moment, pointing to a group of thorns about halfway down the wall. "It's so quick, you almost miss it, but not all the thorns are the same. Some of them have a patch of illusory magic right below them. It looks like they're concealing a small metal plate."

"Big enough for a fingertip?" Tess asked, her excitement rising.

"Probably," Cazrin said, meeting her gaze.

"Point them out to me as they appear," Tess said. She grinned. "Let's see how quick my reflexes are."

They crowded as close to the wall as they dared, and one by one, Cazrin called out the hidden metal plates beneath the thorns whenever they speared from the wall. Each time they did, Tess shot out her hand, pressing on the plates with her fingertip. There was a loud *click*, and the thorn locked into place and didn't sink back into the wall.

A few minutes later, they had ten thorns locked. Cazrin held up her hands, fingers splayed so that one hovered over each of the locked thorns. "I think it's another blood puzzle," she said.

"Of course it is," Anson said with a groan.

"Get ready," Cazrin warned, lightly pricking her fingers on each of the thorns. "Something's about to happen."

No sooner had she said it than a low rumbling echoed in the tunnel, and Tess felt the reverberation of some sort of mechanism or tumbler falling into place.

The thorns pulled away from Cazrin's fingers, glistening with blood as they sank into the stone wall. The last thing Tess saw before they disappeared was a flare of blue radiance as an arcane script suddenly shimmered into being where the thorns had been. Cracks formed in the stone wall, fissuring out from the depression and widening, until the entire wall broke open in a cloud of dust, revealing a searing disk of blue light, roughly as tall as Tess and as wide as the tunnel that they stood in.

"It's a portal," Cazrin said in a hushed voice.

"I guess we really are on the right track." Tess met Baldric's gaze.

The dwarf gave a curt nod. "We are, but somehow it doesn't reassure me."

"I should go first with the Ruinous Child," Cazrin said, stepping forward. "There might be protections on the portal to prevent unwelcome visitors to Alagesheth's lab."

"Think they'll stop Lorthrannan?" Anson asked.

Cazrin's wince was answer enough for Tess.

"We'll be right behind you," Tess told Cazrin as the wizard stepped up to the portal. "Be careful."

Cazrin nodded and, with the book held tightly in her hands, stepped into the glowing circle, letting the light engulf her. Tess put away her cat mask and followed, her heart thudding in her chest. The light was cool on her face, like a misty breeze after a spring rain.

Then, a physical force settled in her gut and her chest and *pulled.*

Tess felt like she was coming apart at the seams, pieces of her scattering to the wind as her stomach heaved and her vision went dark at the corners. She clung to consciousness by sheer force of will, and the next instant she was stumbling out the other side of the portal, gasping for breath, with sweat pouring down her face.

She looked down at herself, expecting to see her limbs rearranged or some other horror, but she was fine. Everything was right where it should be.

Cazrin stood a few feet away from her, propped against a tunnel wall, examining herself in much the same way Tess had. Their gazes met. "All in one piece," Cazrin said. "Let's not do that again."

"Agreed."

A soft *pop* echoed from behind her, and one by one, the others came bursting through the portal. Lark skidded to his knees, clutching his stomach, while Baldric and Anson leaned on each other for support. Uggie alone seemed unbothered by the journey. She came bounding through the portal with her tongue lolling happily out the side of her mouth. Then again, she was probably used to strange churnings and roiling in her gut.

"Does *everything* about this lich's magic have to be painful and unnatural?" Anson asked, wiping sweat off his brow.

"I think you answered your own question there when you said 'lich,'" Baldric pointed out.

Giving the others a moment to collect themselves, Tess looked around at their new surroundings. To her disappointment, not much had changed. They were in a tunnel lit by the portal's glow that seemed to dead-end at a wall about fifty feet away. But when Tess made her way cautiously down the tunnel, she heard wind whistling and discovered a hole in the cavern floor, roughly six feet in diameter. A set of stone steps led deeper into the ground in a tight, dizzying spiral.

"Fallbacks, get yourselves together and come look at this," Tess called out to the group. Uggie trotted over immediately, while it took Lark a moment more before he reluctantly picked himself up off the floor to trail behind Anson and Baldric.

Cazrin gazed down at the hole. "That looks promising," she said, pointing to the stairs. Spell lights were arranged at regular intervals along the wall on the way down, so they wouldn't need Cazrin's magic or any torches, at least for the time being. There was also a strange, glowing rune etched into the wall between two of the lights.

"What's that?" Baldric asked, pointing to the symbol.

"I think it's an elder rune," Cazrin said. "Alagesheth mentioned them multiple times in his notes. They're imbued with magical effects. If you trigger them, they'll sometimes give you a boon." She winced. "Other times, they'll harm you. It depends on Halaster's mood."

"Let's be safe and not mess with this one at all," Tess said, and the others nodded.

As Tess approached the stairs, a low rumble echoed down the tunnel, and the ground beneath her feet began to tremble.

An earthquake? All the way down here?

Instinctively, Tess braced herself against the tunnel wall, but the tremor ceased almost as soon as it had begun. Soft puffs of dust drifted from the tunnel ceiling, but otherwise there didn't appear to be any damage from the quake.

"That's less promising," Cazrin said.

"If these caverns are prone to tremors, those stairs could be unstable," Anson said as he gazed down into the hole, the wind stirring his hair.

"Wonderful," Baldric muttered. "Painful, unnatural, *and* unstable."

"If someone falls, I can catch them," Cazrin said. "Well, not catch, exactly, but I can slow them down."

"What if we all fall?" Lark asked dubiously.

Cazrin hesitated. "I can catch most of us," she said.

The bard nodded. "All right, as long as I'm one of them." He glanced at the others. "Ready?"

"I'll go in front," Tess said. "Cazrin and Anson can come behind me, and Cazrin can be ready to catch me if I hit a bad spot. The rest of you stay near the walls and watch your footing if another one of those tremors happens. Let's get moving."

They descended the steps slowly, testing the stability of the stone, but it was surprisingly secure. Tess stopped them once to disable a trap that would have triggered a section of the wall to sweep open like a door, knocking an unsuspecting person off the steps, but other than that, they encountered no obstacles.

Until they got about halfway down, and a second, much stronger tremor rumbled through the cavern, strong enough that the magical illumination on the walls flickered and danced.

Tess pressed her back against the wall and grabbed on to Anson, who in turn grabbed on to Cazrin, and so on. Tess's teeth clacked together painfully as she tried to keep her footing. She looked up at the stone stairs above their heads, willing them to stay intact and not break apart and bury them.

The tremor seemed to go on forever, but finally the shaking lessened and ceased. Baldric coughed on the stone dust filling the air, and Uggie went into a violent sneezing fit.

"Everyone all right?" Tess asked when the dust had settled.

There were nods and murmurs of assent, though everyone was looking up at the spiraling stone above their heads with trepidation.

"Let's get moving," Anson said. "I want to get off these stairs."

Tess wasn't about to argue. She led the way down the stairs again, quickening her pace because she could see the bottom of the shaft at last. It lay about fifty feet below them, and there was a door in the wall made of what looked like carved obsidian.

Another tremor struck.

Tess's foot slipped on the edge of the stair. She teetered dangerously forward, but Anson grabbed the fold of her cloak and yanked her back. She bumped into his side, and he put an arm across her shoulders and pushed her against the wall. The others managed to crowd close, but Uggie got her legs tangled up on the shuddering steps, and she slipped off.

"Aw, Hells," Baldric growled, and he lunged for her, reaching for the closest tentacle he could grab. He didn't have the leverage, though, and Uggie fell off the stairs, yanking Baldric after her.

"Hold on!" Cazrin whipped her staff off her back, chanting the words to a spell as she pointed it at Baldric and Uggie.

Instantly, their plummet became a slow, meandering float, and as the tremors slowed and stopped once again, Tess leaned over the side of the stairs to watch them drifting gently down to the floor.

"My thanks, Cazrin!" Baldric called up to them, then, "Get off me, beast!"

Uggie was trying to run in midair, using her tentacles to grab on to Baldric's leg and pull herself toward him.

"Well, now I've seen everything," Anson said, shoulders shaking with laughter. "Baldric just risked his life for Uggie."

"I heard that, and I did not!" Baldric shouted back indignantly. "It was a reflex, that's all! I was afraid she'd snatch at everyone with her tentacles and drag us all off the stairs."

"Makes perfect sense," Lark said as Tess ushered them the rest of the way down the stairs to catch up to Baldric and Uggie. "You were just protecting the group."

"And don't you forget it!"

Finally, they reached the bottom of the shaft. Tess leaped off the last stair with a sigh of immense relief. "Well, now we know why Alagesheth abandoned this hideout," she said. "Too many earthquakes."

"Makes you wonder if the way forward is going to be blocked by cave-ins," Anson mused.

"Only one way to find out." Tess strode over to the door and examined it for traps. To her surprise, she found nothing, which gave her an uneasy feeling. Why were there no protections on the door?

"Cazrin," Tess said, "can you see if there's any magic guarding the door that I'm missing?"

Cazrin stepped up to the door and made a sweeping gesture with her staff. Her gaze narrowed on the latch. "There is magic on it," she said, "but the book is also reacting to it." She held up the Ruinous Child in one hand. The arcane symbols on the cover flashed with a deep crimson glow. "I think we'll be all right passing through, but a group that isn't carrying the Ruinous Child is going to get a nasty shock." When Tess just looked at her, she amended, "A literal shock, like a lightning bolt to the face."

"Good," Lark said from behind them. "I don't know about the rest of you, but I, for one, wouldn't mind the lich's group getting a lightning bolt to the face."

There was also a chance that the traps might take out a few of the Zhentarim, Tess thought. All of that gave them an advantage, and they were going to need it.

Cazrin handed off her staff to Anson so she could hold the book in one hand and grab the latch with the other. Slowly, she pulled the door open. It moved easily, unaffected by the tremors or the passage of time down here. Beyond the door, there was another short tunnel, this one choked with debris from past cave-ins. At the end of it, the passage appeared to open up again, but there were piles of rocks blocking their way forward.

"Looks like we have some digging to do," Tess said grimly.

There was a chorus of groans, but they set to work anyway, digging, shifting aside larger boulders—or magically lifting them away, in Cazrin's case. By the time they cleared a gap in the pile, they were sweating and dirty and tired. Luckily, there were no more tremors to slow their progress, but Tess had a feeling the calm wasn't going to last.

"I think this is big enough that we can squeeze through," Baldric said, tossing aside a large, flat rock and peering into the space they'd made. "Hope so, anyway, because I'm tired of playing excavator."

"What can you see in there?" Lark asked. He was standing at the bottom of a pile of rocks, one leg propped on a large, lumpy boulder. "Please don't say more rocks."

"Nah," Baldric said, sighing. "Worse than that. Bones. The biggest pit of bones I've ever seen in my life."

CHAPTER 31

L ark wasn't a superstitious person by nature.
However.

As he crawled through the opening they'd dug out of a tunnel in the darkest bowels of Undermountain while yet another tremor rolled through the cavern, making him stumble and nearly plunge face-first into a pit of bones, he was beginning to question whether some divine entity or force of nature might be having a laugh at his expense.

Every sensible instinct he possessed told him that it had been a mistake to stay with the party after the first night they'd spent in The Wander Inn. He should have just slipped away quietly in the night, and he'd never have ended up in a bone pit in Undermountain on a fool's errand to destroy an evil book.

But he hadn't left, and he'd been more than a little indignant when Gustan had suggested to the rest of the party that he would cut and run at the first opportunity. That they couldn't count on him.

He was *here*. Wasn't that enough?

He flattened himself against the wall of the chamber. A narrow lip of stone encircled the huge bone pit, offering them a path to the other side of the chamber, where there was another door half-blocked by a cave-in. The bone pit itself was filled with as much stone as bones, from all manner of humanoids and monstrous creatures.

"Is that a dragon skull?" Lark demanded as he shimmied along the wall. "Did that lich haul a dragon down here? What is this place *for?*"

Tess turned to look where he pointed. There were more magical lights arranged along the wall, casting bluish-purple glows across the elf's face. "The entity Baldric spoke to called it a laboratory, so it was probably some kind of experiment."

"Something to do with Alagesheth's quest for immortality," Cazrin said. She was paging through the Ruinous Child, looking for more information. If Baldric was the dowsing rod leading them through this place, the book had been like a master key, granting them safe passage.

Lark should have been happy about that, but for some reason, he grew more rattled every time he looked at the thing. Part of it was the aura the book gave off. He felt it like a physical weight on the back of his neck, like eyes staring at him, finding fault.

That was what was most unsettling: the idea that the thing was observing them, making them dependent on it to survive this place. Lark didn't want to be dependent on an evil magical tome.

They reached the other end of the chamber, where a set of stone steps led up to an octagonal platform suspended above the bone pit. Out of the corner of his eye, Lark caught something that gleamed golden at the top of the stairs.

Tess was examining the door that led out of the room, her lockpicking tools in hand. The rest of the party gathered around her, clearing away the rocks blocking the door. Lark drifted away from the group, wanting to put some space between himself and that damn book.

And it worked. With each step he took, he felt lighter, as if a yoke he hadn't known he was wearing was suddenly removed from his neck. He breathed a sigh of relief and walked up the steps, drawn by the golden gleam and the sense of freedom.

Arcane symbols were etched into the platform, forming a rough circle that pulsed with golden light. Lark was faintly disappointed. He'd hoped the gleam was a pile of gold, maybe something culled from the unfortunate victims who'd ended up in the bone pit.

"Lark, what are you doing up there?" Anson called to him. "It's not safe to wander."

"It's all right," Tess said. "He knows what he's doing. Lark, you find anything up there?"

"There's a magic circle," Lark said, bending closer to inspect it. "Cazrin, you might want to take a look." As much as he hated to bring the Ruinous Child into his orbit again, this might be something they could use.

"I'll be right there," Cazrin said, but Lark wasn't paying attention. The arcane markings were pulsing faster now, and little sparks jumped from one carved symbol to the next, the light pooling in the grooves like liquid gold. There was a song lyric somewhere in that, Lark thought absently, squinting against the light to see if he could translate any of the symbols.

He detected the faint hum of energy an instant too late.

Lark reared back just as twin ropes of golden light sprang from the circle and wrapped around his wrists. Lark found himself yanked to the floor in the center of the circle, spread-eagle as two more golden ropes wound themselves around his ankles. Pinned on his stomach, Lark felt the energy humming against his chest, like the magic was building up to something.

Gods above, he'd done it again. Panic welled up inside him. Tess had lectured him and lectured him about following instructions, and the minute she'd trusted him to act on his own, he'd fallen into disaster anyway.

She was going to be unbearably smug about this.

"Help!" he cried. "Little help here!"

"Lark!" Cazrin said, as her soft footsteps came running up the stairs. "Why didn't you wait? I said I was coming!"

"Cazrin, I did not *ask* to be grabbed by the magical golden grabby hands and stretched like a rabbit over an open flame," Lark said irritably. "Just get me out of here, please!"

"We've got a problem," Anson said, as his heavier footfalls came up the steps.

"What?" Lark twisted his head around, trying to look back at the two of them, but he couldn't move his body much, and the magical humming was beginning to give him a headache. He could feel it rattling his teeth.

"It's the ceiling," Baldric called out. It sounded like he was still over by the door with Tess. "There's a metal trapdoor right above the circle. Sounds like something's about to be dropped on top of him."

"Hold on," Cazrin said. Lark heard the end of her staff rap sharply against the floor. A flare of light filled his vision, Cazrin grunted, and then . . . nothing.

"What's going on?" Lark demanded. He flexed his arms against his bonds, but they held fast. "I thought you were getting me out of here—ouch!" A stinging pain shot along the length of his forearm and rapidly became a burn. "What in the Hells is that?"

"Acid," Anson said, his voice strained as if he were trying to lift a boulder. "Dripping from the ceiling. Cazrin used her magic to keep the trapdoor mostly sealed, but there must be a waterfall of the stuff waiting behind it, and it's seeping through the cracks. I'm trying to move the platform out of the way."

"This will help." Baldric muttered a quick prayer, and a shimmering aura settled over Lark's body like a blanket. "That shield will protect you from the acid, but I can't keep it up forever, and it isn't impenetrable. We need to get him out of there."

"The bone pit." Lark's mouth had gone dry. "So, the lich brings his victims in here and dissolves their flesh and just . . . what . . . keeps the bones as trophies?" He swallowed convulsively and began yanking at the golden ropes. "I'm sorry. I was a fool. I'll never wander off again. Please, get me out of here right now!"

"Lark, stay calm." Tess had joined them now. "Anson, stop trying to move the platform. It's not budging. Keep an eye on that door, and make sure nothing comes through. Cazrin, can you dispel the magic in this circle while Baldric keeps the shield up?"

"Probably," Cazrin said, "but my magic is the only thing holding the trapdoor shut at the moment, and if I let the spell go . . ."

"I don't want to be dissolved by acid, thanks very much," Lark said. He resisted the urge to beat his head against the floor. "Isn't there another way?"

"There's always another way," Tess said. "I just need to get up there to the trapdoor and jam the thing shut. Won't take a minute."

That was exactly what Lark wanted to hear, but he was distracted from his relief by movement from the bone pit below him. He couldn't see the whole of it from where he lay, but he could just glimpse a small portion of it in the corner of the room near where they'd come in. Several of the bones there were shifting minutely, as if something moved underneath them, a swimmer coming up for air.

"Um, Anson," Lark said, trying to pull the fighter's attention. It was probably just a rat, that was all, some scavengers looking to pick the bones clean. "Can you see what's happening in the corner over there?"

"What do you mean?" A boot scraped, and then Anson let out a blistering round of curses, followed closely by the sound of his broken sword leaving its scabbard. "Tess, we've got company! There's something hiding in the bone pit!"

It wasn't hiding anymore. Centered in Lark's line of sight as he lay helpless in the circle, a sinuous, twisting column of bone rose slowly from the pit, crowned by a serpent's skull with jaws that creaked open to reveal uneven rows of teeth and a pair of impressively long fangs.

"Oh Gods," Lark breathed. His heart hammered in his chest. "I take it back, let the acid come. I'd rather this was over quickly."

"Just hang in there," Cazrin said tightly. "It's a bone naga, Anson. Alagesheth had notes on them in the Ruinous Child, and now I see why. Be careful! It'll have magic."

Wonderful.

The bone creature fixed its empty eye sockets on Lark and corkscrewed through the air toward him, skeletal jaws flexing to take a big, juicy bite. Lark wanted to shut his eyes, but somehow, he couldn't make himself look away from the undead monstrosity.

A shadow fell over him, and a pair of booted feet stepped into his line of vision.

Anson.

"What are you doing?" Lark yelped. "Get out of the way!"

"Nah," Anson said, his voice darkly humorous. "I like the view from here."

Lark raised his head just in time to see the bone naga strike at Anson, who caught the blow with his broken sword, wedging the blade into the corners of the thing's mouth to keep its jaws at bay. The creature tried to pull back and flee, but Anson drove the blade in deeper, halting its retreat. An unearthly hiss filled the chamber as the creature thrashed on the end of Anson's sword, its body stirring up small tornadoes of bones from the pit while Anson stood calm and still as a sentinel, guarding Lark.

Despite his terror, Lark found himself wanting to compose an epic ballad in Anson's name.

"Hold him there!" Tess shouted.

Lark wrenched around to see the elf scrambling up one of the chains securing the platform. Baldric had his mace out, the head glowing like a hot coal as he brandished it in front of him. The blue gem in his helm flashed as he continued to channel his divine magic into shielding Lark.

"Indefinitely?" Anson shouted back, his voice strained with the effort of holding the bone naga at bay.

"Next hour or so," Tess said, then launched herself from the chain, grabbed on to the trapdoor mechanism attached to the ceiling, and dangled there by one arm. With her other hand, she grabbed a tool from her glove and proceeded to try to jam it into the mechanism.

They were all fixated on trying to save him, Lark thought with no small amount of wonder. They were standing under an acid waterfall fighting a bone serpent when they should have just left him there and strode out the door. He wouldn't have blamed them. Much.

A loud metal crunch sounded above his head, followed by Tess's triumphant shout. "Got it! The mechanism's jammed, so the trapdoor should stay shut. Let the spell go, Cazrin, and help Lark!"

"Letting go!"

Should? Lark thought.

He braced himself as Cazrin began casting.

"Heads up!" Anson shouted, just as the bone naga twisted out of his grip, driving him to his knees at the edge of the magic circle. Lark was afraid the magic of the glyph would reach out to trap him too, but it seemed it could hold only one target at a time. Small blessing, that.

Anson lunged, slashing at the naga's body. Bone chips flew, and the creature reared back with a pained shriek, an eerie, hollow echo through its bones. The shriek softened, turning into something that sounded like whispers. Or maybe . . . chanting.

Oh no.

Cazrin's voice rose as she finished the spell. Lark felt the magic tethers at his wrists and ankles loosening just as a ball of sparking light formed at the back of the naga's throat and burst out in a bolt of lightning.

"Watch out!" Lark vaulted to his feet, and the party hurled themselves off the platform and into the pit of bones just as the lightning bolt struck the platform with a teeth-rattling *boom.*

CHAPTER 32

Tess was still dangling from the trapdoor mechanism when the lightning bolt struck her. There was the briefest instant of white-hot pain shooting up her arm and the sensation of her heart spasming in her chest as if someone had gripped it in a fist. Then there was nothing.

When she came back to herself, she was lying in the bone pit with what felt like a human skull digging into her lower back. Baldric crouched over her, healing light fading from his fingertips.

"Was I knocked out?" Tess mumbled as she struggled to sit up.

Baldric grunted. "Your eyes were open, but you weren't moving, and you took that blast point-blank. I thought you were dead." He wiped the sweat from his forehead. "Scared some more years off my life."

"Thanks for the save," Tess said, giving him a tired smile.

She surveyed the impromptu battlefield. A few feet away, Cazrin and Lark were struggling up a rough ladder of bones they'd constructed to pull themselves out of the pit. It didn't look as if they'd taken a hit from the lightning bolt. Uggie was waiting for them at the top. It looked like she'd been bitten at least once by the bone naga, but she was still trotting around happily with a bone clamped in her jaws.

As Tess climbed to her feet, she noticed that small patches of her clothing had been charred black, pieces of cloth flaking off as she moved.

That was disconcerting.

Up on the platform, Anson still faced off with the bone naga. He had a long black scorch mark down one leg and bled from a crescent-shaped bite wound on his left shoulder. But he'd landed a fair number of blows himself. Pieces of the bone naga's body had been chipped away, and Anson showed no signs of tiring, despite his wounds.

"He's going to drop dead if he keeps up that pace," Baldric said, wading through the bone pit toward the fray.

"Story of Anson's life," Tess muttered, following him. He'd sooner get bitten in half than let anything get to them while they were vulnerable. It was what she loved and feared most about him.

Baldric let out a roar as he charged the naga. Fire erupted along his mace as he slammed it into the creature's body, knocking a flaming chunk out of it. The serpent hissed and swung round to face them, but Tess was there with her dagger, hacking at the base of the thing's body, chipping at bone, and harrying it from the opposite side.

"Share some of the fun, will you, Anson?" Baldric called up to the fighter, who'd paused in his relentless assault when the creature swung away, out of his reach. "Take a breather . . . and a healing potion," the cleric commanded with a dark frown.

For a second it looked like he was going to argue, but Anson met Baldric's gaze and nodded gratefully. He stepped back and reached into the bag of holding for a potion. Tess and Baldric kept up their attacks from either side, and the creature appeared to be slowly weakening.

"Back up, you two," Lark shouted. He and Cazrin had made it out of the pit and were poised to attack, Lark's hands on his lute. Cazrin was already chanting.

Tess ceased her attack and scurried backward over the bones. Baldric did the same, just in time for a sphere of fire to come streaking across the room, engulfing the bone naga at the same time a thunderous wave blasted it back across the pit. Blistering heat rolled over Tess's body, and she was certain that when she looked in the mirror later, she would find she no longer had eyebrows.

The naga exploded, sending flaming shards of bone in all directions. Tess threw up her hands to protect her face as she ran, tripping on imp skulls, human thigh bones, and dragon teeth, toward the bone ladder Cazrin and Lark had used to escape the pit. Baldric came stumbling and cursing behind her.

Cazrin reached down to help pull her out of the pit. "Sorry about that!" the wizard said. "I thought I gave you plenty of time to get out of the way!" She caught Tess feeling for her eyebrows and said sheepishly, "They're still there. Mostly."

"Good enough," Tess said. "Thanks for finishing it off."

The sound of grinding metal drew her gaze to the ceiling. The tool she'd wedged into the mechanism had burst free, and the trapdoor opened, spilling a deluge of acid onto the now inert glyph on the platform. The acrid smell made Tess's nose scrunch, and her eyes streamed from the burn.

Lark stared at the spot where he'd been tied down only a moment ago. "That was close," he said in a choked voice, looking up at the others. "Thanks for, you know, not running out on me."

Anson gave him an incredulous look. "Did you actually think we would?"

"Well . . ." Lark's shoulders hunched defensively. "Maybe, if there was no other way to save me. It would have made sense. Even I wouldn't have been able to fault you for it."

"Well, we wouldn't have done it," Tess said. "We're all together in this, remember?"

Slowly, Lark nodded. He reached out a hand to Anson. "Thanks for keeping me from getting my face bitten off."

Anson clasped his forearm. "Anytime," he said with a grin. He stepped back and held up a gleaming silver key, its triangular bow engraved with a lightning bolt. "Looks like I've joined the tavern club," he said. "It appeared while I was resting, when Tess and Baldric stepped in to cover me."

"That's great," Tess said, trying not to feel the sting of still being without her own key. She glanced at Lark, and their eyes met in a rare moment of commiseration.

"Saving the best for last," Lark said with a shrug.

"Obviously," Tess agreed, taking stock of the party's condition. They had bigger problems than who had or hadn't been admitted to the tavern club.

The potion Anson had taken had closed his shoulder wound, but he limped a bit on his leg. Tess still had lightning burns, and the rest of them were more beat up than she'd realized. They needed to rest and regroup. Maybe they could just take a minute here by the side of the pit to regain some of their strength.

"Let's take a breath before moving on," Tess told the others. She didn't expect them to argue, and indeed, no one did. They slumped to the floor near the door and took out their waterskins and some food to pass around.

Tess automatically checked on Cazrin and the Ruinous Child. The wizard was sitting cross-legged on the floor, the book beside her. She was holding a slender, moldy pouch in her hands.

"Where did you get that?" Tess asked, sliding down the wall to sit beside her.

"I found it in the bone pit while Lark and I were rummaging around making that ridiculous ladder to climb out," Cazrin said. "As soon as I touched it, I felt something. I think whatever's inside might be magical."

"I found one too," Lark said, emptying the contents of a black leather pouch onto the floor in front of him. Platinum coins gleamed in the light from the wall sconces. "Just as magical," he said on a sigh of pleasure.

"Finally!" Baldric slapped Lark on the back. "We might turn a profit on this job yet."

Cazrin lifted the pouch flap, revealing two long, slender sticks tucked inside. She carefully eased them out of the pouch, and Tess realized they weren't sticks at all.

They were wands.

Cazrin murmured a quick incantation, moving her fingers over the wands. Her brow furrowed in curiosity. "One's a puzzle," she said, laying the longer one next to her on the floor. "Its capabilities aren't clear. The other is for channeling offensive spells. "

"Can you make use of them?" Baldric asked.

Cazrin tossed aside the empty pouch and slid the wands into her own satchel. "Oh yes," she said, smiling. "I'll need to study them later, but I can definitely make use of these."

Tess leaned back against the wall and closed her eyes. Things were looking up. They just needed to find the lich's lab and get rid of the Ruinous Child. Then maybe they could take some more time in the bone pit and whatever other rooms this place had, strip it clean of its treasures, and turn a profit on the job, just like Baldric said.

A tingle started in her fingertips where her hands rested on the ground. At first, Tess thought her hands had gone to sleep, but then the feeling spread up her back, a subtle vibration that heralded another tremor.

"Not again," she groaned. "How many of these stupid—"

She stopped. Her eyes were drawn to the pit in front of her. The tremors were making the bleached bones dance and rattle in an unnerving cacophony, but that wasn't what had attracted her attention. It was the fact that the bones were *sinking*, as if they were being pulled through a sieve. The tremor intensified, and if they hadn't already been sitting down, Tess knew they would have fallen. She grabbed Cazrin's arm on one side and Baldric's on her other side, and together the party made another human chain to keep themselves steady.

"What's happening?" Lark demanded. Now pieces of the cavern ceiling were falling, loud rumbles and crashes filling the chamber.

"We need to get out of here," Tess said. "Anson, can you reach the door?"

"Look!" Cazrin shouted.

Tess didn't want to look, but she did. Within the bone pit, a massive sinkhole had opened. Bones dropped away into darkness, but something else was rising from the pit, something round and dark and massive. Tess's mouth dropped open as she recognized the shape emerging from the pit.

It wasn't any natural earthquake that caused the tremors here. It was an immense tunneling creature, eating its way inexorably through the rock as it carved out a home in the honeycomb of caverns. Tess had read about these creatures, though she'd never dreamed of seeing one up close.

A purple worm.

The drawings Tess had seen of the creatures hardly did this one justice. The mouth of the worm came into view first, a ten-foot-wide gaping maw ringed with jagged teeth like massive stalagmites. It burrowed straight up out of the bone pit toward the chamber ceiling, its segmented body pulsing and heaving, bruise purple in the light and covered in bone spurs the size of a full-grown human.

"Get to the door," Tess barked, pushing Cazrin toward the exit from the chamber. The only thing saving them from being swallowed was that the worm had tunneled straight up and past them without noticing the tiny cluster of prey clinging to the side of the bone pit.

The tremors caused by the worm's passing made it impossible to stand, so the party crawled to the door and hurtled through. Anson came last and slammed it shut behind them. The six of them huddled on the floor on the other side of the door, waiting for the tremors to stop.

Finally, after a few minutes, the shudders quieted, and the only sound left in the tunnel was the party's harsh breathing. Tess inched back to the door on her knees and opened it a crack to look through.

The bone pit was gone, leaving a gaping hole into a dark abyss. In the ceiling, there was now another tunnel going straight up into the unknown.

"Well, at least we know where the earthquakes are coming from now," Cazrin said breathlessly. "I bet that's why Alagesheth really abandoned his lab. He made notes in the Ruinous Child about 'disturbances in the caverns,' but I didn't know what he was referring to. If a purple worm moved in next door, it would make conducting research terribly complicated, don't you think?"

"Or maybe Halaster sent it to drive Alagesheth out of the neighborhood." Tess felt a hysterical laugh bubble up inside her as she closed the door on the chamber. "Either way, I think this certainly complicates things," she said. "Maybe we'll get lucky, and the worm will eat Lorthrannan too."

"Wouldn't that be grand?" Lark said dreamily. "There's a story in that. The titanic struggle of a lich and a purple worm."

"And the adventuring party caught in the middle," Baldric said.

"No songwriting right now," Tess declared. "We're moving on, as fast as possible."

Getting to her feet, she scouted ahead. She hadn't taken much time to study these carved passages, but now she could see they were about ten feet in diameter—just like the other tunnels they'd encountered, the roughly scalloped edges of the walls mimicking the burrowing pattern of the worm.

It was possible the entirety of the lich's lair had been carved up by the creature over the centuries, which would explain the collapsed tunnels, the rooms all spread out and half-buried by rubble and debris.

Tess led the party down the tunnel, silently praying this wasn't an often-used path by the worm, or at least that it had tunneled far enough away that it wouldn't be back anytime soon.

When they came to another intersection, Tess called Baldric up so that he could use the memory of his vision to guide them. She also reluctantly called on Cazrin to consult the Ruinous Child.

Cazrin dutifully opened the tome, and as the pages fluttered from one side of the book to the other, Tess wrinkled her nose at the stench of rot and decay. Cazrin confirmed via passages written by Alagesheth that there was a ritual chamber somewhere in the center of the mazelike caverns. She wasn't sure how long it would take them to travel there with the worm's having carved up the space, but at least they knew they were on the right track.

Still, Tess was uneasy. Did the Ruinous Child know what they intended? Cazrin had explained that while the book was sentient and contained aspects of Alagesheth's personality—specifically his malicious nature and cruelty—the tome seemed unaware of the events happening in the world outside its pages and unconcerned with the passage of time.

As far as Cazrin could tell, the book's sole desire was to pass on its terrible legacy, but only after causing the person who sought its knowledge as much pain and despair as possible. A terrible price for terrible power.

Joke's on it, then, Tess thought grimly, *since we're here to end it.* She wondered if Alagesheth himself had been a little afraid of his own creation. Maybe that's why he'd made sure to devise a way to destroy the book. An inanimate object becoming a threat to its creator—there was some dark humor in that.

"This way," Baldric said, turning them down yet another worm-chewed tunnel.

They walked on. Time had begun to feel meaningless down here, and Tess didn't like that either. She could never live so far underground, away from the sun. And the idea that they were following the path of a gargantuan creature that could swallow them all whole wasn't doing anything to boost her confidence.

Anson caught her staring at the bite marks on the tunnel walls and gave her a reassuring smile. "You know, I served on a merchant ship for a while," he said, pitching his words to carry to the rest of the group. "We sailed a route between Baldur's Gate and the Moonshae Isles once, and we stumbled on a kraken's lair. Just this little nub of rock—nothing to look at above the surface—but in the depths, it was hiding a creature that was more terrifying than anything I had ever seen. We watched it breach, close enough to our ship that I thought the wake it made would capsize us."

"Did you try to run?" Tess asked. She thought she'd heard all of Anson's stories, but the man was full of surprises.

"Of course we did," Anson said. He shrugged. "It wouldn't have mattered. If that monster had wanted to tear our ship to pieces, it would have. But it swam the other way, like we were nothing to it, and we lived."

"So, you think if we keep our heads down, the purple worm won't notice us?" Baldric said dryly.

Anson grinned. "No, I just wanted to tell you my kraken story."

They all laughed, and some of the tension eased as they continued on into the dark.

Finally, Baldric pointed ahead to an opening, a slender crack in the stone that led into another chamber.

"I'm hoping this isn't a second bone pit," Lark muttered as they approached.

Tess looked inside and then turned to Cazrin and Baldric. "No, but it might be a treasure trove for some of us," she said.

Cazrin peered in next, and her whole face lit up.

"Must be the lich's private study," Baldric murmured, looking around her into the room.

The chamber had been hung with tapestries of ancient cities along two of the walls, but they were faded and eaten away by time and whatever small creatures had made their way down here to feast on them. A large stone fireplace dominated the back wall, with moldy leather chairs and a threadbare rug placed in front of a cold hearth. On the fourth wall, there was a large oak desk that appeared to be in pristine condition—magically enhanced, Tess guessed—and behind that, a sealed glass display case with several tomes arranged inside on a bed of red velvet.

Tess moved ahead of the others through the room, scanning the floor and walls for traps before motioning the rest of them inside. She went over to the glass case and performed the same inspection, then nodded to Baldric and Cazrin, who immediately came over and lifted the lid to look at the books on display. The Ruinous Child stayed dormant in Cazrin's hand, and the books in the case seemed unbothered by its presence.

That was some luck, Tess thought with a sigh of relief. She didn't think the group could take on another monster springing out of a tome, even if they had managed a rest earlier.

Lark and Anson searched the room for hidden treasures while Uggie munched on the rug by the fireplace. Tess examined the tapestries and found a door hidden behind one of them. It wasn't a great attempt at concealment, but Tess didn't imagine Alagesheth had been worried about unwanted guests.

She examined the door for traps and then tried the latch, only to find it locked. Taking out her picks, she set to work. In just a few minutes, the lock yielded, but Tess didn't open the door just yet. She went over to Cazrin and Baldric to see what they'd discovered in the books.

Cazrin was beaming. "It's wonderful, Tess," she gushed. "Historical texts and at least one ancient spellbook. As far as we can tell, neither of them was composed by Alagesheth. These were tomes he acquired and magically preserved."

"Best part is, they aren't alive either," Baldric said.

"Well, that is a welcome change," Tess said. "They'll be safe in the bag of holding. We can examine them later, but we need to keep moving."

When the room was searched and stripped, they gathered around the door, Anson holding back the tapestry. Tess eased it open with a creak and peered through.

"I don't want to get anyone's hopes up," Baldric said, "but if my vision's right, this should be . . ."

Tess's heart fluttered in her chest.

"It is," she whispered.

They'd found the lich's laboratory.

CHAPTER 33

The chamber was massive, the cavern ceiling arching at least a hundred feet above their heads, riddled with stalactites that gleamed with magical light at their tips, another example of the lich's magic enduring long past his demise. The magic created a starlight effect above their heads that Cazrin marveled at.

Even Alagesheth, buried in his research and obsessed with creating his awful legacy, missed seeing the stars.

The purple worm had been through this chamber, many times by the looks of it. Fissures gaped in the floor. Some were shallow and small enough to step over, while others were yawning chasms that disappeared into untold depths. Faint skittering and squeaking sounds could be heard from the darkness within, as if creatures clung to the walls.

To her left was a slight depression in the cavern floor. Within it was a nest of cages and stalagmites that had rusted chains dangling from them. Old blood stained the cavern floor black. Some of the chains looked like they had been made to hold humanoid creatures, while others were big enough to restrain small dragons or other similar-sized beasts.

"That must have been where Alagesheth kept his live victims when he wasn't conducting his experiments," Cazrin said, pointing to the prison. If the lich had spent most of his existence searching for a way to protect his soul with an indestructible vessel, he would have needed to have many victims on hand to practice his methods. She gave a shudder. "Once he was . . . finished . . . his servants probably took them to the acid chamber to be . . . disposed of."

"Bastard was efficient—I'll give him that," Baldric muttered as they spread out through the chamber, moving cautiously in case there were more glyphs or other traps waiting for them.

In the center of the room, there was a stone island dominated by a lectern that looked like it had been carved out of the surrounding rock. Arcane symbols covered its surface, faintly glowing with red light. There were more bloodstains here.

"That would be Alagesheth's murder lectern, I expect," Lark said, wrinkling his nose in distaste.

Cazrin hovered her hand over the lectern, not touching the stone. She didn't have to. She could feel the power emanating from it, a subtle hum that was echoed in the Ruinous Child. The resonance was so similar. She felt something that was almost a sigh coming from the book, like a traveler returning home after a long journey.

"This is where the book was enchanted," Cazrin said softly. "It was imbued with Alagesheth's essence here. This is where we destroy it."

"Excellent news," Tess said. "How do we do it?"

Cazrin turned in a slow circle, scanning the rest of the room. On the back wall, a series of indentations in the stone formed rough shelves filled with row upon row of books, with what looked like a printing press sitting nearby. Affixed to the wall above the press were various diagrams. She was too far away to make out many details beyond that, but there had to be something useful there.

Unfortunately, there was a rather large, deep fissure separating her from those items.

"It looks like his staging area is back there," Cazrin said. "The place where his books were printed and bound. If we can get over the fissure, I might be able to find what we need."

"That won't be necessary."

The voice came from her left, near the cages. The hairs on the back of Cazrin's neck lifted, a crawling sensation sliding over her skin. She whirled in time to see a group of figures emerging from a door in the left-hand wall, one she swore hadn't been there before.

Lorthrannan and the Zhentarim had arrived.

In an unspoken accord, the party closed ranks around the lectern, putting their bodies in front of Cazrin and the Ruinous Child. Without taking her eyes off the lich or the six Zhents making their way into the chamber, Tess leaned over and whispered to Cazrin, "If we buy you time, can you get what you need and destroy that thing?"

Cazrin's stomach clenched with dread. "You can't fight Lorthrannan. He'll kill all of you."

"Well, that's very pessimistic," Lark said. "Aren't you the one who's always supposed to be about rainbows and happiness and 'magic is beautiful' kind of stuff?"

"None of us intend on dying, Cazrin," Anson said calmly. He patted Uggie's head, and the otyugh curled a tentacle around his knee. "It's going to be all right."

"It *is,* because I have an idea," Tess said.

"There it is," Baldric said. "I was waiting for the plan stage of this operation."

Tess shot Cazrin a quick, reassuring smile. "Just do what needs to be done. We got you." She turned to the others. "When it all starts to go bad, keep moving or find cover, but make as much noise as you possibly can. Do you understand?" She shot each of them a meaningful glance. "So. Much. Noise."

"All right," Cazrin said. "I'll try."

"Well met, Lorthrannan," Tess said, pitching her voice to carry across the cavern in a cheery greeting. "We didn't think you were going to make it."

"How *did* you make it?" Lark asked. "We figured you'd be hours behind us without that Ruinous Child to help."

Lorthrannan tossed back his hood, revealing the withered, papery flesh clinging in patches to his skull. His mouth—what remained of it—twisted in amusement.

"Did you truly believe those obstacles would slow us down?" he asked. His arms were folded, tucked into the sleeves of his black robe. "Your sojourn at Candlekeep should have shown you that neither you nor the tome can travel in secret for long."

"We managed to keep it hidden from you on the road back to Waterdeep," Anson said, "so we must not be doing too badly."

The lich laughed, a soft, dry sound that chilled Cazrin. "You weren't hidden from me," he said. "I prevented other interested parties from destroying you for the Ruinous Child, for which you should be thanking me, and I allowed you to live long enough to lead me here to Alagesheth's laboratory."

Tess sucked in an audible breath, but her expression didn't change. "Looks like we did you a favor, and you did us one," she said. "I'd say we're even, but who was the other person after us? Wait, let me guess. Valindra Shadowmantle? She can't be too happy that you're also chasing a book she covets."

Lorthrannan's expression hardened as his skeletal fingers clenched into a fist at his side. "On the contrary. She will be my partner in unlocking Alagesheth's research."

"Yet she's not here helping you now," Tess said, an edge of mockery in her voice. "But what do I know about secret lich clubs? They're so insular."

"Such a shame," Baldric agreed. "Members just gossiping and tearing each other down."

"*Literally* tearing each other, if Lorthrannan's face is any indication," Lark said.

Red light flared in the lich's eye sockets, and Tess muttered, "Too much, Lark."

"Listen, I never back down from a good insult."

Cazrin softly began casting a spell, channeling the magical energies through her staff into a spectral armor to protect her body from whatever was to come. Then she slowly began to back up, stopping when the heel of her boot reached the edge of the nearest fissure. There was about a three-foot gap, something she could easily traverse with a jump.

As long as she didn't slip.

Cazrin's palms began to sweat inside her gloves.

Lorthrannan made a gesture to the Zhentarim, who fanned out on one side of the cavern. In front of Cazrin, Anson shifted and cursed under his breath. Cazrin thought it was simply the presence of so many enemies that had unnerved him, until she followed his gaze to one of the Zhents.

It was the man they'd interrogated on the road outside of Waterdeep, the one who'd revealed to Anson that his brother was working with the Zhents and Lorthrannan.

"Isn't my brother going to show his face here?" Anson demanded of the man. "Or were you lying about that all along?" Baldric put a hand on his arm, but he shrugged it off. Uggie whined and bumped his knee.

The man's face twisted into a sneer. "I tried to warn you that you were in over your heads. Your brother ran like a coward the first chance he got. He—"

"That's enough," Lorthrannan said. He didn't even raise his voice, but the Zhent fell silent at once. The lich turned his gaze to Anson. "Your brother is a hunted man now, but don't worry, we'll find him soon. He stayed just long enough to tell me all I needed to know about you." He cocked his head. "How is your left knee, Anson? The one you favor ever since you impaled it on that nail as a child."

Anson opened his mouth, but no rebuttal came. Hurt crept into his eyes, though he struggled to hide it. Cazrin realized he'd been holding on to the slim hope that his brother really wasn't involved in this, that it had all been a lie.

Now that hope had been dashed.

Lorthrannan addressed the others. "All of you still have a chance to leave this chamber alive. Give me the Ruinous Child and swear yourselves as my servants. In time, you might prove useful to my plans."

Softly, Cazrin chanted the words to another spell, and when she felt it take hold, she drifted three inches off the ground, doing her best not to draw attention to herself or the flying spell.

"I don't believe that for a second," Tess interrupted, and the elf's musical laughter echoed in the chamber, nearly making Cazrin fumble her magic.

What was Tess doing?

"You don't believe you can be useful?" Lorthrannan said. "Then by all means—"

"Oh, we're much more capable than the band of merry fools you've brought with you," Tess said, cutting him off. "But that's not what I mean. I don't believe for a second that the only reason you haven't attacked yet is that you want to recruit us." She crossed her arms. "I think you've expended too many resources tracking us and fending off your Lady Shadowmantle friend, or whatever she is to you." She glanced at the rest of the party, who were gaping at her just like Cazrin was. "Think about it," she said. "That night we hid in the tavern and saw that unnatural storm in the east." She nodded at Lorthrannan. "That was you, wasn't it? You tried to convince Valindra Shadowmantle to partner with you, and you were going to use the Ruinous Child as leverage because you know how much she wants that tome."

Baldric nodded slowly. "Bet she didn't like the idea of dealing with a middleman, not when she could just rip the information she needed out of your desiccated body."

"She got fed up, and the two of you had a spell battle that reshaped a bit of the Sword Coast." Tess swept her gaze over the lich. "Since you're standing here in one piece, you didn't exactly lose, but I'm betting you didn't win either. You don't want another fight, so you think you can intimidate us into serving you."

"You two are brilliant," Lark said, grinning. "I've just noticed the Zhents are looking worse for wear themselves. Even your brother's little friend looks beaten down, Anson. No offense," he added, smirking.

"None taken," the man growled. "Don't worry, I'll make sure I have just enough energy left to finish *you* off."

"Stop," Anson said, taking a step forward.

The Zhents' hands tightened on their weapons. Everyone stood tense, waiting, then Lorthrannan raised a hand, and the warriors relaxed a fraction. "You can't master the Ruinous Child," he said. His gaze found Cazrin behind the group. "It's already left its mark on you," he added, in a sympathetic voice that made her want to scream. "You weren't meant to carry the kind of darkness with you that your ancestress did. It will hollow you out." He made a beckoning gesture. "Give it to me, and I'll reward you and your friends handsomely for your loyalty. Enough coin and powerful magic to enable you to go wherever you want. You need never return to Waterdeep and be hunted. The whole of the world will be open to you." His eyes flashed, and Cazrin drifted back, hovering at the edge of the fissure. "If you refuse, I *will* kill you and your companions, and I can ensure your deaths are excruciatingly painful. Make the right choice and save yourselves. There's no shame in choosing to live."

Cazrin swallowed, caught by the lich's hypnotic gaze. The fact that he knew of her ancestress had her feeling off-balance, adrift. What else could he have learned about her and the others?

But he offered her empty promises. She knew that as surely as she knew her own feelings for this group. The lich's eyes burned with barely concealed rage. He would make them suffer no matter what they chose. More than that, she knew all too well what lay within the Ruinous Child, and she knew no bargain was worth what the lich was offering.

But could she really destroy the book? It was a powerful, ancient, evil artifact, and it had already trapped her once. Why had she ever thought she'd be able to handle this? She was in over her head with magic, just like her family had always told her she would be one day. Her party was counting on her, and she was on the verge of failing them.

The doubts and fears crowded Cazrin's mind, keeping her frozen, unable to act.

Then she felt Baldric's hand rest on her shoulder, and she sensed Tess's presence nearby, silent as a shadow but an undeniable comfort.

"Out of all of us in this chamber, I'd put my best odds on Cazrin to handle that beast of a book," Baldric said gruffly.

"So would I," Anson said.

"Me too," Lark said, "mostly because I'd be terrible at it."

"Our answer is going to be no," Tess said cheerfully. "Anson, would you care to—"

Anson was moving before she'd even finished speaking. His sword was in his hands, and he charged to the edge of the fissure separating the two groups and jumped, the muscles in his legs flexing as he easily cleared the gap and landed on the other side, right in the midst of the Zhentarim. Uggie thumped after him, moving far less gracefully, but she still made quite an impact as she crashed into one of the Zhents, sinking her teeth into his leg.

Tess threw one of her paired daggers, burying it in the thigh of the closest Zhent, and she vanished, teleporting across the space into the fight so that Anson wasn't alone.

Lark sent a thunderous wave across the chamber that hit Lorthrannan head-on, driving him back several paces. It didn't seem to leave a scratch on him, but that wasn't the point. The cavern shook under the force of the spell, a beacon for the purple worm lurking somewhere out there in the dark.

Baldric finished casting a protection spell that settled over the group like a curtain of warm light. He stepped in front of Cazrin and drew his mace. "Go," he told her tersely. "I know you can do this. We'll face our demons together."

Emotion clogging her throat, Cazrin jerked her head in a nod. She didn't want to leave her companions alone in this fight, but Baldric was right. This was her chance to get what she needed to destroy the Ruinous Child.

Turning, she flew across the chamber and over the gaping fissures. She landed near the shelves carved into the cavern wall and immediately began to scan their contents, looking to the diagrams on the wall for guidance. They were covered in barely legible scribblings, and some of the parchment, without the benefit of magical protection, had rotted away over time. It would take hours to go through everything here, looking for clues.

Cazrin's hands shook as she ran them along the shelves, trying to think what to do. Alagesheth likely wouldn't have left the means to destroy the Ruinous Child just lying around for anyone to find. On a sudden inspiration, she reached into her satchel and pulled out the book. Holding it in her hands, she moved slowly along the shelves again. This time, a small section of the back wall gleamed with illusory magic—shelves of books that weren't actually shelves at all. Cazrin hurried to that section of the wall, moved aside the books, and placed her hand flush against the back of the shelf, her fingers finding a concealed latch.

An explosion filled the chamber behind her, the force of it slamming her into the wall. A curtain of heat spread across Cazrin's back, the worst of it thankfully absorbed by her spectral mage armor. The hidden door swung open, and she stumbled inside. Glancing over her shoulder, she could see that the remains of Lorthrannan's fireball had ignited all the flammable objects in the chamber. Nonmagical books on shelves along the walls, bits of ragged tapestries, and rugs laid out across the floor were all ablaze, filling the chamber with acrid smoke.

Her friends were scattered, running for cover. Baldric was furiously patting his cloak, which had caught fire, while Lark's right arm had been blackened from elbow to wrist. One of Uggie's tentacles flopped at her side as she chased a Zhent around the room. There was no sign of Tess, but Anson fought against three Zhents on the opposite side of the chamber, including his brother's friend. Another lay in a charred heap on the ground. Lorthrannan obviously didn't care how many of his own mercenaries he took out trying to get to the Ruinous Child.

But as the lich raised his hand to cast another spell, a massive tremor shook the cavern. Cazrin took to the air again to keep from falling. She held her breath, not quite daring to hope that Tess's wild plan had actually borne fruit . . .

The area of the cavern with the cages and chains began to sink. The rumbling in the ground became a deafening roar as the entire back half of the cavern collapsed in on itself, fissures opening wider, new cracks in the ground racing toward Lorthrannan, swallowing another of the Zhents along the way.

The lich vanished, reappearing safely behind the group of Zhents fighting Anson just as the purple worm burst from the cavern floor in a shower of rocks and debris. Its massive body loomed over the scene. Moving faster than Cazrin would have thought possible, it came crashing down to the floor, chewing through the stalagmites in its path as if they were kindling, surging toward the closest sound of movement, which just happened to be the group of Zhents and Anson.

What had they done?

"Anson, watch out!" It was Tess. She'd somehow gotten back to the stone lectern with Uggie and was firing her crossbow at Lorthran-nan.

Anson jumped out of the way of the worm plowing through the chamber as Cazrin frantically searched the secret room. It was empty except for a small table pushed against the back wall that held a single piece of parchment weighted down by a jar filled with glowing green liquid. The parchment appeared untouched by the ravages of time. Cazrin snatched it up, scanning the text quickly.

It was an unbinding ritual, a way to separate Alagesheth's essence from the book. He must have had it as a fail-safe in case the Ruinous Child grew too powerful. He hadn't wanted the child to supplant its creator while he was still alive.

But Cazrin was connected to the book now too, because she'd given it her blood. That bond was her way in.

This was it. This was how she could destroy the book.

She grabbed the jar and flew out of the room, across the chamber to the lectern, landing behind it. She let go of her flight spell just as another violent tremor rolled across the cavern, buckling and shattering the stone under her feet. Cazrin fell to the ground but clutched the glass jar to her chest, protecting it with her body. Rolling onto her side, she came up onto her elbow just as another sinkhole opened in the ground roughly thirty feet away, making room for a second massive purple body to explode from the floor.

Cazrin stared.

Another of the Zhents screamed as the emerging creature snagged his leg and bit it cleanly off at the knee. With another surge of its segmented body, it swallowed the man whole, his scream abruptly cut off as he disappeared inside the creature.

Two of them.

Two purple worms had made their nest in the lich's former lair.

"It's a party now!" Lark hollered. The worm's body swung toward the pile of rubble where he and Baldric were taking cover.

"Loviatar, if you could have my back here, I'll make this thing suffer!" The cleric reached out, his hands glowing with necrotic energy instead of healing light. He raked the worm in passing, leaving behind a dark, ugly slash in the creature's body. The worm recoiled, which likely saved Baldric and Lark from being swallowed whole. But they couldn't dive out of the way fast enough as the worm smashed into the stone, sending them and tons of rock flying across the chamber.

CHAPTER 34

They were all going to die.

That had been Tess's initial thought when the second purple worm burst from the cavern floor—rival, twin, mate, or maybe just best friend to the other worm, because the two of them somehow made space for each other in the cavern and immediately made it their mission to eat everything and everyone in the room.

Her plan had worked beyond her wildest dreams, and it was very possible that same plan would kill them all.

The sound of Lorthrannan's hissing, sibilant voice filled Tess's ears, distracting her from her panic. She looked up just in time to see the lich point in her direction. Green light illuminated his fingertip, and Tess and Uggie were up and moving, diving behind the lectern with Cazrin as that light became a beam that speared in their direction. The light sheared off part of the bottom of the lectern, leaving behind a cloud of dust that slowly drifted to the ground.

Tess's heart beat like a drum in her ears, her body breaking out in a cold sweat. If that beam had hit her, she had a feeling she'd be the pile of dust right now.

Cazrin uncurled from the ground next to her, a determined look fixed on her face as she stood up, took the Ruinous Child, and placed it on the lectern. She uncorked a jar of green liquid she carried in the crook of her arm. As Tess watched, she poured it into the runes carved in the lectern. The liquid spread fast and sure from rune to rune, as if it had a mind of its own, leaving a glowing green trail. A soft hum filled Tess's ears as ancient powers awoke within the lectern.

Cazrin glanced at Tess. "I know what to do," she said.

Tess's heart leaped, going from despair to hope and back again so quickly that it made her lightheaded. Her hands shook as she went for her crossbow again, ready to cover Cazrin while she worked, trusting her to get the job done.

The remaining three Zhentarim were running scared, trying to keep out of the reach of the purple worms. Lorthrannan had retreated to the edge of the pit where the first worm had appeared and was casting another spell.

There was no sign of Baldric or Lark from the pile of rubble where they'd been thrown, but Tess got eyes on Anson as he ran parallel to one of the fissures, sword ready, veering in the direction of the other purple worm.

"Oh no," Tess breathed, just as Anson jumped, landing on the back of the worm. He raised his sword and drove it to the hilt into the thing's body to create a handhold as the monster thrashed and slammed into the cavern wall, trying to dislodge the insect that was stinging it. But Anson was tenacious. He held on to the sword and closed his eyes, as if he were actually meditating in the midst of all the chaos. The wounds and bruises covering his body didn't slow him. He was in complete control, unshakable, immovable, and the worm could do absolutely nothing to stop him. Pure force of will drove Anson on.

"He's going to get himself killed if he stays up there!" Cazrin threw aside the empty jar. The lectern was glowing a vivid green now, the runes standing out in sharp relief from the rest of the stone.

It would be a very Anson thing to do, Tess thought grimly, but the fighter was in his happy place and was holding his own against the creature. With the monster whipping around the chamber in a frenzy, Lorthrannan was distracted from his casting and forced to move aside as a shower of stalactites rained from the cavern ceiling right where he'd been standing.

Tess took advantage of the distraction to shout across the cavern. "Baldric! Lark! Are you alive over there?"

Moans sounded from across the chamber, and a dwarven hand rose from the rubble to give a weak wave.

"We're in one piece!" Baldric called out.

"Stay under cover!" Tess shouted back. "Anson has one of the worms. Sort of."

Hysterical laughter—Lark—was the only answer. Tess understood the feeling completely.

Cazrin began to chant over the Ruinous Child, her eyes half-closed, hands spread above the lectern, not quite touching the book or the runes. Flickers of red light danced between her fingertips. The air around them shimmered for an instant, like a heat mirage on the horizon. Tess felt warmth caress her face and realized it was emanating from the lectern itself, or maybe the book, or both.

"Stop!" Lorthrannan shouted from across the chamber. He'd recovered from the stalactite shower and saw what Cazrin was doing. With a snarl of rage and frustration, he pointed at the closest purple worm and chanted a spell.

The monster rose in front of the lich—and then froze in place, a quiver going over its body. Slowly, it sank down before Lorthrannan, its toothy maw flexing. Tess tensed, hoping the worm was going to try to swallow the lich, but it seemed to be simply waiting.

Lorthrannan smiled.

A horrible feeling settled in Tess's gut. The purple worm was waiting for *instructions*. The lich had taken control of it with his magic.

"Kill them!" Lorthrannan shouted, pointing at Tess, Uggie, and Cazrin.

"We have to move!" Tess hadn't realized until that moment how horribly exposed they were in the center of this room beside the lectern. "You hear me, we need to—"

The words died as Tess turned to Cazrin. The wizard gave no sign that she'd heard Tess, and she didn't move. Her eyes were blank and staring, and she continued to chant under her breath.

"No, no, no," Tess murmured. "Is that still you, Cazrin?"

No response.

CAZRIN WAS NOT in the library now.

She was still in Alagesheth's lab, but everything was different. The purple worms, the lich, and the Zhents—even her friends—were gone. The chamber was unspoiled by cracks and dark fissures, looking as it must have in Alagesheth's time, with those same spell lights glittering above her like stars. The printing press hummed busily behind her, the only sound in the chamber.

But the shadowy figure loomed large from the lectern. Finger-sized thorns curved from its body as it towered over Cazrin. She could feel the weight of its malice like never before.

I would have given you the world, the shadow screeched. *I still can. It's not too late to turn back, to embrace all the gifts I offered you. You've already seen all the good you can do with the knowledge in these pages.*

Cazrin couldn't deny it. Ever since that day in the library, when she'd won the struggle with the Ruinous Child, the book had yielded to her. It had given her the tools to help her friends come this far. It hadn't threatened her. She'd been the one in control.

The shadow pressed closer, as if sensing an advantage. *You are more worthy a successor than any who have sought me before. The family who never valued you—you can show them how wrong they were, child. Embrace my legacy, and I will watch with a parent's pride as you go forth and thrive in the world.*

Each word was like a thorn digging into Cazrin's heart. It hurt more than anything else the Ruinous Child had tried to do to her. It hurt because there was a seed of truth wrapped in its promises and lies.

"You *are* everything I could have wanted," Cazrin admitted. "The knowledge I glimpsed in you was vast, and I could have turned that into something that made the world better. I could have tried to make my family approve of me." She swallowed, and her voice hardened. "But I know now that I'm enough, just as I am, and I don't give a damn about making *you* proud."

Cazrin called upon the bond in her blood, forcing her way into the connection between Alagesheth and the Ruinous Child.

Stop! Panic filled the shadow's voice now. *Upstart child! If you do this, I will take your life. I will ride the connection between us and boil the blood in your veins!*

"No, you won't," Cazrin said, feeling the tiniest thread of pity for the formless remnant in front of her. In trying to tempt her, the Ruinous Child had shown her too much. She knew how to defend herself now. "Your time is over. It's all right to let go."

She waited for the book to argue, to threaten her again. Instead, the sound of disembodied laughter filled the chamber, raspy and cruel.

Then may you enjoy the brief time you have left. You will pay the ultimate price for the path you've chosen.

THE PURPLE WORM was rising, turning in their direction, moving at Lorthrannan's command.

Tess panicked. Beside her, Uggie pranced and whimpered, tugging on her pant leg. Tess was just about to grab Cazrin by the shoulders and shake her out of the magical trance when she noticed the Ruinous Child quivering on the lectern. Even the runes on the cover seemed to be shivering, curling in on themselves and then flattening out again, as if the book itself were writhing in pain.

All the while, Cazrin chanted over the tome. But there was no darkness in her eyes as there had been at Candlekeep, and she stood calm and straight, no unnatural contortions to her body like there had been when she'd lashed out at Baldric and the others during her possession.

Realization struck Tess. The book wasn't controlling Cazrin. Not this time. She was holding it with the power of whatever ritual Alagesheth had devised for the book's destruction. Against all odds, their plan was working.

All right, then. Tess knew what she had to do. Guard Cazrin's back.

Against a purple worm.

She could do that.

"Ready to help out, girl?" Tess asked, looking down at Uggie.

The otyugh bumped against her hip in solidarity.

Tess turned to face the oncoming purple worm. She spread her arms wide. "Come and get me, big fella! I got a snack for you right here!" Buoyed by her enthusiasm, Uggie howled right along with her.

"Tess, get out of there!" Anson was trying desperately to hold on to the worm he was riding, to turn it back toward Lorthrannan. "It'll swallow you!"

Baldric suddenly jumped up from behind the pile of debris and pointed at Lorthrannan. "Regards from Kelemvor, who hates liches so much that this one was on the house!"

A beam of radiant light shot out and struck Lorthrannan in the chest. The lich grunted in pain and staggered back. For an instant, the purple worm faltered, and another shudder went through its body, but then Lorthrannan recovered and closed his hand into a fist, shouting, "Kill them now!"

Following the command, the worm lunged right for Tess, striking faster than a snake. Its open maw, ringed with bloody teeth, filled Tess's vision, but just as she was about to dive out of the way, the worm slammed into an invisible barrier. It must have activated when the ritual started. There was a deafening *boom*, and Tess's ears popped as the shield shattered. The worm recoiled, sinking into the closest fissure, stunned and disoriented.

At the same time, the other worm slammed its body into the wall again, this time dislodging Anson and his sword. The fighter went flying and landed near a wounded Zhent who was hiding behind some broken furniture and debris. The worm whipped around, forcing Baldric back and driving Lorthrannan behind some rocks and out of view.

Tess's knees were weak, and she leaned on Uggie for support. "That was fun, wasn't it, girl?" she said shakily.

Uggie was standing in a puddle of liquid. Tess gave the otyugh a sympathetic smile. "Don't worry, I won't tell anyone. I nearly did the same thing."

Behind her, Cazrin gasped. Tess whirled just in time to see the wizard stagger away from the lectern. She gripped Cazrin's shoulders to steady her. "Are you all right?" Tess demanded.

"I'm f-fine," Cazrin said, laying one of her hands over Tess's. "It's done. The ritual's complete, but something's . . . there's danger, I think, and we . . ." Her voice trailed off and she clutched her head, rubbing her temples.

"What danger?" Tess said urgently. "What are you talking about?"

Light from the lectern distracted her, drawing Tess's gaze to the Ruinous Child. The book was glowing a deep green, just like the runes surrounding it. As Tess watched, a pulse of bluish energy burst from the book, passing through her body and continuing outward in a wave. Where the magic touched her, Tess felt a blast of searing cold, strong enough to make her gasp and clutch her chest.

She turned, tracking the wave as it rolled through the chamber. When it reached the walls, it dissipated, and there was the sound of slow-grinding stone coming from both sides of the room.

"No!" Anson shouted. He and Baldric had regrouped on the other side of the cavern and were now running toward the door Lorthrannan and the Zhents had used to enter the room.

A block of stone was sliding down from the ceiling, covering the entrance, sealing it off before they could get to it. Together, the two of them yanked and strained to pull it back up again, but they couldn't move the stone slab. Tess looked toward the door their own party had used, only to see a second slab had slid into place to block the only other exit from the room.

They were trapped.

"Oh no," Cazrin murmured, gripping Tess's arm. She was gazing at the book in horror. "The Ruinous Child . . . or . . . no . . . it must have been Alagesheth himself who designed this trap."

"What are you talking about?" Tess demanded. "Why are we sealed in?"

Cazrin looked stricken. "I should have realized it before. Alagesheth made certain he had a way to destroy the Ruinous Child if it ever got too powerful for him, but he wouldn't have wanted to give anyone else the means to destroy his legacy without consequences, so he put a punishment in place for if that ever happened."

Her words sank in with a terrible finality. Tess didn't doubt she was right. It explained why there'd been a shield erected around the lectern when the ritual began. It wasn't intended to protect them but to trap them, because someone other than Alagesheth was performing the ritual.

The Ruinous Child would soon be gone, but it was going to cost them all their lives. A senseless game designed by a lich who'd been dead for centuries.

Tess felt a terrible anger steal over her, but with it came an odd veil of calm. She loaded her crossbow and fired at a Zhent who was climbing out of one of the shallow fissures where she'd taken cover. The crossbow bolt struck her in the neck, and with a wet gurgling noise, she slid back into the fissure and didn't come up again.

"This is not happening," Tess said coldly. "We are going to move one of those slabs and escape this chamber if I have to go over there and lift it myself."

"You don't understand," Cazrin said, her eyes wide. She pointed to the Ruinous Child. It was still vibrating, and it looked like another pulse of energy was building for release. "The book is being dismantled bit by bit. It's going to release its power in waves. You felt the pain of the first one, didn't you?"

"Yes," Tess said, not liking where this was going. "You're saying they're going to get stronger?"

"Much stronger," Cazrin said. "I don't know how exactly it will manifest, but when it gets to the end, the explosion will probably . . ." She trailed off and gestured helplessly to the cavern around them.

"Kill us all instantly in the best-case scenario and cause a massive cave-in that buries us under a ton of stone in the worst-case scenario," Tess filled in for her.

Cazrin opened her mouth as if to object, then closed it again. "Yes, that summarizes it," she said bleakly. "I'm sorry, Tess. I should have seen this coming and warned you all away."

"And we would have ignored you and stayed," Tess said, waving a hand impatiently. "You did what you had to do. So, let's deal with the situation. First of all, we need to get away from this lectern and find cover before—"

Boom!

A second wave of energy mushroomed from the book, and for an instant, Tess was back in that moldy, rat-infested warehouse where she and Cazrin had first met, and there was a tower of crates getting ready to flatten the wizard.

This time, Tess's reflexes were faster than Cazrin's magic. She grabbed the woman around the waist and spun her, with Tess putting her body between Cazrin and the energy wave. The last thing she saw as the magic slammed into her was Cazrin's horrified expression and a view of Lorthrannan climbing out of the rubble on the other side of the cavern.

Still, as Tess sank to her knees and let darkness claim her amid Cazrin's frantic shouts, the only emotion she could bring herself to feel was relief.

She'd saved Cazrin. The party leader had protected her own. Sometimes, that was all you could do.

CHAPTER 35

Uggie didn't feel good.

She'd been hit by a cloud. Except this was an evil cloud because it had hurt.

It had hurt so much.

She tried to get up, but the room was spinning, and her legs didn't want to hold her. Stupid legs. The air smelled and tasted like something she wanted to spit out. She'd never felt like this before. There were loud noises and huge, scary monsters everywhere. Uggie had never imagined there were such monsters in the world. She didn't like that she knew about them now.

She wanted her persons.

Whenever she was scared or hurt, she looked for her persons, and they made her feel better. Her Baldric person, with his magnificent beard, made her warm and happy inside. Cazrin person created wonderful, sparkly things with her hands, and she was always giving Uggie treats. Sometimes, at night, her Lark person would sing to Uggie with the most beautiful voice in the world. Whenever she wanted pats and scritches and the finest belly rubs, her Anson person was there.

And her Tess person.

Wait . . .

Her Tess person was lying on the ground. She wasn't moving. Had she been attacked by the evil cloud too? An angry growl came from Uggie's chest. If someone had hurt her Tess person, she would rip them apart and eat them. Then she would vomit them up just so she could rip them apart and eat them again.

But her Tess person wasn't getting up. Why not? All of her persons had been hurt before, but they'd *always* gotten up.

Why wasn't her Tess person getting up?

Uggie planted her three feet beneath her, and with a mighty grunt, she pushed herself up, using her tentacles to keep herself steady. Her back foot dragged behind her as she moved toward her Tess person, but that was all right. Uggie had been hurt worse than this before. Uggie was tough.

When she got closer, she saw that her Tess person's eyes were closed. She must have fallen asleep. Well, Uggie could fix that. She went right up to her Tess person, scrunched down, and gently head-butted her shoulder, whining the way she did when it was time for treats. Those headbutts always made her Tess person laugh. Uggie adored the sound.

Her Tess person didn't wake up.

Uggie nudged and whined again, even going so far as to lick her cheek—even though her Tess person did not prefer this—but it didn't do any good.

Uggie hated this. She was scared and hurt and nothing she did made any difference. There were still monsters everywhere, and her persons couldn't help her.

She would just have to help them instead.

Standing straight, Uggie planted herself beside her Tess person and made her body as big as she possibly could, stretching her tentacles and bulging her eyestalk. She knew she would never be as big as the other monsters, but that was all right too, because even though she was afraid, Uggie could be brave. She would be brave, and she would protect everyone.

Because that's what you do for your persons.

CHAPTER 36

"Tess!"

Cazrin guided the elf's unconscious body to the ground beside the lectern as the wave of magical energy poured out through the room, striking the Zhents and Lorthrannan with its necrotic force, although the lich seemed to shrug it off with no ill effects. Cazrin crawled to the other side of the lectern to check on the rest of the party. Baldric and Anson had dived behind some stalagmites, and though she couldn't see him, Lark was presumably still behind cover on the opposite side of the room. He hadn't shown his face since the appearance of the second purple worm.

When Cazrin returned to Tess, Uggie was standing guard. The otyugh was trembling in pain. Frantically, Cazrin cast a spell to conjure a floating disk that hovered just above the ground. As gently as she could, she lifted Tess beneath the armpits and moved her onto the disk. Then she sprang to her feet and ran for cover near one of the blocked doors, the disk and Uggie following.

At the moment, Cazrin's only goal was to get them as far away from the lectern as she could, and then they would try to figure out how to escape the chamber before the Ruinous Child exploded.

She found some cover behind a large, squat stalagmite that had so far survived the spell attacks and the worms' assault. Once Tess and Uggie were settled, Cazrin peered out from behind the stalagmite to assess the situation.

To her relief, the worm that had been under Lorthrannan's control seemed to have broken free of the spell. The lich waved his hands and shouted at the monster, but the worm ignored his commands. How had the creature done it?

Cazrin's gaze went to the book on the lectern. It was lying open now, and an inky black smoke leaked slowly from its pages. It looked like the writing itself was curling up and vanishing, becoming a dark mist that drifted down from the lectern, spreading across the stone and into the fissures. The worm was passing in and out of the black fog.

It was the book's magic. The ritual was dismantling it little by little, and that effect was now bleeding over into the area surrounding the book. It had broken Lorthrannan's spell and was likely disrupting all other magic in the immediate vicinity. If Cazrin had waited a moment longer to cast her floating disk, the spell likely wouldn't have worked.

The other worm was on the far side of the chamber, striking at Anson. The fighter let out a roar, and a bright purplish bolt of lightning, stronger than anything she'd seen his weapon produce, sizzled down the blade and into the worm. The force of the blast ripped through the creature's body, making it writhe in agony. Through it all, Anson kept his grip on the sword, channeling the lightning into the creature and then slashing at the thing repeatedly, desperation in every swing.

Cazrin frantically waved across the chamber at Baldric, who'd just knocked a Zhent to the ground as he worked his way over to help Anson. The cleric caught her eye, and Cazrin motioned for him to come to them. He had to help Tess.

Baldric gave her a tired, sympathetic smile and gestured to the ten-foot fissure that separated them. Cazrin's heart sank. Of course. He had no way to cross the fissure, and even if he could get to them, Cazrin didn't know how many healing spells he might have left.

"It's all right," Cazrin murmured to herself. She pulled back behind the stalagmite and went to Tess. "It's going to be all right." She began to rummage in Tess's pouches, looking for a healing potion while keeping one eye on the book. It was still bleeding smoke, thicker now, and for the moment, that seemed to be keeping Lorthrannan at bay as he reassessed the situation. The lich was probably afraid of the book sucking his magic away.

But how long would that effect last? The Ruinous Child was expulsing its powers one by one. Sooner or later, once he got around the worms, Lorthrannan would make a play for the tome.

"Lark!" Cazrin yelled across the chamber. She wasn't even sure if the bard was still conscious, but he was the only one who might be in a position to help. "Lark, can you hear me? The Ruinous Child! You have to protect it! Lark, please!"

Her hands closed on a vial, and Cazrin triumphantly pulled a healing potion from one of Tess's pouches. She unstoppered the vial and leaned over Tess.

She was so pale. What if the spellbook's magic had done something to her that couldn't be healed with a potion? She'd been guarding her back so Cazrin could complete the ritual, and then she'd stood in the way when that energy blast would have hit her in the chest.

Cazrin's vision blurred. Furiously, she blinked back tears and held the vial to Tess's lips. "You're not going to die," she said firmly, tilting the vial so that the liquid slid down the elf's throat. "This potion is going to work, you're going to wake up, and then you're going to come up with a brilliant plan to get us out of here before we're all killed by the Ruinous Child. Because that's what you do." She wiped her face. "You make big plans, you have huge ambitions—too many for your own good—but that's what I like about you."

She smiled down at Tess. "You don't look at things and see obstacles. You see opportunities. You don't get stuck on people's weaknesses. You find the best in them." She swallowed a lump in her throat. "Do you know how few people in this world bother to do that for someone they don't know?"

A loud crash echoed from the other side of the chamber. Cazrin tossed the now empty vial aside, the glass shattering on the stone as she looked out from their hiding spot.

Lorthrannan was hovering in midair, dodging the attacks of one of the worms. Stone rained from the cavern ceiling as the worm tried to maneuver close enough to take a bite out of the lich. Anson and Baldric were moving toward Lorthrannan as well, drawing the other worm after them, probably trying to get it to engage the lich.

There was still no sign of Lark.

A terrible suspicion crept over Cazrin. What if the bard had slipped away before the chamber had been sealed? It would have been the perfect opportunity, while everyone was distracted by the entrance of the purple worms. What if Lark had decided that this was one battle too many and tried to escape on his own?

If he had, she couldn't do anything about it now. Cazrin focused on Tess instead, crawling back to the elf's side just as Tess's chest heaved on a gasping breath, and her eyes snapped open. "What happened?" she demanded. "Why are you crying? Are you bleeding?" She sat up quickly, then immediately grabbed her head. "Oh, that hurts."

Cazrin put a hand to her mouth to stifle a little sob of relief. "The Ruinous Child is dying, and we're still trapped in the cavern."

A burst of white light filled the chamber, blinding Cazrin. She covered her eyes and ducked deeper behind the stalagmite, feeling Tess bump against her shoulder as the elf got down too. Slowly, the glow faded, and Cazrin looked out.

Lorthrannan was reeling in midair, and the purple worm he'd been fighting had a sizeable chunk of its body ripped off by the radiant expulsion. Anson and Baldric were down on their bellies, blinking the light from their eyes. The Ruinous Child had torn itself in half, and pages of it fluttered off the lectern, still bleeding black smoke, which was slowly solidifying around the lectern into a strange, tar-like substance that reeked of brimstone.

Tess wrinkled her nose. "That thing's going to be a bastard right up until the moment it finally explodes and kills us, isn't it?"

"I think it's going to be soon," Cazrin said. Each expulsion built on the one that came before it, and if that last blast had been any indication, the next one would bring down the whole cavern. "We have to do something—no!"

"What?" Tess had been reaching for her crossbow, but she turned to look where Cazrin pointed.

Amid the fire and falling rocks, the blast of radiant energy, and even the worm trying to bite him in half, Lorthrannan was still flying around the chamber. He'd conjured duplicates of himself that flew alongside him, mimicking his movements and confusing the monster. As a group, they dodged a strike from the worm's tail stinger and flew around the creature, heading straight for the lectern.

"No!" Cazrin cried again. Tess fired her crossbow, but the bolts tore into one of the illusions of the lich, making it flicker and vanish.

"Someone get to the book!" Tess screamed. "Lark, help us!"

CHAPTER 37

This is ridiculous.
   Everything hurts.
Lungs on fire.
Chest caved in.
Benevolent gods, grant me the sweet release of death.

"Lark! Get . . . Ruinous . . . Child. Protect it!"

Lark would rather wander the howling wastes of Pandemonium naked than attempt to sit up, let alone raise one finger to protect the vile trash tome that had caused this whole mess in the first place.

"Lark, help us!"

That had been Tess. Asking *him* to save all their lives?

Well, he'd wanted a chance to prove himself, although there was such a thing as putting too much faith in a person.

He cracked open one eye, then the other.

Two purple worms rampaged through the chamber. Now *that* would make for a song, a grand bardic tale no one would ever believe. Not that Lark could have reached his quill anyway, owing to the broken bones and blood loss.

Come to think of it, maybe his chest wasn't caved in after all. He was still breathing, and his head was beginning to clear a bit, though there was still a vicious ringing in his ears and stars floating in the corners of his vision.

He took a chance and glanced down at himself. Huh. No blood, no bones sticking out of his body or limbs twisted in a direction they shouldn't be. Gingerly, he fumbled with the drawstrings of his pouch and reached inside, coming up with a healing potion. He chugged it, feeling the cool liquid slide down his throat, putting out the fires of pain all over his body. Now, if only he had a nice glass of Zzar to go with it.

"No!"

Cazrin's shout and the healing potion abruptly cleared Lark's head, and he sat up. Across the room, the Ruinous Child was breaking apart, but that wasn't stopping Lorthrannan. The lich had magically duplicated himself and was flying across the room toward the book, heedless of the purple worm surging up behind him, ready to swallow him whole. His entire attention was fixed on the tome.

Lark rose to his feet and leaped nimbly over the rubble and the smaller fissures, miraculously finding a path right to the lectern. He scooped up the broken halves of the Ruinous Child, looking up to see Lorthrannan and his duplicates bearing down on him. The red pits of the lich's eyes smoldered. Bits of papery flesh had peeled off his face, exposing more of his skull than Lark was comfortable seeing up close, to be honest. The lich raised his hand and pointed at him.

At the same time, the purple worm coming up behind the lich opened its mouth wide, obviously intending to get Lorthrannan, his duplicates, *and* Lark into its mouth all at once. Lark had just enough time to throw himself into the fissure in front of him in order to dodge.

He landed on a soft surface, what remained of the book clutched in his hands. He looked up over the lip of the fissure in time to see the purple worm swallow Lorthrannan.

Triumphant laughter bubbled up inside Lark like a song, but he couldn't properly enjoy the moment, because the ground beneath his feet shifted and swelled, and he realized what it was he'd landed on.

The other purple worm. The bottom half of its body was wedged down in the fissure, while the top half was still attacking the others in a frenzy.

Time to get out of here.

The Ruinous Child shuddered in his grip. Oh yes, he'd almost forgotten he had the thing. Lark looked down at his hand and was surprised to find it bleeding, stabbed by a hundred or more thorns that protruded from the torn halves of the book. The pain came over him all at once, as if his mind had been blocking it out while he dodged the vicious worm.

"Ow!" he screeched. Blood dripped down his arm, and the worm beneath him bucked again. The book pulsed, and a loud hum filled Lark's ears.

Lark wasn't a wizard like Cazrin, but he knew enough about magic to recognize an impending explosion when he felt one, and the vibration in his hands was steadily growing.

He looked up the purple worm's back. There was a clear but steep path all the way to the thing's gaping maw. Song lyrics flashed into Lark's mind, ones he would never remember later because he was too terrified, but in that instant, so he wouldn't lose his nerve, he sent his mind a world away. He pictured himself onstage, singing to a rapt audience.

Walking the path of nightmares
They'll never know my name
But it doesn't really matter
Because all legends end the same

And the con-artistry

Of my history
Will be all that's left
To judge

Lark took off.

Using the bone spurs along the worm's body for handholds, he half ran, half climbed up the monster's sloping back, all the way to the edge of its cavernous mouth. Without ceremony, he chucked the Ruinous Child down the thing's throat.

"Choke on that!"

He dove off the creature's back.

He landed at the edge of a fissure, off-balance and stumbling toward oblivion, but suddenly Anson and Baldric were there, grabbing him and hauling him back. Then Tess, Cazrin, and Uggie were coming up behind him, and Cazrin was hugging him, and Lark realized that maybe a few of his ribs were still broken after all because that hug *hurt*.

Then Tess was shouting and grabbing them, herding everyone toward the fissure's edge. Lark thought the elf might have finally lost it, but then her shouts penetrated his fear- and victory-addled brain.

"The book's still going to blow!" she bellowed. "Get in the fissure! We'll follow the tunnel the worms used. Go, now!"

They jumped into the fissure, a confused tumble of bodies falling into the dark. Lark had the impression that another of the Zhents—Valen's little friend—jumped with them at the last second.

Lark hit the ground just as a massive explosion deafened him, turning the air in his lungs to fire. All he wanted to do was collapse in a ball of pain. Someone grabbed his shoulder and hauled his sagging body up and made him *run*. Outrageous! His legs, ribs, and back screamed in protest, and he cursed whoever it was that was towing him along—probably Tess.

Distantly, he was aware that rocks were falling all around him. The tunnel behind them was collapsing. Maybe it was a good thing that he was running, even though he was almost certainly bleeding internally and probably so horribly disfigured that he'd never play the lute again. He was never letting the others hear the end of this.

Then a rock struck him in the temple, and he went away.

WHEN LARK CAME to, Baldric was healing everyone with the lantern he'd acquired in Oghma's temple. Lark basked in the golden warmth flowing over him like honey. His body was no longer moving, thank the Gods. He was lying facedown with his hair spread out over his face in a very unattractive tangle, but he couldn't have cared less. He reached for his lute to assure himself it was still in one piece and strapped to his back.

"You'll live," Baldric declared, and leaned his face down next to Lark's. "I'm not carrying you any farther, sunshine, so you'd best be waking up. I know you're not unconscious anymore."

Lark groaned but obediently sat up. He regretted it at once because Cazrin hurtled at him out of nowhere and wrapped him in another bone-crushing hug.

"You did it!" she said. "That was brilliant! It muffled the explosion just enough to buy us time to get out of there. You're amazing, Lark!"

"Don't compliment him too much, or it'll make him insufferable," Anson said with a tired grin. He was sitting across the tunnel, tying up the Zhentarim who had escaped with them—the only survivor, it looked like.

"Too late," Baldric said, lying down on the ground and closing his eyes with a sigh. "He'll be insufferable after this, no matter what."

"He means to say that you did really good," Tess said, coming over to Lark and offering him her hand to shake. "Thanks for being there for us."

Lark had to clear his throat several times before he could flippantly say, "You're welcome, I suppose."

Tess looked a little worse for wear herself, with several bleeding cuts on her face that she dabbed at with a cloth, and as she turned to assess the others, she was limping a little.

"I thought you'd abandoned us," Cazrin was saying to Lark, her eyes gleaming with moisture. "I shouldn't have doubted you."

"No, you shouldn't have," Lark said in mock affront, "especially since I followed instructions this time." He sagged against the wall, taking in the sight of all of them, bruised and battered but undoubtedly alive. Even the otyugh had survived.

Something shifted in Lark's chest. Relief, elation, exhaustion—he didn't know how to sort it all out. One thing was certain, though.

He was here. He hadn't run. The moment of truth had come on him again, and this time, he hadn't turned his back. As he sat there, contemplating all the good decisions he was suddenly racking up, he felt a warm, solid weight in his hand. He looked down and discovered there was a silver key in his hand.

Well, it was about time.

He supposed this was his life now, for better and for worse. The world was in front of him, and these were the people he was going to experience it with. He wasn't going to be alone.

He rested against the wall of the tunnel, deep in the caverns of Undermountain, and marveled at the strange and interesting hand fate had dealt him. Maybe he wouldn't always feel this kind of loyalty. Even if he did, the group would probably get him killed eventually.

But he had a feeling it would be a fun ride.

EPILOGUE

WATERDEEP—CITY OF SPLENDORS

ONE MONTH LATER

The theater still smelled like fish. It was even worse on the roof, but once Lark had shared the secret of how good the acoustics were up here, and how you could hear each and every performer as well as if you were sitting in the third-row center, Tess had decided she'd prefer to sit outside and look over Waterdeep Harbor.

So, that's what they were doing. The sun was setting over the harbor, and Tess sat on the edge of the roof with her feet dangling over the side. The others were sprawled in safer positions, but Tess liked the feel of the wind in her hair right here. The sunset promised to be spectacular, deep blue and purple streaks glazing the sky below a swirl of red and pink clouds.

Anson scooted across the roof toward her. "That seat taken?"

Tess patted the space next to her. When Anson had made himself comfortable a safe distance from the edge, Tess said, "How are you doing? Have you had any word about Valen's whereabouts?"

Anson shook his head. "I know he's alive—his Zhent friend confirmed that much, and he was seen in the city as recently as a tenday ago—but the trail's cold. Not that I'm surprised. The Zhentarim are hunting him now, looking for revenge. I might have had more luck tracking him down if the Watch hadn't kept us in custody so long."

Tess winced at the memory. Two grueling tendays of explaining their story, waiting for the Watch and the Magisters to interrogate the Zhent prisoner they'd hauled out of Undermountain, and waiting for word from Candlekeep confirming the parts of their story that could be confirmed. It helped that several eyewitnesses had sworn to seeing Lorthrannan on the streets of Waterdeep the day they'd all descended into Undermountain. The presence of a lich, walking the city streets openly and using destructive magic, had raised more than a few security concerns, which had somewhat overshadowed Sefeerian's murder investigation.

They hadn't escaped completely unscathed. The authorities had laid a hefty fine on their heads for fleeing a murder scene and leaving the city. That had taken a significant chunk of the coin recovered from Alagesheth's lab, but it hadn't been a total loss. They still had the magic items they'd found, and there'd been no sign of Lorthrannan or any further trouble from the Zhents. Tess knew it was extremely difficult to kill a lich, but she also knew that being swallowed by a purple worm and then being at the epicenter of the magical explosion of an ancient and powerful spellbook would probably mean a difficult and lengthy recovery for even the most robust undead. And if Valindra Shadowmantle was still out there somewhere hunting for Lorthrannan, he had much bigger problems to worry about than an adventuring party who no longer possessed the thing he'd been seeking in the first place.

So, without a target on their backs or a murder charge hanging over their heads, they were free to do as they wished.

They also still had the tavern, which they'd been slowly working on making their own. Tess removed the magical figurine from her pouch and examined it thoughtfully. She'd actually been hoping to use it tonight, once it got late enough.

She put a hand on Anson's arm. "We'll find your brother," she said. "Don't worry."

A hint of sorrow touched Anson's face. "Maybe we shouldn't," he said. "He joined an organization that tried to kill us, after all. I don't even know why I'm still trying so hard to get to him."

"Because you need closure," Tess said, "and he's the only one who can give it to you."

Anson shook his head. "It's not just that. I have to be honest with myself and with the rest of you." He stared off into the distance. "I wanted to save him. I always have. I suppose that makes me a fool."

"It doesn't," Tess said, squeezing his arm. "But some people can't be saved, Anson. Or they have to do it themselves."

His lips curved in a rueful smile. "Baldric said something similar."

"Well, we're both very wise," Tess said, and got the chuckle from him that she'd been hoping for. "I don't know what happened between you and your brother, but we're all here for you, the same way we're here for Baldric. We're going to help him figure out what this entity is that's dogging him, and we're going to help you get closure with Valen. I promise."

"That's a big to-do list," Anson said, his eyes suspiciously bright as he cleared his throat. "You sure we're up for all that?"

"I know we are. Just think about all we've gone through." She glanced over at the rest of the party to make sure they weren't getting so drunk that they were in danger of falling off the roof.

Things would be different going forward. They were learning to trust and to open up to each other. That would make them stronger in the long run, even if it wouldn't always come naturally.

Eventually, sunset turned to full dark, and the performances in the theater wound down. By the time all the staff had left, locking the doors for the night, it was late, and the rest of the party had had a considerable amount of wine, to the point that Tess was starting to seriously worry that Lark would trip on his tail and end up in the harbor or smash his face on the cobblestones below.

Right. It was time, then.

"All right, Fallbacks, gather up," Tess said, clapping her hands and sloshing the ale in her tankard at the same time. Maybe she was a little bit drunker than she'd planned to be, but that was fine. Even the party leader could cut loose every now and then.

She led the group to the flattest part of the roof and produced the magical tankard figurine, along with her own silver key, the bow engraved with a cat's paw.

"Hey, when did you get that?" Anson demanded, pointing at her key. "Have you been holding out on us?"

Tess smiled enigmatically. "Maybe," she said.

Actually, she'd gotten her key the day they came back from Undermountain, not long after Lark had gotten his. It had taken Tess a while to understand why she'd been the last, but in the end, she believed that was the way it was always supposed to be. She would never have been able to feel fully at home in the tavern if the rest of the group didn't also feel they belonged there together. She couldn't be the party's leader if there wasn't a party to lead.

"It's time to take this party inside," Tess said, holding up the magical figurine.

"What, here? On the roof of this incredibly tacky dockside theater?" Lark drained his wineglass and tossed it off the side of the roof. It shattered on the street below. "I love it. Let's do it!"

"Ish . . . *is* this a good idea?" Baldric asked, his eyes glassy. "I mean, the weight . . . and the angle." He held out one hand, palm up, and put his other hand on top of it. He hiccupped. "Theater . . . tavern . . . stacking. What if it collpaps–collapses?"

Tess waved a dismissive hand. "Cazrin and I measured and discussed the magical weight, and we determined it'll be fine."

"We did?" Cazrin asked, and Tess dug her elbow into the wizard's ribs. "Ouch! We definitely did! It's going to be fine."

Tess set the figurine in the center of the roof. "Everyone have their keys?"

By some bit of grace, no one had lost theirs. Tess activated the magic, and the familiar silhouette of the tavern appeared in a flash of light, right on the roof of the dockside theater. The building gave an impressively loud groan under the weight, but it held. The sign swaying above the tavern door read *The Wander Inn*.

Later, some drunken passersby would notice the unexpected and ostentatious hat the theater temporarily sported, but with any luck, instead of reporting it to the Watch, they'd chalk it up to an ale-induced hallucination. And even if they didn't, Tess thought the risk was worth it.

She opened the door and led the party inside.

The common room had once again undergone several changes.

In addition to the freshly stocked bar and pantry, there was a new cherrywood table in the center of the room with custom-carved chairs for each of them. A fire was waiting, and in front of it was an Uggie-sized quilted cushion and a basket of toys. The toys were made out of steel, of course, so Uggie wouldn't eat them. Not that that had really stopped her.

She even had her own toy tavern key. It had been waiting for her on her cushion the first time the party had returned to the tavern after Undermountain. The symbol on the bow was something of a mystery. No one could tell exactly what it was supposed to be, but Tess could have sworn it looked a little like Baldric's beard.

Behind the bar hung a large oil painting of a pair of purple worms bursting from a cavern floor. The party had agreed that even though the monsters had tried to eat them, they'd been instrumental in helping the party escape certain death at the hands of Lorthrannan and the Ruinous Child. Therefore, it was only right that the creatures be immortalized in art.

At the back of the common room, a hallway led to comfortable bedrooms for each party member. Cazrin had filled her room with books from the collection she'd recovered at the warehouse and from Alagesheth's lab. Lark had a soundproof music room, while Anson had a dedicated training space. Baldric's was an oversized room with another table and comfortable chairs for card games.

Tess was still working on her own room, but she'd known she wanted a big, comfortable bed and a tapestry on the wall across from it that depicted the whole of Faerûn. Every city, every forest and sea, rendered in fine detail, waiting for them.

She smiled fondly as Cazrin, Anson, Baldric, and Lark spread out in the common room, talking, laughing, and making themselves comfortable. Uggie pranced over to the fire and plopped down on her bed, tucking her tentacles in close to her body.

Tess went to the bar and sat down on a stool. She refilled her tankard and raised it in a silent toast to the tavern and its magic, and to their party. It was officially theirs now.

The Fallbacks.

And they were just getting started.

ACKNOWLEDGMENTS

The right adventuring party makes all the difference on these journeys. Thanks to Alex Davis, Elizabeth Schaefer, and the team at Random House Worlds for charting the course and keeping the party from getting lost in the wilderness. You all are wonderful. Thanks to Paul Morrissey, Sarra Scherb, and everyone at Wizards of the Coast for being an amazing collaborative team. Critical hits, all of you.

To my brilliant agent, Sara Megibow, thank you for being there with me every step of the way. To my dad and to Jeff, I love you both so much. And to Tim, none of this would be possible without you.

ABOUT THE AUTHOR

JALEIGH JOHNSON is a *New York Times* bestselling author who lives and writes in the wilds of the Midwest. She has written fantasy fiction for middle-grade readers and for adults, including novels for Dungeons and Dragons, Marvel, and Assassin's Creed. Johnson is an avid gamer and lifelong geek.

jaleighjohnson.com

ABOUT THE TYPE

This book was set in Caslon, a typeface first designed in 1722 by William Caslon (1692–1766). Its widespread use by most English printers in the early eighteenth century soon supplanted the Dutch typefaces that had formerly prevailed. The roman is considered a "workhorse" typeface due to its pleasant, open appearance, while the italic is exceedingly decorative.